QUINTEMBER

Paper? Paper? No! One must carve holes *in the air!* (p50)

Illustration by Dione Verulam

QUINTEMBER

The first volume of the misdemeanours
of Dr Felix Culpepper

Richard Major

IndieBooks

Quintember:
The first volume of the misdemeanours of Dr Felix Culpepper

By Richard Major

Illustration by Dione Verulam
Map by Alick Newman

ISBN: 978-1-908041-41-8

Published by IndieBooks
Unit 9, 5-7 Wells Terrace, London N4 3JU

www.indiebooks.co.uk

Set in Minion Pro 12/14

Printed by CPI, Durham

The poem 'Fractures' on pages 236 and 257 was previously published in
Oxford Poetry, and is used here by kind permission of the editors.

To
K.L.F.,
my brilliant wife:

THE COLLEGE OF THE BLESSED SAINT WYGEFORTIS IN CAMBRIDGE
FOUNDED A.D. 1513 BY ADAM WORTHYAL
LORD BISHOP OF ST ASAPH

1. Allegorical Fountain
2. Tower of Lethe
3. Erebus
4. Kitchens
5. Senior Combination Room
6. Lodge
7. Antechapel
8. Tower of Acheron
9. Cocytus Court
10. Temple of Priapus

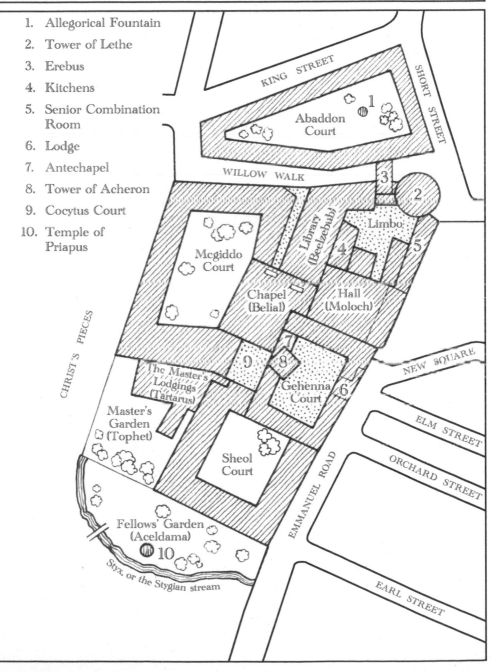

'First point' (said Julien): 'even the cleverest Englishman is stark raving mad for an hour each day, when he's visited by the demon of Suicide – the national deity.

'Second point: Intellect and Genius get discounted 25% upon disembarcation in England.

'Third: nothing in the world is as beautiful, as wonderful and as moving as the English countryside.'

STENDHAL, *Le Rouge et le Noir*

Byblos

i.

'BEAUTY' (I THOUGHT): 'beauty-beauty-beauty; there's nothing else to say. A million varicoloured points tumbling without forethought into one design. As if a gas-main exploding under a kitchen produced – from the racket of copper pans bashing their way through brick walls – order. Calm, symphonic harmony. Every random semiquaver settling into massive chords. Beauty!'

I've never known St James's Park look as wonderful as it did that bright late afternoon in early October, gazing at it from the top floor of the Foreign Office.

And I've never known Benjy, the Foreign Secretary, sound more like the twelve-year-old he was when I first came across him at school, snivelling behind the gym.

But then, who's ever lived up to the Foreign Office? It's a porphyry palace for Greek gods: not exactly beautiful, in fact ghastly, but so swaggering that your littleness is crushed out of you. You've no choice but to exult in the coarse strength of those coffered ceilings. The gilt staircases seem built just for you, addressed to you: in each niche an out-sized mid-Victorian nude gesticulates, waving fist or torch or sword as if to say 'Bah! foreigners!' And your soul (you can't help it) shouts back 'Pah! Let 'em try, that's all!' You find yourself, as you ascend through giantish polychrome marble, ready to tear out an enemy's kidneys and eat them, to fling yourself on the Mad Mahdi's dervishes, to charge massed Ruskies, bayonet adazzle, smoking with gore in the snowy air. By the time you reach the uppermost floor you long to trample Germans or sepoys under your hooves, to fire off a Trident for the fun of the thing, to – but here a severe private-personal-secretary, tautly buttoned into her severe grey suit, subdues you with a look. Miss Litherland's hand pauses on the golden knob of the high door shielding the innermost sanctum. She knows that after those stairs visitors are inclined to bound in, roaring 'Blood! blood!' Therefore she pauses; and you enter hushed, prepared to murmur wisely with the Great Man.

Only to be spun head-over-heels, as by an unexpected wave of surf. For over the shoulder of Benjy Wedgwood, advancing diffidently, mournfully, over the carpet ('Hallo Felix') is the view.

St James's Park, which isn't large, manages to be mysterious. Its sinuous waters bend under their exotic bridge as if Asia opened on the far bank. There's a rich confusion of domes, spires, obelisks against the soft English vault, so that however much you tell yourself *It's only ugly old Buckingham Palace* or *That's the roof of my club*, your imagination prances, as if Trebizond or Karakorum were twinkling out there beyond the candle-blooming chestnuts.

So I patted Benjy above the elbow and went past, ignoring him, leaning over his sill into the Park, wondering how the Foreign Office ever gets any work done. What intoxicating complexity of vision! (And what late-in-the-day bird-music!) Glowing borders of foxgloves and stock, sedgy lake a dozen shades of grey-green, black swans, piebald Muscovy-ducks, scarlet geese, leaves turning ox-blood, lemon and amber. Yet there was ordered simplicity here, too. A coherent formula of bars, appealing to the mind as well as the eye. Lambent darkling-blue sky; heavy red foliage; everlasting English grass. Order!

'...probable complications.' Benjy was mewling behind me. 'There could well be *definite*, I might even say *serious* complications.'

Sighing, I turned from the view. 'Tell us about it, then – Foreign Secretary.' The third man in the room didn't look like someone who should hear the Foreign Secretary called 'Benjy'. 'I attend.'

Which was still only partly true. For the room too was distracting. In its heavy, rhetorical, Italianate way, it was just as overwhelming as the early-autumn Park. The carved ceiling was splendid as the russet sky was splendid, the woodwork was as sure of itself as a living trunk. The green wallpaper, painted with gilt stars, was as aweful as the golden plane-trees. Say what you like about man aping God, human art *does* sometimes seem to come out of the same workshop as nature; and requires the same rapt quiet.

However, this wasn't a moment for æstheticism. I braced my eyes by resting them on the Winterhalter that hung over the malachite fireplace:

a portrait of the Prince Consort in a kilt, gun in hand, welter of grouse about his ghillie brogues.

'You probably wouldn't know, Felix,' began Her Majesty's Secretary of State for Foreign and Commonwealth Affairs, who'd taken refuge behind his official desk, shuffling papers, 'that we've had a major exhibition over the last three weeks. Of a dead American. A' (he consulted a paper) 'Mark Rothko.'

I wouldn't know, eh? True, I don't hold with most modern art. Normally I'd have said 'No', perhaps tricked out as a derisive 'Really?'

But as it so happened I did know, thanks to a conversation last Thursday; a conversation which hadn't gone well. 'What d'y'want for your birthday, Margot?' I'd asked; 'it's Tuesday isn't it?', pretending to be vaguer than I was. It's no small matter having a mistress turn twenty, especially when she's also your student, and in her first week as an undergraduate in your college. A ticklish moment; also, wonderful. I was looking forward to Tuesday. But 'I want Rothko and dinner,' is what she'd said: 'there's a show at the Tate that's about to close. Take me to that tonight, then to the Ivy.' When I'd snorted and demurred, making a short speech about the folly of Abstraction, she'd snorted 'Remote and ineffectual don' and left me, slamming the door.

Remote and ineffectual don. Remote and ineffectual don: the quotation had fixed itself in my mind, obscurely paining me. A childish insult, yet annoying, distinctly annoying. A man of paper. An oldster. *Ineffectual*: me.

But at least I was now able to say, severely, 'As it happens, Foreign Secretary, I was aware of it.' I was examining Albert's wizened thighs, wondering what excuse there'd ever been for such clashing tartan, scarlet squares streaked with mustard and green, flayed flesh, gangrene, pus. 'At the Tate Modern. Closed on Friday.'

'Ah! Finger on the pulse… An *important* exhibition, they tell me.' More papers. 'A dozen massive canvasses done in 1955 for the Shah. Who wasn't *saveur du jour* in New York – Rothko kept the commission quiet. The Shah was discreet too. Hung them in his summer palace on the Caspian. For his private delight, or to dazzle the Western woman he liked to take there. And since the Revolution the ayatollahs have kept them locked up, not saying a word. Although Abstract art apparently doesn't jar on Islamic sensibility – isn't that so, Professor um, um—'

'Jones-Brown', almost 'Joonth-Brown' semi-lisped Jones-Brown, who'd been introduced when I'd entered a few minutes before, and had (my manner indicated) already dropped out of my mind. 'Their existence came as a global surprise. There's no suggestion,' he explained heavily, 'in the *catalogue raisonné* of any 1955 *hiatus* in the *œuvre*. None;' then shook his head as if he couldn't stop.

Jones-Brown had neat features, so tiny they seemed somehow folded away. But here's the thing: whereas neat-faced men should be stocky like pugs or sinuous like ferrets, he scarcely had a body. A favourite picture in one of my childhood history books showed a head paraded on a pike by a *sans-culotte*. That was Jones-Brown: a bobbly head. His shapeless clothes were a tent. Twitch them aside, you'd startle a dwarf wobbling a pole.

I blinked at the head, as if to fix its appearance. It seemed (framed by that Park, by that room) intensely insipid, fading from view as I stared, diluting the air. Had he sinned against the blessèd sense of sight, and been punished with near-invisibility? Damn me if I can picture him even now. I snatch at this or that flaw, not out of malice, but because without his carbuncles he vanishes. Or was it freckles? Warts? Bulbous lips certainly, ajar like an urchin's. A spectacularly commonplace face, an extremely typical weak chin, an unusually usual receding hairline, a freak of normality. 'Even I,' he was drearily saying, 'had absolutely no idea at all.'

'Even you?' I said.

Perhaps my tone was offensive, for Benjy put in, unctuously: 'Our distinguished friend Professor Jones-Brown holds the chair in Modern Art at, at, at...'

'North Newborough,' said etcetera-Brown, half-apologetically, half-truculently.

'Ah,' I found myself saying, 'Northborough – Newborough.' It's odd how fatuity spreads about a room, like a yawn.

Anyway, I was only half-attending. I had to decide how to soothe a nineteen-cum-twenty-year-old who was used to words like *ineffectual*. I needed to ingratiate myself before her important moment; which ought to be marked by something more than a cultural outing; something more.

'The University of North Newborough,' exclaimed Benjy, as who might say *Why not, why not indeed?* 'Professor Jones-Brown, the author of scores of books—'

'Books are obsolete. Eleven online articles.'

'—was academic consultant for the Rothko exhibition, and has kindly come back to town to give me his expert opinion.'

I made as if to reconsider Jones-Brown, now breathing through his nose, arms folded. (*What imposition on intellect of my calibre! Summoned to Whitehall indeed!*) A seriously stupid man; possibly not as stupid as he pretended. Certain marine creatures disguise themselves in hazes of black ink.

'In March,' continued Benjy, 'Tehran revealed its cache of Rothkos, and announced a travelling exhibition to, well, *difficult* nations. Naughty Venezuela and Cuba, Lebanon, Syria. But then they offered to include London in the tour. A thrill for the art world, wasn't it, Professor?' But Jones-Brown was communing with his own rare thoughts. 'And for the F.C.O., cultural diplomacy's so easy – not like the real thing. An enemy loans us a picture, we send an orchestra, suddenly there's *rapprochement*, I'm on the front page of *The Economist* shaking hands with their Foreign Minister, we're accrediting ambassadors, selling them fighter-bombers...'

I smiled thinly. The insignificant third man uncrossed his arms to smooth his forgettable grey trousers.

'Well, the show was a success, queues round the block, wasn't it? Professor... er...'

'Joneth—'

'Jones-Brown. I was about to send an informal note about it to the Grand Ayatollah through the diplomatic bag. *This*, as it happens.' He held up a postcard. 'A Persian rug from the V&A. Apt, yes? Good turns of phrase too. Delicate ambiguities, openings for further discussion...' He read his beautiful phrases, having for the moment forgotten us. (Benjy's never been a dab hand with prose; indeed it was a particularly feeble *What I Did in My Hols* that caused him to be sobbing behind the gymnasium.) He sighed, and slid the card into a drawer. '*All that effort* gone to waste. You know those lock-ups you see under viaduct arches?'

'I've always wanted to see inside.'

'Me too. At dawn today the Met kicked one in, in Hackney—'

'Did they indeed?' I murmured, staring up into the coffering. 'How'd they come to do that?'

'Anonymous tip-off.'

'Delivered just before dawn?'

'Well no, the call came yesterday afternoon. But they weren't impressed by the fake accent. "An effete suburban travesty of Irish."'

My eyebrows went up. 'Where d'you recruit coppers? Swiss finishing-schools?'

'So they didn't take it too seriously. Don't let that detail rankle, Felix, you have to stop loathing the police. Who naturally prefer to mount their raids at dawn. Sirens, smashing, screaming: that's all wasted on rush-hour London. Be reasonable.'

'Aha. And what *was* inside the cubby-hole?'

'Dank emptiness. And, flung into a corner: *that.*' He waggled his hand toward an easel, sheathed in bubble-wrap, standing anomalously in a corner under the tremendous golden ceiling. (I'd been ostentatiously ignoring it.) 'Which I'd like to show to you and Professor, ah – who is, I should've said, the world authority on Rothko – isn't that so?'

'There is' (this seemed torn from him) 'a young writer in Orvieto...'

'In the British Isles.'

Jones-Brown, low, sullenly: 'Gale of Aberdeen is perhaps...'

'In England then,' said Benjy briskly, rising from his desk. (It's a surprise, after you've listened to him, to find him tall and spry.) 'No false modesty, Professor Smith-Br – Brown-Jones. Too much is at stake,' and he made a showy business of pulling the bubble-wrap off the easel.

It was, or had been, a painting six foot by four: a composition of three unequal bars, yellow and scarlet with a belt of white between. But it had been vilely treated. Most of the canvas was torn away, leaving a wreckage of wooden frame; what was left bore tyre-marks and boot-prints, and was splattered with sticky black corrosive muck.

Brown gasped, sprang up, and flung himself on this dirty ruin, pawing its corners, snuffling, groaning, whipping out a magnifying-glass to interrogate flecks and splinters. Benjy followed this carry-on with reverence. I, with no opportunity to show off my own charlatanism, observed it with disgust. I made as to speak. The Foreign Secretary stayed me with a hand. We waited.

'This is undoubtedly,' pronounced Brown at length, standing upright and facing us, '*Untitled Number 849.*'

'Ah?'

'One of the Shah's Rothkos,' explained the unhappy Benjy.

'I didn't realise any were missing.'

'Nobody does. Officially speaking, all twelve were taken down and packed up two nights ago, and the exhibition reopens in Beirut at the end of next week. But since the Professor thinks—'

'*Thinks?* I know! This *is* genuine!' he snapped, and turned back to it. 'The Master's tonal values are *inimitable.*' (Benjy held up deprecating hands, having no doubts to cast on tonal values.) 'Besides, he was a magician, he employed secret ingredients, not even his assistants knew all. Formaldehyde, salad oil, resin, eggs, boot polish...' He was pressing his face to the desecrated work: fingertips, nose, cheeks. 'But not anchovy paste,' he added, in a muffled voice since he was now using his tongue, 'whatever lies they print! The case for anchovies rests on exaggeration, anecdote, even the *conscious fabrications* of self-seeking greengrocers.' Breezily: 'The whole tenor of contemporary Rothkology – driven, I may say, by my own work – is distinctly anti-anchovy, whatever' (here he turned truculent) 'the *obscurantist insinuations* of Professor Gale.' He turned a fierce face on Benjy, who wobbled his head, disavowing neo-anchovian heresy. 'I've tracked down the Master's bills. He frequented a bodega on the corner of East 70th Street. Anchovy paste: zero. But mayonnaise! Guess how much mayonnaise a New Yorker of the Eisenhower era consumed?' Benjy wouldn't dare. 'He bought *three times* that amount. I've pierced his secrets. I've written papers on his late-period hair conditioners. Bath cleaner, nail-polish, insect repellent: I taste them all.' None of this sounded ridiculous. Jones-Brown was on his own ground. The innate strength of any man, which might be spent on pleasantness, wit, beauty, goodness, he had squandered on occult lore. He was the best-informed Rothkoist of his generation, between the Solent and the Tweed. He could speak *ex cathedra*. 'I, Jones-Brown of Newborough, am convinced of its canonicity. I pronounce.'

Benjy glanced at me. I shrugged.

Jones-Brown saw, and seemed to bridle. '*Diplomatic* doubts? You find it *politically convenient* to deny the truth?'

'Sorry, Professor, perhaps I rushed the introductions. This is Dr Felix Culpepper—'

'Gulper?' Now he was deliberately riling me.

'Culpa. But spelled *cull, pepper* – quaint name, old family.' Jones-Brown looked pitying; my smile thinned. 'He helps us out now and then but he's not *with* the Foreign Office. He's an academic. Just like you,' at which I demonstratively blinked. Jones-Brown's tiny face squinted up into mine. (His eyes were crossed; I remember now.) 'Felix is in fact a distinguished classicist. Well, a classicist. At Cambridge.'

Jones-Brown's squint went blank. 'Classical music?'

'I study ancient poems.'

'Ah! We don't go in for primitivism at Newborough', *né* North Cambridgeshire Polytechnical Institute: I'd remembered it now.

'Here's this,' put in Benjy hastily, pre-empting my riposte. 'Taken two days ago, that's to say Friday, the evening the exhibition closed.'

He'd handed me an enlarged coloured photograph of an art-gallery black-tie drinkypooh; grandees, patrons, connoisseurs, backs to the art, grimacing faces to each other; on the wall between Sir Michael Jagger and the Duke of Gloucester *Untitled Number 849*. Or not.

I passed it to Jones-Brown. 'Yes, yes, crude. Wholly unconvincing even in a photo. Brushwork too vertical, contours coarse, pigments blurred. I am 110% certain – 125%. If,' he added, with surprising bitterness, 'they'd invited me to the reception, I'd have spotted it *instantly*'; and thrust his magnifying-glass back into his pocket, with the air of a sheriff blowing smoke from his six-shooter, then twirling it faster than eye can follow into its holster. On the verandah of the tavern lie six twitching bandits, drumming the woodwork with spurred boots. 'Anyway, you must yield to facts.'

Benjy nibbled a knuckle. 'All right. The buggers *have* managed to lift a Rothko from the Tate. *Damn* the Tate,' he burst out petulantly, 'what did it *do* with the' (another piece of paper) 'half million we gave it for extra security? Eh?' More nibbling. 'Replaced it with a crude fake – made a hash of getting it away. Drove over it, spilled motor-oil *and* trampled it, God knows how.'

'Haste,' I suggested airily. 'Panic. Easily done. Events always go awry, the physical universe has been a muddle for fourteen billion years. Only in the realm of ideas can anything work. Huge painting through a window in the dark, too many men – suburban Irishmen! – manhandling it into a dirty truck, everyone hissing. No, whispering effetely. Crack, tear, swear, stumble, smear. A natural bungle. Frankly, I sympathise.'

'Frankly I don't. Anyway, by the time they examine their loot, it's worthless. They abandon it, feel a spasm of compunction, let us know where it is. But *where*,' he burst out with intensified self-pity, 'is the compunction in that? What about me? Why didn't they consider *me*? When does anyone, about to cause trouble with foreigners, stop to ask "Won't this be hard cheese on the poor Foreign Secretary?" Never.'

'Don't blub, Wedgwood *minimus*.'

'I'm not. I'm just saying: what am I, I mean what are we to do?'

I brooded. 'The fake'll be spotted quickly?'

'Instantly,' repeated Jones-Brown, sitting down again. 'The moment it comes out of the case. It's embarrassingly bad.'

'And then,' groaned Benjy, 'I'll have the most hateful difficulties.'

'It's insured?'

'Oh yes, yes, for' – he fidgeted with his papers – 'twenty-eight million. *That's* all right. But diplomatically! The Americans, who *like* to be unkind, will say... And these cultural exchanges can *backfire*. The Iranians'll claim we're incompetent. Or that it was a put-up job, that I lured the Rothkos here with fell intent. The hardliners will argue: "England never changes: behold, she steals our canvas, she despises us, let us enrich more uranium-238." Iran wobbles on a razor-blade, anything's enough to tip it, God knows where this ends.' He buried his face in his arms. There was a long unmeaning lull.

(I realise this affair seems to amount to very little. Jones had confirmed what Benjy Wedgwood must already have guessed; I, purveyor of clever violence to the British State, couldn't undo the damage; we were wasting Benjy's time. I'm wasting yours. It appears that way; but you see, my talk with these two pawns, these nullities, was a pretence. *I knew what was coming* and, despite my bored swagger, was queasy with fear. *Did* I have to – *was* it worth – *dare* I go through – ? That lustrous room was my torture chamber. Nonetheless…)

I coughed lazily, stirred and stretched.

Benjy had evidently gone down to wallow in the sewer of self-pity (which is never quite dry, even in resolute minds like mine). He was ignoring me.

'Foreign Secretary?' at which he looked up, bitterly. 'I'm awfully sorry and so forth. But why've you called me in? What d'y'want me to do? I don't feel helpful.'

'Now you mention it, neither of you have been particularly helpful.'

'If we had the stolen painting, I might try to swap it back for the fake. But we can hardly let the Iranian have *that*,' gesturing toward the debris on the easel.

'No. That's good for nothing.'

Jones-Brown stared at it enigmatically, shaking head, unfolding insignificant legs as if about to leave. '*That's* worth – nothing.'

'Much less than nothing,' said Benjy morosely, 'think what it might *cost* us.' He was re-swathing it in bubble-wrap. 'Actually this rubbish will be worth a lot, to historians, if it's ever Iran's *casus belli*. And survives,' and the following picture popped into my mind: the Foreign Office a sooty skeleton, staring, through an ash-cloud shrieking in the nuclear whirlwind, at the consummation of St James' Park; every tree a bending flame.

'I'll burn it if you like,' I said, measuring in my imagination the fun of obliterating thirty million quid of paint, mayonnaise and sun-cream.

'No. It's an historic artifact. It goes to the Depository.' He had put on his sepulchral voice. 'I'll stow it where – oh I say.' Benjy had evidently remembered that he had to please us, or at least me; he was suddenly a small boy offering bigger boys a treat. 'Shall I *show* you my Depository?'

I smiled in a superior way (although I was thinking: *This is a killing matter*).

Jones-Brown looked at his watch. (Second-rate minds are never as happy as third; they realise what's missing; they're querulous.)

But Benjy, excited now, jumped up and pulled a tasselled cord. Massive curtains fell, blotting out the darkening Park. He turned on his desk lamp, locked his office door, approached the fireplace; tilted Prince Albert to the left. There was a neat metallic creak, a ping. One of the porphyry panels beside the hearth swung open. Crouching, I saw a steel cavity stretching back and back, stacked with portfolios, boxes, papers bound with ribbon; a baby's coffin; a prosthetic penis (I *think*) in a glass-fronted blue-satin-lined walnut box stamped in gold letters *N.C.*; rusty caskets, a broken sword; skulls.

Benjy's trickier than he looks. He can't write because he can't lie, but he can hustle. When Whitehall throws him out, Hollywood might take him in. When our French master announced, in tears, that his surgical truss was missing, Benjy was above suspicion; in the end they sacked one of the gardeners because they had to sack someone. Yet Benjy was the culprit; he let the whole Fourth Form try it on at two quid a pop, making enough for a new bicycle. Part of him's always been a showman.

'This,' he said, lowering his brows, darkening his voice, 'is the Foreign Secretary's private vault, our Most Especially Secret Safe. Palmerston installed it. "To engulf what we owe it to history not to destroy, yet is too interesting to be healthy in the open air." I get things out on winter afternoons when there's nothing going on. Let's see, what would you enjoy most?' (I was interested despite myself. A bad sign. Benjy only mollifies people when he wants something appalling done. *This,* I was thinking, *is the start of my death*.) 'What about this, then?'

'This' was a bag of dark linen. He untied it, sniffed, put in his hand, and produced – what was merely horrible, a shrunken head: a brown boggling obscenity the size of a grapefruit, with tiny forehead and horrid swollen toothy jaw. Benjy clutched it by its long blonde hair, and it swung back and forth, smirking, defying us to look away.

'What is *that*?'

'Amelia Earhart.'

'Who?' asked Jones-Brown, and, perceiving we were amazed, added with shame and pride, 'I have no outside interests. I only read about Rothko.'

'An aviatrix,' I told him, dreamily, looking away from him, peering into her cowry-shell eyes. There was, despite the distortion, a nightmare resemblance to her photographs. 'She vanished over the Pacific in '37, trying to fly around the world.'

'*Without trace*, as journalists always say,' said Benjy, twirling the head by its yellow locks. 'But here's the trace. Given to our Resident Commissioner in the Gilbert Islands in the 'Fifties. By the headman of a tribe that hadn't liked Miss Earhart's snarky attitude after she crash-landed on their atoll. The Commissioner didn't fuss because they were a friendly tribe, I mean friendly to us, and shipped it back to London. Since the Americans never let us know more than they have to about *anything*, we left them in the dark about *this*.'

The Professor observed stiffly that it had no artistic merit. 'Not Rothkoesque.'

'Well, then,' said Benjy, hurt, dropping Miss Earhart into her sack, 'what about this? A pretty thing?' He pulled out a grease-stained cloth suitcase worked with psychedelic swirls. The dainty Professor turned his shoulder. 'This' (he patted it) 'is an atom bomb. Code-name *Die uiteindelike laer*, the ultimate laager. The South Africans kept it in the basement of their London embassy as the final guarantee of apartheid. We stole it, dismantled the firing mechanism, kept it. Seven kilotons… Or what about this? *This* is significant.' A sheet of manuscript in a stiff plastic case, paper fading to yellow, ink to brown, a jagged-florid hand. *Ex M: Lutherus*, I read, *monachus falsæ sectæ Nazareni: ad dominum nostrum generosum Suleimanum, sultanum sultanorum*… 'We acquired this, well, looted it, frankly, from the Ottoman archives. When we occupied Constantinople in 1919. It tickled Lloyd George's fancy. He thought it might be useful one day. For vexing Ulster Protestants.'

'Luther,' I said, unaffectedly impressed, 'was in the pay of Suleiman the Magnificent?'

'Evidently. This is his annual report. He got twenty-four thousand silver thalers a year to make trouble for the Habsburgs.'

But Jones-Brown was a fanatic who cared only for his idol. Since Rothko owed nothing either way to the Reformation, it could have no fizz for him. 'I must get back, Mr Wedgwood, if you've no further need of me; I've notes to write for a graduate seminar.' He managed to look yet more extraordinarily ordinary, and at the same time sly. He wouldn't catch my eye.

Benjy put Luther's report back in the Most Especially Secret Safe, along with Miss Earhart, the Boer bomb, the mangled canvas that might yet undo Persia, and other broken toys of history. Including the French master's truss? *Was* the prosthesis Chamberlain's? Too late to ask; our treat was over. Benjy moodily slammed the porphyry slab and there was a series of heavy, comfortable clanks.

He showed Jones-Brown to the door. The fellow had a peculiar gait, holding his chest as far forward as it would go, then spinning his little feet forward to stop falling over. 'Farewell, Professor,' said the Foreign Secretary in his blandest voice. 'I hope you have an easy journey back to, to, to—'

'North Newborough,' said Jones-Brown with pathetic dignity.

'Newborough, Newborough, yes. Thank you for coming in. Obviously you'll say nothing about this to anyone ever.'

'You have my word.'

'Oh yes, that,' muttered the changeable Benjy, suddenly not courtly at all, 'your word of honour. You'll *also* remember that the Tate hired you as a consultant, won't you? Which makes you a government contractor under the terms of the Official Secrets Act. Liable to two years in prison if you mention the theft; or my Depository; or Culpepper. Or anything. But especially Culpepper. If you divulge *him*, you'll soon be wishing for a nice comfortable cell.' Benjy has it in him to be formidable.

But then so does Jones-Brown. 'I would never,' he said simply, 'sensationalise the memory of Rothko.' Once at dusk I brushed against a rotten beech stump; a stag beetle reared up to threaten my passing boot. There was nothing preposterous about the insect. Jones-Brown was like that. 'Rothko is the greatest artist who has ever lived.' He sounded perfectly serious (although damn it, that was a wink he was giving in my direction. Hidden shallows). Then, in his impossibly pedestrian way, he got on his shapeless hat and was gone.

Benjy sagged against the door. 'Don't *you* go. Sit. Let me get you whisky.'

'Er – in my own small way I too have work to do. Must get back…'

'No you don't. You need to do something for the government.'

'For the—'

'For the country. For me. Come on, Felix.' The showman was gone; the Depository hadn't won me; the clingy small boy was back. 'Do you want water in it?'

'Yes. No. Thanks… But I don't see what I can do. *Do* you credit the scintillating Jones-Brown? He sounded like the Last Word.'

'I do, he did… Wasn't he dreadful? Oh Culpepper, I'm so glad I'm a dunderhead. My clever colleagues spend all their time having in-tee-lect-shulls in, being told what to do. Appalling people, academics. I don't mean you.'

'We're drunkard idlers at St Wygy's.'

'No, no… But Smith, I mean Jones-Brown! How does anyone get like that, d'y'think?'

'Ah. I know how: I've give pedantry some thought, Benjy. Let me explain.'

Benjy, who couldn't possibly be interested, knitted his brows in concentration: 'You always could get to the bottom of things.' He was doing a good job of buttering me up.

'Saints, Benjy, give up the world without regret, believing the One contains the lesser many within Himself; so they're losing nothing. Pedants are the opposite of saints. They give up the world to pursue one tiny remote thing, one among the many, precisely because it contains nothing but itself. They don't want infinity, but finitude in its most extreme form. They *want*,' I added, shuddering, 'to be ineffectual' (that word). 'They don't aspire to everlasting life, but immediate impenetrable death.'

'Golly. I'll try to remember that next time my Permanent Under-Secretary tries to set up a think-tank… But come on, Felix. What am I going to do about this damned painting?'

'My advice,' I said, teasing, since I knew he wouldn't dare take it, 'is to confess at once. 'Phone. Sound contrite. Better the Persians hear it from you before unpacking a bogus Rothko.'

'That won't be until tomorrow afternoon at the soonest, you know.' Benjy gave me his famous puppy look over the rim of his tumbler.

'What difference,' I said hypocrtically, 'can a day make?' Tragic play with his lip. 'What d'y'have in mind?' More dog-eyes. 'Where are the paintings at the moment?'

'Ah!' said Benjy, brightening and putting down his glass. 'I was hoping you'd ask. Still at Heathrow. Just. On a small Iranian jet. It's scheduled to fly out at nine.'

'Raid it before it takes off.'

Benjy was appalled: 'Good God no, that'd violate the Vienna Convention. It's diplomatically privileged.'

'Then if you can't touch it on the ground, and can't bear to let it carry the fake to Iran, you'd better blow it up in mid-air.'

Benjy looked less appalled. 'They're very careful about bombs. Coming from where they come from. Don't know how we'd get one on board. Anyway, it's too late.'

'Shoot it down. They'll be flying close to Cyprus, where there's a British base – what's it called?'

'R.A.F. Akrotiri. But… do you really think I should?'

Oh, these men of paper. The wickedest statesman only dabbles in crime – does his skulduggery by not contradicting what an underling says he's about to do – or pretends not to hear, hunts about his desk for paper-clips while the essential words are being uttered, looks up with vague smile: "Hm?"

'Isn't there another way, Felix? You're so clever, you always get to the bottom of things.'

I'd known this was coming. I didn't yet have enough of Benjy's single-barrel malt inside me to say yes. The event needed softening. Prevaricate, prevaricate. 'Can't you delay their departure for a few hours?'

'I suppose. How should I do that? – Oh, d'y'want more whisky?'

I did. It was one of those late afternoons that require golden spirit to be poured on them, as haggis requires Scotch, plum pudding brandy – I thought, a bit incoherently; for I was passing through one of those moments when interior and exterior merge. I was lolling in one of the room's magnificent blood-dyed leather armchairs, and my eye was losing itself in the gilded coffering, sun after sun, receding into that self-contained heaven of the ceiling.

'A bomb you say, eh?' murmured the boyish man.

More of this.

Then I was descending the great staircase between marble figures, feeling more human yet more godlike as I passed through the subdued gold light, emerging into a Park that was like a dim furnace of autumn pigments. There I lifted my arms to exult – not least because I knew Benjy (if not already unconscious) would be looking down at me. St James's Park was clamorous with birds saying vespers, cold-warm with the green-red sunset, which seemed to have melted together the million points of colour. In my dark suit, against that rainbow foliage and flowers, I must have looked to him like the photographic negative of a goldfish in a murky bowl. I stood against the colours like death.

ii.

'Camel-diarrhoea on her grandfather's dick,' remarked the pilot, taking his seat in the cockpit, to his new co-pilot, an innocent fresh from a *madrasa* in Qoms. '*Choob too konet* [a brass-studded stick up her arse].'

The Persian language has endured twenty-five centuries of history, all full of occasion for invective.

'Sir! Reza! Whatever is the matter?'

'*Nanat sag suk mizaneh*. They say we can't take off, Hassan, that's what the matter is. The donkey-dung Britishers have telephoned our hyena-scrotum Foreign Ministry saying "Pretty please can you not take back this dreadful woman?" and I've just received orders from Tehran to wait for madam. *Marg!*'

'Who is she?'

'*Antar* [a baboon]! The wife of someone big in the *régime* who's been on a "shopping trip". I know these London shopping trips. Whoring herself to taxi drivers. Raping waiters. Fellating dogs. Anyway she's "overstretched herself". That's what the sparrow-brain in Tehran told me, she's "dizzy." Too drunk to walk is what that means. *And* she's lost her papers. Sold them, doubtless, Iranian diplomatic passports fetch twenty thousand euros on the black market.' The pilot, a hard-bitten man, did not care that the control tower might be recording whatever he said; as, indeed, it was. 'The Infidels don't want to deal with complications, so they ask, as a special favour, now our nations are French-kissing each other like Kurdish goatherds in heat, can't we fly her back with Pahlavi's pretentious grease-smears, and dump her on her husband.'

The eyes of the co-pilot widened with dismay. 'Is not Mark Rothko greatest of all Expressionists?' It had been a most broad-minded *madrasa*.

Reza shrugged disgustedly, he would not discuss such matters.

'Whose wife is she, Reza?'

'*Molla nanato kard* [a mullah fucked her mother]. Who cares? All big-shots are pigs from the same herd, and their wives are worse. If someone makes a pious speech in the Majlis about revolutionary purity, be sure it's his hangover speaking. He's just back from running amok in New York, Dubai, Bombay. Tel Aviv, even.'

'Reza. Surely not.'

'Nothing would amaze me. The things I've seen flying government 'planes. In Brasilia once' – and he retailed an anecdote that immediately undid five years of ethics classes at that excellent *madrasa* in Qoms.

When it was over Hassan gasped: 'Tell me the truth, Reza. Are there indeed such heinous places?'

'Everywhere. Why, in Paris airport itself, for the convenience of transfer passengers, there's an establishment where the tarts' – and he finished the rout of Hassan's education.

It was a very dry-mouthed co-pilot who managed to ask: 'Which terminal?'

Reza uttered a terrible laugh, but broke it off to exclaim '*Zamino bokoni* [fuck the soil]! Look!'

Hassan peered out of the cockpit window. A long black Jaguar was creeping toward them across the dark tarmac, British flags aflutter.

Reza leapt up. There was nothing he could do about his stubble, beer-breath or blood-shot eyes, but he smoothed his grizzled curls as well as he could and patted down his moustache – dashed back to the cabin-door, slapping aside two of his crew who tried to help, and got it open. He sucked in his paunch and struck a wide-armed pose of welcome at the top of the steps, just as the driver and two policemen extracted a figure in a cyclamen-coloured burqa from the back of the limousine. It seemed unable to stand. They propped it.

'*Khosh amadid!*' exclaimed Reza. 'A thousand greetings to you, most gracious lady. May the starry heavens in which it it is to be my privilege to waft you be to – be to you – '. It was too obvious his guest wasn't listening.

The face was (perhaps happily) covered. No light shone though the eye-grille. But the enormous folds of the *chador* could not disguise the grossness of that tall body. 'She must weigh a hundred kilogrammes!' exclaimed young Hassan, peering out of the cockpit window. It was his innocent custom to utter his thoughts aloud. Until tonight no harm had been done, his thoughts being like dew on almond-orchards in the high Zagros. 'She could be hiding a youth in there! Vile thought!' He sucked his teeth in a way he'd learned from Reza. 'Praise to The Merciful we're carrying so little baggage,' and this utterance too was recorded by the control tower; recorded so that I could hear, and bear witness to his debasement.

With a tremendous burp, the pink, ogrish figure lurched from car-door to aeroplane step, clutched the hand-rail, swayed a moment, began to pull itself up. The left leg was stiff, hurt perhaps in some drunken tumble, the black-gloved hands groped like blind crabs; the head rolled sightlessly. The policemen, who had a sense of humour, saluted. Reza, horrified at the idea of touching such a one, made a ceremony of standing back and gesturing her into the cabin with bows and rolling forearm.

Hassan was distractedly readying the 'plane for take-off, muttering: 'How can the Compassionate Fashioner-Of-All-Things permit wickedness in the wife of a Guardian? Do opportunities for such wickedness exist even in Iran – if I look hard enough? … Turbos off, throttles closed': that's how the drill goes. 'Inter-coolers cold, gyros uncaged; lights switched off; on; idle cut-off checked, cowl-flaps open right.' Usually this rigmarole soothed him, it was like telling worry-beads, or reciting the ninety-nine names of the Effacer, the Subtly Kind. But tonight it flustered him. The routine words had been dirtied, they inflamed him. 'Wanton idling, flaps open, inter-heating'. When Reza came back to the cockpit, shaking his head, he was startled to hear his *protégé* muttering 'Up-thrust, *kosefil*,' like any foul-mouthed veteran of the sky.

Back in the fuselage their monstrous guest was slumped in a seat – seats; draped over three of them.

'What about her seat-belt?' murmured Dr Naqdi of the Teheran Museum of Fine Arts, Curator of the exhibition. A cautious white-haired man in suit and no tie, he'd long since buckled himself in. But when he glanced back at the other two passengers, bleak-faced bearded young men who obviously had no use for seat-belts and seemed not to hear him, he gave up. 'Not a moment to quibble.' Instead he re-read aloud the plastic card of emergency instructions.

I suspect he exacerbated his anxiety about water-landings to take his mind off more pressing unease; for the men, lightly dangling sub-machine-guns, wore the dark-green uniform of the Iranian Revolutionary Guard. These two rogues were, by definition, guilty of atrocities, they were free of compunction about killing, and although they were onboard to protect the Rothkos – *his* Rothkos, as Dr Naqdi thought of them – they were sure to regard him as a changeling and half-infidel. Whenever he glanced behind, to the baggage compartment at the back of the 'plane where his precious Rothkos were stowed, he was careful to display a faint mordant smile, a model of ambiguity and moral detachment. No one could fairly interrupt it as impudent criticism of their fellow-passenger, who might be anyone at all; no one could justly infer he condoned her excess, should there have been excess and who could say; it was just a smile.

The Revolutionary Guards had no use for such nuance. They glared at the massive pink bundle, their faces livid with the imagination of stoning.

Then everyone heard the engines.

⊗

What a piece of work is man! How adroit, unkind, inventive, base; how nearly godlike, how much more troublesome than an insect! Without fault the man-made machinery spun, the cunning vessel sprang on to its ærial road, bearing a cargo of luminous man-made beauty. But it also carried six actual people, a fairly typical sample: that is, one satyr, one half-corrupted faun, one coward, two cruel bigots; and one more, who stirred, snored, belched, farted and scratched.

☙

Take-off was just after midnight; it's five hours from London to Beirut.

Outside the window wheeled the deathless stars, for it was a fine night; and the extravagant mortal lights of Europe twinkled below.

Around four the stars began to pale.

You'll have gathered who was lurking in the *chador*. I waited another quarter-hour, then put off my (almost-entirely affected) drunkenness, opened my eyes, adjusted my tremendous pink folds, and looked about.

The lights were low. Naqdi was anxiously dozing, dentures exposed, a distinguished glitter on his *pince-nez*. From the closed cockpit came a low mutter: Reza was further debauching his minion.

One of the Guards had deigned to sit, and was thoroughly asleep, face set in stern Islamic lines. But the other was alert, standing, gazing at me unkindly, cradling his gun. He was my difficulty.

This was a small low-slung jet, with ten seats and a tiny servery. There was no cargo-hold: luggage went behind a partition, aft, beyond the single loo. I knew all this from studying a plan of the 'plane during my journey from Whitehall to Heathrow, in that very embarrassing Jag.

So now I heaved myself up and began to move down the fuselage, hobbling because my left knee couldn't bend.

The Guard made a peremptory gesture as if to say *Sit, wretched harlot*, but I performed a charade of vomiting, and he shrugged in distaste. *Here then is the lavatory, much-befouled daughter of Shatan, make haste*. His glare as I approached him was so savage he must have expected more abandoned behaviour on the spot. Perhaps I'd produce noxious stuff, forbidden by the Prophet, and tempt him. As a matter of fact that's almost exactly what I did. (Here was one of the moments I'd foreseen. I'd foreseen it might kill me.) I was holding up a silver hip-flask and his eyes, which had been widening in rage, blurred, for a gas came hissing out as I unscrewed. If you did not hold your breath, as I did, you at once swayed, as he did – .

The bore of being a conspirator is that you keep looking ahead, not to what might happen, but to what you need to do if it does. When the future arrives you stop thumbing one version of the script and grab at another. Actual events pass you by. Thus I barely noticed, and could scarcely enjoy, the sight of my enemy toppling, for he made such a crash at my feet (at least it sounded tremendous to me) I had to swirl about. Here was another moment I might not survive.

But the other goon slept on, doubtless inured to the shrieks and thuds of police stations. Naqdi flinched but did not wake. The hum of the captain's conversation continued without pause over the rival hum of the engines, too engrossingly pornographic to be broken. All was well.

I turned back to the partition-door. Would it be locked? It *was* – no it *wasn't*. Glory, glory. I pushed it open, kicked the Guard through, bent awkwardly, left leg straight, to scoop up his AK-47, squeezed my own tremendous bulk through sideways, pulled the door behind us, let out my breath, and groped for a light. Click.

An untidy, windowless cabin. Suitcases piled over there, more guns and such unpleasantness *there*. But here, here, directly before me, were a dozen upright pine cases, an inch apart, each case three inches wide, five foot high, seven foot long, like coffins for folk crushed by steam rollers. It was the horde.

Edifying to see how well the cases were secured against turbulence and other airy troubles! Each was fixed to the floor with steel brackets.

Less delightful to find there were no labels. I might have to open them all.

I looked at my very complicated watch and swore. Late, late, late! It said 04:44 Greenwich time, and we were 33° 29′ East: already beyond the coast of Cyprus. And we had (as I could feel myself) begun to descend: 27,000 feet; 26,500. I'd not given myself enough time.

Fast as I could I wriggled off my horrible robe. My fatness was composed of sacks of equipment strapped to my torso; these I flung about the floor. One sack was a toolkit; I got out a short crowbar, and after a second or two had prised open the first of the cases.

Remarkable, this: the famous Rothko glow works even on its side in a wooden box. Such white-green-yellow shone in my face, it might have contained a spring meadow. However, white-green-yellow bars were no good. It wasn't *849*, and I hammered it shut. Nor was the next case, full of burgundy-crimson-brick light, right. Nor the third, nor the fourth; and we were now at 21,000 feet. The fifth case was lavender-purple-black (odd that black should glow so much) but the fun was going out of the thing. When I looked at my watch I found we were thirty-five miles from target, four minutes off, which was too soon; and I cursed Benjy for his pathetic eyes which seemed likely to get me killed. Why hadn't I left him whimpering behind the gym? Sixth case; no. Of course this wasn't really about Benjy, it was about – seventh case; no. Eighth – yes yes yes. Portcolour, green, a border of radiant sea-blue: this is what had caused all the fuss. I lifted it from its case, astonished at its weight. *Why?* Of course, the frame: black resin, simple, tasteful, geometric, massive.

Despite my rush, I leaned the hefty black thing against the stack of suitcases, and sighed over it. Jones-Brown could say what he liked of 'crude fakes'; This canvas was beautiful. I let my fingers patter over its extraordinarily thick patina...

We were at 12,000 feet; 11,500. I got stuff like coloured Plasticine from one my packages, and applied a sausage of it to the cargo door. My admirable hands did not tremble. I inserted a fuse and clipped on a detonator. Good. I studied my watch. We were thirty miles off the coast of the Lebanon: good again. 10,000 feet: good once more. Forty-two seconds to go. Anything else? I bashed the empty case about with my crowbar to create the right impression. I dropped the tools, kicked them aside, frowned a little over the Revolutionary Guard's sombre young face, zipped my jumpsuit to my throat, pulled on a woollen cap. Thirty-four seconds; thirty-three; thirty-two.

At thirty-one came disaster: a sudden noise over the speakers. Reza was addressing his four passengers in a loud babble of Farsi. I caught the word *Beirut*. He was rousing them far sooner than I'd expected, blast him.

The other Guard was roused. I could hear him saying 'Jafar?', then shouting, 'Jafar! Jafar!' Jafar heard him too, and moved pitifully at my feet, trying to groan. One more moment and his comrade would be through the door, beating me unconscious with his rifle-butt.

We weren't yet in the right place but I couldn't wait. I touched the detonator, and although the bang was not much more than a Christmas cracker, the world was overthrown in the twinkling of an eye.

The cargo hatch tore itself free – shrank at incredible speed, was a dot in the roaring dawn air, gone, nothing. A fresh violent sunrise filled the cabin, gold, cold – tearingly-deathly cold – there was unbelievable roaring, every atom shrieked, kept shrieking – an alarm pulsed red overhead, its wail inaudible in the howl of the sucking air. The air was full of rockets, a thousand things firing themselves through the blazing gap that had been the hatch – all the bags erupted outward, some thumping me in the head as they crashed past – my *chador* whipped by, was gone – Jafar the Guard went to his reward – the hefty black thing –

And me. I'd clung to one of the brackets, letting the furious outward wind tear me with its hundred claws. Now I loosed my fingers.

Crack! Hell vanished. I was in ethereal free-space, burning red-gold, gently whistling, turning over and over, plummeting into the enormous dawn.

iii.

An interlude.

Since boyhood I've been prone to dreams that strike me, even when they're finished, as wiser than most waking thoughts. Such dreams come to me even when I'm not asleep – which isn't a sign that I'm a visionary, or incipient lunatic, but that the wanton part of my mind remains open by day, when in most people it hibernates. My languor, which (among other things) makes me so unpopular with undergraduates, isn't entirely feigned. I'm never perfectly asleep, never entirely awake.

Therefore I'm not shy to record what I saw during the half-minute I fell.

One particularly atrocious dream plagued me as a child. A noise of hurrying cataracts rouses me: something's abroad. I sleep with curtains open (closing them makes my visitations worse), so I sit up and look into the night. And out of the night, swimming through the burbling air, comes an eye. Unable to scream, I cringe against my headboard. The eye floats up to my glaring window. When it presses itself to the glass I discern the head of which it's a part: wolf, giant lizard, pale decapitated woman…

I'm sceptical about these complications. I suspect my imagination concocted them to blunt the insane horror of the eye itself. Or perhaps I invented them to *cheapen* my nightmare, so it could profitably be retailed at breakfast to dull Agatha, my sister. (A mere eye wouldn't make her scream; she was never very subtle; a born teenage suicide.) Certainly the adult form dispenses with such gothic touches. There's only the eye.

I'd suffer horribly, except I've discovered that my work blanks the eye out. When I'm beset, I get out of bed and go to my desk, to pore and scribble and thus cocoon myself in paper.

But there was no paper to hand that dawn, tumbling out of the sky; the eye visited me, unveiled.

And there was this difference: it soared out of the continent of Asia, from the east and a bit to the south; it came closer and closer; and as it approached it enlarged. A hundred yards off it was huge beyond words, blotting out the sun; by the time it was within arms' length it was vaster than the cosmos. I was a speck within a mote, and the mote was the physical universe, hovering faintly in front of the eye.

The eye! I was beyond terror now, my emotions had boiled off. All I could do was witness the unspeakable, unendurable beauty of that eye: glowing-black pupil, hazel iris flecked with yellow, white sclera; an abyss of seeing and being seen.

It was only a flash, but then everything's a flash when you're accelerating at thirty-two feet per second per second. I'd seen what I needed to and looked away. Behold, I was far out from land, far above the water, deep in the golden air, still dropping, and wonderfully alone.

iv.

'Um – yes, hallo? Hallo!'

'Foreign Secretary? Have I woken you?'

'Most definitely not, Miss Litherland,' Benjy whispered severely; speaking might crack his skull. 'Up since dawn,' which was technically true. He'd fallen asleep on his immense leather sofa as soon as I'd left, and first light had roused him with crinked neck, rasping eyes, throbbing brain, parched gums, churning stomach. He'd rung for crumpets and tea, and sat nibbling until it seemed likely he'd live; then returned to the sofa to regroup. (He owed as much to England.) Thus he'd been prone, dreaming of Bumper, his boyhood cocker-spaniel, who'd understood him. 'Consulting. Experts.'

'I have the Iranian Foreign Minister on the private line.'

Benjy sat up sharply. 'Put him through.' Click. 'Ali!'

'*Benjamin.*' A refined New England accent. 'Good morning. I have sad tidings.'

'Don't say that, Ali. Not today. We're exhilarated. Success of the Rothko exhibition, y'know. So gracious of the Islamic Republic to send.'

'It's that of which I have to speak. The aeroplane bringing it on to Lebanon suffered a mishap as it was coming in to land. A loose cabin door.'

'Good G – gracious, Ali. Was all well?'

'Sudden decompression. They landed safely, although the Curator gave himself thrombosis. But it grieves me to report that the distinguished lady you asked us to transport was lost. As was one of our Revolutionary Guards. I doubt their remains could be retrieved. Those waters teem with sharks.'

'Ah. Ali, I'm saddened, appalled, more than I can say… The artworks themselves?'

'One, alas, was sucked out – its case disintegrated. It too is unrecoverable. Although, of course, insured. The others are apparently undamaged.'

'The exhibition?'

'Goes ahead. The catalogue will be rewritten with just eleven paintings. The Curator, happily, is in no state to object. Nothing need be heard of this sensational incident. Sensation distracts from the calm spiritual beauty of art, don't you think? As well as embarrassing us. The authorities have their media under control in Beirut. As have we.'

'As have we, Ali. Or rather they control us, which works just as well. Rest assured, they'll henceforth refer to *eleven* Rothkos. Nothing can, or indeed should, disturb the, the course our media have set, of ' (he was groping for the postcard; got it! Not wasted work after all) 'of renewed friendship between the ancient nation of Britain and the yet-more-ancient nation of Iran, a renewed and renewable energy-source for both.'

'That is very well put, if I may say so, Benjamin.'

But something struck Benjy. He put down his precious card. 'I say, Ali, if negligence by our ground crew was in any way—'

'Tut-tut. It was the pilot's responsibility. He has already been shot. And his co-pilot. Uttering, I gather from our gallant friends in Hezbollah, obscene blasphemies. More important matters. This tour, which we have allowed *nothing* to disrupt, surely augurs further exchanges between our peoples.'

'How wonderful you should say so. Ali: the Worcestershire Morris-Dancing Troupe is finishing a tour of India. If an invitation were to come – through the British-interests section of the Swedish embassy – we could arrange...'

'It will be despatched this morning. After *that*, I see my schedule allows a stopover next month at the Cork Film Festival, where an Iranian animated short is in competition.'

'I wouldn't dream of missing it. And if we run into each other...'

'Benjamin, I feel we might...'

'I look forward to discussion which could...'

'Range beyond art?'

'Art?' purred the Foreign Secretary, 'what is art?', and put the 'phone down knowing he was among the great. (Bumper had guessed; Benjy had seen it in his eyes.) The race is not to the swift, nor yet favour to men of skill. Was Talleyrand candid? Was Disraeli deep? Was Lincoln pious? Was Bismark upright? Was the Borgia pope scrupulous? Whimsical history passes over paragons to lay its finger on *this* chance statesman, murmuring 'He, he shall be first of his generation.'

Thus Benjy nuzzled in the lap of fate; fate cooled his forehead; his hangover was gone. In a twinkling, his youthful self-doubt, his innocence, had become, as it might be, historic curiosities, worthy to be stowed in the Most-Especially-Secret Safe. He contemplated (he told me; for he gratefully recounted this *dénouement*, sparing himself nothing) the Nobel Peace Prize. He contemplated *rapprochement*, reopened embassies, freighters cutting wakes through greasy blinding mirror-smooth Gulf waters; state visits, a knighthood, global realignment, the vindication of Shi'a. He thought of exported fighter jets and shortbread, of imported oil (oil!), dates, pistachios, Caspian caviar, of – of breakfast.

He strode across the room, flung open the door, and startled Miss Litherland by the booming fashion with which he uttered certain words of command; words they'll be quoting in Whitehall corridors when I am dust, when they gossip about the moment statesmen put off mortality and take on grandeur. 'More crumpets, Miss Litherland, *if you wouldn't mind too terribly?*'

v.

'So I let go of the steel bracket and bang! the 'plane whipped away. I was turning and turning in space. It wasn't like falling. I spun, hanging, like a god. But the sparkling sea grew wider, rushing up to embrace me.'

Frankly, I think I was telling my story rather well. But my tiresome chit wore her face of exaggerated interest – pretty expectation, jolly amazement – which is her way of at once suppressing and expressing a yawn. (Lady Margot ffontaines-Laigh is tall and her hair, redder than what's usually called auburn, is so massive and heavy it gives her the cachet of a statue. She's often still, partly from pride of caste, partly because she's not yet certain which note to sound. Intelligence and beauty came on her suddenly – she's a crimson-white lump in photographs from five years ago – and has yet to calibrate her displays of wit, voluptuousness and command. She already knows to understate her alarming self-sufficiency, and to dissimulate her boredom with male puppy-likeness. Me she both underrates and reveres. I fear she regrets being born female. Her eyes are very green.)

I tried harder, heightening my effects. 'The sea! Stippled, gilt and black. The Levant an immense craggy mass, deep grey. Coming out from behind Mount Lebanon, the sun. The same sun I'd seen politely descend into the lake in St James's Park the evening before. But it'd turned violent, going round the back of the world. It came roaring out of Mount Lebanon, burning red. A cauldron in a foundry, tipped over to pour out molten iron.' Really I should take to the stage, I should rent myself out for children's birthday parties. Which is what this was, after all. 'The air was steaming with white vapours and flakes of gold leaf. But above me, all about me, was pure bullion. Not a scrap of blue. It was impossible not to think of that vault as solid.' Why was the minx not delighted with me? Wicked birthday-girl: she went so far as to raise her eyebrows (her admittedly excellent eyebrows, thicker than most girls or women would dare). 'Only far off, far to the west, was black. On the furthest edge of the planet, bending over into space, there was still night. There, this astonishing vast day had yet to begin.'

She held her *demitasse* for me to notice it was empty. To punish such coarseness, I attended to my other guest.

'More coffee, sir? No? Oh yes and what about *you* young Margot? And more Bénédictine?'

'Thank you, only coffee,' she said, dryly. She must be impressed despite herself; she must. 'Tell me, Felix, had you been sky-diving before? You obviously found it dreadfully exciting.'

'No, I was virgin. Read what to do in a book.'

'In a book. I see.'

'You?'

'Oh yes. Only the once, I think. Last year, when I was travelling. The Maldives. Or Seychelles? One of those places. It rained.'

'Then you know what it's like and I shan't bore you with more details. Have *you* ever been parachuting, Professor – um, um, Professor?'

Jones-Brown tittered weakly. 'I've no interests outside my academic field': again that gawky note, blending defiance or discomfort. For he was certainly uncomfortable.

We were in my rooms in College, although they were unrecognisable. My sitting-room had put off mellowness and become a silvery cavern. No longer did books or unbound papers form effete heaps, here and there, on upholsteries of silk. My desk was scattered with maps of Africa and the Amazon. The waterproof camping trestle I'd unfolded in the bay window bore an arsenal of spiky metal: skates, crampons, tent-poles. The mantel was stacked with hard plastic equipment, ration boxes, ammunition boxes, sky-diving helmets topped with cameras. (Thank God the Foreign Office was paying.) A complicated backpack was propped against a wall beside an inflatable mosquito-net. Two heavy hunting-rifles made themselves at home on an ottoman, for I was considering a safari. Wouldn't shooting elephants, now that it's so illegal, be more fun than it had been in my grandfather's day? His diaries make depressing reading: bustling officials, crafty local chieftains, pilfering bearers, unspeakable insects, never enough to drink in the evenings. But of course grandfather, poor booby, always missed. Surely modern poachers must shoot straight? In the Carpathians there's still bear; I've always wanted to see the Carpathians…

The outdoorsy mood doesn't visit me often, but when it does, it gets indulged, despite my slightly creaky limbs and very slightly receding hair.

I'm sure outdoorsy moods never visit Jones-Brown. Invisibility clung to him: amidst these dense mineral shapes he resembled a human figure cut from tracing paper. He was perched spinsterishly in the corner of a sofa he had to share with a brace of oxygen tanks. Gutting knives on the coffee-table glittered so wickedly he seemed nervous about putting down his cup. Or perhaps his discomfort came from within. He'd just lunched with me on high table, although – as he told me, then all his neighbours, one by one (this was a man who used thought sparingly, recycling what he used) – he usually didn't bother with lunch, there being so much to read. Now he was sipping strong black coffee, which he was obviously not used to either, one hand pressed to his belly.

He had no interests outside his field. 'Oh well, I plunged two miles out of the sky in the usual way. But I'll tell you this. When I used to go to confession—'

'You did?' Margot was amazed at last.

'During a pious period, very brief, at school. I found going through the confessional door was like stepping into the Tardis.'

'The what?' asked the impossible Jones-Brown.

'Be quiet,' I said before I could stop myself, then softened it a bit with a smile. 'It's nothing, Professor, just pop cult. But listen: it's much more like dropping out of the door of a 'plane…'

It was refreshing to have Margot interested again. 'You catalogued your sins on the way down – once you'd finished itemising the colour scheme?'

'I thought of this and that.' I wasn't going to confess the eye in the presence of Jones-Brown.

'Let's have a *précis.*'

'I hurtled downward for half a minute. Like death. Obviously. Also, birth. Glorious to be so alone. The 'plane receding off to the east, losing altitude quickly but clearly in one piece. Beirut a congealed blur. In shadowed folds of mountains to the north, villages with their lights still on. A tiny white wake behind a tinier black dot: a boat returning from a night's fishing. But all about, for miles and miles and miles, just me. Me, and this ecstatic brightness.'

I'd lost Margot. She was shaking her hair. Without making a sound so she managed to tell me: *This is my birthday; I've many pleasant things to do; it's not pleasant wasting my afternoon with your cardboard joke of a guest, this* parody *of you.* (Ouch! Is that how I seem?) *Why exactly am I here?*

Why exactly was she here? I'd noticed her in the crowded body of Hall as we dons and our guests filed up to high table. All the undergraduates stared; her stare was particularly hard. I'd vanished on Friday morning; it was now lunchtime on Tuesday, her birthday, and I was reappearing without explanation, bringing with me this sordid little man. She'd caught my hand-signal *Come to my rooms after lunch* – and obeyed, but she wasn't being gracious. My account of being consulted by the Foreign Secretary, which had made Jones-Brown giggle, squeeze his knees with professional vanity, and turn almost human, had blackened her face. My stint as a fat Persian woman left her cold. Even my assault on the Guard and parachute jump seemed to weary her.

Yet I kept talking. 'D'y'know Doré's engraving of the *Paradiso* – the souls in bliss hanging in radiant circles?'

'Retrograde art,' sniffed Jones-Brown, 'of no developmental significance,' and was ignored.

'Heaven *was* like that. An untainted world. The new day felt impossibly fresh. To match the impossibility of being alive in mid-air. Too much joy for one man. The universe jangling from the final hammer-blows of creation.

'However, Professor, we seem to be irritating Lady Margot with these flourishes. At 1,500 feet I pulled a cord. Thwack! A lime-green canopy jerked upward between me and the sky. What? Oh yes, Professor, one of my parcels was a parachute.

'I was jolted, then floated, not attempting to steer. Slight offshore breeze. Sun in my eyes. Freefall is godlike, parachuting's merely fun.

'When my wrist altimeter read twenty-five metres I yanked at another package, a hard yellow cylinder the size of a magnum of claret. It split in two, and started hissing, writhing, spinning over itself, unfolding, inflating – officiously turning itself into an inflatable raft.

'I didn't enjoy this. For last seconds in the air I wrestled a soft fatness that *would* press its swelling belly into my face, however I grappled with its handles.

'Hit the water upside down. Smothered and blinded by rubbery skin. Like every sea, colder than it looked. Raft on top, parachute an affectionate giant squid. I was unhappy.

'Two or three strokes. Clear. Got hold of the raft's soft side. Got breath back. Loosed parachute straps, clumsily clambered aboard. Would've been easier if my leg could bend. Tumbled in face-first. Gasped and gaped for a bit. Slowly got my wet things off. Chucked 'em overboard.

'The last of my packages was a waterproof bag. Towel, denim overalls, silly hat, electronic beacon, whisky flask. Gentle swell on the sea. Southern sun already warm. I lay drowsily sunning myself, content.'

'Pshaw,' said Margot, becoming exasperated, 'you must've been nervous. You'd blown the door too soon. Landed in the wrong place.'

'By half a minute. A bit high, a tad north, a smidgen too far off the Lebanese coast. But my beacon uttered friendly beeps, flashing its reassuringly unimaginative red bulb: *beep, beep, beep…* No, I wasn't concerned. They'd find me. Meanwhile I was on the bosom of the Inner Sea, still entirely alone. Watching the sun mount. Watching its waters flush silver, then indigo, then turquoise.'

Margot turned sarcastic. 'Perhaps the Mediterranean was gaudy from having a fake Rothko dissolved in it.'

'A pretty fancy, my dear. But here's the thing: I *couldn't* be scared. What with nearly being killed by Revolutionary Guards, falling through air, being cradled on sunny water…'

'Not to mention your hangover,' she said, unnecessarily.

'A wisp, the least wisp – my mind was transfigured. It beheld simplicity. I wasn't chugging through a thousand atoms of experience each second in the usual way. Nor did it waste energy thinking. The cosmos had resolved itself into broad, radiant elements. Which I had simply to observe. Admire.'

'All hangovers are like that.'

'Silly teen. I've been in an elevated mental condition, not just on the 'plane, but all week. A state of grace. Don't suppose it'll last, but it's interesting. I floated at sea unworried, unworriable, because the world is just as Rothko says. Luminous bars of orange sky, black land, turquoise sea. Visible abstraction.'

'That,' said Jones-Brown, putting down his coffee cup with a clatter and sitting up smartly, 'is reductionist. A crypto-naïve representationalist approach' – but I've seen that cross look on academic faces before, I know what it means: they object to *any* approach. Jones-Brown was a vestal who'd given up whatever chance he'd had of normal life to stand before his tiny temple, burning paper on the altar, paper, more paper. It was cruel for him to see a normal man come up whistling, hands in pockets, and stroll past him into the shrine.

I laughed, and gave myself the last of the Bénédictine. 'Then let me share less controversial thoughts that occurred to me as I lay embosomed on *mare nostrum*.'

Margot rudely pushed away her cup. 'Don't. Conclude. *Were* you eventually rescued? Or did you die at sea?'

I smiled at her insolence. I was spinning out my story for a reason, a reason I'll keep from her; she'd find it creepy. She was born, I happen to know from Lady Rievaulx, her incontinent mother, at 16:41:22 on 9th October 1992. It was now a shade after four. If I could detain my impatient teen another half-hour, I'd witness her infancy cease.

Wasn't there a mad New England doctor who installed fine scales beneath deathbeds, to weigh his patients' departing souls? Didn't Wordsworth observe the visionary gleam dwindle through youth to the instant (the *instant*) when *the Man perceives it die away and fade into the light of common day*? I couldn't get Margot to stand on bathroom scales, but by God I was going to watch her carefully. The moment might prove as suggestive, as abysmal, as death.

So: 'I feel oddly safe at sea,' I said discursively, 'like all Englishmen. Even as a castaway. Don't you?' Jones-Brown, tainted no doubt with unmarine Welsh blood, shrugged. 'Continents groan with aliens.' He was shocked. 'But as soon as we're offshore we're in the keeping of the Royal Navy. Such as it is. Now, the flagship of our Mediterranean Fleet was close at hand. Eighty fathoms below my own craft, bolt upright, nose buried in slime. I knew this because my Great-Uncle Wilfred (bless him) liked to recite William McGonagall.

> 'Twas on Thursday, the twenty-second of June,
> And off the coast of Syria, and in the afternoon,
> And in the year of our Lord eighteen ninety-three,
> That the ill-fated Victoria *sank to the bottom of the sea.*
>
> The Victoria *sank in fifteen minutes after she was rammed,*
> In eighty fathoms of water, which was smoothly calmed;

(as it was yesterday). Our Fleet was on manoeuvres off Beirut. Admiral Tryon, a furious fellow, couldn't bear being corrected. "Sixteen points to port!" "Surely you mean starboard, sir?" "Port!" bellowed the nation's hope. "What are you waiting for?" and they obeyed, shutting their eyes. *Victoria* was chopped in half by *Camperdown*. Tryon went down with his ship. So did most of his men.

'What colossal egotism! An admiral throwing away a perfectly good battleship rather than suffer contradiction!' Margot scowled, as if to contradict. 'Naturally Tryon was god of my boyhood.

> *For he was skilful in naval tactics, few men could with him cope,*
> *And he was considered to be the nation's hope.*

When I grew up I too wanted to sacrifice one incomparably beautiful thing to whimsy. Ideally, toss it into the *same* sea. To lie beside the wreck of. H.M.S *Victoria*. Meanwhile, what joy to have my hero lying near! The old boy's shade raging on the sea-bed, unassuaged—'

Jones-Brown made a *moue* of indifference. 'Slithering into mysticism, Dr Culpepper?'

I glanced at my watch. More. 'Then I raised my eyes and let them play along the shore. Directly opposite me was the town of Byblos. During that recent event, the Trojan War, Byblos was already renowned as the oldest city in the world. It had been standing for 7,000 years. Unimaginable! For millennia, its ships went about this blessèd sea carrying papyrus – what the Greeks called *biblos*. Byblos caused literature. Alas. I'm no bibliophile, Jones-Brown, are you? I regret paper. Once you've got paper, you shrink to its level, you need it; it creates addicts; it's an export sinister as opium. Byblos, Byblos, Byblos: every time we enter a *bibliothèque* or consult a (horrible thing) bibliography, we're commemorating the city. Yet how can we criticize it, staring at it down such an abyss of time? A century of centuries!'

'What's antique cannot be relevant to the twenty-first century,' pronounced Jones-Brown as if it were an aphorism. Perhaps it is in the staffroom at North Cambridgeshire Poly.

Margot audibly groaned, and stood. 'Thank you for coffee, Felix. I'm glad your weekend exploits amuse you. I should go and read an irrelevant Latin book. Professor – um.'

It was only quarter past. 'Oh sit down. I've nearly finished.' A lie. She sat. 'While I was thinking these and other wondrous thoughts (now lost to you both for eternity), there came a tiny whirr, which grew to a whine, then a ridiculous deafening roar. A jot on the northern horizon had swelled into monstrosity and crouched over me, flickering my raft with shade.'

'In short,' said the impossible man, 'a helicopter.'

'The sun, high now, had painted the universe to match itself. The vault was an almost-solar gold. I was awash on a pool of molten tinsel broad as the planet's face. It was dazzling to look up. Impossible light burned on the curved glass of the helicopter, burned and fled, flashed at me from steel – I covered my eyes.

'Something flaccid thumped my face. Rope. A ladder had dropped from the sky. I made a poor job of hauling myself on to the lowest rungs, what with my stiff leg, and the dazzle and bewildering racket, but I managed. Four hands stretched down and heaved me in. It seemed horribly crowded after such perfect solitude. Bizarrely dark. Suddenly the racket got worse: one of the squaddies was leaning out, shredding raft and parachute with his machine-gun. Nothing was left but a meaningless litter of rubber, untraceable, shrinking, shrinking – we were ascending now. With a swoop we were off over the sea to Cyprus.

'I would have liked to get off the base and look round the island of Aphrodite – R.A.F. Akrotiri's a scruffy sort of place – but orders were to get me back to England at once. I tried to be discreet. Which wasn't hard. Picking unexplained people out of the sea was apparently everyday work. These airmen knew better than to ask how I got there. They all seemed to be twenty and thought of me as an old man, especially with my irritating limp.' A stiff-legged old fellow with an excessively young girlfriend. Another twenty minutes until she turns. 'They were patronisingly polite. Hardly any swearing at lunch. Which was surprisingly good. Barbecued octopus. We kept away from the one inflammatory topic, Abstract Expressionism. Afterward I was put on a twin-turboprop. We landed at R.A.F. Wittering last night in time for a less good dinner. I got back to Cambridge this morning by train. How wet England looks after even a few days away. You were kind enough to drive over for lunch, Professor. And here we are.'

Smug Jones-Brown raised an eyebrow.

'Oh yes,' I said, 'one last thing. The point of it all, really. I 'phoned the Foreign Secretary from Wittering. He sounded relaxed.' True. 'Clearly the crisis is averted. He didn't say but I could tell he was thinking' (a lie, this) "Thanks to the artistic acumen of um, Jones-Brown".'

There was a pointless pause for a second or two. Then Jones-Brown began to snuffle and twitch, and at last slapped his knee. 'To make a very long story short – you're defeated.'

'I am.'

'I've worsted you.'

'You have.'

Margot looked bewildered

'Ah well. Don't take it too hard.' He got to his feet and peered over Megiddo Court. 'It's pretty here in its way, but the real work's being done at more progressive universities. That's where the brainpower is. You see that, don't you?'

'Yes,' I said humbly, as Margot slumped back in her armchair, dazed. 'Do you need to get back to New Northborough? I imagine vital research calls.'

'North Newborough.'

'I beg your pardon.'

'Yes. There's just the matter of...'

'Of course! To the victor the spoils. Over there,' and I gestured to a wooden case under a ski-helmet.

Jones-Brown shuffled over, peered down, hesitated.

'"Port!"' I mock-bellowed in hoarse naval fashion. '"What are you waiting for?"'

He sniggered, pulled out a bottle of 2002 College tawny, squinted at the label, dusted it with dampened forefinger, spelled out the lettering, admired his prize, looked round for something to clean his finger, didn't dare touch the wetsuit at his feet, and at last rubbed it on his trousers. 'Well, well,' he wittily remarked.

'Would you mind signing for it, Professor? Winners always sign my book.' I produced from a drawer a leather-bound ledger, heavily tooled in loopy gold in accord with *fin-de-siècle* taste.

'Ah yes, your funny old notebook,' said Jones-Brown condescendingly. 'Quaint reactionary customs,' and signed with a ballpoint pen. 'Now I'd better be off.'

But it wasn't to be. He couldn't get the case more than a hand's-breadth into the air. It came down again with a distressing tinkle of glass. He stared at me haplessly.

'It *is* heavy. For a man of such brainpower. Let me carry it out through the Lodge. Where's your car? ... Good. Meanwhile you—' said I to Margot, dropping the diffident manner, 'stay here and read this.'

I thrust the ledger into her hands, and went across Megiddo with the port jingling in my arms. Jones-Brown rolled along beside me: I think I've mentioned his extraordinary gait. I ignored him, smiling as one smiles who communes with Admiral Tryon and the King of Byblos.

> *'Twas only those that leaped from the vessel at the first alarm,*
> *Luckily so, that were saved from any harm*
> *By leaping into the boats o'er the vessel's side,*
> *Thanking God they had escaped as o'er the smooth water they did glide.*

I smiled as one smiles who dictates what goes on in another head. My ledger's familiar to me; I knew precisely what it must be inciting in Margot. The point of making other people read is to penetrate them and possess. The point of reading I cannot imagine.

vi.

GERALD CULPEPPER'S
BETTING-BOOK

reads the title-page in school-boy handwriting (but BETTING has been blotted and corrected to BETING, itself struck through. The third time, perhaps having canvassed his peers, great-grandfather gets it right.)
Next page:

> *Harrow, 4th Feb 1890*
> WAGED: *that Sibley of Rendalls House cunot eet as many*
> *jamtarts as Culpepper of Moretons.*
> STAKE: *two shillings*

There are childish initials in the margin: *J.S., G.C.*

> *Harrow, 5th Feb 1890*
> VICTOR: *G. Culpepper (27 tarts).*

The greedy brat goes on to win a number of similar contests. At Cambridge his gambling progresses from food to drink. After Cambridge the entries take a more baleful turn; whores are mentioned; then:

Brooks's Club, St James's, 14th March 1900
WAGED: *with Charlie Baine that I cannot make the acwaintence*
of his cousin Miss Margaret Baine, who has 4000 a year in the
Funds, woo & be acceppted before midsummer's day.
STAKE: *a week's jaunt to Monte Carlo.*

[C.B., G.C.]

Monte Carlo, 21st June 1900
VICTOR: *Culpepper*

After marriage Gerald's atrocities taper off. There are a dozen pages of innocuous wagers about the weather. He generally wins. Finally:

To my son
Osbert Baine Culpepper,
on the occasion of his XXIst Birthday,
22nd Jan 1922;
hoping he will employ this book as profittably as has
his affec: & profligate father,
G.C.

In fact Osbert was a more cautious fellow, profligate only when it was safe. His bets concern shooting and fishing; they are seemly, modest, without gusto. It comes as a shock to find, from his time as a colonial judge in Kenya, this:

The Club, Balambala, Tanaland Province
Tues 2/6/1953
WAGED: *with Mjr Cyril Maze of the Lancashire Fusiliers,*
that I can condemn a dozen damned rebels before Tuesday next
STAKE: *as much gin as can be drunk in an evening.*

[C.M., O.C.]

The same,
Tues 9/6/1953
VICTOR: *Maze*

Osbert, having failed to hang enough Mau Mau, seems to lose interest in gambling. There's nothing more until a brusque note, dated 1990, to say that he's leaving his ledger *to my troubling grandson Felix.*

I've used it occasionally, mainly to settle spats with other dons about Latin adjectives. But here's my latest entry.

> Morpeth Arms, *Pimlico,*
> *Fri 5.x.2012*
>
> WAGED: *that Prof. Jones-Brown of ~~New~~ North Newborough does not possess such standing that he can persuade the authorities a genuine painting by Rothko is a forgery, to the length of having them destroy it.*
> STAKE: *a dozen bottles of middling St Wygefortis College port.*
> *[S.J-B., F.C.]*

> *My rooms, St Wygefortis', Cambridge*
> *Tues 9.x.2012*
>
> VICTOR: *S.J-B.*

and then an uncouth signature, *Steve P. Jones-Brown, PhD (Keele).* The final two-thirds of the book are blank, awaiting whatever mischief can be thought up.

vii.

In the six days since matriculation, Margot had acquired from St Wygy's perceptive and unkind undergraduates the nickname *Abishag,* after the girl who shared the bed of the senescent King David to keep him warm. But *did* she warm my age (I'm thirty-four); didn't I rather chill her youth? Now, as she read, she certainly felt cold all over.

But did she? Perhaps she felt *stricken.* Or: *for the first time in her life she considered the possibility of fainting.* Or: *she turned numb.* Or – very well, this is guesswork. You can be a person looking at a book, you can be in a book looked at; you can never quite look out. I don't know why I bother. Except that she did look old as death when I bounded back into my sitting-room. I'd achieved that much.

'Huzzah! We're rid of Jones-Brown.'

She said nothing at all.

'Self-absorbed brutes, these red-brick lecturers. I'm making myself whiskey and soda. Do you want? A hunter's drink... He's devoted his life to one dead artist. Worships him, collects tertiary relics – laundry-bills with Rothko's name on. Yet he's prepared to throw away his Master's masterpiece for a case of port.'

She said nothing at all. She was a silent teen.

'No, not even for port – I don't imagine he can tell wine from beer with the lights off. Just for the thrill of scoring points off Oxbridge. Isn't that sinister?'

Then Abishag burst out in horror: '*He's* sinister? Dear Christ. What are you?'

I enthroned myself on the oxygen tanks, stirring the ice with my finger, stealing a look at my watch. Not much longer.

'I follow it all,' she continued, wildly – 'this derring-do was just about reproving *me*. There was no robbery. On Thursday when I asked you for a visit to the Rothko exhibition you didn't merely refuse me. You decided to *act out* an ultimate No. You slipped off to London yourself the next—'

'True. Taking my betting-book. "Something sensational to read on the train".'

'—next morning. Went round the exhibition. Chose the best of the paintings. Found that dingy muppet Jones, flattering him with conversation on some technical point—'

'Cleverly guessed.'

'—took him out to some pub, got him tipsy, made your bet.'

'Wrong,' I said mildly, feet on sofa. 'He sipped a half of shandy. Booze was unnecessary. He *leapt* at my wager. That's why I say he's—'

'Then you had a Rothko forged—'

'Wrong again. Did it myself. Half an hour in my sister Gertrude's garage applying house-paint with a roller. Rather more time smashing and trampling the result. It only had to impress detectives, whose artistic taste rises no further than fox-hunting prints. And Benjy, who now and then admits a certain baffled awe for "Bellini, and Tiepolo, and all those fearfully clever Italian foreigners." Benjy probably doesn't grasp there *can* be American painting. Painting's something done in Italy the way champagne's made in Champagne… My daub wasn't remotely like the real thing. I don't know how Jones kept a straight face, keening over it, groaning about tonal values, egg-whites—'

'—stowed it in a lock-up, then put on a bad brogue—'

'*That's* simply a slur, I spoke a shade of County Wicklow—'

'—to 'phone the police—'

'—*southern* County Wicklow, which I could hardly expect the police to—'

'*You 'phoned the police.* And waited for that innocent, Benjamin Wedgwood, to beg you to save him. As he always does. Knowing he'd call in Jones. God, I feel quite sorry for him, sitting there in agony, expecting a diplomatic crisis, with you two villains playing him along. Pretending not to know each other—'

'Credit where credit's due. Must've been harder for Jones. There are so many things he really doesn't know, think of the strain of *feigning* ignorance.'

'All so you could—'

'Feigning not to know *me.* The unknowable.'

'All so you could have the government help you get your hands on the loveliest thing Rothko ever painted. And *obliterate* it. A sacrifice to whimsy. *Then* come back and crow over my weak taste. On my *birthday. And* risk international chaos. *And* risk ruining Wedgwood, not that I care about him. *And* – O God, I can't endure to be in the same room as you.'

'You're overestimating my perversity.'

'But it's *true.* You just told me. Your crime's witnessed in this cursed ledger.'

'Oh that. Don't worry. I needed Jones to sign the receipt as a confession. We're quite safe from him now. He can never boast about what he's done. If the Official Secrets Act doesn't silence him, the thought of what art-lovers would do to him *will.* I mean if they knew he condemned a genuine Rothko worth thirty million pounds, just to win a bet... Don't think I like whisky and soda.' I put aside my tumbler. (She made a wild gesture of rejection.) '"Worth" in some abstract sense, of course. It can't ever be sold, so it doesn't matter what it's worth, does it? We can only measure the delight it brings its possessor. And it *is* delightful.'

'Felix, I'm going mad before your eyes. Why are you using the present tense? Did you chuck it in the deep or not? Was the story you just told a lie?'

'*The monster war vessel capsized bottom uppermost, And, alas, lies buried in the sea totally lost...* No, every word was true. I left out certain details.'

'Have mercy. Where is *Untitled 849?*'

I glanced at my watch. (What a lot of our life we waste staring at clocks, watching the hands brush away the most precious commodity. Thirty-five seconds to go.) 'Deduce, deduce. You affect to be my disciple. Think like me.'

'About *what*?'

'Begin with my leg. You ought to've noticed – the infamous stiffness has cured itself. See?' I performed an improvised dervish swirl round the room, which metamorphosed into a matador pose, watchful, menacing, graceful: I snatched up a mortarboard as cap, a long metal tube from my desk as sword, I twirled my scarlet doctoral gown as a cape. Death-incarnating, the bull lowered its massive head, blacker than night, pawing the yellow dust of an arena where a thousand beautiful women in black mantillas clutched lace fans, begging the Madonna to protect me; the sequins on my *traje de luces* scarcely glittered so still I stood, awaiting the beast's heavy onrush. Oh, I felt pleased with myself that afternoon.

'Your stiff leg was a fraud?' murmured Abishag, battered into stupidity.

'A container was strapped under my trouser-leg. Stuffed into my sock. To hold, don't you see, the canvas.' Her face, bewildered, almost bovine, was quite unlike itself. 'Which I cut out of its frame on the 'plane. Before I blew the door. D'y'follow?' I paused: seven; six. 'You seem not to follow.' Tick, tick: *ping!* Time. She transformed before me. In a moment, in the twinkling of an eye, the trumpet sounded, the young were made old, corruptible; as we shall all be changed. 'Darling Abishag, it was just the black frame that went flying. To lie beside the *Victoria* and the bones of Sir George Tryon, on whom be peace.'

'Where,' my twenty-year-old persisted, in the heavy blurred voice of a sleepy child, 'is the painting now?'

'Here.' I handed her the metal tube. 'Happy birthday. Sorry I didn't have time for gift-wrap. Please never again call me ineffectual. Or remote.'

She held the tube in both hands and stared, and stared.

'I admit there are splashes. Sea-salt. But that tube's designed to withstand blizzards, it'll be all right inside.'

Like a sleep-walker she swept her arm over my trestle, sending studded-boots and ice-picks clattering to the floor. She unscrewed the metal cap and slid out the canvas, unrolling it with blind, unerring hands.

It was luminous; how are we to handle this fact, short of Jones's alchemical bibble-babble? Here were blocks of red, green, blue, formed of brushstrokes without any sign of effort, poised beside each other without mingling or jarring, radiant from each other's purity. Their harmony was so absolute the glow was like a zone of music – no, silence: perfectly new silence when the last throb of a gong has died into air, compelling as the silence of the spheres.

(Generally speaking, mind, I don't care about paintings, 'though I like them as *décor*: the important thing in a picture is matching the sofa cushions.)

I looked up from the canvas. My handsome sitting-room looked cluttered and dusty. Margot had lost the power of speech. To clear the mood I transformed myself into her tutor, and chatted.

'Y'know, it strikes me that Rothko paintings are made the same way as the universe. It's made to be seen by us, and whatever we see's an arrangement of colours. We can detect seven million colours, but each is a cocktail of three raw ingredients, red, blue, green. There are three types of cone in our retinas. We're what the biologists call trichromats. Trichomacy's the absolute limit of simplification.'

Margot, who wasn't listening, let her hand pass an inch above the surface of her birthday present. It would be sensationalist to say the colours shone through her hand. Yet I did perceive this hand (wont to caress me) dissolve into its constituents: it broke down into pure form, nerves, molecules, atoms, down to the level of the quark, a trillion-trillion-trillionth of her hand. And above her appeared the planes of college, country, planet, sun, galaxy, finally the invisible plasmic edge of the universe, a trillion trillions as large as she. Abysses within, abysses without of much the same dimensions; and at the fulcrum her hand, moving over the glory.

A banal wheedling donnish voice, mine, kept chattering. 'So what I want to know is why it's *not* simple. If this is the bedrock of trichomat perception, why are we seeing something *behind*?' (The face she turned to me was dashed clean of its usual intelligence.) 'Someone said the secret of the world's that we only see the back of things. We see trees and clouds from behind, and they appear brutal. But if we saw the face… Here's mere colour, the elemental root, the base material. Yet it seems to be looking elsewhere. Bouncing back elemental light.'

(I meant more than that, too, more than I dared say: that the light seemed uncreated as well as unmingled; that the element almost showed a face; that it was human, and seemed to converse with the viewer, as if we could be comradely with an atom, or go drinking with a wave function. Also: that the painting was the apple of an eye. Also: that it would be her companion when I no longer was. It would hang above her bed and dye her body with its colours. I'm glad I said none of this, it would have been out of character.)

She sighed, collected herself, and began to roll up the canvas as if it stung her.

'Off you go. No, don't bother putting it back in the tube. Don't hide it.

Carry it across college, pin it up in your room. In plain sight. Don't worry about discretion. If anyone gushes "Where did you get that fantastic Rothko copy?" you know what to say?'

'"It isn't a copy."' She spoke as if out of the ground.

'Exactly. "It isn't a copy, my lover nobbled it for me at ten thousand feet, then jumped into the sea." You'll get quizzical looks, shrugs. Not the police. Always rely on double-bluffs. Understand?' She nodded and stood. 'Now go and change. Be back here at seven for bubbly. Then I'm taking you out. You wanted Rothko *and* dinner I think? Be off with you, child.'

It's swell being a man of action: one can address mistresses in brisk imperatives, and carry off gestures that would be camp or theatrical in a bookworm.

Of course this couldn't last. I was bound to relapse into languor. A few weeks, or days, and I'd once again be ineffectual, a slave to the King of Byblos. But now I took her hand and chivalrously bent to kiss it.

And she said, a bit damp-eyed, '*Felix...*'

No doubt she'd never before loved me so much, and probably'll never love as well again. She said '*Felix...*', clutched the rolled canvas to her breasts, was gone; but for that moment none of my usual mental fidgets got in the way. No sheet of writing slid between us, not even this present writing (which of course I foresaw; for which I was posing). For that one moment everything, even this story, went clean out of my mind. In that moment her eyes shone into mine, my eyes into hers, my hand rested in hers, hers in mine.

Bah: what's the point of putting black scratches on a white page? Pointless as pinning butterflies to cork. Nothing worth seeing can be captured, nothing worth describing can be described. There's only the instant of sight, given once. There is only the glance, with its millions of points: irreducible, irrecoverable.

Thinking which, I sprang up impatiently. It was scarcely five, but the autumn day was already well gone in rottenness. White and yellow were leeching out the corrupt daylight, blue was seeping in. Beyond my windows Megiddo Court was turning into a lead model of itself. Within, each bit of furniture threw a shadow like a fresh bruise.

Roughly I pulled my curtains to, groped about in the sudden thick grey, found a caving-helmet, switched on its light, banged it on to my head. Sweep-sweep went its nervous beam over ceiling, walls, furniture. For cuirass I pushed arms into a life-jacket (white-water-rafting grade).

I snatched up the hollow tube Margot had left behind and sketched a salute: '*En garde, monsieur!*' Paper? Paper? No! One must carve holes *in the air*! There. Better. *Prêt? Allez!* Aha!—' A fine slashing upstroke; it was parried, but I gained ground on what we swashbucklers call a *tempo patinando* (slow step, fast lunge). 'That you did not expect, eh, *Monsieur le Roi de Byblos*?' The bar of light from my head twitched back and forth in mid-air; I hacked at it in riposte; it caught the cheval-glass above my desk and stabbed my eyes – that old trick! I twisted aside my head. He was attempting a *croisé* now, taking my ski-pole on the *forte* of his own blade to thrust it down, across my torso. I leapt back and countered with a *raddoppio*.

How masterful he looked in the dimness, my morbid self-conscious! How fast his shadow arm flickered over the wall I'd hung with so many pictures! How much he knew!

'A *Prise de Fer*? Bah, I saw it coming!' – and I brushed it back. Now I almost had him: '*Touché? Pas de touche? Bien!*' But when I brandished – ah! Aha, a-*ha*—

If the assassination
Could trammel up the consequence, ...
here, upon this bank and shoal of time,
We'd jump the life to come.

                                            MACBETH

Iolë

AFTERNOON OF THE FIRST DAY,

WEDNESDAY, 14 NOVEMBER 2012

—which was so irritatingly *wrong* (I can't bring myself to record it) that I, Felix Culpepper, threw myself back in my armchair and at once launched into

the first story (2:23 p.m.)

'Once upon a time, Ollie, Hercules sloped into view. Tripping along beside him, trying to keep pace with his enormous strides, was Deïanira. Deïanira, Hercules' lovely new tiny timid bride. They reached a torrent called the Euenes.'

'The—'

'Euenes. No, don't write anything down. And shut your Ovid which you're never going to master. No, shut it. Listen. The Euenes leaps, oh the glory of it, Ollie, it makes your guts leap against your ribs, leaps down through the mountains of Ætolia, in a gorge so deep the sun scarcely reaches the water. Where, here and there, it does, the pebbles on the river-bottom flush red-gold. An amazing colour. And the twisting banks of gravel glitter like silver. The pines soar up steeply on both banks, black not green, unimaginably dense. They're virgin, no axe has ever fallen in these woods. Here they hunted the Calydonian boar – Meleager, and Nestor, and Atalanta most wonderful of women. They made me look up from my kayak, through the spray, to see the very hillside where the boar charged Telamon and Peleus, out of a water-course choked with willow. It would have slain them if Atalanta hadn't shot it, just behind its left ear. Pppp-*thwack*.' I gazed off.

Ollie Vane-Powell peered at me from beneath his expensive coiffure, his bloody, bloody coiffure. He wanted his tutor to tutor; my poetic mood was new and unimpressive. *This isn't much of a revision* – I could see the thought forming beneath his kiss-curls: *it's only eighteen months to frigging Tripos. C'mon, Culpepper, enough tourist brochure. Let's have another bash at the lines I slightly fucked up a moment ago.* He reopened his *Metamorphoses*. '*Uberior solito,*' he recited aloud, 'which means *something unusually more than something—*'

But I remained irritated. 'Do *shut up* you horribly uninteresting boy. Just listen. Imagine a pure Hellene backdrop: sun, black sunny crags, forests. An aura of glory. We went down the Euenes in March, when the snows melt on the peaks above Delphi and rivers are in spate. The sky was already hard-blue, busy with eagles, but the air stayed cold 'til mid-morning. Swiftly, swiftly we flew down the white water. It took two days.' Ollie visibly imagined the anguish of two days away from shampoo. 'At Rigani, when I capsized and tore my forearm, I saw my blood gush into the stream, faster and paler than I'd have thought possible, gone in an instant. Below Trikorfo, the Euenes reaches the lowlands and turns mellow. It meanders through the plains, and muddies itself into the sea at Missolonghi, where Byron died for your sins.'

'Nah that can't be right, Dr Culpepper. Byron was back in the olden times. Before even you.'

'I mean that classically-educated knuckle-heads like you drove Byron out of England, and made him want to die for Greece. In certain moods I – anyway. That's what the Euenes is like. Was like. I'm told they've dammed it since my visit. They trap it in a reservoir and pump it to Athens. Remember that next time you're staying there, on your way to a beach-rave on Mykonos. In some grotesque hotel with a disco and a buffet and a biddable *masseuse*. When you flush away your feeble piss, that'll be the sacred Euenes.'

Ollie was doubtful. 'None of this will be in Tripos, will it?'

'Will lustral loo-water be in Tripos? No, I don't suppose it will. But you *are* going to face unseen gobbets of *Metamorphoses* book IX, and since you're too stupid to translate Latin, you need to know the stories and fake it.'

Ollie perked up at the prospect of something for nothing. 'It's a scam!'

'A scam. This is how it works: *I* speak; *you're* silent. Close your eyes.' I made an eye-poking gesture with two fingers. '*Hercules* is about to appear to you – more than you deserve. Nessus too. Even silver-footed Deïanira…

As I was saying. No, as Ovid was saying. *Venerat Eueni rapidas Iove natus ad undas.*

'Er – the son of Jove came—'

'Pluperfect, cretin.'

'Had come to the rapid, or swift, Eue – um – Euena—'

'Euenes, Euenes. Hercules and Deïanira reached its banks in early spring, sunny and brisk: the same season I saw it. Dark, boiling waters full of bobbing boughs. The current tugging at low branches. The little beaches submerged. An unspeakable racket from boulders the size of shepherds' huts grinding along the bottom. See it?'

'Yes!'

'Then try again: *Uberior solito, nimbis hiemalibus auctus.*'

'Um, um – richer than usual.'

'*Uberior*, more copious, yes—'

'Rains of winter. Bigger *because* of the winter rains.'

'Good. Crowded with *verticibusque frequens*, frequent torrents, and *inpervius amnis*—'

'Impassable rapids!'

'You've done it. Yes. And those whirlpools you've brilliantly discerned: they frightened Deïanira. Hercules was *intrepidum pro se*, afraid of nothing himself, being just a walking fist.' I walked my fist across my Ovid; how tempting to clout my student just below his curl-line! 'But he was concerned for his wife, *curam de coniuge*. Who clung to his elbow, mightier than the shoulder of a normal man, moaning.'

'Bit of a goer,' sighed Ollie, puckering his eyelids.

'You make me numb… They looked about and saw – a prodigy. A tall man cantering toward them, four hooves kicking up the meadow dew.'

'That can't be right. Centaurs don't exist.'

My voice hardly shook. '*Te, Nesse ferox*, says Ovid: You, ferocious Nessus—'

'Oh. I thought that was about the Loch Ness monster.' My fingers tightened on the arm of my chair. 'Which science has seen through too.' It's remarkable how much Ollie denies, given how little he knows.

'*Te, Nesse ferox*: "Bestial Nessus, what *ardor* you felt for that poppet!" *Ardor*: frenzy. Desire *more* than human, but also less. A centaur can speak with us, mislead us, war on us, mate with us. But it can't pity us. It's an animal, with no more restraint than an avalanche. A cunning animal. Knowing it was no match for Hercules' strength, it concocted a whopper. "You're in luck. The gods have appointed me ferryman of the Euenes.

Swim across, you incomparable, while I carry this sweet baggage dry-shod through the flood." Hercules believed his story. So—'

'Wants to show off to his squeeze by swimming. Hoping for an admiration blowjob on the other side.'

'—swinging his tiny quaking wife on to Nessus' warm withers—'

'Mistake!'

'—flinging his club and bow across, he dives in. Even for him it's a pull. When he reaches the far bank, over the waters' shrieking, *coniugis agnovit vocem.*'

'He, er, recognised the spousal voice.'

'Deftly put. Deïanira's howling. *Biformis* is galloping her up the piney slopes, venting joyous human neighs. "Rapist!" bellows Hercules, in sopping lion-skin, "she's mine! I'm coming for you! With wounds not words!" His curses are strong, like everything about him.'

'But he shouldn't *be* cursing. He ought to do something.'

'He is, he is. *Ultima dicta re probat*, that last word he proved real. He's getting an arrow on the string. Just as Nessus flings Deïanira on her back in a convenient clearing and prepares to fall on—'

'I don't buy this.' His eyes were still scrunched. 'I saw a centaur statue in the what's-it in Paris. Horse-willy between its back legs, not at the front. It couldn't fall on a girl, it'd either have to squat, or get her on her—'

'To fall on her,' I continued through my teeth. '*Thwack!* Hercules' bolt, stinging with Hydra-venom, goes straight between its shoulder-blades and out its chest. Down it goes, horse-body on top of man-body. The woman-body rolls out of the way, splashed by blood, semen and death-sweat.'

'Arrow arrived in the nick of time.'

'You wouldn't say "nick" if you'd seen that hole. Hercules' arrow-heads are like elephant-bullets, meant for big scaly monsters. The exit wound's the breadth of a fist. The mess is unspeakable. Deïanira has to rub gobs of horse-plasma out of her face before she can shriek. And when she shrieks no one hears but the gods and poets. The Euenes is thundering away. Even Hercules' roaring is inaudible. The centaur murmurs to itself "I shan't die unavenged" and, with a smile, annihilates him.'

'Er – what?'

'Kills the son of Jove.'

'Can't be right.'

'Anyone can kill anyone.'

'*I* can't.'

'You're subnormal. For the rest of us, it merely calls for some off-the-cuff ingenuity. Fatal moonshine. Hercules can turn his words into wounds because he's unusually muscly. Nessus turns its dying words into wounds because it's commonly clever. *Ultima dicta re probat.*'

'Um—'

'Strength is nothing, it can always be bent against itself. Deceit is power.'

'Er—'

'Listen: every instant reality comes pouring over us. It's too vast to describe, it's ineffable. But chop it into a narrative shape, hand it on to someone. If he takes it – he usually does – he's yours.'

'That can't—'

'What's language? A Darwinian struggle between stories. And what's a story? A lie that lives and therefore kills. A falsehood big enough to inhabit. Listen to my untruth, enter my miniature world. Inside it I'm God, troubling you at whim. Or blessing, or slaying.' Ollie wrinkled his brows. Sculpted curls jostled, much as thoughts jostle each other. 'That's what the horse-man does. As it dies, it thrusts its gory tunic at Deïanira. A mess of guts, venom, *et cetera*. But it'll do to hang a story on. *Dat munus raptæ velut inritamen amoris.*'

'*Dat*, it gives, *munus* a present to – er. Er. Give us a sec.' (I gave him that second, thinking: *He's not naturally doltish. If the time spent fabricating curls were spent reading, he'd get a First; if the same energy went on writing he'd have finished a novel. That mane's a waste of fiction.*) 'Nah. Can't get *raptæ*.'

'It means *rapee. It gives its rapee a prezzie, naming it an incitement to love.*'

'I wouldn't buy that if I were De – whatever she's called.'

'If you deny centaurs exist, how can you disparage centaur-blood? *I* can't think of a more plausible aphrodisiac. Anyway, Deïanira does accept this cock-and-bull story. Cock-and-stallion. She keeps her centaur-fluid in a stone jar. Treasures it as the years pass. Until a certain young woman comes along. Even younger than herself, even slimmer. A new wife. Iolë.'

'Natural, that. He's muscle-bound. Likes 'em small, likes 'em tender.'

I frankly shuddered. 'Hercules is off on Mount Œta with Iolë, making sacrifice to this god and that. Before dawn, sleepless Deïanira gets out her jar. Soaks a wad, dabs it over a nice new shirt. Wraps up a parcel. Gives a slave the gift, watches him jog off down the road. For the rest of the morning she's happy. She's preoccupied by Nessus' bosh about love-philtres. She even adds to it, I mean she tacks on a final episode: as hubby does up the buttons he claps his forehead: "What am I doing? Naff off, you horrible small tart, I'm going home. I'll bring my darling wife flowers…" Then she sees what makes her scream: the wad, discarded on the tiles of the courtyard, spitting and smoking in the sunlight.'

Ollie, still with eyes closed, allowed himself a guffaw. 'Can't be right – they didn't have chemicals like that in th'olden times.'

The nails of my left hand nearly pierced the fabric of my chair.

'*The chemical's not the point.* What caused Hercules' blood to hiss like a bucket in a smithy? *Not* Hydra-venom. The centaur's invention.'

'Oh – a fib.'

CB

I put down the book and growled 'What exactly are you doing here, Ollie? What're you reading? Why waste three years studying Latin and Greek "fibs"?'

'Can't do maths.' His eyes, open now, were bland as a child's.

'Why be at Wygy's at all?'

'My family always comes here. It's the stupid college and one of our traditions is being stupid.'

'I mean, why come to 'varsity?'

'Girls. That's where they keep'em. The rich ones who are up for it. Supply's pants everywhere else.'

The comfortable way Ollie said this made a hand grenade go *boom* in my mind. I dropped my Ovid, reared from my armchair; I loured over the horrid youth and his strawberry corkscrews, genuinely enraged. 'You're less than human. A donkey-centaur. No, hair-centaur – this great *do* is welded to the scrap of you that's man.'

Ollie looked mildly alarmed. 'That's not right. In fact, isn't it a bit superstitious? I'm not special. Wygy's *is* the dim randy college, I'm like everyone here, Seb, Toby, Hugo, Rajiv, Tristan—'

The vulgarity, the justice of this made me go limp. I turned away and pressed my forehead against the pane.

It was a classic St Martin's summer; I've never seen College look so gorgeous and futile. My wholesome outrage dribbled away. There was no one to reproach but myself. 'Why am *I* here? Why did I choose—' I took a sudden jump – 'or rather, why, having chosen to drop myself into this ditch, do I see *the Foreign Secretary* hurrying toward me?' For, in a swirl of good tailoring, face swaddled in silk scarf, that very grandee,

Benjamin Wedgwood himself, was coming with furtive speed straight across Megiddo Court. 'Incredible!'

'Secretary coming here?' prattled the boy inattentively; he was ogling over my shoulder a triplet of strolling girls. 'A foreigner?'

'Out! Out, out, out! Go and prey on credulous females like the half-human you are. Story's done, supervision's over. Ovid's too good for you. Begone! See you Friday. I've got a serious politician coming up the stairs.'

'That can't be right,' said the insupportable Ollie, 'why would he come here?' I bundled him out of the door, mock-kicking the brat in the buttocks and rumpling his curls, as the Foreign Secretary came in. Expensive damage.

'Oh, hello,' murmured the diffident Foreign Secretary to Ollie.

'Don't bother with him, he's sub-human,' I cried, elated by Benjy's greatness. 'Come in, come in.' I slammed the door and got his scarf off. 'Sit. Drink?'

'No.'

'Cigar?'

'*No*. Stop prancing, Felix. Can't you sit? Something to tell you.'

'Oh God – *something* means a narrative,' I thought, and indeed, before I could get myself properly comfortable, Benjy launched breathlessly into

the second story (3:12 p.m.)

'It happened in Soho last night. Just before twelve. Young couple, knocked down and killed. Professionally done. Dark green Mercedes cabriolet. Veered on to the footpath, splatted them against a brick wall, stopped, reversed over the girl's head (she was still wriggling), roared away.'

'Were they important people?'

'She was a primary school teaching assistant, he worked in a bookie's. They shared a flat in Harringay. No.'

'Were they *really* that? Not spies or blackmailers?'

'Really just that. Labour voters, too, I gather.'

'Have you been demoted, Benjy? This doesn't sound like your usual beat.'

'They'd just left a nightclub on Shaftesbury Avenue. A louche place called *Déshabillé*.'

'Good God, that takes me back. Round the corner from Great Windmill Street, isn't it? There used to be a woman there—'

'*Do* pay attention, my car's waiting outside the Lodge. I need to get back for a Cabinet meeting. But I didn't dare telephone you with this. It's too important.' I subsided. 'Someone'd rubbed mud over the Mercedes' licence plate, but the plods enhanced a security camera picture. They're pretty sure it had diplomatic plates.' I looked more interested. 'In fact, an Harani embassy car.'

'Ah!'

'And 'though the driver wore a woolly hat low over his forehead, it seems to have been the ambassador himself.'

'What nasty habits it instils, Benjy, diplomatic immunity.'

'Quite. Well it dawned on the coppers, after a few hours' hard thinking, that this was politically ticklish. They got in touch with the Foreign Office. The problem worked its way up the chain and reached yours truly in time to ruin my day and obliterate lunch.'

'God. Sherry, then?'

'*No.* Thank you. Meanwhile the police had found some witnesses from *Déshabillé*. It seems the dead couple had been involved in a *fracas*. A shortish fellow had propositioned the girl. To put it politely. Doesn't seem to have had nice manners. In fact he'd been making a general nuisance of himself before molesting the Harringay girl. Groping left and right. The Harringay boy wasn't particularly upset, but she was, so they—'

'*Intrepidum pro se*,' I murmured, '*curam de coniuge.*'

'—knocked the intruder about. Not much, he being so scrawny. Everyone cheered. Then the bouncers threw him out. There's a camera over the road, on Great Windmill Street, and we have a good picture of him dabbing his forehead, and whimpering, and making a 'phone call. Here's the photo, by the way.'

'Humph.'

'We got a positive identification around noon. The boy's visiting—'

'From Haran.'

'Yes, from Haran. And staying at their embassy.'

'Does *he* have diplomatic immunity?'

'Much worse. He's the President of Haran's youngest son. Idris ibn Ali al-Mutlak.'

'Hm. What's he doing here?'

'Shopping, basically. And whoring and drinking. His excuse is that he's being interviewed at, let me think, the University of the Mid-Pennines.'

'The *what?*'

'There are 115 universities on this island, and in every list Mid-Penn's

115th. You mustn't smirk, remember I'm in the government, it's partly our fault these places exist.'

'Was I smirking? I'm sure not. This is St Wygy's. *We* have no prejudices against chuckleheadedness.'

'Young Idris aspires to study office-design at Mid-Penn, and last week satisfied the entry requirement, which is possessing a daddy who can write a cheque.'

'Whereas *you're* an intellectual snob. Inexplicably.'

'He's due to fly back from Gatwick to Paddam Aran tomorrow evening.'

'You're not going to arrest him?'

'Ticklish, Felix, ticklish. The Met say they don't have enough to charge him. And my lip quivers at the thought of annoying the Haranis. Especially' (he put on his portentous face) '*just at the moment.*'

'Then overlook his naughtiness and let him go.'

'Her Majesty's Government,' said Benjy with grandeur, 'does not countenance foreign hooligans coming to the West End and having our citizens squished.'

'Proles from N15.'

'Felix, *your* snobbery's always been preposterous.'

'A teaching assistant. Crushed at the command of a Mid-Pennines office designer. *Really.*'

'In fact I suspect it's just a pose.'

'All right, let's pretend the dead boy was a paladin. And the girl a mitred abbess of Merovingian descent. It's still not much of a case, is it? Purely circumstantial. Young al-Mutlak *might* just have been reporting to his embassy he'd been beaten up. The hit-and-run *could*'ve been the ambassador's own naughty idea. Vindicating the honour of Haran and the al-Mutlaks.'

'We don't take that view. Of course we'll declare the ambassador *persona non grata*. At some point. But what about Idris? At eighteen he's already got the name of a murderous little bastard. The President's middle son was machine-gunned at a camel race last year, and public opinion around Paddam Aran blames Idris.'

'I see. Not a good sign, is it, if the ambassador thinks it worth his while obliging Idris? I mean to the extent of running over girls who annoy him.'

'No, not a good sign. In such a very young person it implies pushiness.'

'What would the President think? I mean, if you told him?'

'Papa has a dicky heart, he's probably past doing anything. But the oldest son, who'll soon be President, we hope, might not mind seeing the last of baby brother. Name of Jasim. A Sandhurst man. Fairly decent as Haranis go' – Benjy looked sly saying this.

෴

I pondered the Foreign Secretary for a moment.

Cagey is the word. He's curiously unembodied. It's hard to believe there's simply a column of flesh or solid bone beneath his bodily movements – which are rather good, a charming fluttering motion in the hands, a boyish fidget in the feet. His eyes are sea-blue and slightly epicanthic (Benjy is one of those people so English as to look Chinese), and he shakes them about like pretty marbles, not as if he uses them to look through.

This is all curiously appealing on television. Even his obvious shiftiness has charm; since no one can credit his lies, he can never be said to mislead. As he dwindles into late middle-age I foresee Wedgwood will become a national treasure, unassailable, ageless.

'So that's the end of your yarn, Benjy?' He did his tossing-back of the head, slightly disarranging hair thin and platinum as it must have been in the nursery, washed back over his skull like an otter's pelt. 'I'm to do something unofficial about Idris al-Mutlak?'

Now he performed with his vivid eyelids, ears and hands: it could not be defined as *Yes* or *No*.

'You want me to find out exactly what he did last night? And then, so forth?'

More of the mime.

I exhaled heavily and pulled the 'phone toward me, pretending to be wearied, in fact tremendously excited. 'Where's this wretched youth staying?'

'A suite in the Savoy. Number 322.'

I paused, drumming his fingers. 'Does he have a rank?'

'He's notionally governor of Arpachshad Province.'

'Hmm.'

'Directory enquiries,' said a depressive.

'The Savoy Hotel, London… Yes, please put me through.'

'A wonderful morning to you!' said a manic euphoric. 'This is the Savoy!'

'Room 322, if you would.'

'Course at once sir! Been a pleasure.'

The 'phone rang and rang. 'Yeah?' came a surly boy's voice at last.

Smiling murderously at Benjy, I adjusted my tone. 'Can this be His Excellency the Governor of Arpachshad? You elate me. Your servant, the Tutor and Fellow in Latin at St Wygefortis' College, Cambridge;' and at once I launched into

the third story (3:29 p.m.).

'May I first bid you welcome to our chilly capital, Excellency? At this remote seat of learning we barely regard the pleasures of London, but rejoice that such a distinguished youth should savour them, having heard so much... Nonsense! You are too modest... Oh, from the dutiful *fellaheen* of Arpachshad Province. And the intelligentsia of Paddam Aran, who speak of you as the hope of Haran.' Idris became more lively; I covered the receiver to whisper to Benjy. But he'd already vanished. I went to my window, and saw him receding across Megiddo Court. '...Hm? Oh yes, England holds Haran to be the light of the Near East, and Your Excellency as the light of...' I wasn't paying much attention to what I said. 'How often we discuss you on High Table. Let me tell you a story: last week the Master remarked... And the Bursar cried "Young al-Mutlak! I've heard..."'

The larger the lie, the harder to see round it. I didn't stint. I think my story finished with the Fellowship leaping up to toast Idris and sing the Haranian anthem. It doesn't bear repeating.

'You are honouring, I understand, the University of the Mid-Pennines? An institution in a league of its own. Nonetheless, should Your Excellency care to consider instead classics at Cambridge...' Much more of this. 'It would be,' I concluded, after some minutes of fantastic fiction, wandering about my rooms poking at piles of books with my feet, 'a privilege for this College to invite you here. If it were possible for you to come for an interview tomorrow. A mere formality, of course... What? Oh, at your convenience... Four? Four would be surpassingly excellent. Until then. *Ma'a as-salāma!*' Perjury complete.

ଔ

A little nauseated, I replaced the 'phone, sported my oak against visitors, picked up the half-finished translation Ollie had left behind, dropped it in my bin, drew my curtains, fell on my bed. It was past my usual siesta time, but sleep's sleep, *ennui ennui*. I'd had enough of the fourteenth of November for a while. For an hour I would opt out of that tiresome narrative. I shut my eyes, disgustedly, which brings us at once to our

fourth story (3:46 p.m.).

Idris ibn Ali al-Mutlak had been expelled from three international schools in Switzerland for increasingly grave offences. He spoke gutter-American and gutter-Swiss-French as fluently as Arabic. He'd travelled all over this sorry globe, admittedly not often getting beyond the beach, where his hotel possessed a beach. He had squandered many fortunes and was guilty of things grown politicians only aspire to commit. Yet the embarrassing truth is that he was at heart a child.

Only three generations separated him from a camel-hair tent in the wilderness. His great-grandfather had been an illiterate sheikh whom the British had taken up toward the end of their Mandate, needing a strong man to hold Nahor Province. And this old sheikh, for all his cunning and flocks and wives, could not gainsay the young British officers who came to see him because they spoke so well, so wonderfully! It was delight surpassing all delights to sit with them.

His great-grandson had inherited this susceptibility. To look at Idris – slight but wiry, heavy-lidded, long-fingered, hawk-nosed, loose-lipped, well-tailored, drug-worn – you'd think his twenty years had already rendered him jaded and cynical. But part of him remained a child of the desert, capering delightedly before the baubles of the towns. And language was for him the gaudiest of all baubles, as for most Levantines. The Hebrew scriptures and *The Thousand and One Nights* were composed with bedouin toughs in mind. The Prophet denied his warriors wine; he dared not forbid the deeper drunkenness that comes from words crushed, fermented, aged and strained.

Idris al-Mutlak had denied himself nothing: not wine (although he usually cut it with Coca-Cola), not white chocolate liqueur, not heroin-morphine speedballs. But no excess mortified his addiction to stories. They were his one secret vice, amidst many vices well known to all. When he locked himself in his suite in the summer palace, in the hills above Paddam Aran, the servants assumed it was women, or boys, or some terrible Western drug of which they had not yet heard; or that he was plotting against his father with Colonel Adeeb of the Presidential Guard; whereas in fact he was lost in the world of Brazilian *telenovelas*.

His favourite was the gloriously interminable *Dias da Paixão*. Idris scarcely noticed real people being shot or hanged before him on his own orders. Yet when he fell to wondering whether even now, in episode 899, Fábio might emerge from his coma to reveal what he knows of the helicopter crash that killed Glória (or her secret twin) in episode 324, his face became so rapt that personality was chased away; he looked almost pleasant.

Even so, Idris' terrible great-grandfather had sat before the opening of his tent in the Nahoran waste, chewing dates slowly with his sparse teeth, spitting them out, nodding for his Somali slave to bring him more tea in bronze bowls, shading his eyes (although he was nearly blind) as the sun declined toward the mountains of Pildash. Behind him, in the odorous gloom, his four wives crouched on their haunches, chins in their henna'd palms, embroidered veils pulled low. Fat Daborah, ever the favourite. Thirteen-year-old Aanaa with her frightened eyes. Beautiful unloved Raaheel, shrill, a scold. And pale-haired green-eyed Frida, a half-Bavarian camp-follower captured from the Ottomans in a raid, long ago.

Before the tent, uncomfortably cross-legged on a rug, as if back at prep school, sat British officers with toothbrush moustaches. Twenty years had worn away since the romance of the Arab Revolt. These were a hard-bitten generation, who got their ideas from *Scrutiny* and the Left Book Club. They spent a lot of time feeling silly. 'Honestly,' they'd tell each other apologetically, bouncing back to H.Q. on their dromedaries, 'don't you think this T.E. Lawrence carry-on's a bit shopworn? I mean to say, amusing a feudal oppressor all afternoon, it's a bit thick.' But holding down the Nahor meant charming wicked old Sheikh al-Mutlak.

Therefore they gorged him, with everything they could remember: tales from Shakespeare and Kipling and Boccaccio and *Pickwick*, Ealing Studio comedies, smoking-room stories, anecdotes of the War, reminiscences of *Punch*, slithers (lightly disguised) of the Bible, nursery tales, muddled opera plots, shoddy problem plays, expurgated sagas.

The sheikh's wives (who cared only for love and heavy gold jewellery and quails braised in a certain way over embers in a mess of pounded almonds) were tremendously bored by these stories. So were his tribesmen, sitting a respectful four paces off, keeping their views to themselves; the mildest criticism of the sheikh was apt to lead to being pegged out on a dune and eaten by jackals. They were indifferent to other men's adventures, dreaming only of their own. They dreamed of how it would be when the conspirators of the capital, with their soft hands and womanish European suits, staged a Nationalist revolution; for then, they'd been promised, the British would let the Mutlaki clan ride, whooping and cavorting, to the sack of Paddam Aran. Meanwhile, why concern themselves with the profane doings of the *bint* Becky Sharp?

But the sheikh himself never wearied. He demanded hours and hours of fiction before he would discuss the shipment of rifles.

Three-quarters of a century later, Idris did not enjoy his great-grandfather's liberty. Obviously he could be as degraded as he pleased; indeed, he could scarcely be degraded enough, everyone found it useful to push him further down that path. But innocence was forbidden. The al-Mutlak dynasty had moved beyond noble savagery. Their regime had postmodern fittings: there were elections to manage, websites to hack, visiting celebrities to bemuse. Beyond Haran, the al-Mutlaks ran a complex of offshore shell companies, not to mention two American Congressmen; they owned houses in Chamonix and Hampshire and Long Island, and retained lawyers in many countries. By choosing nannies carefully they'd acquired chirpy Californian accents. They had arrangements to keep fresh with Al Jazeera and Fox News. International press barons sometimes took their calls. Such was the family business. The last thing it needed was a younger son with an atavistic barbarian heart.

Idris was no *naïf*. He was aware of his outrageous innocence and realised its peril. If Jasim found out about the soap-operas he'd certainly inform their father Ali, a hard, serious, dangerous man even now he was so sick; Idris didn't like to think what would happen.

But what (he asked himself) could he do? He was a throwback, as simple-hearted as his great-grandfather; he inherited with his one-sixteenth of Bavarian blood the irresponsible romanticism of the Danube. He couldn't escape his debauching thralldom; indeed he longed to sink deeper.

For he'd heard of an even stronger narcotic than Brazilian soap-opera, lush, fulsome, humid; he craved it. It was called literature, and was manufactured in Europe. One line can be enough to intoxicate. Take it and you're transported into a lie, a lie vast as a city, far out beyond the ergs of non-existence: gleaming, with pinnacles beyond number, walled about, rose-coloured, watered by springs, visited by storks. The mere rumour of that city had been enough to bewitch his great-grandfather; Idris wanted to enter it, to get lost in its alleyways, push past unicorns laden with panniers of roc eggs, with the shadow over him of a tremendous wooden horse…

He'd heard of schools (not, admittedly, Mid-Penn) where this drug is administered. And now Cambridge had rung! Idris was overcome by my call. I wasn't just some smarmy teacher who would have to be bribed. I was a *djinn*.

For hours he lay on his hotel bed, dabbing at bruises and cuts left over from last night's brawl at *Déshabillé,* while his imagination rioted with pleasure at the thought of what lay ahead. He was so happy he didn't think of his cocaine stash in the bathroom, or revisit his ornate plans for the torture and dismemberment of Jasim once he was President. He forgot the glaring infidel city beyond the plate glass of his suite, pulsating with lawlessness. He pictured himself as a Wygefortis undergraduate: fornicating expansively of course, boozing and snubbing and shopping; but also (to do him justice) sitting at night in the College library turning pages.

Thus Idris, while loathsome as to morals, was *imaginatively* in advance of Ollie Vane-Powell, who couldn't see the point of Ovid.

It was ten o'clock before Idris remembered what he owed to himself and to the House of al-Mutlak. He rose and showered, doused himself in unfortunate cologne, and went to a nightclub to pull, still hugging to himself the fabulous ecstasy of education—

03

It's shocking that you're swallowing all this. How can anyone possibly know what passed through Idris' head, alone in his room in the Savoy? We can't even be sure what he *did* there. The police didn't have a camera or microphone in the suite itself, they merely staked out the corridor, and observed from across the road. This hazy stuff about rocs and sheikhs and Frida the German is the daydream I, Felix Culpepper, spun for myself as I dozed.

The only facts are these: at 23:04 the Suspect emerged from his room (it's perfectly true, it's in the police report, that he reeked of cologne). He asked the concierge the way to a nightclub, found it, sat at the bar, and ordered (23:14) a grilled cheese sandwich. He consumed three Jägerbombs, looked around for a woman, found same or was found. By 23:22 he'd got her on the barstool beside him and bought her a drink, buying also, as he clearly assumed, her attention, adulation and sexual obedience, and launched into his familiar, coarse, reliable technique, beginning, 'Hey! How's it going? Great to hang out. You cool? You a secretary or whatever?'

'Whatever.'

'Whatever. Feeling all right? Great. Me too. Really cool. More about me. I'm like a student at St Wygefortis'. It's part of Cambridge College. I'm going there to study Latin stories. They're kind of all right.'

'Are they? Coo,' said the undercover policewoman, who was wearing a wire, 'you must be ever so clever.'

'Yeah, I got smarts.'

'And you're really a provincial governor?'

Idris hadn't mentioned this fact, but he was too pleased with himself to notice. He smirked.

'Tell me about governoring.'

the fifth story (11:24 p.m.)

He told her, holding back no crime. Idris' innocence did not, of course, make him good. His cruelty was gleeful, his greed for money and women childish: a piling-up of pretty things. Possibly he embellished the horrors (although many of them are, alas, verified by Foreign Office reports on Haran). He'd read in dirty magazines how excited women get in the presence of masterful men, shedders of unrighteous blood, whip-wielders.

In any case the detective sitting a mile away in earphones, listening to the boy's boasts – a detective never one to hold back in the thrashings of prisoners or the fixing of evidence – found his mouth swinging open. 'Never in my born days have I heard the fuckin' like—'

MORNING OF THE SECOND DAY,
THURSDAY 15 NOVEMBER 2012

Naked, rosy, tanned (but snoring and very slightly dribbling), Margot ffontaines-Laigh lies with her hair spread over pillow, counterpane and shoulder, an incredible aureole of orange-brown. There's never much sun in England, but what there is, is doing its best: enough has worked its way through a flaw in the autumn clouds, and a gap in Margot's curtains, to turn her hair to fire.

I, Felix Culpepper, having just stolen up staircase II of Gehenna Court, through her sitting-room and into her bedroom, stand over her with folded arms, mingling indecently my roles of tutor and lover.

But can these roles be mingled? Walking across Gehenna just now I was officious and stooped, as a don should be when crossing a College court; coming up the stair I was eager but unsure of myself, two steps at a time, face held up to glory in the approaching door, the ideal lover. Dissonance, you see.

And dissimulation. Even at St Wygy's, where the shameless undergraduates nickname Margot *Abishag*, Fellows are meant not to sleep with students; certainly not with Freshers they tutored over the summer and got into College in the first place; and the other dons (many with similar arrangements of their own) have to be helped to overlook it.

Now, standing over her, the lover recedes and morbid empiricism reasserts itself. 'Yes she's lovely. But,' I tell myself, 'it's beauty of quality, not form. Not one of these shapes is particularly fine. Certainly not the nose. Yet if it's not the best tailoring, the fabric's superb. Tall, loose-limbed, flawless skin, perfect bones, clear eyes. And the hair, the hair! Of course there are days when she's not wonderful at all. If she's tired or out of sorts, the bloom dims, the hair's just lurid and unkempt. Consider, though, the decades to come! Stuff outlasts shape. She'll be splendid in old age, when all forms sag and blur. Still splendid eyes, still ruins of uniquely splendid hair.' She snuffles in her sleep.

Not that she is unique; no one's that. We're all twice-told tales; slaves of heredity, with each generation crushing the next to its own shape. Left to his own devices Ollie would be inoffensive enough, but he conceives his purpose on earth to go to bed with as many females as he can, because that's what Vane-Powells do; and fusses with his curls as a spider tends its web, much as his Victorian ancestor must have fussed with macassar-oil, and his Georgian ancestor with horsehair perukes.

Erudite Margot is even more enslaved than oblivious Ollie, because she knows exactly where she gets her red hair, and much else. They're inherited from her great-great-great-grandmother, the intellectual Urania *née* Romilly, Lady Rievaulx. It's Urania who compels Margot to be so artfully self-possessed, crushing, slatternish. She'd no doubt be a normally timid, well-groomed, dull, sweet-tempered girl, if she weren't self-conscious about being a reverberation.

I adore Margot. I think. Would I have liked Urania ("patron of the theatrical Kemble, friend of John Stuart Mill, comfort of the elderly Coleridge, *confidante* of Disraeli" – who all, in their different ways, were besotted with her colour)? Could she have abided me? She's almost as familiar to me as her descendant; indeed she must seem almost as intimate with my darling as my darling is with herself, since the girl spends so much time poring over the privately-printed memoir (1904), *Urania Rievaulx, A Merry Life, by various hands*. It's her private Bible, the infallible scripture of her religion of herself; I study it myself so that I can understand not Urania but Margot.

Here it is on the shelf above her bed. I take it down, open its soft green leather covers, lettered *U.R.* in gold, and consider the frontispiece: a sepia photograph of Lady Rievaulx in court dress for the Golden Jubilee, still emphatically handsome, still with her amused, sardonic smile. Despite the grisly late-Victorian upholstery, Urania manages to look indefinably lax, as lax as she must have been in her Regency girlhood, when she ran about in loose muslin, listening to loose Jacobin talk at Holland House. Urania was never subdued to the age; she subdued.

Yes, Margot too will be splendid in old age. In her eighties she'll have become entirely Urania, a magnificent reproduction. Not that I'll see it, being dead.

I open *A Merry Life* at random, and on page 64 find a letter from the Leader of the Opposition, Disraeli, which tosses me into

the sixth story (8:44 a.m.)

1 Aug 1862. <u>Confidential</u>. My drst Ldy Rievaulx I write in t^h wildest haste & w/ t^h most fervnt congrat:ns. We have hd a proper coup d'etat in t^h H. of Commons t^h evening! As we feared, that wearisome bigot t^h Chan: of the Exch: launched upon an insulting survy of American affairs. D-v-l take Mr Gladstone! he seemed perfectly bent on giv: offense. A few more such provocations & I verily believe we wd find ourselves at war w/ t^h Union hand-in-hand w/ t^h slaver Confd:r'cy & t^h Empr. of t^h Fr. However I sent over an anon. note to the Govt. benches intimating wh: you told me of t^h conduct of Gl:'s ~~hussy of a~~ wife (which by-the-by I learn fr/ Ldy Warboro' was not – & <u>cannot</u> have been so – that Mrs Gl: was w/ her t^h whole evening you allot to her criminal rendez-vous w/ Mr Radvers – that in fact t^h whole ~~wild~~ scintillating & plausible tale not excepting Mr Radvers himself sprang Minerva-like fr/ yr own head). However this the Lib'ls. were not to know & as t^h passed my note fr/ hand to hand I cd see mingled consternacion & astonishmt. At last Ld Palmerston tugged on Gl:'s coattales and whisp'd; upon wh/ he quite blew up before us & subsided into fragments. 'Not a rack remained.' He begged t^h H.'s pardon, sat. We rose w/out a division, & I have bustled out to ~~pay~~ lay at once my tribute at yr feet. Of course Gl: will soon estb. his wifes innocense & the nonexistnce of Radvers but t^h moment for mischief over t^h Amer: war is passing, &

since Parlmt is soon to be prorogued 'til t^h close of Oct I verily beleve
we need dred him no more. Thus drst Ldy R you have outdone t^h
romancers of t^h age & warrant t^h admirat:n as well as gratitude
not only of yr own Dizzy but of t^h nation. T^h olives of peace (tho' of
necessity <u>secretly</u> bestowed) are more precious than t^h bays of war
nay even than t^h laurels of the noveliste & I hasten to press them on
yr brows, my thrice-precious friend. A 1000 adieux, D.

I shut the book; the gentle noise wakes Margot. She smiles, raising
golden-brown arms to pull me down, saying nothing true or false. I,
unworthy brute, baring my own body in all haste, leap to her. Warm flesh
for the moment casts out even the possibility of words.

ख

Afterwards, we lay for a while in immaculate silence, her head on my
shoulder, her glorious hair half-covering me. She smiled up at the abstract
canvas fixed above her bed with drawing pins: the shining blocks of yellow,
white and scarlet, from which her hair, perhaps, draws its strength. She
was thinking (I think) of me. I thought, not of myself for a wonder, but
blessedly of nothing.

Not for long. The beastly fidget of meditation resumed, the stories that
outlive us, cascading from father to son to son, the main reason I suppose
fathers bother begetting.

I didn't consider her: when a Culpepper's mind's not gnawing at itself,
it pesters the infinities. Wobbling between narcissism and metaphysics, it
finds the middle range, that is, other people, comfortless – which isn't my
fault, in more sensible ages I'd have made a tolerable monk; I'd have had
a skull to finger in my cell, instead of making *memento mori* of a healthy
girl of twenty years and one month…

Meanwhile I wound a strand of her incomparable hair about my
fingers and tried to read her thoughts in her eyes. *How he likes my hair…*
How disgusted Urania must have been, she reflected (perhaps), *when the*
Pre-Raphaelites made heavy negligent chestnut hair fashionable, therefore
common. Of course the fashion didn't last; it went out before she died, and
it's gone in and out of fashion since her day, in and out, displaced by all sorts
of ringlets, bobs, shingles, peroxides; now in this year of grace 2012 it's as out
as it's ever been, thanks be to the merciful and infernal gods. How he likes it.

I do; but what I was wondering was whether Urania could have prevented a war with the United States if she'd been a watery blonde; and, conversely, what Abishag might be capable of, given the colour she has.

Her green eyes turned to mine. There's always a postcoital danger she'll whisper 'I love you', which is after all not quite true. To pre-empt her I sat up, and launched abruptly into

the seventh story (9:14 a.m.)

'Last summer, travelling through the Basque Country disguised as a priest, I met—'

'Why?'

'I'd been ordered to go there and settle someone.'

'No, why that disguise?'

'Englishness reads to foreigners as fussy clericalness. I don't have to adapt my manner, just make people understand it differently. A useful mistake.'

She said 'Ah,' clearly repulsed.

'I met an old woman, in a mountain village called Urdax, near the French frontier, which I needed to cross without being seen. Urdax is a tiny place in the folds of gigantic valleys, set about with gaunt beautiful rocks. The crone was gaunt but unbeautiful. Cheeks like rotten potatoes, teeth like crumbs of coal. She was probably in her early fifties. I was in a hurry but she saw me passing and pulled me in, insisted on giving me stewed elvers, unburdening herself to me in appalling French. People always tell me things when they see me in my cassock. They can tell I care for their stories.'

'But you're entirely self-absorbed.'

'"Aita!" she told me (*Aita* is Father), "you must hear me. I grew up on a farm high above this village. As my parents were dead I belonged to my grandfather, a harsh man bent double who needed me to work our bad holding. We had few sheep and moreover our flock had *la tremblante du mouton*", which means scrapie. "Terrible was our wool, the shame of the district. My grandfather would not let me marry. I was never allowed to come down here to Urdax for the *festa*, and there were no young men in our heights. I began to suffer *la chlorose* and—"'

'Suffer what?'

'Known to physicians – meaning the physicians of the sixteenth century, in whom I put my faith – as *morbus virgineus*. Green-sickness.

Listlessness, bad stomach and moodiness in maidens.'

'What is it really?'

'By *really* you mean *according to the nineteenth-century materialist quackery*. Hypochromic anæmia in adolescent females.'

'Oh *that*. Go on.'

'I will. But do try not to be such a credulous materialist. So-called science is obfuscation, little else. Men in white coats are tame witch-doctors.'

'Yes, Felix.'

'"I began to suffer *la chlorose*, Aita, and became pale as goats' milk. The night before All Saints' Day an immense storm settled on the peaks of the Pirinioak and—"'

'Is that the Pyrenees?'

'Yes. "And the thunder was so terrible one of our ewes miscarried. But I went and lay in the field above our hut, in the angle of the stone wall, with my skirts pulled up. At each stroke of lightning I cried *Bai, bai*," *bai* is yes, "with each roll of thunder I groaned as with delight, and when the rain came, big and hard like pebbles, I opened my legs. At midsummer I gave birth to the most beautiful son. Neighbours, enemies, said it was my grandfather's but how could that be, seeing my grandfather was small and crooked and squinting?"'

I think my story was chilling Margot, who stirred uncomfortably on my warm shoulder. 'Were the elvers nice?' she said, to say something.

'Pale wriggly worm-things browned in oil, with lots of chilli. I had thirds. "Never has a boy like Absalon been seen in these hills," the witch told me during my second bowl, "never in all the Pirinioak. So good, so obedient, above all so clever. His thoughts came fast as lightning, they rolled in the mind like thunder. Where all the rest of us would say what we felt, he would calculate, calculate. Listen to his cleverness, Aita. I inherited the farm and flock when with three grammes of black hellebore cooked with onions I poisoned my grandfather, who ought never to have touched me: Absalon taught me how, and he was but eight. *There is a one-in-six chance any one of our lambs has* la tremblante, *mother,* he would say, *we must sell them to the butcher at a fifth less than the usual price and with the margin we'll have enough to silence him should anyone sicken from our meat.* Or: *If we pay the notary eleven thousand* pesadas *to muddle our wool with the wool of Txabier we need sell but eight bales to cover the bribe.* By the time he was fourteen we were rich and bought this splendid house in Urdax, where folk live who have never known hunger. My Absalon was the marvel of the schoolmaster, who said that when he grew tall he must go to the university and study the mathematics and be a great man. Meanwhile it was like hearing music to see him cheat at his exams. Like the *ezpatadantza* which is the great sword-dance of the Basques and most hazardous if an error is made which it is not."'

Margot's mental discomfort was tainting her physical ease. There seemed no comfortable place for her head along my whole warm flank.

'"The dreadful thing occurred, Aita, because the summer before his matriculation I tell him *Always you work too hard, go down to Irun and make merry with Gillermo*, who was his great comrade at the *lycée* and the son of a wealthy fisherman, for by now we had acquired magnificent friends. Absalon went and was back two days later, before the dawn. He scratched on my window and almost I suffered convulsions when I saw his face through the glass, so haggard and owl-eyed. When I opened the door he fell through, dripping with rain, went to that dark corner there beyond the wooden chest painted with the saints (do you see it, Aita?) and dropped himself down with his face turned from me. For a long time I could get nothing from him. Then he told me." Here she paused to give me my third bowl of elvers. "Absalon and Gillermo had had too much of the strong beer they sell in Irun and gone out in Gillermo's father's motor-boat, and bashed her prow on the jetty but ignored it and went many kilometres out and turned off her engine and floated, singing and drinking and telling each other what they would do in the wide world, and how many women they would have, and how many men they would cheat. They sang and they boasted, Aita, until they found her sinking, with her engine flooded beyond revival. Then they began to bail but the ebb took them and they became afraid. The *bateau* sank lower and lower until the seawater was around their ankles and the sun began to sink also and the coast to fade in the haze. Gillermo wept until he was breathless but Absalon suffered more, for he could not stop calculating. He was bailing thirteen or fourteen times a minute but Gillermo, a fat boy as are the sons of the rich, only eight or nine. Moreover Gillermo weighed seventy kilogrammes whereas the small metal plaque on the gunwale said that the boat was to be loaded only to 220 kilogrammes. Therefore taking the boathook he struck Gillermo over the head and pushed his body under the sea while his eyes measured the gunwhale, which rose four centimetres for she rode much more lightly in the water and he was safe. Then he went on bailing more slowly than before from weeping over his friend whom he had loved, until a short while later he was rescued by a yacht of Russians which against expectation was making its way along the coast at dusk. He had the Russians land him on a strand with no folk about and walked inland until he got a ride with tourists with German licence plates who would be gone and not testify of him. When they let him off he trudged by backways and so came to me with no one having seen him. The next morning Gillermo's father appeared in Urdax, wailing that his son and mine were drowned and lost. And now you must have yet more of my stew. No? Then you shall take some *patxaran* which I make myself from the best sloes.

'"I had to have a requiem Mass said for Absalon who was hidden in our old hut up in our fields, may the Virgin forgive me the sacrilege, and the day of that unholy requiem our flock took the murrain. Within the week the drains in this fine house were disturbed and there had been a fall of hail, most unseasonable. And there were other things, too, forgive me for naming them in your hallowed ears. The *iratxoak* and *lamiak* grew sportive (these are imps and nymphs, Aita, *plus puissant et maléfique*), and there were rumours that the other thing was abroad, that which has not been glimpsed since our fathers' fathers' time."'

'*What* other thing?'

'That's what I wanted to know. Her voice sank to a whisper: "The *basajaun*, the *basajaun*." When I pressed her she just mumbled "*Chut, chut, assez*."'

'What—'

'"Understand, Aita," she insisted, stilling me with more of her fiery *patxaran*, "Absalon was a good religious boy for all his book-learning. *I am accursed, mother*, he told me, *unclean things run riot because of me*. What could I do but weep and hold his head to my breasts, not daring to let him know the *basajaun* itself had been seen trotting along a high ridge of pines at sunrise? *Hélas*, had I not had Mass of the dead said for my poor son while he yet stood upon soil? Had I not surrendered him to the other realm? Made him over as prey to the prince of the air whose spawn he perhaps was? *Hélas! hélas!*"'

'I'm more interested in the *basajaun*.'

'So was I. But my garrulous old woman clammed up. From what she let slip I gathered he's something like the woodwose – y'know, the wild hairy man of the woods the mediævals knew about.'

'I've always hoped the woodwose was the yeti.'

'That's because you, as I keep pointing out, are a shallow materialist. Cryptozoology seems solider to you than respectable legend because, even if it's vulgar and imbecile, it at least pretends to wear a white coat.' Margot pouted. 'Why can't a woodwose be a folk memory of fauns? Or satyrs? Or, yes, yes, of centaurs? Or not even just a memory?'

'Why can't the woodwose be a confused report of chimpanzees?'

'I disown you. Anyway, you're interrupting. Absalon thought these bugaboos, whatever they are, were drawn to him, and wanted to be exorcised before he died. His mother found a Dominican, a theologian – he must have been a clever man, God knows what he'd done to be exiled to those benighted mountains. Anyway, she brought him to the hut. "I left him alone with my poor son, Aita, and stood without listening to voices rising and falling and rising, then a howl so terrible I looked about lest the *basajuan*... But it was just Absalon. The friar emerged from the hut, pale, with his mouth set. *I cannot absolve him, Madame: alone in all the Pirinioak your son can never be redeemed, for his great sin came not by perverse appetite but by what he calls* calculating, *that is according to right reason, of which man cannot repent. He is assuredly damned.* With that he hurried away down the path to the village, the coward, to be far from that font of evil, my son, my beautiful son.

'"I went into the hut, Aita, expecting to find Absalon dead or raving. He was standing like one of the carved figures on the front of our parish church. *I have grieved enough,* he said, and I scarcely knew his voice, *I am dead to the world and now to Heaven also. There remains only America. Mother, give me your money,* also he took the money of the schoolmaster who loved him too, and fled to a city on the far side of the world which is called Seattle, because that, the schoolmaster certified us, is where those with *capacité surnaturelle* in the mathematics are employed writing spells to cast on machines and where no one exorcises anything. The schoolmaster is wise and reads on what he calls the Web of Chuck or Mikey or Lance, which cannot be their true names: men who have acquired riches writing mathematical spells in the city called Seattle. I am sure one of them is my Absalon and wonder if he is at peace. Do you think it is possible, Aita?" I said I hoped so and thanked her for her stew and got away, because I had to be in France before the light failed.'

Margot had snuggled down into a position that involved no contact with my skin. 'Do you really believe Absalon made it to America?'

'I forgot. "Aita," she told me, "every month an envelope with many banknotes arrives from the United States." Her house in the village was quite opulent. And she had a servant, a cringing girl who spoke only Basque and kissed my hand because I was a priest. So I'm sure the brilliant

Absalon did triumph in Seattle.

'What *I* wonder is whether he's hidden invocations in the machines to which we bare our minds. The code that runs them is almost infinite, no one can get to the end of it, it could harbour anything. Three-dimensional *simulcra*, for instance. When you switch on your computer and dive into its parallel world, what unthinkable thing comes to the surface to welcome you? What clatter of implacable hooves, what lustful neigh-saying, what black incredible whinnying?'

☙

'Felix,' said Margot presently, 'have you ever really been to the Basque Country?'

'No. Have you?'

'Only the beach at San Sebastián. My mother had a thing for the yoga-instructor at the *Hotel Splendide.*'

We were both silent for a second, wasting that second reflecting on the desolating incontinence of the present Lady Rievaulx.

'You invented the whole *canard*?'

'Yes.'

'When?'

'Now. As I went along.'

'It's unsettling how good you are at lies.'

'It doesn't *feel* like deception. More like brass-rubbing. Y' know, you scrub your pencil over the paper. A ghoulish mediæval face shades itself in.'

Margot may have been trying not to be a credulous materialist, for what she said next was: 'Ever wondered if you're demonically possessed?'

'That theory's occurred to me.'

'What was the point of your story?'

'I'm not sure...'

'The friar struck me as the hero.'

'Yes, didn't he... I suppose the point is that he's right: a man's the sum of what he's done. A shuddering misshapen tower of rocks. He can repent of this deed or that – tear out a stone. But can he remove his foundations? Repent of what he *is*?'

'He can regret a murder, but not being essentially a murderer.'

'Exactly. Absalon went off to program calculating-machines after a calculated crime because he *was* a calculating-machine.' I'd ungallantly bounded from bed, and was briskly getting dressed. 'What's man like? Murdererous; Cainesque. Few fulfil our doom. Where's my other sock?' She pointed. 'Ta. Those few, homicides by nature, are a different species. Fully human, fully damned.'

'Er—'

'There's a boy coming this afternoon. *He's* the point of my story.'

'Why's he coming?'

'Candidate classicist.'

'Clever?'

'Direly stupid. Cufflinks?'

'There and there. Too dim even for Wygy's?'

'Even for here.'

'So why's he here really? *He's* not "fully human", is he?'

'I need to find out. A couple were run over on Tuesday night. He may' (trousers on) 'have ordered it.'

'Beat it out of him?'

'In fact' (one shoe on) 'I'm going to do just what the *basajaun* did.' (Other shoe.)

'*Frighten* him into confession?'

'Just that. So I need to recruit a bogeyman. Ollie, I think,' and I was gone before she could volunteer. It's not that I'm chauvinist; I daren't employ Urania-Margot for my capers. Who knows what she might be capable of?

03

Was Margot annoyed? Did she feel snubbed? Yes, she told me later that crowded day, she was, she did. To soothe herself she reached above her head for *A Merry Life*.

the eighth story (10:01 a.m.)

The world thoroughly neglected the broken Coleridge once he retired from it; Urania Romilly did not. Such friends as visited the Sage of Highgate would often find Urania already there, still little more than a child, already famous as a wit.

She delighted Coleridge with her grace; she bore with him, too, when he was fuddled by his morning laudanum; and softened his apprehension of his own decline with kindly deceits. It was, for

instance, the custom of the prematurely aged poet to sit beneath an
oak in the garden with the long view down to London behind him,
and regale his guests with ghastly or demonic stories, so effective
in the days of Lyrical Ballads, *so tame in the era of the* Biographia
Literaria. *She would slip behind that chair, and the poet never*
guessed that the starts and shudders of his audience were due to
horrible faces she pulled over his shoulder.

   'It is strange,' *records one visitor,* 'that a ruined man should
yet sound so sublime; stranger still that Miss Romilly, a lissom,
lovely creature, should be able to flash the very visage of a Gorgon.
At sixteen she is already mistress of fiction; perhaps, too, of
abomination—'

Margot, who had known this passage since childhood, put down the
book, as she always did at this point, went to her bathroom, and began
rehearsing abominations in the looking-glass. She rolled her eyes so only
the whites showed, she waggled her ears. 'I shall rule the world with scary
stories,' she informed the mirrored monster. She sucked her cheeks hollow,
she protruded her eyeballs, she let her tongue hang like a dead thing, pulled
her hair over her chin, fixed her mouth like a marauding shark's. 'Surely
more frightening than a *basajaun*? Anyway, more frightening that anything
Ollie Vane-Powell can manage,' and satisfied, expectant, ran her bath.

જી

But meanwhile you, reader, if you had been poised on top of Acheron,
would have seen me emerge from staircase II looking like a lover
(distracted, happy, vaguely disordered), glance about, shake myself,
metamorphose back into a don, and cross Gehenna Court with that rapid
round-shouldered shuffling known only to Fellows of Oxbridge colleges.
You would have seen me vanish beneath Acheron, and – if you were
nimble enough and moved quickly – emerge on the other side, striking
across the grass of Megiddo Court toward my own set.
   Acheron, although officially the Chapel tower, bears no particular
relation to Chapel; nor to any known style of architecture. Guidebooks
hardly prepare you for the mere bullying menace of the thing, seen for
the first time from the railway station. It gouges the low soft flat grey vault
of Cambridgeshire like a battle-mace. On the brightest day clouds gather
behind it, as if the wound festers; the glow of sun, the sheen of rainfall

seem alike powerless to soften the curious deadness of its black stone. And its shape!

> *Acheron rises, slightly swelling, in audacious incoherence: spiralled fluting gives way to inverted fanvaulting like the wings of bats, from which howling turbaned gargoyles jut into the void; then come immense ossified cobwebs holding up a storey of rusticated stone nearly irregular as a crag. This, dangling stalactites, is topped with a crazy dome set about with a crown of spikey balustrade. Finally five ribbons of stone, for which there seems to be no term, leap overhead and knot themselves together. Acheron seems to owe nothing to the Gothic, the Moors, faërie, nor even Milton's Pandæmonium. It makes an infernal impression which seems wrung from the unmediated experience of some overtaxed soul.*

I excerpt this paragraph from my *Quincentennial History of St Wygefortis' College*, a book I am laboriously composing at the command of the present Master, Sir Trotsky Plantagenet ('You have so little teaching to do, Culpepper'). I am indulging myself in my *History*, shamelessly. Nor am I embarrassed to quote myself.

> *The tower was designed by Theophilus Knipe, Master of Wygefortis', who, about the time the House of Brunswick usurped the throne, turned from being a sound scholar and Churchman to an informer, a double agent, and something like a satanist. He was, at least, the only man to be expelled from the Hellfire Club for excess. Knipe corresponded recklessly with the Old Pretender; one by one the men involved in these intrigues fell into the government's hands. He was a Hanoverian creature, but the government so dreaded and despised him he found it prudent to retire to Wales, dying there by his own hand in a goatherd's hut. He willed the College an immense sum, £33,300, on condition the Fellows erect a tower, for which he left detailed drawings. They accepted the bequest and built Knipe's Turret; but the late Master had such an evil reputation no one calls it that; it is universally known by the gentler nickname 'Acheron'.*

Imagine you had spent that morning, the fifteenth of November, on the walkway running between Acheron's bulbous dome and the balustrade. You would have observed, once I was out of sight, all the sluggish life of St

Wygefortis' College acted out beneath you.

Thus you would have seen undergraduates slouch into the Porter's Lodge and out again, loitering with cigarettes and joints in cobbly Gehenna Court, the oldest portion of College, which Acheron overhangs, looking down into it as into a well.

You would have seen Margot *alias* Abishag emerge from staircase II, bathed and severely dressed, sail across Gehenna indifferent to her peers, and head out through the Lodge into the world.

You would have seen Ollie, or rather Ollie's pampered locks, drifting across Gehenna in the opposite direction. Beside every female head of hair, the curls pause.

You would have seen Tristan Bolswood's brown hair come out from the far side of Sheol Court, which is Art Deco on one side, spacious and Victorian on the other three: polychrome brick, bas-relief of saints, sandy paths, herbaceous borders, much like an opulent prison.

You would have seen bedders come and go with their buckets.

Would have seen workmen come and go with ladders, which are their excuse for doing nothing.

Would have seen traffic in and out of the Library, which stands to the north of Chapel and Hall; but not much.

The low, pale, clear sun, oddly warm, would be approaching its zenith above you. Directly below is a curious indecisive whiffling, and looking down you would see the College Chaplain, Dr William Leigh – *Woll*-yam *Leee*, a tall Ulsterman, always known as Woolly – stand haplessly before the doors of Chapel, turning this way and that, trying to decide what to do with the last of the morning. What fine dead heavy long white hair he has! How well it goes with those tremendous fog-lamp eyes! (He lifts them blankly now, toward the sky, toward you; but you can tell they see nothing.) If a traveller above the Arctic Circle, having dug a latrine in a floe under the midnight sun, would pause for a moment to watch it fill with pale-blue water, he would know what it is to look into Woolly's eyes, those wide, flawless, featureless shallows. No definite thought ever soils their colour; it harmonises wonderfully with his cassock, which is very pale green. Anything more emphatic he thinks too 'denying' (a favourite word). Apart from the eyes Woolly has no face to speak of. He's like a tree frog in a judge's wig. Yet he is beautiful. His fatuity is cosmetic, it makes a blur to which imagination gives generous shapes: mystic, bard, wistful Old Testament prophet.

And you would have seen Sir Trotsky Plantagenet come out of Tartarus, as his Lodgings are called, and cross pinched, sunless Cocytus, his belly preceding him. He is bound for the Senior Combination Room and an early drink.

You would have seen, as soon as he was out of the way, the staff of Tartarus – butler, chef, secretary – slip into a shady corner of the Master's Garden with a lion, not quite full-grown, which they methodically set about buggering. Its stiffness and awkwardness give it away: it is long dead and stuffed. Sir Trotsky, then a young man on National Service, shot it in the Sudan. ('Anyway, some oppressed proletarian shot it, and by purchasing it in the Khartoum bazaar I paid for the shot; least said.') He is rightly proud of his lion cub; it is his favourite possession; he keeps it in his bedroom, despite its puzzling stink. If he were a good man to work for his servants would honour that lion cub. But he is cruel and tetchy, and this is the recompense they permit themselves every non-rainy day. God knows what put such a macabre idea into their heads.

You would have seen (noon having rung from Lethe, the other tower) the outflow of student slow, the influx increase, the aimless mob in Gehenna increase. Lunchtime is close.

You would have seen the kitchen staff spill out into the chaotic area behind Hall called Limbo for a final smoke. They have brought with them a cauldron full of what is pale and bubbling. When they are done, they add their butts to the stew, one or two spit in it; they stir it well and carry it back inside to feed their foes.

Fabulously tinny with distance comes the tinkling of the lunch bell. There is a surge of young heads up the steps to Hall. We dons, however, approach Hall dramatically, over the roof from our Combination Room. Our gowns billow behind us. Sir Trotsky, a little unsteady, leads. Woolly can barely fix himself in a straight line. I, tall Dr Culpepper, disconcertingly, have my head back and am looking up, directly at you.

The crowd vanishes, is engulfed. Suddenly Wygy's is empty. Wygefortians, old and young, take victuals seriously. In the sudden absolute hush you might have heard birds sing and trees move; also, from within Hall, Woolly's over-ripe voice chanting the notorious College Grace: *Domine, qui in novissimo die os gehennæ omnibus indignis pascet...* He hesitates painfully, self-searchingly, over each phrase, for his Latinity's as uncertain as the rest of his mental equipment.

> *O Lord, Who at the last day will feed the maw of hell with*
> *all the unworthy, grant today (we beseech Thee) worthy meat*
> *to us, unworthy as we are, that we might live on to endure all*

Thou hast appointed for us to suffer in these latter days.

– and when at length he is done the entire community of the College sounds out a rumbling *Amen* resonant enough to reach you atop Acheron, as if all were eager to eat and drink damnation on themselves.

AFTERNOON OF THE SECOND DAY,
THURSDAY 15 NOVEMBEFR 2012

Now that everyone's at meat, you feel so lonely up there it's a relief to spy movement.

A dirty mop of blond hair is emerging from the corner staircase of a Georgian polygon built around a lawn. This is Abaddon Court, standing to the north, apart from the rest of College, beyond Willow Walk, which is spanned by a covered bridge. In the midst of Abaddon is the shimmer of falling water, and a bewildering mass of stone: the College's celebrated allegorical fountain. Scholarly Endeavour, a dowdy goddess in academic cap and gown, pours eternally from a tremendous stone inkpot the pure water of learning, while fending off the javelins and slingshots of Indolence, Error, Concupiscence, Indulgence and Spleen – half-clad nymphs much more alluring than herself, particularly Error.

The dirty mop of hair, which belongs to Sebastian Hawicke Trocliffe (*hoik trosly*), sways a little in the mild air. A hand comes up to shade the hungover eyes against the afternoon sun, the only sun Seb ever sees. He is, as usual, evaluating the water splashing on Error's stone bottom. But this is as far as he gets from bed. After a sad moment the mop turns and recedes back into the staircase, defeated by the throbbing within. Seb will not rise today.

You lift your eyes from unpeopled St Wygefortis', and are relieved to see undergraduates from other, better colleges, whipping along Emmanuel Road on their bicycles, distorted by your perspective to two slashes of black. You cast your gaze further, looking north to Jesus College, west to Christ's, south to Emmanuel, east to nothing at all, the tremendous nothingness of East Anglian mud-flats, North Sea, half-tamed steppe of the Germanies, Russia, the Urals. Returning, you regard Cambridge spread out below you, sweet as an apple in the still quiet air of the Indian summer, that season outside the seasons, perfect, apparently incapable of wearing away.

Suddenly the doors of Hall open again and you see people once more, disgorging themselves down the steps. Some undergraduates hesitate, retrieve bags of books, pass through the Lodge, presumably to lecture-rooms. Most frankly go back to their rooms in twos or threes, for the wines of Wygy's are quite remarkable.

There are no gowned figures yet: evidently the Fellowship lingers on high table, waiting for the Master to ground his gavel. At last you see us, a single black-clad undulating body, pocked with bald heads, reeling back across the roof, clutching at the stonework for support, hiccoughing gently. It reaches the shelter of the Combination Room – coffee, for God's sake coffee, brandy and snuff and asafœtida.

Two figures do not go in. The shaggy white hair of Woolly slouches off unsociably in one direction. And another, more wholesome head of hair separates itself as well: myself. I toss my gown over my shoulder; fix another troubling glance on you, invisible (surely) in your perch; and stride about Gehenna Court, back and forth like a fish of prey through the shoals of idling undergraduates. I stop before a mass of curls – Ollie! – and you see me produce (a flash) a silver case, and offering (distinguished flick of black) a Turkish cigarette. Then we two conspirators sidle into a corner just beneath Acheron itself, which stands arrogantly at an oblique angle to the western range of Gehenna. Since Acheron overhangs we have made ourselves, as if deliberately, invisible to you.

Impatiently you lift your eyes and see a taxi pulling up in Emmanuel Road, just outside the Lodge. A black, lavishly oiled poll emerges, topping a well-developed brownish nose and slight figure in shiny clothes. The driver takes two, three, four matching suitcases out of the boot (does the boy mean to stay here forever?) and piles them on the pavement. The luggage is matching, it is too bright, it twinkles with a gold monogram, *I.i.A.a.M.* The boy in the bad white suit looks about, with deadly innocence, for someone to carry them for him.

The victim, in short, has arrived. It is time for you to come down and witness the mischief.

This is a little easier said than done. Your route is halfway down the tower by its treacherously smooth stair, then across the roof of Chapel.

The Chapel interior is empty enough, after a bewildering history of being expanded, lopped, remodelled, reoriented, de-gothicised, plastered, frescoed, re-gothicised, unplastered, re-catholicised, de-christianised, and finally carpeted, as religious fashions have drifted here and there; it now resembles a shapeless ashlar auditorium, with a few anomalous pointed arches; except where Woolly has erected Buddhist and Hindu shrines to reveal the breadth of his mind.

But the Chapel roof remains a chaos. Steep gables of slate run in every direction, tracing the spine of side-chapels long since demolished by Cranmer, or Cromwell, or the abominable Knipe (who moved a wall to annex the altar of the Holy Innocents to the College kitchens. He liked to enter the kitchens in the full glory of his doctoral robes, to watch live lobsters being strapped to the grill, or turtles boiled in their shells, or eels flayed). It has been trimmed, too, with complex iron parapets, lacework and spiky lilies. It's easy to get lost up there. Each undergraduate generation initiates the next into the maze, although in principle no one is allowed up; the Chaplain's second-floor rooms guard the only window with access to the roof. However, Woolly is so vague he can never persuade himself he is hearing a footfall ('*as such*') in the corridor that runs behind his sitting-room until it is too late.

You descend the tower, cross unerringly the labyrinth, and step through the little window. You are not perfectly silent. Woolly lifts his baffled head, a bush-baby head rolling loosely on the torso of bony Ulster farming stock. His face is particularly blurred after lunch. 'One hand clapping,' he thinks, 'feet that are and yet *in a profounder sense* are not, unfixity of the cosmos. God is love, all is one' – and so, unchallenged, you pass his door and descend into the bloody shambles.

EVENING OF THE SECOND DAY,
THURSDAY 15 NOVEMBER 2012

The sun has descended the sky, broken up on the edge of the world, gone to America like Absalon. November dusk is folding Acheron into a larger darkness, making it minute by minute less horrible.

Day has dwindled slowly in this idle wicked place. There is nothing much to be said about the afternoon; now the inmates are wasting the evening. They dine early at St Wygefortis' to make sure there is time and appetite left for a large supper at eleven. From the Junior Combination Room comes a monotonous baying and the occasional bash of thrown crockery. From the Senior Combination Room comes a lower rumble: the College elders are also at play.

Otherwise a splendid quiet lies on Cambridge and on St Wygefortis'. Ten days of unseasonal warmth has produced immense peace in everyone's mind. In the pubs and courts there is mellowness. There is mellowness in the green places, except where fanatics lope along sweatily in shorts. The scholars themselves are contentedly turning pages, doing no harm of any sort, in every college library.

Every college library but one. A Wygefortis undergraduate seen reading at this hour would risk debagging. Only Abishag the Great, who is beyond criticism and can do as she wishes, kneels in the bay window of her set, amusing herself as usual with *A Merry Life*, waiting (arrogant child) for me to turn up and admit I need her as my bogeywoman.

the ninth story (8:12 p.m.)

Lady Rievaulx remained a devotee of Coleridge for the rest of her long life, and was always fond of retelling his eerie tales, most memorably to her grandson Reginald, the present Earl of Rievaulx, on the occasion of his sister Edwina's coming-out ball.

Urania, although now only the Dowager Countess, insisted on giving the ball herself. 'Edwina's a dry stick of a gal, sure to throw herself away on a stockbroker,' she told anyone who asked, 'don't care for her one bit. But there's family honour to consider and Constance,' she added, Constance being her daughter-in-law, present mistress of ffontaines House, 'gives such thunderin' dreary parties.'

Lady Rievaulx did not give dreary parties. Edwina's ball was the triumph of the 1890 season according to everyone, or rather everyone except Reginald, who was compelled to remain upstairs in bed. 'I'm not having that beany cub spoil my blow-out, grandmama, d'y'hear?', said Edwina, crossly and coarsely. Constance backed her up; which was a mistake.

As soon as the Dowager Countess's first guests had arrived, including the Prince and Princess of Wales, she was seen to slide upstairs in her wonderful jet-bead frock, bearing champagne, a plate of foie gras, *cold truffled ptarmigan, and other titbits unsuitable for a thirteen-year-old. She fed these to Reginald, and as he scoffed, recited from* The Ancient Mariner:

Her lips were red, her looks were free,
   Her locks were yellow as gold :

Her skin was as white as leprosy,
The Night-mare LIFE IN DEATH was she,
Who thicks man's blood with cold.

The lines are evocative rather than descriptive. But Lady Rievaulx was happy to expatiate on their full dreadfulness, and to act out the rôle of Life-in-Death: her wiles, her mingled heat and coldness; above all, her terrible faces.

When she had done her worst she tucked her grandson in and came downstairs, and an hour later was still smiling her famous smile (no one had ever been able to analyse it) when Reginald's shrieks started rolling down the great staircase: shrieks so terrible that Deepford the butler, who drank, dropped a bowl of punch, the orchestra tripped over its waltz and foundered, the dancers stopped, everyone looked upward.

Reginald did not miss his cue. He appeared at the top of the stairs, naked, horribly pale, flecked with blood, with Edwina's pet budgerigar, pierced by a hat-pin, hung about his neck. He was sleepwalking, more or less, but still managed to put up an excellent fight against the footmen sent to tackle him.

Meanwhile the Prince of Wales was heard to utter a guttural oath, and Edwina – 'Her temper's gettin' frightful bad,' remarked her grandmother, cheerfully – flung down her bumper of champagne-cup, which unhappily shattered over the shoe of a young Marquess who had been working his bashful way towards confessing to Edwina that he 'cared'. (No more was heard of that, and she has indeed recently, at a mature age, taken the hand of Mr Alfred Nuttall, of a reputable City firm.)

After a year's convalescence at Baden-Baden, Reginald was declared well enough to return to Eton. But he was soon asked to leave, and has not since recouped his health despite a world tour with his tutor. He succeeded last year to the ffontaines-Laigh title and property, but despite—

Margot sighs, closes her book, and stares out of her window. It is too lovely to think about Great-great-uncle Reginald, his blood thicked with cold.

Yes, even here in Wygy's-the-damned it is a delicious evening. The burble of the allegorical fountain weaves a fugue with its echoes against the severe Palladian walls of Abaddon; the clatter of servants washing the surviving dishes sounds not unmusically round Limbo; from Tartarus comes scratchy music (Sir Trotsky is keeping the faith, playing L.P.s of the Red Army choir), but the mild November softens even that to a harmony.

All things go at peace with each other. In the furthest, southernmost end of College, leaves die and fall from their trees gently, gently, on to the lawn of the Fellows' Garden.

And from the Fellows' Garden comes suddenly CRACK! CRACK, CRACK! CRACK! – immensely loud bangs; then a metallic crash as of a garden gate slammed; gasping, terrified gasping; a lone figure pelting across Sheol Court (ignoring the paths, a College offence, but no one sees it), through the tiny abyss of Cocytus, across the lawn of Megiddo, still at top speed, up the wooden steps of staircase IV three at a time, thud, *thud*, tumbling over himself as he (it is Ollie) crashes through the double doors into my rooms, and still hurtling through the air, not quite having steadied himself by the grasp of an armchair, shrieks, bellows, red-faced, slick with sweat, launching at once into

the tenth story (8:27 p.m.).

'He has a gun! You didn't say he'd have a fucking *gun!*'

'Then you weren't thinking,' I purred, shutting inner and outer doors and pushing Ollie into an armchair. 'Course he has a gun. Dictators' sons can't go about unarmed. Now, d'y'want scotch or Drambuie?'

'You didn't say he'd *fire!*' Ollie was unmanned and nearly blubbering.

'No, I couldn't be sure of that.' I lifted Ollie's nerveless right hand and folded its fingers round a tumbler. While the boy sucked at this, I picked up the 'phone on my desk and pushed zero for the Lodge. 'Lint? Lint? Evening, Lint. Culpepper here. Those slight bangs a minute ago – oh you heard them, did you? *Shots?* No, no, good heavens no...' ('The head porter says he heard *shots!*' I said in a stage whisper. Ollie didn't smile.) 'No, no, Lint, don't bother coming to have a look. It was just that fool Ebbe. He's been doing smelly experiments in his rooms again. Blew up a retort by the sound of it... Yes, with luck! Although I think I still hear him stomping about... Good night, then.' I hung up, sighed, and contemplated the wreckage of Oliver Vane-Powell. 'Can you speak?'

'All right, all right. I'm over it.'

'Then speak. Tell me what happened.'

'I did all you said. Took him out drinking—'

'No, no, this is important. Slowly. Small things may be significant. I want nuances. You went to his room—'

'All right, I went and banged on his door. Abaddon IV, 5. There was some sort of video playing. In foreign.'

'Foreign.'

'Um… Portuguese! Yeah, that's it, I had a Portuguese nanny after Marcellite got one up the duff and left us.'

'You're a sophisticated fellow, Ollie.'

'Funny Portuguese, though.'

'Brazilian?'

'Maybe. God. Is *that* significant? How can it be? He turned it off and opened up. Haughty little fellow in whites. Estate-agent-in-Barbados look.'

'Yes, yes. I've seen him. Get on.'

'Nervous, too. He looked up and down the staircase before he said "Hallo?" "Hi, I'm Ollie," I say. "I'm upstairs. You're Idris. You're the candidate. You're here for an interview. Did it go well?" He didn't look very well. In fact, he looked drunk already and his room smelt of brandy. "It was a triumph," he said. *Was* it?'

'"*Amo, amas,* um um um, *amum.*" No, he's hopeless. I've never interviewed such a one. *Infinitely* ignorant. Makes even you look like a Latinist.'

'He *said* it had gone well and that he was sure to get in so I said "Cool, come upstairs for a decent drink", and we finished a bottle of the claret my father sends and then I said "If you're coming here next year, you'd better see College," and I took him round. We stopped off at the Bar first. Where he got really drunk. On Jägermeister.'

'Exactly how drunk?' I asked, with my severe judicial precision.

This is a science well understood at Wygefortis'. 'Drunk enough to talk too quickly and loudly but not slur his words much. Slight stagger but at least half a dozen pints below passing out and could easily get it up.'

'Hm.' Sober enough to know what he was doing.

'I showed him the courts, showed him Hall, turned on the lights and showed him the Library, not that he'll be needing that, showed him the whatsit, the Chapel. He liked the big gilded Bodhisattva, so we sat cross-legged in front of it and I unscrewed its head-dress and got out a couple of joints. That's where Woolly keeps them, y'know. He thinks we don't know.'

I sighed again. College is never sure what to do about Woolly.

'He told me about what his family used to do to people they caught worshipping images. *Cripes.*'

'Really? Who could they have been? Armenian Orthodox?'

'Yeah. S'pose so.'

'I didn't know there were any Armenians in Haran.'

'There aren't now. According to Idris. Strewth, the things his family did to them.' Ollie paused, obviously wondering what Idris would do to *him* if he caught him.

'I'm sure it was good for the Bodhisattva to hear atrocities,' I said comfortingly. 'Take that smug smile off its bronze face.'

'Yes. Anyway, by the time he had finished telling me about massacres the spliffs were gone and he said "Back to the Bar!" But I said what you said to say: "First you've got to see the Fellows' Garden. We call it Aceldama." "Why?" "Don't know. But it's way creepy. The stories I could tell…" Well, he wanted to get back to the drunk girls but he seems to like stories even more than he likes girls, so I got out more ganga and told him all about Aceldama.'

The eleventh story.

All about Aceldama!

This is lore all Wygefortians know, no matter how ignorant. There's a tradition that newly-matriculated undergraduates and newly-elected Fellows must spend an hour there alone. The experience sinks in, and is not repeated. It isn't a place for old men with bad consciences, the most morbid youth won't strike poses there.

Aceldama is a fantasia, a *jardin anglais* in high Romantic style. But how are we to speak of its clumps of yew, sideways-pyramid of porcelain, bent columns, herms, looking-glasses embedded in trunks, abstract topiary bushes? These elements defy rational analysis without quite suggesting randomness. Perhaps they accord to an order which is not human at all. Perhaps they're a coded picture of somewhere far away.

There is a river in Cambridge no one has seen complete since the reign of Elizabeth, when it was dammed, diverted, run through conduits and otherwise tormented, before being allowed to drain into the Cam below Peterhouse, in the boggy ground called Coe Fen. This buried river resurrects itself here and there. It breaks ground in the strip of green called Christ's Pieces, rushing through a deep ditch; after twenty yards it vanishes beneath Emmanuel Road. This stretch, which is called the Stygian Creek, cuts off from the rest of the world a tongue of land lying under the blank south wall of Sheol Court; a patch of ground serving as the College's vegetable garden until, in the fat years after Waterloo, it was laid out formally by Myre.

Josiah Myre, florid, red-haired and well made, was another Master elected in the odour of piety and learning, who went suddenly to the bad. It happens at Wygy's once a century or so.

'In robust middle age Master Myre was guilty,' reads my luscious *Quincentennial History,*

> *...of an infatuation with the youthful wife of Alcock, the saintly Archdeacon of Ely.*
>
> *Lady Fanny Hervey had by all accounts been born as desperately wicked as she was rich. She was undeniably handsome and shapely, as we can see from her infamous portrait by George Romney, as Iolë, dancing in dissolving draperies on Mount Œta; a painting refused by the Royal Academy as 'conducive to the decay of public morals'. By seventeen her family thought it best to marry her off to a clergyman. By the time she was nineteen her affair with Myre was the common talk of the University.*
>
> *Septimus Alcock was a devout, abstracted man. He might have overlooked the Myre scandal which was not, alas, the first. He might have borne the wrong to himself, as he had done before.*
>
> *But Fanny, who was witty as well as lovely, committed an act of unwise cleverness. She persuaded her husband that her frequent visits to St Wygefortis' College were 'occasioned by orthodoxy': that she went to the Lodgings bearing improving tracts and Patristic commentaries, with the object of reclaiming the Master, who notoriously inclined to the errors of Rousseau. She would read Bishop Butler's works aloud, until tears (she told the Archdeacon) ran down Myre's lovely red cheeks, and into his wonderful foxy whiskers.*
>
> *Perhaps Fanny was a thwarted novelist. In any case she must have been a bewitching storyteller, for she made Alcock, who was no fool, credit this pretty tale. The result was that when he learned the Master was boasting of Fanny's personal charms on high table, he found insupportable not Myre's wrong against himself, but Myre's calumny against her.*
>
> *The two men met at Grantchester at dawn, with no witnesses but their seconds, a doctor, and a tipsy undergraduate who turned up in a brougham. It is possible that the Master fired first, too soon. In any case Alcock's pistol misfired and he fell, fatally wounded in the lower*

abdomen. His dying words were of forgiveness, but Myre did not hear them, having already fled in the brougham. The tipsy undergraduate was Lady Fanny herself, shamelessly disguised. They drove to Harwich and took the packet to Holland.

Even during the Regency, it was not good form for Heads of House to shoot Church dignitaries. Attempts at prosecuting Myre, or simply depriving him of his Mastership, went nowhere, for Fanny was an heiress with connections at Court. But it was made clear to her family that she must never return.

So the guilty couple wandered. They reached France and shocked the Parisians, not least by staying in the château of 'Kitty', Viscount Courtenay, who as a boy had been Beckford's paramour, and was still dragging out his life beyond the reach of English prosecution. They reached Venice (there is a scabrous sonnet about them by Byron). They reached Greece (Myre carved a Greek hendecasyllable in praise of Fanny on a column of the Parthenon; tour guides refuse to translate it). They had an audience with the Sultan, who jestingly offered Lady Fanny a place in his seraglio; Myre jestingly asked his price. When the renegade Princess of Wales led her entourage of hundreds into the Holy City, bare-breasted on a white mule, Fanny and Myre rode behind on a dromedary, and were duly enrolled in the Order of St Caroline of Jerusalem created to mark that occasion.

All these doings were reported in England, and the standing of St Wygefortis' College fell very low.

At last came news that the notorious Fanny had died at Smyrna, of the pox (although rumour was not slow to allege her lover had throttled her for infidelity with a dragoman). Myre came home like a pirate, bearing nothing but an antique bronze treasure-chest of Coptic design, having, he said, burned all their chattels against infection. There is an unkind aquatint by Rowlandson of Myre standing on Dover Cliff, with his threadbare Armenian tapestry cloak snapping about him in the breeze, his lilac-and-silver ribbon as Sacred Chancellor of the Order of St Caroline about his neck, clutching his outlandish casket: a grim, lawless figure.

Then for a while Myre was a fixture of the Chancery Court, a spectacle, a hissing, an indecency. He wanted Fanny's fortune, and claimed they had been married by the English chaplain in Florence, a sottish unreliable man. It was only after bitter litigation that Myre won his case.

Little good it did him. He was shunned in London, even more thoroughly shunned in Cambridge, and spent his last years as a virtual recluse in Tartarus, the Master's Lodging. Too worn for further debauchery, he wasted his money on grotesque improvements to the College he, perhaps, loved. It certainly abhorred him then, and resents him still. He also bought the unfortunate Romney portrait of his mistress or wife and hung it in the College Library, where it has distracted generations of undergraduates from their work. He also perpetrated the rose window in the chapel, showing the dalliance of the Nephilim, the copious asses of Ezekiel, and Moses as a bloody bridegroom; generations of scholarship have failed to explain it away.

Worst of all, Myre is responsible for the Fellows' Garden, so sinister in appearance that Cambridge called it Myre's Horror, or the Rape Garden, and even worse things, before settling on 'Aceldama'.

You can laugh at Aceldama if you haven't seen it. It sounds like a grubby toy of a sort common enough at the time, or rather a little earlier. By 1821 dirty pleasure-gardens were old hat, and Aceldama was dated even when it was laid out. For instance, it contains, just as you'd expect, that hackneyed eighteenth-century joke, a white-marbled Temple of Priapus, tiny, with miniature colonnade of blue-veined marble, and a miniature cupola in rose-coloured Carrera. The Temple is embellished with mock-Pompeian murals of Cassandra being forced, Chrysippus, Tamar, and Leda. Lest anyone require tactile titillation, there's a bust on a plinth of Lord Courtenay. (When Lord Courtenay heard about Aceldama he sent his portrait. 'Didn't realise,' he remarked to his dubious hairdresser, 'chaps back home still went in for *questo genere di cose*, that sort of thing… *Sì, Beppe, il solito,* the usual.') Yet no one who actually sees Aceldama laughs it off as a period piece. Significantly, even the degenerates of St Wygy's never employ it for its obvious purpose. No one but Myre ever found a use for Aceldama.

What did he use it for, exactly? In a niche of the priapic Folly he kept his 'idol', his Coptic box. Did he spend his hours in Aceldama worshipping it? Rumour said so. On his deathbed he spoke so curiously of *passion that has defied the grave*, of *favours if not love enjoyed even beyond death*, that the College chaplain sent the servants out of the room, along with Myre's spinster niece, who hoped for a bequest. Soon afterward Myre began to scream. When the screams were over, the butler, prising open the door, found his master stone-dead, and the chaplain in strong hysterics.

The spinster niece was thwarted. Myre left all his fortune to the Fitzwilliam Museum 'for the purchase of antique herms', a direction the Trustees quite properly ignored. Myre's desire to be buried beneath his Temple of Priapus was also not honoured. And Aceldama, although College has never quite nerved itself to tear it down, was neglected. The casket vanished; the loathsome frescos of the Temple grew stained and faded; the weird topiary grew confused and inoffensive with generation after generation of College gardener. True, a mid-Victorian Master added to Aceldama's ferocious, inviolable gloom by burying his pugs there, one after another, each with its miniature headstone and Greek epitaph. And in the 'Twenties some high-brow published an article, '*Un certain jardin à Cambridge et les origines du Surréalisme*', which however did no harm because a vigilant customs official at Dover glanced at the photographic plates and had that number of *La Nouvelle Revue Française* seized and burned. Aceldama is so extremely evil, so supremely repellent, that, paradoxically, from Myre's day until that unseasonably warm November evening in 2012, when I found a use for it, it did little harm.

the tenth story, resumed (8:32 p.m.)

'*All* about Aceldama, Ollie? You told him all *that*?'

'I skipped the boring bits. Skipped the really nasty things too. I got it just right. He wasn't *too* scared. Just spooked enough. He said: "Let's have a look at it then." I wish he hadn't.'

'So?' But Ollie was silent, listening for further gunshots, listening to the thunder in his own chest. 'Ollie? Come on.'

Ollie took another swig. 'All right. So we went across Sheol into Aceldama. Through the garden arch. The gate was unlocked for a change.'

'Did you go first?'

'Yes. God it's dark in there. We were both a bit jumpy. I don't think Idris often gets jumpy. But as soon as we were beside the little temple thing I said what you said to say. I mean I whispered it. "Oi, Idris, look out. There's someone lurking behind that funny-looking bush." He looked terrified. So I said, as you said, "He looks like you. I mean, Arab. He's holding – is that a rifle?" And that's as far as I got because instead of being frightened he reached under his armpit and got out this gun, this fucking gun, and starting blasting away. A *gun*. You didn't tell me. Blasting away. Bang bang bang bang. Mad bugger. Mad bugger. So I scarpered. You didn't tell me he'd have a gun.'

I heard out Ollie with my hanging judge face. Which is exactly what I was. 'Guilty, guilty, guilty. Al-Mutlak started at a shadow: that's conclusive. To fire once might be panic. *Four* times is bloodguiltiness. One shot, he hears nothing, no one fires back; yet he still pumps another bullet into the bush; and when the lurker must surely be hit, another, then another. Only someone with blood on his hands, recent blood, could be so nervous, cowardly, savage. Absalon has to kill Gillermo, because it's his nature; Idris is a homicide not a human… Am I sure of that, am I *sure*? Yes. Four times: that's proof. Trial by imagination's a real trial. Forces the mind to judge itself. Good enough for Prince Hamlet, good enough for me.' I smiled in condemnation; smiled again passing sentence. 'If the mousetrap makes you start, it's time to wheel on the guillotine.' Then I looked a shade more troubled.

'You did well,' I told Ollie. 'Very very well. One more thing to do before bed. Find Idris—'

But Ollie turned tearful again. 'Fuck that. Fuck fuck *fuck* it. I'm not going near him. He's a fucking loon. He's got a *gun*. He'll put a bullet right through my hair. Head. I'm going to my room and I'm locking myself in.'

'Oh come on, Ollie.'

'No. End of story.'

○3

'Ollie—'

'I've had enough of your—' but he evidently didn't want to define what it was I had that he rejected. It seemed safer to put down his tumbler and blunder out, wiping his nose with his sleeve.

I watched him critically from his window, running across the court toward the looming silhouette of the Library and the shortcut over the covered bridge to Abaddon Court.

'This,' I told myself, 'is no good.' I paced up and down. 'It's no good using children as helpers if they snap like this. But I do need someone to lure Idris.' I knew perfectly well what came next, and was curiously alarmed.

I was even more alarmed a minute later, standing in Gehenna Court and looking up at Abishag's window, open to the mild evening. She was so obviously *waiting* for me. She raised her eyes from Urania, saw me, smiled in triumph.

CR

After his experience in the garden, Idris required drink and he required talk.

The boy was not, you'll understand, distraught. He was used to shooting shadows in the course of an evening – shooting people, indeed. Why, one morning he'd supervised an interrogation of one of his bodyguards from the cafeteria of the Berne International School, muttering instructions into his mobile 'phone, looking at his watch. The man had, probably, been spying on him for his half-brother Jasim; he had to be broken in the next quarter of an hour because he, Idris, had an algebra test, and then Jasim would be back from Beirut at lunchtime. The staff, swabbing the tables before setting lunch, glanced about curiously: even with the earpiece covered, they could hear squeals down the line from Arpachshad. The man broke and Idris got a C+, which was all he needed.

This evening he was hurt, nonetheless. Ollie had seemed so friendly. Idris was not used to friendliness untainted by fear. It pained him to be the victim, after all, of a trick. Once he had kicked and trampled the bush and made sure Aceldama harboured no assassins, his impulse had been to go back to Ollie's room and – and – well, pistol-whip him at the least.

But then he remembered he was about to be admitted to St Wygefortis'. There would be plenty of time for revenge. In the meantime, he needed drink, he needed chatter, and he needed a woman.

It is not etiquette for a candidate, who is not a member of College and statistically unlikely to become one, to go into the bar alone. But Idris was so prodigal in buying strangers drinks that he was tolerated. When, an hour later, Margot found him loafing on a barstool, he was looking almost at home.

She floated to him. There was a miasma of awe about her, because she was meditating on her ancestress and Life-in-Death. *Her lips were red, her looks were free.* She's beautiful (most of the time) without being the least bit pretty, and was wearing what could have been, and in fact was, a dress made in Paris in the 'Fifties, an unadorned cylinder of grey. It was a College saying that if Abishag would give up tiresome King David she could rule Israel. She was a paragon, and had no business going up to Idris, this mere stranger, and putting her hand on his shoulder. The two of them had nothing in common but the roles I had assigned them in my plot.

She said 'You're new,' and he, looking up, felt dazzled by the wisdom of her remark.

She flicked her head. The lesser females on either side of Idris vanished from their barstools. She sat beside him. A faint tremor went through the watching crowd.

'Well?' she said, quietly, so no one could hear, when he had got her port. 'They call me Abishag.'

'I'm Idris.' He had nothing to tell her, there was nothing in him true and interesting. But lies are always to hand. He leant forward so as to gloat over her breasts and launched into his staple chat-up: 'Listen to this. A guy walks into a sperm-donor bank wearing a ski mask and holding a gun. He goes up to the nurse and says…'

He observed her weary look and stopped. His story was stillborn.

'Perhaps,' he said lamely, 'you've heard it before?'

the twelfth story (10:22 p.m.)

'My great-great-great-grandmother Urania,' said Abishag, a little shyly, 'once snubbed The Prince of Wales for telling her the same dirty story twice. "You grow tedious with age, Sir!" she said, and turned her back. She was forty years older than he was, too. Poor Bertie went puce, couldn't speak, nodded brusquely to his hostess (the Duchess of Devonshire), and had to be helped to his carriage. He wasn't seen anywhere for days, and he didn't forgive great-great-great-grandmother for years. But she stayed on at Devonshire House and was still dancing when the sun came up.'

the thirteenth story (10:23 p.m.)

'My great-grandfather,' said Idris, even more shyly because he was in thrall to this redhead, 'didn't know many stories, not 'til the British came to the Nahor. Once, when he was telling for the thousandth time the tale of the Woman who Made her Husband Sift Dust, one of his men yawned. He had him buried up to his neck in the sand and sat watching until the kites had finished with his eyes.'

ന

'Princes of Wales aren't allowed to do that. Still,' she added, not wanting him to think she was criticising his ancestor, 'I like men who take things seriously.'

'I could take you seriously. I think,' said Idris, who had never fawned on a woman before, even to this extent. Being gallant gave him vertigo. He didn't like the sensation. She would pay for his discomfort later. 'I like what I see.'

'The best view in Cambridge,' said Abishag primly, looking away and folding her hands, 'is from Acheron. That's the big tower beside Chapel. We're not supposed to go up there, but of course we do. It's quite easy. Up Megiddo staircase VII, along the corridor past the Chaplain's rooms – he's deaf and very silly, he won't catch you. Out through the window at the end. There are catwalks all over the roof. Go left. Take the third turning on the right, first left, first right, and you'll find yourself in front of a dark stone arch. Through that, up three turns of the stairs, and you're on the platform. You'll see everything. Be there at exactly twelve. I'll be there at two minutes past. My sable is bulky to wear on such a mild evening but it's lovely to lie on.' She laid two fingers on his lips to stop any reply, and glided away. The mob of drinkers parted before her as she went, sightless.

That is all she said. I'd told her nothing, merely giving her her orders: 'Get that Harani yob on top of Acheron at midnight.' But she went back to her room feeling a bit like Idris' great-grandfather, who slew his own men because of his own bad stories. Possibly she felt, for the first time in her life, that she was getting beyond Urania. For although she loyally kept *A Merry Life* open, it is to be doubted whether she read. When the yell came (twelve was still tolling) she rose without starting and went out, with her finger between the pages marking her place. She reached Cocytus, and gazed about the cobbles. Nothing. Slowly, slowly, though, she raised her elegant head and found what she was looking for. It had not cleared the roof after all. It had got snagged in the steel lacework on the way down. Indeed – a rabble of shouting, gesticulating undergraduates was forming behind her, the windows were flying open, someone had got a big lamp and was shining it on to the Chapel roof – it was impaled. One of the metal lilies had pierced the shoulder-blades, and stuck out through the chest. Another fixed the groin. The dreadful white suit was stained with what looked black in that bad light. 'Get a ladder!' someone was bellowing. 'A ladder!' A semi-circle of slate below the untidy figure was shiny with gore. The tracery of ornamental ferns was festooned with loops of gut.

The body looked freakishly funny, as surprising carnage does, until you noticed that it wasn't a body, but feebly moving, twitching one of its dangling arms, jerking its foot, still, moving, still again, flopping like a landed fish.

THIRD DAY:

THE SMALL HOURS OF FRIDAY, 16 NOVEMBER 2012

Not since the tumults of the Protectorate had so much blood been on offer within College walls. Never had College hoped to see so many agitated policemen in its Courts. *And* a police helicopter overhead, *and* three fire-engines at the gates, *and* half a dozen television trucks, although the ferocious Lint had kept these outside the walls in Emmanuel Road, where they told each other on camera 'I'd say the mood is tense, Tom.' 'Yes from what we're seeing Shazia, I'd certainly characterise the mood as tense.'

The police, with little else to do, had made a great aggressive business of clearing the mob of undergraduates from Cocytus, and roping it off. Margot had managed to remain.

'Hop it, you, *now*.'

'But I spoke to him in the Bar.'

'Who?'

'That – person up there.'

'Oh you did, did you? Well stand over there and don't go away.'

'I spoke to him too,' said Tristan Bolswood, most jaded of the first-year classicists. 'I spent half an hour teaching him ride-the-bus.'

'What's that?' The detective clearly hoped for muck.

'Just a drinking game. We played it with Jägermeister.'

'Oh you did, did you? Very nice I don't think. You stand *here*, see. And don't you go talking to each other.'

So Margot stood beside Tristan and watched the constables push everyone young out of the little Court. She watched them, once there was no one left to boggle at the roof, boggle at it themselves. She heard the ambulancemen who had climbed on the roof call to each other pitifully from between the gables, lost. She watched the firemen bring in a mechanical ladder and try to approach their quarry from below. She would have seen more, but a bald detective had thought of a searching query and strode over to her. 'What did you talk to him *about*, miss?'

'Nothing in particular. We exchanged stories about our ancestors.'

'Stories, eh?' He wasn't sure about putting that equivocal word in his notebook; but had a flash of brilliance. 'Would you say that these so-called ancestors were *dead* at all?'

Another, younger, hairier detective had thought of something to put to Bolswood. 'How would you describe his state of mind?'

Lascivious, thought Bolswood. 'Tense,' he said, 'and drunk.'

The bald detective, who was writing *Conversachun about dead persons* in his notebook, nonplussed by his rival, appropriated his wit and flashed it at Margot. 'How would *you* describe his state of mind?'

'Drunk,' she said. 'Drunk but intense.' The hairy detective, who was writing *Morebid state mind?* in *his* notebook, glanced at her piercingly, then held up the page to his colleague, who blenched. This young fellow would go far, he could see him at the Yard one day. Very well: best to co-operate. He gave a Napoleonic nod, and the two policemen strode off together to compose their Preliminary Report.

Sir Trotsky Plantagenet, Master of Wygefortis', and a few other College officers too great to send away, stood in an arch of Cocytus. I was conspicuously nowhere (watching and listening, as it happens, from a darkened window). Tristan and Margot, forgotten, stood beside the dons, watching the firemen prise off the corpse – for that's what it clearly was, long before they reached it.

'Poor loves,' breathed fat wheezy Mrs Oathouse, the College nurse, creeping up from behind, 'this must be ever so awful for you. Do you need a little something?'

Bolswood was bored more than anything else, but it was Junior Combination Room policy never to say no to Nurse's barbiturates and risk freezing her generous heart. He held out his hand.

The detectives were squabbling again. 'Actually I think you'll find *self-destructive psychological traces* sounds better than *self-destructive remarks*. More smart-like. See?'

'Not if you spell it without a *p*, I think you'll find.' They flashed looks of hatred at each other, for art is the cruellest tyrant and English prose most exigent of all the arts.

The firemen were handing their burden down the ladder now, its head sprawled backward at a terrible angle. A paramedic hopped about below with a stethoscope, trying to be the first to get at the gory chest and pronounce the obvious.

'Manners,' sniffed Mrs Oathouse. 'This is my patch and I think they might have asked me to have a little listen.' Tristan patted her hand and was rewarded with two more Seconals, which Nurse keeps loose in her cardigan pocket like doggy-treats.

The mangled thing lay on the stones of Cocytus with a stretcher beneath, muffled with a blanket. The uniformed men stood back. Margot and Tristan lowered their heads. Mrs Oathouse became snuffly. Even the police detectives put down their duelling-notebooks.

This is a moment painters and playwrights love (although there's nothing novelists can do with it): the instant after martyrdom, before the spectators resume their chatter. Groaning is done, specious last words are out of the way. The human body as such, all passion spent, is allowed to express whatever it expresses, before being bundled away. Then *Take up the bodies. Go, bid the soldiers shoot*, and so forth. But first comes the moment when dead flesh casts out even the possibility of words. In the particular silence flesh suggests – well, it hardly matters what, for in this case there was no silence.

Enter stage left the Rev'd Dr Leigh, burbling. (The Court had become very stagey, roped off and floodlit as it was: a cube of dressed stone on four sides, cobbles below, night sky above.) He threw himself down over the corpse, and broke into long, fervid speech, while everyone else stood about shyly.

In justice to the Chaplain, let's make clear that there were no journalists about, only one indifferent police photographer. It is greatly to Woolly's credit that he knelt so long and photogenically over that blanket, and that he outdid himself in his prayers. Idris was promised (Margot noticed; she was at first the only spectator attending to Woolly's words) the Catholic resurrection of the body, *and* blissful obliteration in nirvana, *and* reincarnation as whatever is even better than an al-Mutlak, *and* Primitive Protestant exemption from hell, *and* Modern Protestant quality time with Jesus; as well as the more orthodox *Jannat al-Na'īm*. 'Which means Garden of Delights,' Woolly explained to that bumpy part of the blanket, not much stained, where the face was hidden. He had an anthology of *hadith* in his hands and leafed through it nimbly. 'You'll soon be finding *houris* so light and pleasantly-scented that their very *hijabs* are better than the world and whatever is in it. You'll soon be selecting your new soul. Already the fever of Being is being abated by ineffable Nothing.'

These firemen, like most firemen, were rugged papists, and here one of them coughed. *Houris* he could tolerate because the buggers hold with that sort of thing out there in Arabia, but what was this heretical faffing about new souls? It wouldn't have passed muster in Holy Name parochial catechism class.

Woolly turned hungrily at the cough, because it was what he'd been waiting for. His brand of willful moronism isn't fulfilled in itself; it needs to know that it is offending sense. '*Don't* you see,' he whined, eagerly, plaintively, and belligerently, still on his knees but shuffling slightly sideways, away from the unresponsive Idris, toward the more promising fireman, 'don't you *see* all these promises *are the same*? All truth is in the most special sense *one*. We all look out to the same point. We need never deny. The essence of every faith…'

He was doing no harm and really might have been allowed to blather. But Tristan, who couldn't abide Woolly, found that his own slight capacity for reverence was now used up. Seconal, on top of all the liquor, was making him belligerent. So he suddenly snarled: 'What d'y'mean, Mr Leigh, *every* faith? My daddy's a pantheist, he doesn't believe we look *out* at anything. You slighting that?'

A quiver of dismay went through the crowd. Everyone glanced anxiously at the body, which expressed no embarrassment. As for Woolly, he relished desecrations. He liked folding them into his routine. It was one of his party tricks at weddings to urge the bride to explore her lesbian impulses, and then pounce on any wriggling or intolerant leg-crossing amongst the congregation. So now his pulse quickened from its usual sluggish forty-four beats per minute to the low sixties. 'Idris ibn Ali,' he pronounced, twisted back toward the blanket, 'merge with our Common Mother the Cosmos whence—'

'Ee, 'o you callin' common?' protested Mrs Oathouse, the only mother present in that ruck of youth, burly firemanhood, sadistic policemanhood, and barren dons. This time the crowd's rustle sounded like approval. The Oathouse folded her arms, pleased with herself. '*Cosmo* wench indeed.'

'Idris ibn—'

'*I'm* a pagan,' said one of the medics, angrily. He had a ring in his nose. 'And *I* don't reckon he's merged into anything.'

'Yeah, he's gone to The Summerland.' This one had reddish dreadlocks.

The crowd was closing in on Woolly, who grew confused and excited (72 b.p.m.). 'Pass, Ali, for a space to the warm, gentle realm of reflection, of recuperation, in the—'

'Not Ali, Idris!' corrected half a dozen voices. 'Idris ibn Ali!' Even the dons were joining in now.

'– in the company of *sídhe* and faerie sprites—'

'Aam a haythin tay,' growled a backward under-porter named Scurf who, to my certain knowledge, has never been north of Loughborough.

'I'll thenk ye nae tae belittle Sell-tick Reconstructionist Pag'nism wi' thes toffy-nosed gab ay summer resorts.'

Like Scurf, but in a different way, Woolly has been educated beyond his intelligence. 'Come, O Ibn, unto *Tír na nÓg* – which means,' Woolly informed the dead boy, 'Warrior Land of the Young—'

'Idris!'

'*Tír na,*' he insisted. He seemed to himself to be surrounded by bigots who wonderfully spurned, as they always did, his one idea. One minus two is three, One God No God, good God, oddgod, Godforsaken, many gods, doggone: all the same. How he cherished denying bigotry. Farrago was his nirvana (or Summerland, or *Jannat*), but just as a drunk can't get giddy until physics pushes back against his staggering, only contradiction could release pure muddle into Woolly's blood. Still kneeling in his lama-hat and cassock, he lifted vague and ineffectual hands, begging to be heckled, to be tussled (lightly). More, more. A martyrdom of pushes and gentle pokes! The veins stood out in his pale forehead.

'Our friend Idris is discovering that all is one!' His pulse had reached a plateau of 96, and he could barely sustain such throbbing. 'I feel almost orgasmic,' he thought; 'I imagine.' Soon, perhaps, would come the faint, the plummet into perfect and infinite confusion. He'd achieved it only once before, at a wedding when an infuriated bridesmaid had thrashed with him the bride's bouquet.

But tonight Woolly's timing was off. He had enraged his audience too quickly. 'Get off!' they said. 'Buffoon! Idolater! Show-time over! Amen!' Mrs Oathouse gave his shoulder a push and he swayed. Tristan wondered if he dared kick the ridiculous man's buttocks.

There is a God, just One: there'd be no point in writing novels if that weren't so. A novel is a pretend God's-eye-view, a trespass into the Royal Box at the opera house, an impudent attempt to picture things as they must look to the Patron. If you can bear novels, you'll know there are certain breaches of theatrical convention not to be borne. Woolly couldn't grasp this.

Sir Trotsky did. He was a devout Marxist with clear ideas, who dreaded and loathed the opiate of the masses: dreaded it in a fashion that betrayed an anxiety that it might be true. Woolly's fruit salad of the masses offended him to the marrow. History was, Sir Trotsky hoped, a comedy of manners with the Communist revolution for *dénouement*. It might, terribly, be a mystery play. But in either case it was not *this*. And so the Master strode across the court, pushed through the ruck, seized his Chaplain by his dog-collar, heaved him up, dragged him away – exit Clown stage right; a dissipation of noise, a recrudescence of dignity.

Enter an ambulance crew. They came forward to the blanketed shape, with its pulse of exactly zero. (Yet Woolly's receding babble could still be heard testifying that everything means everything. No one has ever refuted silliness. The abject have access to underground pools of complacency which you and I will never understand. He was happy.) It was nearly three. The helicopter was gone. Darkness, quiet. Night-time is night-time, even in Wygy's. Death is death. When the ambulancemen heaved up Woolly's prop, a rectangle of dark dampness remained on the dry stone. The quietness turned to absolute silence. Then the ambulancemen's footsteps were loud on the cobbles. They passed offstage and there was a gust, everyone releasing breath at once. A sterile pentecost.

Such was the passing of Idris ibn Ali al-Mutlak, favourite son of the President of Haran.

LATE MORNING,
FRIDAY, 16 NOVEMBER 2012

College got out of bed late, and groggily, as after a debauch. The impaling of al-Mutlak had inebriated the most unimaginative undergraduate – Ollie, that is: although in fact Ollie kept to his rooms. It had inebriated everyone else, that's what I mean to say: inebriated them with the enhanced possibilities of life, its weirdness, brutishness and glitter.

But blood hangovers, like the usual sort, ooze backward through time. The past warps and spoils in memory, the only place it exists. When the morning feels so unsatisfactory, we become agnostic about the dwindled pleasures of the night. Were we really so gay?

Margot gazed through the drizzle on her window. The Indian summer was suddenly over, and it too shrank in hindsight. Normal, unsatisfactory November had resumed, blustery, drizzly and dim. It was hard to see, amidst such greys, why a scattering of pink intestines had seemed such gaudy fun. In this unsatisfactory universe, everything grated, or itched.

She'd had ill-omened dreams. Their thrust was simply: last night's butchery had been so indiscreet I'd certainly go to prison; she'd go too, as my accomplice, and not enjoy it. Even Urania hadn't experienced gaol.

It was close on eleven before a wary, puling Margot emerged from her rooms. She made her way across courts dotted with haggard undergraduates, like her crapulous with gore.

Cocytus was still blocked off. She could hear the sploshing of firehoses rinsing the Chapel roof. *Down goes the al-Mutlak bloodline,* thought Margot, hoping to ease her depression by being ornate. *What held the Nahor for six generations gurgles into drains; what keeps all Haran in awe is contained by guttering.* But her terror would not relax. *It washes underground into the Styx, runs through pipes to the Granta, dilute but vengeful, toward the – oh damn it. Damn damn damn. What a clumsy performance. He'll have fled. He'll have been arrested.*

Nonetheless: 'Come in, come in,' came my voice when she tapped tentatively at my door. I was still there. Indeed she entered to a breezy Culpepper, an airy Culpepper, a jovial Culpepper in whom guilt was sublimated into jauntiness. No, not jovial; some lesser god than Jove. Hermes the thief.

I was in my grand crimson silk dressing-gown. I smiled at her but didn't speak, for I was traipsing back and forth from sitting-room to bedroom, packing a suitcase.

She sat on the arm of a sofa, trying to place my mood, regarding the suitcase sideways. 'You're running away?'

'Venice,' I called happily from the bedroom. 'I'll be – *what*' (re-entering the sitting-room with two pairs of shoes) 'did you say?'

'Are you escaping the police?'

'*What*? No. Of course not. *The police?* You mean about young al-Mutlak? Good God no. Why would I? They're entirely satisfied.'

'They are?'

'They're quite certain he flung himself from Acheron, yes. You'll see no more rozzers stomping about College and a good thing too. They smell.'

'The case is closed?'

'Where d'you pick up this vocabulary? Been watching telly?'

'If they become unsatisfied, I mean about suicide,' she persisted, heavily, 'do you have an alibi?'

'I wish you wouldn't use words like that. *Alibi* isn't proper Latin.'

'*Do* you? I want to help. I need to know where I stand.'

I sighed. 'Thank you for what you did last night. Cozening, gulling, snaring. But don't worry about the consequences. There are none. And don't try to expand your role. I have no need of a regular sidekick.'

'At least tell me what happened.'

'Nor do I need a Dr Watson. To explain my cleverness to after the fact.'

I was expecting her to persist. (I'm genuinely clever, but easily manipulated; if you say something thick I become annoyed; when annoyed I'm indiscreet, and tell you all you want. Stupidity trumps cleverness. The dimmest undergraduate – Seb, that is – knows how to play me; so does my three-year-old nephew. I'm so nearly a fool.) But instead of annoying me tactically, she simply said: 'Tell me what happened. Because I'm afraid for you. Also, afraid.'

I stagily consulted my watch. I looked sceptically from the oxblood shoes to the brown, sighed once more, put them both beside my suitcase, deferring a hard choice, sat down and folded my legs. 'Really there's no hurry. It's three-quarters of an hour before I need to leave for the airport. And you have a point. About fear.' And thus, ungraciously, I launched into

the fourteenth story (10:45 a.m.)

'Here's what happened late last evening. I went to your rooms and recruited you. Then I came back here and rang Woolly. I told him I needed to come and see him at five to twelve.'

'He can't have liked that.'

'No, it's cocoa and beddie-bye at ten for our Woolly. With a mystical paperback to put him to sleep. That's how he preserves his glittering mental clarity. But he can't say the word *No*. He said "Well perhaps in a certain sense," which is Woolly for *Yes*.'

'Meanwhile I went to the bar and found al-Mutlak—'

'Yes yes, we know all that. In due course I went over to Woolly's rooms and tapped tenderly on his door. You know how deaf he is. Nothing. I let myself in and called "Leigh", and he came shambling out of his bedroom. "Ah," said he in his dead-alive way, "um, Culpepper. Here you are": he looked reproachful. "Didn't we say ten to twelve?" "Oh yes," he mumbled, unfocused, peering at his clock. You know what his rooms are like: grisly, pale, ostentatiously Franciscan. Bad posters pinned to the panelling. The carriage-clock on the mantel is the only decent thing he's got, no doubt inherited from his mum. There are sad little pencilled notes propped against it, including one reading *F.C. 1155*. "Time flies. I was reading… what is it?" He had to look at the cover. "A book called *A Handbook of Rituals of Thelema*. Concerning" – he had to look again – "Aleister Crowley. Terribly um denying. Yet affirming in an esoteric sense. As denial, paradoxically, often…" You know how bemused he gets in the presence of thought; even his own. "Would you like to sit down? Would you like some cake?" *Like* is a strong word. Woolly's confectionery is not so much inedible as uneatable, so crumbly with age your fingers can't get it into your mouth. Like his ideas. And his armchairs look and feel woven of porridge. If you're not careful he gives you mixed-berry squash. His least horrible hospitality is ginger-wine. I was fussily given a mug of this and propped myself against his sideboard. "Leigh, old thing," I said, "it's about those statues in the antechapel," and of course a pallid light flared up in his eyes. You know how he craves persecution, he's such an Ulsterman despite all his infidelities – defending his rainy province against bigoted Zouaves of one sort or another—'

'*Felix*,' said Margot despairingly.

'Well, to get on. "I'll give you one minute, Culpepper," he said severely enough, and I explained what was objectionable about his bronze Buddha and his soapstone Shiva. His attention wandered a little because when I said "Half-human!" very sharply he sat up abruptly, blinking at me. "Did you hear a shout just then?" I asked. "A shout?" "I thought I heard someone shout *Wygefortis*! Didn't you?" "Well I don't know. That's not to deny – what a strange thing to – I suppose in a sense I did." "It seemed to come from out that way. Over across Chapel. Toward Acheron"; meanwhile I'd jumped up and opened the back door of his sitting-room, the one that opens on the forbidden corridor. "In fact I think I heard a slight patter a few minutes ago." "Oh dear yes, yes, they will go creeping over to the Tower. Despite such a clear rule. But in a way to break a rule is to acknowledge –" and at that instant Lint burst in. "Padre, Padre, someone's jumped off Acheron. Come at once," but Woolly can't do anything at once, he was fully three minutes pottering around finding his purple stole, wittering "This is dreadful, dreadful. He must have come this way poor soul. We, you might say, heard him. Or *her* of course. Culpepper and I have been sitting here for the last five minutes. Discussing – what is it we have been? – oh yes, gods. The unity of all faiths. And we heard in a sense a certain cry and we opened the door and of course no one came back … A shout of – what was it? Just *Wygy's*, so ambiguous…" until Lint led him off. I came back here. An hour later a dull policeman came and talked to me. I told him the dull tale I've just told you. Then, despite the racket of that helicopter, I went to bed. End of story.

ᛣᛈ

'Now I must get on.'

Jollily I headed back into my bedroom, jollily I came out again carrying a dark suit. I started squeezing this into my case. I was trying not to smell fishy.

Margot considered me and sniffed. '*That's* what you told the police?'

'That's what I told the police. That's the story they took down in their little notebooks, that's the story that'll be in the evening paper. That's the story that'll be printed in Harani history books, which I imagine are mainly concerned with the fortunes of the al-Mutlaks. And that' (I lowered my forehead to give Margot a hard look through my eyebrows) 'is the story you'll tell anyone who asks.'

'Ye…es. Yes, I will, Felix.'

'Most importantly, that's exactly the story Woolly will have told the police. Bless him, he inspires absolute confidence in policemen, they adore senile tenacity – prize it above everything except fear. They can see he's too muddled to fabricate anything. Especially now. I looked in on him earlier. He worked himself into a state last night. From his mild martyrdom. His being jostled. Mrs Oathouse's sitting by his pillow feeding him Mogadon tablets as if they were lumps of muesli. The police are in awe. Virtually took his statement on their knees. He's a drugged prophet. What he says must be truth. And what he says is that no one went past his door but one.'

'But Felix. Your story *doesn't make sense.*'

'Every word of it is so.'

'Yes. But there's a lot missing.'

I weighed her expression, and finally let out a long breath. 'There is. My account leaves out

the fifteenth story (10:58 a.m.).

my running across the roof of Chapel in my socks, dashing up the stone stair, catching the fratricide staring out over the lights of Cambridge. The racket of midnight was sounding from Lethe Tower. He didn't hear me patter up behind. I caught him by his belt and at the scruff of that atrocious suit. It's easy to throw a man off balance if he's not expecting you. Also, the boy was undersized. He went sailing into the abyss so smoothly he hardly had time for a cry. A breathless half-hearted sort of cry it was, too. Probably unsure whether to bellow in rage or scream with fright. One should decide beforehand. Always be prepared for sudden assaults,

Margot. *He* fell between two stools. Speaking of which, I did intend a good clear splat on the rounded flints of Cocytus. But I got the angle wrong. He was so puny. He got spiked. The end.

೦ಙ

'*Do* I need a mac for Venice? It's supposed to be wet.'

'No, your mac's vile. Buy an umbrella at the airport. But Felix, I still don't understand. Stop! Stop doing whatever it is you're doing to that poor suit. Get dressed. You have thirty-five minutes. I'll fix your suitcase.' I disappeared back into my bedroom while she heaved the case to the floor to pull out the top layers of packing, which went to ruin. Had gone to ruin – pluperfect, cretin.

'I don't see,' she called after me, 'how the two bits of your story fit together. One of them must be a lie. They seem to require bilocation.'

'They do,' I called back. 'Or time travel. Which is the same thing. Listen. I had a magic carpet. It took me beyond fixed space or time. Of course I mean Woolly's mind. In him the noble comprehensiveness of our Church of England has cankered into…'

She looked up, started, and shook her head in disgust. I was still in my boxer shorts, but had strapped over my shirt a parson's vest-stock (a high starched-linen dog-collar on a black watered-silk false-front). Among the remarks that must have queued in her brain, hoping to be uttered, was *Take that rotten disguise off if you're going to tell about your slaughters.* But the remark that made it through her teeth was: 'Do you really need two pairs of black shoes?'

'Yes. Venice is dressy but subdued.' I went back to choose a suit.

Angrily, she began to repack. I returned in navy blue, seated myself in my favourite armchair, folded my legs neatly, and made a spire of my fingers. The clerical miasma was settling on me.

'You know that mad thing they demand in court, "the truth, the whole truth and nothing but"? No one's ever dared produce it. Imagine a barrister asking you "Did you see your wife put rat-poison in your Ovaltine?" The only truthful answer would be to begin *In principio verbum erat*, then work forward through *all the innocent blood of those murdered on earth, from the murder of righteous Abel.* What of any importance has happened since the world began *except* homicide? Finally you'd give an account of yourself, sitting in the witness-stand at a murder trial, deciding which things to leave out. *That* would be accounting for events and their causes.

That would be telling the whole truth.'

'*That* would be contempt of court.'

'Yes, my child.' (How quickly the clerical mask settles on the brain behind.) 'That's what stories are: leavings-out. Chisel away at stone, toss shards behind you, what's left has a human shape. That is, a falsity. The stone never had that shape. You're not really freeing what was already there. But Woolly's mind's different. He can't cut away, he won't reject. If he were ever forced to make a choice about his own life, willing *this* possibility and therefore dooming *that* to oblivion, crediting *that* and thus denying *this* – he couldn't endure it, he'd die. Even a small choice in real life would make him faint. And in a story, a choice must make him – can you guess? Do you see why he's a magic carpet? How I need only say the words of incantation, and be taken wherever I will?'

'No,' sighed Margot, although I think she did. She triumphantly shut the lid of my suitcase, fastened the catch, and offered her master a small weak grin, apologising for doing anything better than I can. She sat. 'Tell me what you did with Woolly. Tell me the whole truth.'

'I shall,' I said, and with an untrustworthy smirk launched into

the sixteenth story (11:01 a.m.)

'Here's what happened yesterday evening. When I got to Woolly's rooms, about half past eleven, I—'

'Aha!'

'Yes. I walked into his sitting-room without disturbing him, put my finger on the minute-hand of his carriage clock, pushed it forward to just before twelve. Then I called him in. I got my unspeakable drink, I got him sitting, then I talked about his Asian idols. "I'll give you one minute, Culpepper." He expected me, of course, to denounce their presence in a Christian church. That's what he wanted. Not a bit of it. "Leigh, Leigh," I said, "you are so doctrinaire. What about the Yazidis?" His hands made vague wild gestures of deprecation or synthesis, then subsided in his lap. "Why is there no image of the Peacock Angel, the penitent Satan?" Woolly's lovely white hair sleethed up and fluttered like an aureole, then collapsed to his chin. "Where is our portrait of Joseph Smith?" He had no answer. "We must have the chapel walls painted!" He was staggered. I talked of what was needed. Such a pandæmonium of goats' heads and sacred fires and mandalas and Assumptions and flying saucers you never heard. Cronus with his castrating hook, Mohammed with his face veiled, Hades with Persephone shrieking across his shoulders, silver Tianlong the Celestial Dragon, blue Krishna, the Green Man, snowy Pegasus: hundreds of figures. The whole cast of *The Golden Bough,* Hesiod and Dante, bedlam, *The Naked Lunch.*

'What's a story? A forged weapon. But weapons do their good work in different ways. Gas burns lungs, maces shatter skulls, hydrogen bombs vaporise. In this case I didn't want to break up the order in Woolly's brain. I needed to suffocate. I needed to hound him beyond time and into oblivion. It worked. He fell into more than his usual state of disintegration. His eyes swelled and wandered 'til they'd erased his whole face, his lips popped like goldfish lips. There was a silence. "Leigh!" I said, experimentally. His eyelids fluttered: "Quite quite, possibly so." I spoke further and his torpor became profound. His clock said 12:23, so it was really just before the stroke of midnight. I slipped off my shoes, ran out, did the needful, ran back, turned the clock back to the right time, and exclaimed, "We need to be able to worship gods animal, human, and especially" (very loudly) "half-human!" Poor Woolly. He was awake at once, or what passes as awake with him, terrified that I was going to start hurting his head again. "By the way, did you hear a shout just then?" He half thought he had, in a sense. I got the door open. Half a minute more and the dreadful Mr Lint was upon us shouting "Padre, Padre!" and dragging him off to glory. What an evening Woolly had. More fun than a month of Sundays.'

'You wouldn't call it fun if you'd seen the way he behaved over the corpse.'

'Bah. The police are perfectly happy with him. *I* am happy with him. There's only one way up the Tower, and two distinguished members of College were happy to swear they were sitting beside that corridor. Only one person went by, a few minutes before twelve. We heard his cry; we pushed the door open at once; we can swear no one came back. Idris was alone on Acheron, his suicide is airtight. And *that* is absolutely the end of the story. *C'est fini!*'

☙

Nothing was satisfactory that morning. Margot frowned. Rain went on making rude noises on the glass. '*Ce n'est pas tout à fait fini.* What if Idris had lived long enough to whisper to a fireman "I was pushed, Margot ffontaines-Laigh lured me"? That'd be awkward.'

'Um – yes. But drop of a hundred and fifty feet is a drop of a hundred and fifty feet. He wasn't going to survive.'

'And anyway, it's not nice. Tearing open a boy.'

'*He* wasn't nice.'

'No, I know,' she said uncertainly. 'He had his half-brother machine-gunned. He had two people murdered on Tuesday night. That sweet couple from Harringay. At least they're avenged.'

'Er, well, yes,' I said absently, not liking to add *if they existed*, which as a matter of fact I didn't know and still don't. I sincerely hope they were real. But I avoided looking into the question, by checking for instance whether there'd been any recent runnings-over in the West End. I was aware the sweet couple might be an invention of Benjy's. Who, if pressed, would say, "Very well, Felix, yes; that's something I carefully didn't tell you. We *did* need to straighten out the Harani succession. Al-Mutlak junior really *was* murderous. And even victims *in stories* ought to be avenged, don't you think? I mean the better sort of story, the true-in-spirit sort."

I didn't mention this possibility to Margot. Nor did I point out that I could have arranged the necessary butchery anywhere, yet called the wretched boy to College – *Dirtying your own nest*, you say; yes, if you must – to prove (to Benjy, Margot, myself) the plenitude of my immunity. I concoct the stories, I control time and space. I shred my victims at my own door, and nonetheless stand aloof.

Margot was still wrinkling her brow. 'If the police are happy, *why* are you rushing off to Venice?'

'I've been given, um, more work. By Her Majesty's Government. As a reward for work well done. Benjy rang this morning.' I didn't say that he had been cock-a-hoop with news of a natural gas concession for a British company, signed that morning by Jasim. The Haranis had been holding out for a year; sudden bereavement had given them a fresh perspective on their friendship with England. 'An assignment on the Grand Canal.'

'I thought virtue was its own reward,' said Margot, softly and bitterly. I stood, frowned, and popped back into my bedroom. 'How *can* you go, though?' she called after me. 'There're still two weeks left of term.'

'Oh, that. I've only got Ollie this morning. And you this afternoon. If a chap can't skip the occasional supervision, where's his ease in life?' I emerged complete in clerical costume. 'God, is that the time? I *am* going to miss my flight. Will you let Ollie know I'm off? Discreetly? Kiss? Filthy rain, isn't it?' And I was gone.

Gone; but here's what Margot reports.

From my window she watched me hopping boyishly across the court. Her expression, she was aware, was sour. 'I'm going to grow up looking like my mother. Her everlasting pout… *Am* I growing up? I seem stuck at child-helper level. Little boys forced up chimneys to scrape out the soot. Useful *because* puny.'

She wrote out the most indiscreet notice she could think of (DR CULPEPPER HAS GONE TO VENICE, GO AWAY UNTIL AT LEAST NEXT WEEK, THIS MEANS YOU), taped it to my door, pulled the door locked behind her, and almost stepped into the arms of Ollie, who was bounding up the stairs.

'Don't bother. He's gone,' she said, pouting. 'To Italy. Until next week at least,' and waited for what must follow. A greasy lascivious fire would flare up in Ollie's eyes ('A whole week!'), an appraising stare, an insinuating smile – but none of this happened. He just sighed, turned, and started down the stair. She glanced sharply at his descending profile.

Ollie's hair was simply not old enough to go grey. But since yesterday it had definitely unravelled a little with shock. The curls did not spring and spiral as they used. Moreover Margot perceived a new element in his face. 'Not precisely sober, not even subdued. Just … inward. Great God, I recognise it! He's turning *human.*' And because she was young, for all her sophistication, and because he was her friend (even though she thought of him as a scampering puppy, yapping for girls as if for walkies), she called 'Wait!', and followed him down the turn of the stairs.

They sat side by side on the landing, staring hopelessly out over the back wall of Wygy's, over Christ's Pieces to the typewriter-shaped wedge at the back of Christ's College. *Tt-tt,* went the rain, *tt-tt, tt-tt-tt. This planet is experimenting,* thought Margot. *It's refining a new improved grey. A shade so crushing all thinking people will simply prefer to die. We are bacilli, this November dinginess is antiseptic. Yes, that's right, planet, a touch more mud in your sky. A little more blurring of blackness in your light… And on this morning of universal dissatisfaction, Ollie Vane-Powell'* (she glanced at him sideways, humbly) *is joining the doomed ranks of the thinking. The man element's predominating over the rampant quadruped. How? Why?*

It was gunfire that had done it: gunfire, that great educator. What the poets of the Great War learned from years of the Western Front, Ollie, more sensitive, was taught by two seconds of Idris' revolver. The bullets had gone nowhere near him, but had penetrated his froth. The fact that bullets exist had pierced his soul. Which now twitched with weird, galvanic life, like an electrocuted dead frog. *Death,* said a violent spasm, and his mind kicked; *love; essential seriousness; wrong; chance; time—*

Of course he wasn't going to say any of this to a girl, especially not a clever girl like Abishag. So he said, sounding aggrieved as any child: 'Culpepper might have been here. Y'know, I stayed up all night. Waded through *Metamorphoses* IX. Translated the whole frigging thing.'

'Really?' She stared with a certain awe at the papers in his hand: a plastic envelope, acid-green, rain-spattered. She thought of him "pulling an all-nighter" with his curtains pulled against the helicopter and the sirens and the blood-drunk undergraduates.

'Yeah, I've translated it. And I still don't know what happened to Deïanira. It doesn't say. I wanted to ask him.'

'*Deïanira?*' Ollie caring about a female he couldn't touch? Abishag nearly laughed. Then she considered his woeful look, and the violence they were carefully not discussing. So she put her arm round his shoulder, as if he were eight, and she were anything old, thirty-eight let's say, and told him

the seventeenth story (11:27 a.m.)

'What happened to Madame Hercules? I'll tell you. A messenger came pounding up to the palace in Tiryns—'

'Oh. One of them,' said Ollie bleakly.

'Yes. There must have been a whole corps of them in ancient Greece,' she said, sounding, even to herself, every instant more like the vanished Felix. (*He's so imitable. I am eventually, through mere slavish imitation, going to* become *him*.) 'A corps of men trained to cast their news into metre as they jogged along through the dust. They sat waiting in post offices for the gods to be annoyed, for heroes to be destroyed. Then off they went, trochee, trochee, rat-a-tat-tat.' Ollie had lifted his face to the bleeding pockmarks of water on the skylight. 'Deïanira was pacing the *stoa* of the palace: ten paces, turn, ten paces, turn. She was tearing the backs of her beautiful hands, scratching, scratching. Had her second messenger, the one with the warning, outrun the first, the one with the venom? She thought of what the venom had looked like, the day she'd collected it beside the sunny Euenes—'

'Culpepper says the valley's too deep to be sunny.' Did it hurt the rain more if it smashed into another drop, or if it hit the glass cleanly?

'The sunny Euenes. Nessus' blood had been brighter—'

'He went down it,' said Ollie's far away voice, 'in a canoe. Ages ago.

When he was young and not so nasty.'

'Been brighter, thicker, hotter than the blood of men. It seemed to come from—'

'Culpepper bled into the river too. He said.' He sounded miserable, but not with simple boy-misery; more like a man stripped raw to mourn. 'Gashed his arm on a rock below a village called I can't remember what.'

'From the horse part of him. How could she not have guessed the stuff was murderous? Or *had* she guessed? That near-rape was as close as she'd come to adultery, while her husband violated their vows constantly, heroically – the fifty daughters of King Thespius in one night—'

'That doesn't sound right.'

'In one night, said rumour. He was always lying to her. Had she lied to herself about Nessus' lies? Was she, deep within, vengeful? But there was a dot on the road by now, getting close, closer. She stopped pacing, she stood with her ruined hands at her sides waiting to hear the fate of the son of Jupiter, her fate too. The palace slaves assembled behind her, in the shade of the columns, getting ready to raise the ululation of lament. The messenger ran toward her, *slowing down* now, the wretched show-boater, in order to get his breath. He'd been on the road for two days and now he wanted to make a good entrance. The dust of every kingdom from Phocis to Tiryns stuck to his sweat. "He looks like a man made of sand," thought Deïanira, horrified that such fancies could occur to her at such a moment. It was the beginning of her horrors. "Your husband's dead on Mount Œta," cried the messenger in passable verse. "Hydra-poison in centaur-blood".'

'Burned him. I know, I know. Tore off shirt, flesh came too. Bones showed. Knew what was happening. Tore down trees.' CRACK, CRACK. Revelation, mustard gas and barbed wire. 'No more fluff or fighting for Hercules. Built a pyre and climbed on. Torch. Whoosh.'

'Yes,' sighed Abishag, bilked. 'That is exactly what the messenger told Deïanira.'

'But it wasn't *true*. I mean, the important thing's left out of the story. He didn't burn. Papa Jove whisked him up to Olympus.'

'She wasn't to know that. She was consumed by partial news. Undone by too much guile,' said Abishag sadly. 'An overconsumption of lying stories, a superfluity of mendacity. One porky too many.'

'But how? I mean, what does *consumed* mean?'

'I don't think anyone bothers to record. Hanged self, stabbed self, drowned self. Evaporated into mythology.'

CR

'I don't think,' said Ollie grumpily, 'I'm any the wiser. I'm sliding,' he said shakily, getting up, 'my translation under Culpepper's door. Then I'm going to bed. But thank you,' he added grudgingly, 'for the bedtime story.' The old Ollie could never have said such a thing, or not without a leer, and as he ascended the stair toward the pittering skylight, and she descended, Margot brooded in a way common to clever children approaching twenty. *He matures, I deteriorate. He ages, like a side of beef; I'm corrupted, like an apple. He learns to read, I learn fraud.* But that wasn't quite what depressed her so much. It was more the feeling (which causes terror) that such developments, although they seem enormous, are small deliberate movements in something else. Dance steps. *In what, in what?* she wondered, stepping into the rain.

A WEEK LATER:
BEFORE SUNRISE, THURSDAY 22 NOVEMBER 2012

"Wygefortis", says our College prospectus, "has always had a special place in Cambridge"; and so it has. No sooner had Bishop Worthyal founded it than it acquired a reputation (says Caxton) for

> *yᵉ moſt cvrſt & vncleenlie ſtvdies in yᵉ ij. vniuerſities of Englande too vvit diuinacions aſſtrologie alchymie caſtinge of oroscvpvms conſortinge vvith hobbgobbelyns ſattirs feyfolke and yᵉ lyke euen vnto svmmoning vpp of famillyerr ſpyrits &c alle yᵉ moſt deuilyſhe cvnninge knowyn to yˢ vnhallowyd ayge: vnto yᵉ vvhyche clerkes chorryſters ſckolars fellovvs & yᵉ maſter of ſainte VVigifortes collyge are moſt greeuiovſlie addycted to yᵉ perill of yʳ ſooles & yᵉ ſcandille of chryſtendoome nay euen of yᵉ ſarraſſennes beeyonde yᵉ ſees.*

Under Henry and Mary, Wygy's was the most heretical college. After the Restoration even Emmanuel dons could console each other by saying *We were not loyal, Sir, but we were not like St Wygefortis'.* In Georgian times no other college had to worry about being quite the idlest, drunkenest or most deistical. And now that dons make such a shabby suburban fetish of exam results, the comfort is: *Thank God for Wygy's: whatever happens, we can't fall below second-worst on the Tompkins Table.* That's why the University has always coddled College. Cambridge not only tolerates our undergraduate illiteracy, it cherishes it, for it allows every other college to recalibrate its own youths; the same goes, thank God, for the Fellowship. As far as it can, the University overlooks even our grossest scandals. Thus there was no inquiry into the spectacular plunge from Acheron of one of our admissions candidates. It was tacitly agreed he killed himself out of anxiety about the interview process. No blame was assigned.

The event caused far more outcry among the Saracens beyond the seas.

The death of Idris killed his father, Ali al-Mutlak. The next day there was an infectious outbreak in the clinic in the Palace where the old president lay sick. With him perished his doctors, Colonel Adeeb and the entire Presidential Guard – it was a wonderfully virulent infection – and even certain Ministers who had not been sufficiently careful about cultivating Jasim; who stepped into his father's shoes without opposition.

One of his first acts as President-for-Life of Haran, after the purges, was to email Sir Trotsky Plantagenet.

> *In the circumstances the Harani Republic does not desire the body of my beloved brother Idris to be flown back to Paddan Aram. There might be popular demonstrations, overflows of our double national grief. So I have an unusual request to make. I wish my dear younger brother to rest forever at St Wygefortis' College, desire for which was so strong it killed him.*

He proposed a donation from mournful Harani people to Wygy's as a memorial. Although the Master was still in dudgeon about all Mutlaks, the sum mentioned was really too much to refuse.

Woolly was still luxuriously prostrate, and in no condition to lead one of his syncretist services; the entire College was sulky and petulant, a reaction against the excitement of last Thursday night; Sir Trotsky wanted nothing to do with it; the Haranis wanted it to happen quietly. 'Quietly,' they insisted, 'very very quietly.'

That was the situation when I got back from Venice. I was a bit taken aback to hear my victim was returning to College; I felt like Saturn being made to vomit up the children he had devoured. But I rallied. After the death of the hero come the funeral games: of course. I volunteered to arrange the burial, and no one got in my way.

'You won't want the body carried through College,' I told the Harani ambassador in lordly fashion; 'collect it from the hospital morgue and deliver it across Christ's Pieces at dawn. My suite and I will receive it.' I put down the 'phone. 'The ambassador,' I told Margot, 'will deliver Idris at seven tomorrow morning.'

'The ambassador? He's not been deported then?'

'Hm? Oh. No. That is – not yet.'

'Who is "your suite"?'

'You. Of course. And get Ollie and Tristan along. We don't want outsiders mucking about.' I could see she liked the idea of being an insider. 'Not Seb, he can't do anything before noon. Tell them to wear something rough.'

So at raw half-light the next day the boys, in rugby shirts, and I, in my regal brand-new Italian overcoat, and Margot, in dark grey and heavy silk scarf (black being too heavy-handed), found ourselves forcing open the tiny rusty spiked bridge that spans the Styx and is hardly ever used. We stood formally in a line on the far side. The pompous melancholy of funerals had infected us. We didn't speak.

Of course the Haranis were late. I was dreading a dark green Mercedes, and that's exactly what turned up. (I couldn't detect any suspicious dents.) It parked illegally in Earl Street. The driver, a burly fellow with moustaches and a trench coat, got out and opened the door; a burly fellow with moustaches and trilby worked himself out of the seat and got himself upright. Then the driver opened the boot and lifted out a parcel, which might have been two sacks of potatoes laid end to end, sewn up in sacking.

'God – is that *him*?' whispered Ollie out the side of his mouth. '*It*?'

'The Mutlaki clan,' I whispered back, 'belongs to a particularly severe strain of Islam.'

'Its tenets,' Margot murmured (why at funerals does everyone mutter in this snide fashion?) 'didn't seem to cramp him much.'

'Not while he lived. But they forbid coffins… *Mr Ambassador*.' I mingled all too ably grief and unction. The ambassador, edified, shook my hand, nodded slightly at the boys, leered then bowed at Margot. He wasn't unpleasant and my *protégés* couldn't decide what to feel when later, just after Christmas, he was recalled to Paddam Aran and shot.

Meanwhile, that was that. The driver heaved the parcel into the boys' arms; stood back; didn't quite salute. Then the Haranis wobbled back to their car and drove away. Not a word had they said.

I led us back over the bridge. We shut and locked the gate behind us with a creak, placed the cadaver on the damp step of the Temple, and dug a grave.

Not that I actually dug. Margot stood beside me handing tools to Ollie and Tristan, who did the digging; I lit a cigar. Why does everyone behave with muted affectation at funerals?

A cold windy half-sunny dawn in November: bracing, sceptical weather. But Aceldama's always an uncanny place, and it was hard to laugh off its menace. There'd been no rain for three days, so the air was crisp and dry, but everywhere in that neglected garden was water. Every tree dripped. The Stygian Creek gurgled out of the ground and back underground through a grille. The soil was waterlogged a foot below the surface. The deeper the boys went the vaguer the distinction seemed between Aceldama and Styx. They soon sank to their knees in the mud, and proceeded by spooning rather than digging.

Deep in the runny mud they came across the bones of a puny dog. Then more; far more. 'The pugs!' I cried, breaking out of my funeral spirits. 'The pugs of Master Wakefield! Let me have them.'

I sat on the step of the Temple beside Idris, unconcerned, wiping the soil off the little bones and assembling a complete dog. The boys, moodily, kept digging.

Cling! *Cling!*

'Eh? What's that now? Gently, gently!' I jumped up and peered in. They were poking round what looked like a block of mud. When they worked it (swearing and groaning) up on to the grass, it still looked like a block of mud. But when I had soused it thrice with the gardener's watering-can, it became metal: metal so rotten that it crumpled under the pressure of a spade, but distinctly a metal box, with rusted bands and bosses, of vaguely Eastern design.

'Perhaps Coptic?' suggested Margot.

'Perhaps,' I muttered, pretending not to be excited. She handed me a screwdriver, with which I broke off the rusty ruins of a padlock and prised back the lid, and...

There was a mass of straw, which I scooped out delicately. My impression was of a muddy coconut, some rusty piping, and a faint stench. I sniffed, scowled, and, too feline to dirty my paws, took Margot's silk scarf, wrapped it round my fingers, and groped for the coconut. I got the thing on the grass. My snort of revulsion turned into a chuckle; I spun it suddenly round toward the two gravediggers, who went 'Fuck' and 'Urgh' at once.

A face – the head of a woman! And quite unlike the clean shrunken head I had been shown last month in the Foreign Office. This was life-size, death-size, half rotted away, and smelt of the earth. But it was a head rather than a skull. Enough skin remained to make it a person.

'Loathsome,' said Margot, and Tristan added:

'Chuck it in the stream.'

'Nonsense. Don't be unfriendly. You know her. You see her every day. Or would if you did any work, you—' Here I paused suddenly. My fingers had jagged on a fissure in the lowest part of her skull, just above the highest vertebra. My thumb caressed it. No doubt about it. A bullet-hole.

Tristan was peering into the face. 'It's the woman in the Library.'

'Nah,' said Ollie, more out of habit than anything else, 'not her. That can't be right.'

'The one draped in shower curtains,' said Tristan. 'With nipples and thighs coming out at you.'

'Goddess-like limbs, I'd have said, floating amidst translucencies.' My voice had taken on a mystical sheen. I was suddenly dazed by the impenetrable dark glory of sacrifice. This little hole opened into the underworld, it was an abyss, bottomless. (I wasn't going to mention it to the children. If I don't know things they don't, what am I for? Besides, it sets a bad precedent. Who knows if one day …?)

I'd got the head sitting upright now on a nest of Margot's scarf, and rocked back on my hams to worship the goddess. 'This,' I pronounced in my public voice, 'is Iolë! The wonderful nymph Fanny Hervey, who had become Fanny Alcock, and later, perhaps, Fanny Myre! Wonderful!' And even Ollie couldn't deny it.

She was no longer wonderful. The state of her hair was depressing; her skin showed the pox; her eyes and mouth were fixed open. But it was the gape of her lying mouth that was most disquieting. It suggested – what? Astonishment?

('The endless howling O of a tragic mask,' suggested Ollie that evening in the bar, where the three of us met to ease our secret – Ollie, newly awake to the possibilities of pain, said odd things that term. 'It was like an inflatable doll's mouth,' offered grubby-minded Tristan. 'It'd have to be doctored to stay open like that,' said practical Margot. 'Fixed open with a nail. Although *my* fingers weren't going in to find out.')

Meanhile, at dawn in Aceldama, I shook out the casket. 'What else?'

All this time Idris lay on the step of the Temple of Priapus.

The metal pipes were guns: a brace of duelling pistols. I scrubbed and scratched at them, murmuring to himself. 'Ollie, Tristan: back to work.' Shrugging, they continued gouging out a grave. 'Too rusty for any maker's marks... no, no, look. You can read it here. *Wogdon & Barton – London.* Must have been lovely things in their time. Ten-inch barrels. Identical, of course.' I can never resist explaining. 'Perfectly weighted. Feel them.' I handed the muddy things to Margot.

'But they're not. This one's heavier.'

I frowned and snatched them back; swapped them from one hand to another, frowned again. I squinted down the barrel of one pistol; considered; squinted down the barrel of the other; frowned some more; then took the second pistol and carefully bashed it on the steps of the Temple, just by Idris' head, four times, until the barrel cracked and I could tease it open. Then I began to laugh so much that for a moment I couldn't speak.

Tristan gazed at me malevolently over the lip of the grave. 'What's amusing him?'

'Oh, it's too good. This one's been tampered with. It's still got its bullet in it.'

'It wasn't fired?'

'It *couldn't* be fired. There's a... pin. A hairpin. Yes, a jewelled woman's hairpin. See? Hammered down the barrel.' I rolled back on the damp grass with my feet in the air. 'O Iolë. *Io triumphe.*'

'We've finished,' said Ollie, not so very sulkily considering how much mud there was in his hair, and how too much conditioner debases the timbre of the cuticle.

Death's death. Even I, remembering what they were about, sobered up. I took out my cigar and balanced it on the balustrade of the folly; took off my fedora and hatted the bust of Lord Courtenay with it; slipped the hairpin into my pocket. Then I got Margot to take the feet of the thing in sacking, myself heaving the shoulders. As decently as we could, we handed the parcel to the boys, who settled it in its cocoon of mud and scrambled out on to the grass.

I had a sick spasm of imagination: how seedy we'd look to Idris, if he'd been able to open his eyes and measure us through his sacking as we stood over his raw grave, hands crossed over groins, guilty heads bent: Margot's chestnut hair, Ollie's soiled blond love-curls, Tristan's dull

English sandiness, and mine. Ollie had proved him a murderer, Margot and I had hoaxed him to death, Tristan had made his death riotous by mocking Woolly. It also struck me that graves, in the moment before they're closed, turn implausible. *You fools, there's a* person *there*: it seems a mistake has been made.

Dong-dong, dong-dong, dong-dong, dong-dong. The bell of Emmanuel, ringing for early Mass, came over the garden wall. Beyond the grim walled garden, Cambridge was stirring; virtuous colleges were already awake; not Wygy's.

Ollie, who is improving and may live to be a good man, coughed. 'Oughtn't somebody to say something?'

I shook my head. 'I think Woolly pretty much exhausted the possibilities of prayer. Don't you? Fill it in.'

But Ollie really is becoming a better person. He dropped his shovel, produced a half-bottle of Jägermeister from his pocket, wriggled back down into the muddy grave, and deposited it by Idris' right hand. 'He seemed so fond of the beastly stuff,' he muttered, apologetically.

The rest of us were stung. Idris must not be buried like a dog. His funeral took a Viking turn.

'In that case,' I said, entering into the spirit of the thing, and I handed Ollie the pistol, the unsabotaged one with which Josiah Myre had slain the Archdeacon of Ely. 'Put that in his other hand. Young Mr al-Mutlak liked firearms.'

Then Margot did a brave thing. She stooped, picked up Lady Fanny's head without flinching, and handed it to Ollie. 'Put that on his knees.' I stirred in my expensive overcoat, but Margot, not glancing at me, asserting herself against me for the first time, said: 'You're *not* keeping it, Felix. If you want a human skull you'll have to kill one yourself. On his knees, Ollie. Like a trophy.'

I sighed. But I used to rub tomb-brasses in boyhood; I enjoy doing what is no longer done. 'If a man was a Crusader who'd reached Jerusalem, the legs on his tomb effigy were crossed. You might cross Idris' legs.'

'*Did* he visit Jerusalem?'

'He's reached Aceldama.'

So Ollie, reluctantly, fidgeted with the legs in their wrapping.

Tristan has an A-level in history. 'If we're getting mediæval … noblemen's feet used to rest on lions.'

'We don't have a lion,' I said. 'And I'm not burgling Tartarus for the Master's.'

'We'll use your pug,' Margot said, coldly.

'My pug! My composite pug! I want that.'

'You can't have it, it's too revolting. You can keep the hairpin. Ollie: here it is.' And so the lower end of the sacking was propped on the canine skeleton. 'And use this wreck of a box to pillow his head.' I didn't dare say a thing. 'No, stop, it looks jagged. Wrap it in this' – and she poured her grimy black scarf into Ollie's hands.

Tristan stared uncertainly at the result. 'All these bits and pieces.' I think he meant that the trench looked like a not-so-unsuccessful experiment in the black arts. 'Aren't we, y'know. *Polluting* College a bit?'

'No, no,' I said, trying to sound breezy, 'we're tidying up. Sorting out the tenantry of Aceldama. Putting them on a more comfortable footing with each other.' Sorting out the crimes that have been done at St Wygefortis' since the beginning. Taking on ourselves every homicide since Cain's. 'They look perfectly decent, don't you think?' We all stared at Fanny Myre's gaping lips. 'Well, not *her* so much. Here.' I retrieved my cigar. 'Plug her mouth with that.' Ollie screwed the burning cohiba between her gums. 'And now' – for the cavity was suddenly unbearable, Ollie had leapt out of it, Margot had covered her face, my voice rose to a sort of wail – 'for God's sake fill it in.'

Which the boys did, frantically. Then they threw down their shovels behind the Temple of Priapus, and the four of us fled, clanging the garden gate behind us so hard every undergraduate in Sheol Court must have stirred in his sleep. Tristan and Ollie ran back to their staircases to shower. But Margot and I fled to my rooms and leapt under a duvet, lying together untouching in that safe dimness like thoroughly wicked children.

TWO MONTHS LATER:
WEDNESDAY, 16 JANUARY 2013

I don't mean to exaggerate the horror. There was a dimness; Margot and I emerged from it and went our ways. Hours passed and became a day. Days passed and completed the term, during which Scholarly Endeavour was once more worsted by Concupiscence, Indolence, and Spleen. Snow fell at Epiphany, hiding the wound we'd made in the earth. Lent Term began – yesterday in fact – and soon enough spring will arrive, grass will spread, the wound will heal altogether; Aceldama will seem no more ominous than usual.

Yet it's remarkable that I've never revisited the garden, except in nightmares; also, that the four of us have a tacit rule not to mention our Harani victim to each other.

Until today. Every 16th January St Wygy's keeps Founder's Birthday, which his statutes prescribe as a unique day of humiliation and winelessness, fasting and lament, until the end of time. Lunch in Hall was grim: rice, rye bread, crab apples and water. As soon as it was done I hurried back to my rooms and, in defiance of College tradition, got out my bottle of Lagavulin. What luxurious iodine, what smoke, peat, salt, seaweed! They'd all been captured on an Atlantic islet, ten years ago when I was still an innocent; now they came forth, and consoled.

The first knock on my door, half-expected, was Margot. Within a few minutes the rest of my undergraduate coterie had shamefacedly turned up: Ollie, who's got his nerve back and is becoming nice, worldly upper-middle-class Tristan Bolswood, and even Seb, that sunny-haired bipedal animal, just out of bed.

The Founder enjoins us to spend the day bemoaning his birth. We were infracting that law; and since every transgression inspires other transgressions, we presently found ourselves being indiscreet about Idris al-Mutlak – to the amazement of Seb, who knew nothing about it. 'Fucking hell,' he said, 'what a spooky thing to do. Doesn't it give you all nightmares?'

The hush was so acute it answered his question; it went on and on, so that it was a relief when Margot boldly drained her tumbler in one, and told

The eighteenth story

'Rot. I dream of rot.'

I refilled her glass, and she reported that she sees Fanny's neck dissolving into Idris al-Mutlak's knee, his thigh into her head.

(A peculiarly disgusting abomination; the comfort is it can't endure. A few more months and this biformed monster, more frightful than any *basajaun,* is bound to fade into clean loam.)

'Meanwhile it likes,' said Margot, 'to join in the midnight chorus.'

Has no one told you about our midnight chorus? Has it not reached the guidebooks? At the moment each Cambridge day becomes extinct, as Little St Mary's rings its twelvefold knell, the dead stir. Freshly laid cadavers scarcely gone squidgy, diffuse lengths of ooze, mere vague pockets of sticky earth, ash urned, ash naked, dust: all of it wriggles, chuckles and begins its purgatorial chant. If you happen to be in a Cambridge graveyard at that hour, do lie full-length and press your ear to the carved stone. You'll hear them at it: *spec, spec, spec* is what you'll make out first, like the meaningless scratching of beetles; then, as you better catch the mirthful sound, *specto, specto.*

Apparently Fanny Myre snaps open her half-consumed eyes, ogles Idris' feet, ogles the Four Last Things, spits out her cigar. Idris' wormy eyes reappear behind his shreds of eyelid. Because the complacent grin of skeletons is so like the complacent grin of seducers, he looks for a moment quite his old self. Then what's left of his mouth starts to move in perfect time with the half-embalmed lips of his baptised lady. The monster (murderer-murderess, murderee-murderee) sings its prayers from double mouth: *Expecto, expecto!*

'Even the pug quivers beneath the monster's toes,' said Margot; 'I see its mandible twitch. Of course it doesn't understand, but you know how dogs are. They always like to woof along. *Expecto resurrectionem mortuorum!'* And she finished her scotch.

ভ

'What does that mean?' asked the imbecile Seb (who reads sociology). 'Is it Spanish?'

We explained. 'The nightmare Life-in-Death,' added Margot, moodily but so artfully I suspected she'd invented her vision.

'Gross-oh,' declared the cheerful Seb. 'That's totally the pits.'

'Not so *totally*,' I said. Why should Margot affect to suffer more than I do? *I* threw him off the tower. 'You only have to *watch*. Last night, y'know,

The nineteenth story

I was Josiah Myre. Once again. Metamorphosed. I found myself putting on my lilac-and-silver ribbon of St Caroline. And my battered Armenian cloak, the cloak Fanny loved when we were outcasts, so heavy now with grime it seems to cling to my flesh. To sear. (I tossed back and forth, trying to wake.) I find myself lighting a candle, I steal from the Lodgings past the stables – Sheol Court isn't built yet – toward. Toward—'

'Yes, yes,' said Margot.

'Toward that odious garden. Cambridge's spires are silver as pepperpots between scudding early summer clouds. Constellations veil and unveil themselves. Winking at what's about to happen. I endure this, and cannot wake. The garden gate groans. I go through. Between silhouettes of yews I make it out, the cupola of Priapus. Gleaming. I open the casket. A skull in moonshine. *Ma chère petite*, I hear, a creaky whisper from my own mouth; *Pardonnez-moi, ma chère, chère petite*—'

'That's enough of that,' Margot said briskly. 'Ollie? 'Fess up.'

The twentieth story

Ollie looked shamefaced. We had to worm it out of him. He's emerging from goatish pubescence, and hardly likes to say that he dreams of – love, most aweful of all frenzies.

What he sees is Fanny as Iolë, dancing for her belovèd on Mount Œta; and it seems to him, sleeping, that her allure is larger than the world. The cosmos is too slight to hold her. Hercules son of God is happy to die for her. Her loveliness abolishes death, and thought, and law. That lift of bare foreleg cancels the weight of mountains. The gyration of ankle undoes Greece, she lifts her arms against the virginal columns of the Parthenon and prevails. In Ollie's dream he both craves her singing and dreads it, for should she sing as she dances, should she sing tales and make them true by uttering them, should she rest her eyes on him, surely he would dissolve—

☙

'Total downer!' said Seb, although the concept of love is naturally over his head (and at that moment it occurred to me how useful it would to have such an oblivious creature as Seb help me in my work. Yes, I will use him). 'What about you?'

Tristan pulled a long face. He's a hard-boiled youth, yet strangely enough the bleakest vision is visited on him. At night he beholds, or so he claimed,

The twenty-first story

the universe turned inside out, with the land of the dead at its apex. The cigar in Iolë's mouth keeps smoking, like a fuming tripod. Its column of infernal incense rises downward, under the bed of the Stygian Creek, past a three-headed pug, exciting the dead with news of fresh atrocities throughout this transient realm of men. Most of all it carries tales of ill-doings at Wygefortis; and these acrid wisps reach the supreme depth, tickling the nostrils of Dis.

The language of sex can be used as a kind of violent invocation, for sex is the great business of the body, and salvation the great business of the soul. People scribble about it on walls as they do about religion. Nobody ever scribbled on a wall about ethics.

CHESTERTON

Sparagmos

i.

'Unhand me, you brute!'

'*Morbleu!* I must have my way with you, Lady Henrietta!'

'Never. I will die before I am yours!'

'Yet I die already! I am bewitched by your glance, your scent, your very being.' He released her and sank awkwardly to his knees, covering his eyes with his left arm. 'What is it in your cool English reserve,' he murmured wonderingly, as if to himself, 'that beguiles me so? What have you that no wanton beauty of the *Faubourg Saint-Germain* ever yet possessed? Why am I stirred as never in my mad ears of um um years of conquest before the outbreak of the deplorable French Revolution? What is this strange thing I feel?'

'Vicomte de Saint-Saleté,' she answered, all her cold cruelty undone by the tremble of her splendid vermilion lip, 'you forget yourself. Stand. You are unmanned.'

'Not so! For too long I have played the wayward boy. Now, only now am I a true man at last.'

With a magnificent gesture she spun on her heel and turned her back on him that he might not see – the young man called Saint-Saleté rose, but she jabbed her finger at the floor and he, sighing, slumped to his knee again. Her back on him that he might not see the unavowed passion that made her breast to heave, daubing with pallor the roses in her cheeks. Heave. Yes. Pallor? Not bad. Done. She spun back and even more impatiently waggled her fingers to get him to his feet.

'Now?' he whispered. She scowled ferociously. 'Then – *alors,*' cried he, slapping his hand to the sky-blue autumn undress-uniform of a lieutenant in the *Garde du Corps*, 'my lady. Very well! I heed your word. At your command I go. On the morrow I sail forth in the amphibious expedition led by Alexander Hood, first Lord Bridport, for – um. Um.'

'Quiberon,' she hissed.

'Quiberon and there doubtless I am fated to fall. *Tiens!* The anguish of a Jacobin poke – pike – can be no sharper than, than the pong of, no. Than.'

'You fucking cretin, why can't you read it? Read it! It's here on the screen.'

'Yes but it's hard to see from this angle. You keep waving your iPad about. All right, no sharper than the pang of your sperming – spurning. Unkindness. A Vicomte de Saint-Saleté may descend far in conduct and reputation yet at least he does not forget how to die know that your name shall be the least word upon—'

'No, just stop. It's too late. It's spoiled. No, keep off. You may as well go. We're done for this evening.' With indescribable violent grace (she thought; she was still watching in the looking-glass on the far side of her room) she tossed back her glorious unruly mane, its locks rebellious as ever against the discipline of Minette's curling iron. 'Get out.'

'Oh – Luce,' he wailed, 'come on. I'll go through the whole business again. I won't make any mistakes this time. Please.'

'This is not *business* for me,' said Lucinda, still dazzling herself in the glass. 'In point of fact. It's not just frigging foreplay. It matters to me, don't you bloody understand? You'd get it right if you took it seriously.' This upward jerk of her cupped right hand was good, she thought, very good indeed.

'But I do try to take it seriously, Luce.'

'"Try"! – I know precisely what that means. "Try"! You think it's just some paperback romance.'

'Well it is a—'

'It's art, as it happens. Woman's art. The one true voice of woman. One hundred percent pure. You think girl writers only matter if they write like boys. Get that jacket off. No, off. They didn't take *Jane* seriously either. I said *off*. And the sword. Put them in the basket and get out.'

Florian felt silly. He was just angry enough to remain excited, so the stiffy in his silk breeches wouldn't go away and he couldn't face the court with it. He groped for the assertive tone he'd heard his father use in the House of Commons. 'Luce, you told me to come here and spend the night. I am going to spend the night. Don't spoil it.'

'Out! Out, out, out! And don't come back. Back. I am speaking literally. Back off. Now. Rapist.'

So out Florian went, and stomped across the rainy court.

It was a dank, sulky night in January, and he was the most irritated young man in the realm. Where else in the United Kingdom of Great Britain and Northern Ireland (he asked himself, angrily), where unfucking else was a fellow expected to dress up and act out novelettes first? The peculiar shame of it.

Although it wasn't particularly cold, the rain had a sullen, leaden, inconsolable quality. He detumesced at once after all. That was a relief. But he felt low, and before he reached the Lodge he ran into Ollie Vane-Powell, of all unholy persons, who smiled at his frilly open shirt, so that Florian's humiliation felt complete.

Vane-Powell, Vane-Powell. He'd been famous, during the four years he'd been at school with Florian, for one thing: slowing down as he went past every window to relish the reflection of himself. Other boys used to stalk him, watching him watch himself, for it was a phenomenon, like echoes and moon-shadows, predictable yet uncanny no matter how often it's repeated: window, pause, glad smile. There was something divine in Ollie's self-satisfaction. It never dwindled, it was immune to derision; jeering fell back on the jeerers, like blasphemy.

Florian Marsh remembered all that; remembered too, Yampton, the most world-weary and retirement-impatient of schoolmasters, telling him 'I can't think why Vane-Powell's thought unusual, there's nothing out of the way about him. A common-or-garden shit, *excrementum excrementitia.* A standard wastrel, not even a rogue. As you, Marsh' (*despite your yellow-brown eyes, your becoming monobrow, your romantically glossy black hair, squandered on you by prodigal nature* – that's what he didn't say) 'are a standard baby-intellectual. More sherry? No? A stopped clock's right once every twelve hours, a face fits the person once in a lifetime.' 'Yes sir. Can I read you my latest draft?' 'Vane-Powell, for instance, doubtless looked suitable at four or five, when hair like his sets off a sailor-suit. And my own expression is still that of the sturdy thirty year old I ought to be. Bewildered by its own grizzling. Afloat among floes. Draft of what?' 'My personal statement.' 'Your Cambridge application? Oh I suppose so.' '*Walter Benjamin once wrote—*' '*Must* it begin like that? Don't look crestfallen, it might as well. But far better, just send them a photo. That beetling expression of yours looks out of place now, it'll come into its own the moment you're bespectacled and balding. They have a duty to offer you academic asylum against that moment. They'll understand.'

And perhaps they had, for here he was, a scholarship boy at Magdalene, fated to live and die here: embowered, entombed. While Vane-Powell (who'd never done anything generous or unusually dangerous, behaving just badly enough to flame in his A-levels) had had to go to St Wygefortis', where people like Vane-Powell do go. And the two boys hadn't set eyes on each other since.

But now he said, in a perfectly friendly fashion, pushing Florian out of the rain, into the shelter of the tower called Acheron, smiling into his face and not at his ruffles: 'Good to see you.'

Florian made an unhappy sort of noise.

'But what are you doing in this borstal?' asked Ollie, which was nice of him because it got them over an awkward point. What was Florian doing here? It was perfectly natural for Ollie to have ended up at St Wygy's, after two depraved years in the Sixth Form and a gap year in Asia encouraging poppy production. But scholarship boys didn't like to be seen even visiting the place, so evil a name it has throughout the University; only partly for its stupidity. Florian looked evasive.

'The obvious reason?' continued Ollie, which was forward; but he spoke in such a comradely way it was impossible to be annoyed.

Florian nodded glumly.

'Can I ask who?'

'Lucinda Crompe,' he said, very low.

Ollie managed not to laugh, merely blowing out his cheeks and raising his brows. (He was crop-headed: he'd taken off his curls. What the little death-by-water of baptism does for billions, death-by-barber seemed to have done for him.) 'Mad as a brush. But you'll have noticed that. Not going well?'

Obviously not fuck you since here I am leaving your shitty college at eleven in the rain in a wet party-costume having obviously been chucked out Florian thought but didn't say, because Ollie's decency was catching. He simply grunted.

Ollie lowered his voice sympathetically. 'She made her last boyfriend act out Mr Darcy.'

'I wouldn't mind that… But she says she's transcended *Jane*. Who was compromised, y'know, by her colonial patriarchal epoch. Luce had moved on. Into it-was-a-dark-and-stormy-night territory.'

'Oho!'

'Tonight we were supposed to be doing *Unlaced by a Traitor*.'

'Ah. Not by *Jane*.'

'By Millicent Shtuphocker. I think that's the name. Anyway, it doesn't matter because I muffed my lines...'

Ollie did laugh now. 'And she threw you out! Christ, what a bitch.'

Florian looked inclined to plunge off into the dark and stormy night and be alone with his embarrassment.

But Ollie, who really did seem to have become a charming fellow, caught him by the shoulder.

'Come with me. I have to collect my pitiful cousin from Abishag. She'll know what to do and anyway she'll give us brandy.'

'Who's Abishag?'

'Real name Margot ffontaines-Laigh. The cleverest person in Wygy's.' (*Which isn't saying much*, thought Florian, trying to keep the thought out of his face.) 'Which is not saying a lot of course. But she *is* clever. Can solve things that can't be solved. Those are her lights over there' – Florian could make out a girl with a lot of hair silhouetted on the first floor, across the court. So because the rain was getting heavy, and because he'd left his umbrella in the cursed Luce's room, and because he'd nothing else to do, he went with Ollie over Gehenna Court and up a staircase and into the first actual peril of his life.

Knock. 'Come in,' said a deep voice; they came in. Here was the possessor of the hair, the silhouette, the voice.

'Hi. Florian, this is Abishag. Abishag, I was at school with this fellow. He's an incredibly brainy historian. At *Magdalene*. Oh, and this' – there was indeed a small girl present, pink and white, sitting curled up yet erect on the floor, like a rabbit, 'and this' said Ollie, struggling to sound entirely appreciative and nice, 'is, in fact, my cousin. Hope Mordaunt. She's coming up to Girton next term. Abishag's been showing her 'round town.'

Florian glanced at her and I grieve to report his systole stayed at ninety-five, dystole in the low sixties; nor did his quietly-thudding heart miss any beats; his thirteen pints of blood went about at a fair clip, but then they always did, dashing through each cranny and back to the aorta every minute. This blood remained inaudible in his ears and did not flush his cheeks, he kept breathing fourteen times a minute, his kneecaps remained steady, his dinner (they dine heavily and simply at Magdalene) continued to descend through his pyloric sphincter to his duodenum without reflux of acid. In short, he did not fall in love. He said 'Hallo, hallo' calmly and looked about to see if he was really going to be offered a drink, and if so, what. As long as Abishag was dealing with the decanter, Florian was thinking mainly of brandy, only a little bit of Abishag (*Hair the reddish side of brown, lovely body but too tall for me, anyway out of my league*),

and not at all about Miss Mordaunt. In all this he did great wrong, for she
– yes, when he'd got his glass and settled in a chair and bothered to regard
her, it was apparent that Hope…

A tear was trembling, it was clear that a tear was most-or-less-always
trembling in those eyelashes. Or even that Hope was herself a teardrop,
glittering in the eyelashes of some higher Power. *Not God or Fate or
History*, thought Florian in his detached inner voice, his essay-writing
voice, the voice that was most nearly *him*. *Some wallflower of a higher
Power. Romantic Fate perhaps. I do like Armagnac more than Cognac, I
must try to remember that…*

Meanwhile these clever young people had begun to talk, to tussle, to
show off; all except Hope Mordaunt.

She was silly and insignificant. However, her face was the sort that
is intensely in fashion now and then. An early Victorian would have
marvelled at its daintiness. In the Age of Aquarius those elfin ears would
have been admired, she'd have been a moonchild. But these features did
her no good now. It wasn't at all a *fit* face. Its eyes were so large that there
was no question of a nose; they strained the dimensions of her skull into an
uncertain shape. Even so, had she held her forehead a few degrees further
back, kept the corners of her mouth firm, lowered her eyelids slightly,
let her pupils rest coolly on this and that, then move on, she might have
come off as aristocratic; which is what she was. Florian might have been
moved. Instead he had summed her up with one glance of his striking
eyes (*Wounded self-concern, self-advertising vulnerability*) and put her out
of his mind.

But *Love me love me love me*, shrieked Hope's parched heart, *give me
your love Florian Florian Florian, give me you to live in*. She'd had her fair
share of boys; that made no difference; she remained a desert sinkhole,
nothing could dampen her. She was a million acres of rusty sand, like
the hinterland of Australia, where the stupid rivers drain inland, nosing
out the driest spot to waste themselves, leaving no damp trace behind.
Hers was the neediness that clutches and clutches until its fingertips are
wrinkled, as after overlong baths.

The first conversational skirmish (on politics) had ended with Florian
driven back to his trench. Now Ollie was telling a story about Yampton,
one Florian had heard before; Abishag was half listening, half summing
him, Florian, up. The rain was getting heavier, spattering on the windows,
in which the blackness was deepening toward midnight.

Florian made himself emerge from his usual self-absorption; the conversation swam into view. The school anecdote was done. He turned his attention to Abishag.

Who was saying: '...clever, suppose I should ask you about your dissertation.'

'My – ? Oh that,' although of course his second-year dissertation was what in the whole world Florian most liked talking about. 'England, eighteenth century. Cultural and religious movements in.'

'Which?'

'Wesley comma John, influence of. I'm wading through his journals. Seven enormous volumes. Wild stuff.'

'Are you a Methodist?' asked Abishag, darkly.

'Certainly not. But Wesley's important beyond Wesleyanism. He may be the most important cultural figure ever.' It's to be remembered in fairness that Florian was a very young intellectual. 'He didn't just invent a parody of Christianity. He invented a way of making all religion subjective. And once you've done that you've subjectivised everything. You're no longer concerned with God, but with your method for making yourself *feel* God – it's why they called them *methodists*.' Florian's intellectual forehead wrinkled his merely decorative monobrow. 'Wesley *tore man apart*, that's it. The eye ogles nothing but its own brain, the brain watches its own guts have spasms. The heart's held up dripping, shorn from the will. Wesley bottled hysteria and sold it on. He's the origin of all morbid self-consciousness. Therapy. Diets. Advertising. Of pretty much everything, in fact.'

Abishag, mildly impressed, refilled his glass. 'You make him sound like the Marquis de Sade. You know, even lust never getting beyond its own skull.'

'Exactly,' said Florian airily (thinking: *I'll use that in my dissertation*).

'De Sade?' gasped Hope. Her nanny had been a Methodist. Besides, she thought it was important to be nice about things like church. But Florian had said *Exactly*, so: 'I think that's true. Very very very true.' Her cousin managed to throw her a flimsy smile; the other two paid her no attention.

'What,' asked Abishag dreamily, 'if Wesley had been born in France? Would he have run amok there?'

'Yes. And if de Sade had been born here—'

'Oh he'd have been a damp squib,' said Abishag. 'In Blighty. Albion, meaning "white". No one pulls off unpleasantness *here*.'

'Swift?'

'Swift. Orwell. There's always a hint of playfulness. Boyishness.' Margot knew the rules for playing with an intellectual. You must knock names back over the net slow as shuttlecocks; he must have time to prepare a return. Such conversations are no more competitive than waltzing. 'Dracula, Dr Jekyll. When the English invent monsters they're funny. We all know no one acts monstrously, not really. Not *here*.'

'Sweeney Todd the demon barber of Fleet Street,' suggested Florian, not quite at ease. This was the wrong sort of cleverness.

'Exactly.'

'Abroad is bloody,' pronounced Ollie very carefully, 'and all foreigners are fiends.' It was one of Mr Yampton's favourite quotations, and Florian laughed.

'My grandmother is French,' said, with a catch in her voice, Hope, for whom all cleverness was the wrong sort. (*I know I'm wet, I know I'm sentimental.*)

'Belgian,' said Ollie before he could stop himself.

'Well, yes, Belgian.' She had the trick of speaking slightly too low, so that listeners had to lean forward.

'That explains it,' said Abishag.

'Explains what?'

'Your delightful accent. The way you said *de Sade*,' and while Hope tried to work out if this was nicely meant or not, Abishag brought badminton to an end: 'Your idea seems very serious, Florian. And worthy and solid. So I have to ask. What's a serious Magdalene historian doing in this rat-hole, at this time of night?'

'Wenching,' said Florian stoutly; Ollie grinned, relieved his school friend wasn't overawed by the regal Abishag. (Hope wasn't going to cry, no no she wasn't.) 'Chambering.'

Abishag raised her remarkably thick eyebrows. 'And yet…?'

'There's a problem, yes,' and he told them with gentlemanly frankness about Lucinda's kink, and *Unlaced by a Traitor*, and how hard it was to read, while kneeling, a screen that wobbled.

The story amused Ollie but made Hope look unwell. Her exorbitant thirst for love could play the very devil with her features. Just at the moment it was making her positively ugly.

'Lucinda Crompe makes you act out bodice-rippers?' exclaimed Abishag, unaffectedly appalled.

'Yes.'

'Before you're allowed to rip her bodice?'

'Not rip, tug. It all has to go back into the basket undamaged.'

Abishag shook her head and Florian looked doleful. (The basket offended his scholarship as well as his manhood: this abominable shirt was rococo – it clashed chronologically with Lucinda's Regency muslin, and with her 1790s wig.)

'Luce is getting worse,' Ollie was saying. 'When she was with Seb he was allowed to bring a paperback *Pride and Prejudice* and use that. With Darcy's part pre-underlined. Seb's thick, y'know, had to practise the hard phrases. Can't you do that?'

'I don't think Millicent Shtuphocker *gets* printed. Girly fiction's gone virtual. You download as many stories as you want on to your iPad for five quid a go.'

'Oh no not at all,' whispered the Hon. Hope Mordaunt suddenly, shyly and intensely: everyone stared at her. '*Oh*' – for Florian had the most wonderful huge eyes, hazel with gold flecks. 'No no no. It's never more that two pounds a book and if you join a fan club it's just 99p.' Florian's mouth swung a little open and Hope, who felt like a ball of soft dough rolled back and forth over ground glass, was dazed: pained by the beauty of his teeth. *And how red his tongue is; O God, O God.* She swallowed, and managed to murmur: 'I know. I read them too.'

'You do?' and 'I don't believe you' and 'Ah' said Florian, and Ollie, and Abishag, frozen in the act of proferring her decanter.

'Really, really. Yes.'

'Nobody does,' said Abishag severely. 'D'y'want more brandy, *Hope*?' Her day-long boredom with the girl was crystallising into exasperated malice.

'Oh no thank you. But I only read one a day otherwise I wouldn't get my homework done.'

Abishag compelled herself to put the decanter down, and not bang it over the pixie head. 'Name one.'

'Well tonight before I go to sleep I'm going to finish *Saved by the Viking Warrior from the Sea* but since there are only ninety pages left it's not a proper read is it so I might begin *'Tis it Love*.' Misreading the silence, she plunged on. 'Which is by the author of *Lasso my Soul* about a cowboy who inherits an Irish castle and falls in love with the village schoolmistress only this time it's the governess and he's a cynical young captain in the Guards. She was so serious she wore *pince-nez* until she lost them in the bog when he rescued her from the gypsies and then she discovered she didn't need them, except for reading, and he thought she had such beautiful eyes. They were lavender. The cowboy, I mean.'

Tempestuous dandies, tender buccaneers, inhibited Vikings, smouldering tycoons: Margot had a vision of these cartoons snatched up into a tin sky by an enormous little hand, one by one, there to be crushed until they dripped ghost adoration, ghost semen, on to the sand below. Unassuaged, a little voice vast as the universe howled *More, more, more.*

Florian was struggling to keep his face free of any expression. He looked like a man about to sneeze, or (thought Hope) like a hero at the instant when his steely heart first thaws and he confesses to himself, angrily pursing his manly lips, that in sooth he cares.

Thus encouraged, she turned confessional. '*A Dubious Duchess* is my favourite at the moment. I read it twice last week, but nothing ever compares with *My Lord and Mistress* because that was my first back in the fifth form. That was when I discovered it. I only thought about science then and didn't think it mattered but it does, doesn't it? Literature. I go back to *My Lord and Mistress* nearly every month and still always cry.'

Florian, remembering his manners so laboriously Abishag could hear the gears clunking, managed: 'So you're coming up to read English?'

Hope hung on this remark (*The first time he ever spoke to me! Oh!*) so fiercely she could scarcely parse it. There was a second's odd pause. *How lovely his lips are.* Then she started vehemently shaking her head. 'No, no no no, not at all.' Her headmistress had declared her too susceptible to pain for French lit., or history, or anything human. 'Just chemistry' (although even so, her heart tore when she heard of atoms rasped from each other, electrons ejected, valencies snapped). 'I'm coming to Girton to study Chemical Engineering.'

Such remarks often create a small silence. But this silence went on for a beat or two longer than was decent; so that Hope decided Abishag, who was staring into the blackness beyond her window, must be pointedly ignoring her, Hope, out of disgust.

In fact she'd forgotten Hope's existence. She was rapt in Florian's case; Ollie was waiting for her pronouncement with reverence; Florian was hoping for a refill.

Suddenly, vatically, hieratically, Abishag flung her heavy hair behind her: 'Intellect!' she declared, eyes cast up like a pythoness. 'What is it? It chugs. Chugs along the rails where there's an argument laid, sleeper by sleeper. But it's imagination that creates the ground on which the sleepers lie.'

Fœtal dons don't care for talk of this sort. 'Y...hes,' said Florian dubiously, swishing about the last of his Armagnac. 'I suppose.'

'It's true,' snapped Abishag, dropping the prophetic manner, 'it's the Truth, it explains everything. You know I'm going out with the Latin tutor?' Florian nodded, although of course he didn't, and was indefinably shocked by her candour. 'Felix Culpepper's the cleverest man in St Wygy's – which isn't saying much – perhaps in the world. He uses imagination as a weapon. He's not just a don, you know, he's a fixer for the Establishment. A mystic assassin. Composes killings the way people compose poems. Controls everything. Sometimes I think he composes me.'

Hope didn't care about metaphysics one way or the other. But her gaze was fixed on Florian's profile, and as she saw him frown (she'd never come across a lovelier frown) she frowned too.

'Felix is gone. He went to London this morning. Otherwise I wouldn't dare apply his methods. But I think this is what he'd tell you if he were here. If he could be bothered.' Resuming the vatic mode: 'I speak not in my own name but in the name of Culpepper and his method. Attend.'

'We attend,' said Ollie, impressed. Florian, who was remembering Wygy's criminal, imbecile reputation, said nothing.

'Felix slays you in a pageant. At first it's delightful being his victim. He twists garlands about your horns, you're led in procession to flute-music, everybody sings. Then the sacral stone axe appears, the sins of the tribe are laid upon your head. At the end of the rite you're not just dead, you're guilty.' Florian cleared his throat. 'He tortures with premonitions, obliterates real people with make-believe. Fiction is a spell to jump reality on to another track.' This was not an intellectual atmosphere Florian could like; this is exactly why he liked socio-economic history, it was so clean. 'Lucinda, in her small way, has made a similar discovery. She makes the feeble pretence of historical romance *incarnate*. She causes you to act it out, *cliché* for *cliché*, heave for heave.'

'Yes, she does,' said Florian with distaste. 'What do I do about it?'

'Out-enchant her. She's practising a weak form of sorcery – because she's also enthralling *herself*. She's subordinating not just her lover but her own love to some other woman's imagination.'

'These brainless stories?'

'Brainless, exactly. So she's ceased to be person, you have her at your mercy. Show no mercy. Treat her as a toy. Take over her conjuring.' And the soothsayer leaned back in her armchair, fatigued.

'That,' murmured Florian, putting down his unrefilled glass, remembering that he had to be up early to row, 'sounds caddish.'

'It's what,' Margot continued in her usual voice, ignoring his fidget, 'she desires. Perhaps you're right about your Mr Wesley. Since his day – for three centuries – human imagination's been swollen but flabby. Shapeless.' The mention of Wesley was crafty, because Florian subsided and listened. 'Most people can't manage their own imagination. They lease it out to anyone who can. Pornographers – pornographers are the unacknowledged legislators of the world.' Margot was rather pleased with this. (No one noticed that Hope was turning pink.) 'If I build a made-up world, it's merely pretty, a puppet theatre. If I get a real person to climb inside, I possess him, as a demoniac is possessed. And Lucinda wants to be possessed.'

'Where's this going?'

'You have to write your own girly story –'

'Good God – !'

'– and make her read it. Could you? I mean, could you get it on to her iPad?'

'I suppose so. Yes.'

'Good. If she has to be a stock character in cheap fiction, it may as well be yours, not Millicent – thing's.'

'Shtuphocker. But how can *I* forge a romance?'

'They can't possibly be hard to write.'

'No, but it wouldn't be convincing, would it? *I* don't know what's in them. I just act them out, I never listen, they're too moronic.'

'Oh I know, I know what's in them,' gushed Hope, 'I know. They're so marvellous. There's always a young woman at the beginning who's not sure of herself but she's really so beautiful if only she knew it and she meets a man and he seems not to care but' – and here her head lolled so far forward that her hair cascaded over it and the other three could see only the violent redness in her ear-tips. 'In the end he does.'

Abishag (it's to be recalled in her defence that she'd been looking after Hope since just after lunch) put down her decanter with a crack. 'I,' she said, in a tone of nausea, 'need to go to bed.'

Ollie remembered his burden of cousinhood. He stood. 'C'mon, Hope. I'll walk you back to Girton.'

'But –', and her unsteady voice went to pieces over the glorious name, 'Fl. Flor. Rian... Would you like to borrow some of my romance novels? I always travel with dozens. You can,' and she lifted her face, white again now but curdled with longing, 'have them.'

Florian was not trying to be a good person, as Ollie was. But he had been well brought up. Magdalene lies in the same direction as Girton.

And what Abishag had suggested might work. So, after a heroic struggle, he managed a smile. 'That's good of you. Shall I walk you back, then? I can borrow a couple and see what the fuss is about.'

'Take them,' said Hope, throatily, 'all. I—'

Ollie pulled his cousin to her feet in a way that stopped her talking, mitigating the shame she was bringing on their kin. 'But what'll you have to read yourself, then? Eh?'

'Here, Hope,' growled Abishag, who had her back to them and was rifling ill-temperedly through her bookshelf. 'Since you're interested in *amour*, and can't take your Viking warrior to bed, have Jake Osgood instead. By way of balance.'

'Oh – not Osgood,' said Ollie, genuinely shocked.

'Who,' asked Hope tremulously, 'is Jake Osgood?' The book had an acid-purple dust-jacket, and was lettered in black gothic. *Making Sandcastles in a Sandstorm: A Nihilist Approach to Sexual Relationships*. It showed one of Lucian Freud's splayed nudes, all on her lonesome across an inadequate sofa.

Abishag was back in command of herself. 'Osgood's the College joke. Our Fellow in Philosophy. A fearful cynic, or thinks he is. You may have seen him being grotesque on the telly. I only have his book to snigger at, and I've finished sniggering' – she handed it over. 'Felix, I think, would say that you need, as an antidote to the poison you've been feeding yourself, poison of *this* sort. I prescribe it in his name': again, the rumble of authority, as if from a menacing oracle you've crossed a mountain range to consult. 'Whenever you feel like a love story, remember you've surrendered yours to Florian' (if this was meant to make Hope gulp it succeeded); 'so read five pages of Osgood instead. That's the rule.'

Timid Hope took the book like a good child taking medicine. She opened it at random, and read, cringingly –

> am merely a transient energy field, like everyone else, yet
> my existence might be described as a success, a positive
> upward blip on the universal downward graph, if I inflict
> more pain than I receive, thus running a credit

– and she snapped it shut.

'Oh. Oh, thank you. Margot. And thank you for looking after me today. And showing me everything. And, and,' *and for introducing me to this god, this god*, she didn't say.

The god was suddenly impatient. He would have to walk home slowly, at girl speed, through the damp, in a ruffled shirt, with a detour to bloody Girton. 'Good running into you, Ollie; pint soon? Good meeting you, Abishag, Margot; thanks for brandy. And' (a little scornfully) 'advice. I'll report back. Shall we go, er, Hope?'

They went.

Abishag and Ollie leaned out of her window to watch. The rain, after a day of flirtatious dribble, had spent itself and cleared. The air was sharper, but stars were out over the turrets and spire. A huge half moon well to the west seemed to blast the earth with her own cold. Florian, walking across Gehennna Court and out through the Lodge, looked genuinely romantic in his white blouse. Hope, skipping along beside him, trying to look into his face and keep up with his stride, did not.

'I know she's your cousin...'

'Second cousin. Not an impressive branch of the family. Drunks and suicides. She's the best of them.'

'Dreadful little thing.'

'C'mon, Abishag, she's not too bad.'

'A waste of space. Literally that. Not worth the twenty-four hundred square yards of blessèd earth that does nothing but grow things to feed Hope Mordaunt.'

'God! is that number right?' asked Ollie, honestly interested, forgetting all about his cousin.

'I think it's the global average. Presumably keeping a person alive takes less ground in England. Rain, fertile soil, more rain. Less, anyway, in Hope's case, she looks underfed even for a runt.'

'I think she's quite pretty.'

'But the way she talks.' Margot mimicked her voice: '"Take them... all." Ugh. Is anything she said today worth the 388 cubic feet of air she sucked in and belched out as waste? And before you ask that's the average when breathing normally at rest, it'll be more now she's panting after your boring highbrow Magdalene chum. Caspian. Crispin.'

'Florian. What I want to know is where these gruesome statistics come from.'

Abishag sighed. 'Felix passes them on. He thinks numbers are magic. Bloody demented pedantic idler.'

'You're cross because he's gone away?'

'In the first week of term. Taking Seb with him.'

'Ah. Did he? For amusement?'

'To *help*, he said.'

'Ah.'

'If Sebastian Hawicke Trocliffe is part of the solution,' remarked Abishag loftily, using very old-fashioned vowels, 'it can hardly have been a very difficult problem.'

'You mustn't be hurt, Ab. *He* doesn't take Seb seriously. Thinks of him as a sort of a puppy and – Good God, speak of the devil', for below them they could hear the truants themselves, laughing raucously. They looked down and there the two of them were, with Clinker and Scurf the underporters following them out of the Lodge, tittering. From this angle Seb appeared entirely composed of grubby yellow hair. Culpepper, in his opulent shoulder-caped overcoat, had doffed his bottle-green fedora, which he was using to gesticulate: flamboyant swoops, indecent cupping gestures, snuffing of candles. He wasn't merely entering Gehenna Court, he was making an entrance; and indeed St Wygy's, like almost all the colleges of Oxford and Cambridge, resembles an inside-out theatre, orchestra and stage facing backward toward the flaps, playing to the stone fabric as the centuries go by. The porters, like stage-hands, fawn on the principals, waiting to carry off bodies immobilised by knife-play or port. The curtain never rises.

Abishag's sulky face half lit up. 'Dammee he looks pleased with himself.'

'Culpepper always looks pleased with himself.'

'Yes, but this is his special after-case look.'

'He's killed somebody, then?'

'I imagine so.'

Culpepper ruffled the matted hair of Seb, who turned and vanished in one direction, toward his own rooms in Abaddon. Then, without betraying himself by glancing toward Margot's window, he took himself off under the chapel tower toward Megiddo Court, where he had his own set.

Margot squinted into her looking-glass, plumped up her generous reddish hair, squeezed her lips, rehearsed a smile. 'I'm off. He'll want to tell me battle stories. How clever he's been. How very deadly.' They were trotting together down her staircase now; she'd slammed her door locked. 'Oh. And Ollie. You won't mention anything to him about the idiotic Crompe? I mean what I told Floris—'

'Florian. Florian Marsh.'

'What I suggested Florian might do. I'm not sure Felix would approve of me practising Culpeppery without a licence.'

Ollie promised, and Abishag, kissing him lightly on the cheek, ran off across the cold treacherous damp cobbles of Gehenna to her lover.

ii.

But we're not to think of Lucinda Crompe as an idiot. That would simply be a mistake. By the standards of St Wygefortis' College she was brilliant. And while she was perhaps unhinged, and certainly a fool like many a cleverer and older person, at least she was not a romantic fool. Her folly lay in the opposite direction. It was precisely the fanciful that Lucinda couldn't bear. Whatever was formless, or gaudy, or threatened to become sublime, was anathema to her small chilly heart.

This antipathy, rather than any positive talent, made Lucinda a good geographer. She longed to tidy away with formulæ the world's eruptions and tsunamis. Her longing made her diligent. She craved intellectual power over the universe: power to rob it of its terrible might.

And she loved to tidy love itself into a formula. If secretly she despised bodice-rippers as much as her lovers did – she would have found Hope's faith in them inconceivable – at least she was in perfect earnest about their utility.

So this evening, once Florian had failed her and been driven away, there were no sniffles. Her manner was dry and rational. She got out of her costume briskly, packing it away in the lacquered bamboo box that doubled as her coffee table. Beneath her fantastic *Directoire* wig she had functional cropped hair, and beneath her muslin were the clothes she invariably wore: black ski-pants and black T-shirt, which went with a black jumper and black knitted cap in winter. These suited her trim, sportive figure (to use smutty language of a different kind). But that's not why she chose them. She simply couldn't picture wearing anything more fanciful. Now she took everything off, folded her things into a drawer, and stepped without nonsense into her quiet sheets. She adjusted her reading-lamp and took up her bedside book of the moment – a solid manly brick of a thing that would have astonished Florian. It had beige boards, it smelt of mould and cigar smoke, it had gilding on the edge of its pages, it was spined with black leather, and it was stamped in gold letters CONSTANTINE PORPHYROGENITUS: *De ceremoniis aulæ byzantinæ.*

She opened it at her bookmark, and read carefully (skipping nothing, worrying apart the knotty mediæval Greek) the Sacred Emperor's account of court ritual when he receives foreign potentates. She mastered the procession from Bronze Gate to Chrysotriclinium, the prostrations upon entering and withdrawing, the formulaic expressions of concern for the health of the Imperial family, the permissible gifts, impermissible questions, coiffures, costumes, number and amplitude of thurible swings, bows, embraces, kisses, music of hidden choirs, salute of undisguised soldiery, ceremonial wine-bibbing, nuances of gesture.

Naturally Lucinda had no historical imagination. She had no imagination of any sort, and thus no sense of humour, which is why she tired so quickly of *Jane*. The energy properly spent on imagination she spent in the opposite way: building up mental ramparts, keeping out the dreaded powers ('mystification', 'wild whimsy'). Nonetheless, being an intelligent girl, she was aware that a great number of details are necessary to create atmosphere; and without atmosphere romance cannot get underway. What romance needs is historical facts, facts shovelled into the flames, grains of incense consumed on the embers, raising a heavy, heady, purple smoke.

Archon, olbios, hegemon: such, she read, are the court titles bestowed by the Sacred Emperor upon visiting chieftains. *Hegemonarches* for special favourites. She accumulated these details as soberly as a chemist might fabricate L.S.D. for his own use. *Prinkips, rex*: the words are too easy, unflavourful. *Eritimotatos* is much better. So is *hyperechon*. Here a *hypertatos* or even a *panhypertatos*, there a *peribleptos* – no, in fact a *peribleptotatos*. The glory of a *phaidimos* is dimmed by the dazzle of a *phaidimotatos*, an *ariprepestatos* looks down on a *periphanestatos*, but is dizzy with awe at a *megaloprepestatos*...

Her lips formed the grand rolling words so proudly it might have been Lucinda herself who stood motionless on the imperial dais of the Chrysotriclinium, in a mantle stiff with silver wire, beside Constantine VII Porphyrogenitus.

And so it was. It was Lucinda who stood by the Christ-Faithful Basileus – Daddy, that is – as he doled out a title of *taxis*, or order, to a tribal king from without the Empire; that is, from the realm of *ataxia*. Yes, to a young barbarian: to a man half-abashed by the dazzling court and half-defiant; overtly muscular, naturally blond, standing before them amidst the silk-gowned courtiers in his outlandish revealing furs; a bronzed specimen of *ataxia*, pent in Byzantium like a stallion in a petting zoo.

Lucinda, feeling she had assembled enough details, marked her place in *De ceremoniis*, put it back on her shelf, turned out her light, and set to work.

'Unhand me, O Eritimotatos and Krim of the Kabardian Bulgars – you egregious savage!'

'*Tŭpite ovtse-tura!*' exclaimed vehemently the handsome warlord, and with a delicious shudder the Constantinopolitan princess guessed he had dared use some profanity in his own uncouth tongue. To her! To the youngest daughter of the Sacred Emperor! 'I must have my way with you, O Panhypertatosess Lucinda.'

What folly it had been to meet such a creature here, by night – here in the seventh bay of the palace library, beneath the chryselephantine statue of the Peribleptos Maximus. Mad, inexplicable folly! She turned from him her blushing face to stare out over the starry black-purple Bosphorus, hissing bitterly: 'You dare insult me, O Eritimotatos, because we are alone. This is not, in point of fact, what your eyes spoke to mine in the Chrysotriclinium.'

'Insult you? Never! Know I am bewitched by your glance, your very being.' And, despairingly, he sank to knees before her, performing the clumsy thing with his left forearm.

Through the thin sheet of polished horn that shielded the library from the cruel wind off the Euxine, Lucinda's glorious eyes traced the familiar outlines of the Tower of Belisarius, of which this wild youth, for all his fascinating droopy moustaches, knew nothing. Behind her, Daddy's triremes and dromons rode at anchor in the Golden Horn. Three floors below were Daddy's dungeons, where the Krim's eyes would be put out if Daddy knew. Below the dungeons was the labyrinth of Daddy's treasury, the rooms stacked with lapis lazuli, the heaped tourmalines and carnelians. What puissance, what pelf! Yet she spurned it all. Her proud heart was with this thing of silver fox fur and brown muscle at her feet.

'What is it' (he was continuing) 'in your haughty Byzantine reserve that beguiles me so? Why has no woman of my own people, richly tattooed though she be, and perfumed even as the musk-ox, won such mastery over the heart of the mighty Krim of All the Bulgars?'

Why indeed? 'Eritimotatos –' murmured the Panhypertatosess more gently, while her little hands sought swiftly beneath her robe, here for a clasp of malachite, there for a tasselled knot. Lucinda had studied a diagram: she knew where all the buttons were, knew it would take a full five minutes' work to get the bloody thing off, massy as it was with jewelled panels, and icons innumerable. She must needs spin out their courtship.

Fortunately there was a formula, there are always formulæ – 'you forget yourself. You are unmanned...'

iii.

Our theme is the ordering and description of the sexual act. Never, in verse nor prose, has there been such explicitness as what follows, further down this page. Now we throw off convention, now we defy moral categories. What has been unattempted hitherto, we dare. We stain this paper with details unspecified since erotic literature was first perpetrated by Gilgamesh, King of Sumerian Uruk (who lured Enkidu from his primal wildness though the scripted contortions of the temple prostitute Shamhat). Let the doors be locked, the lights dimmed, a sentry posted.

Shamhat! Shamhat!

Squeezing her velar palate 'til the pulmonic flow from her diaphragm was occluded while the infolded mucous membrane called *plica vocalis* throbbed; then lifting her lingual organ to the near-back posture toward her calcified structure, at near-high constriction, labially part-rounded; then aptically or laminally, with tip or blade, touching the delectable alveolar ridge while the current (occlusive and pulmonic once more) was forced along only the lingual centre in a perfect alveolar stop, Margot clenched with a touch her glottis; and at once, since it was high time for a labiodental fricative, made a tight crushing motion while the flow churned to turbulence and the still—

I beg the reader's pardon, I find I can't go on with it. (Unlock the doors, you may as well turn up the lights.) I was trying to map in purely bodily terms Margot's evening with Culpepper, which began with her saying 'Good, Felix, you're back' – we've reached as far as the letter *F* – and it seems not to be working. Can there be some mistake in the theory?

Let's say I really held back nothing of the coupling of Margot and Felix. I think I would speak of a field, a bright English meadow, lush with a dozen shades of green, but studded too with yellow blooms, and purple and white. There is a wooded stream behind and a suggestion of low blue hills beyond that, but we hardly attend, for stretching up from the wildflowers is a giantess, not just a very tall young woman, who seems however to penetrate the sunny sky. She's motionless; it is her terrible stillness that makes this Margot seem (even to the work-a-day Margot, who beholds her) other-than-human: a Botticelli goddess, perhaps. She is entirely naked, and her flesh is the honey shade of sandstone. Her eyes are cast down, somewhere in the flowers at her feet, but she does not seem inattentive. She perceives, she possesses, she reigns over this faultless summerland. In her right hand she bears a sceptre, a tall stalk of three white gold-tongued lilies; her left hand bears a large sprigged pear as an orb. Her red-brown hair, braided into a tight bird's nest, is crowned with a diadem of cornflower and iris. Felix is everywhere in the picture, he is who it was painted for, he is the canvas and the oil-paint.

And it would be just as explicit to describe the room their love-making implied: not the bedroom of a Cambridge don, self-consciously cultured, anxiously comfortable, decked out with painfully-chosen art, and lit by candles (for Culpepper was after all a *bourgeois*, and thus not a thousand miles from the sensibility of Lucinda); but a big billowy daylit garret, white-washed and wooden, with three rafters spanning an immense bed in which the linen and comforters are snowy, and two dormered windows at right-angles let the white lace curtains blow in to reveal swift scudding clouds, and bright sea, and high surf, and the start of the islands.

Also, it would just as explicit to record Felix's climactic impression of a trumpet blowing from beyond the bed, beyond College, beyond the world. The blast was not at all vague, it was simply past the edge of what he could turn into words, or even into imagined sensations. So he decided not to consider it; yet it was still there, and somehow struck a chord in his mind with that most bizarre, terrible of all ideas, the resurrection of the body. His body certainly lies, as the bodies of all highbrows lie, deep in the permafrost of detachment; he certainly felt it stir at the trump. And if this was just whimsy, why exactly did he feel, when he got his breath back, such intense after-sadness, such certainty of having fumbled and let a precious thing drop?

iv.

After soggy yesterday, and a rainy night, today revealed itself as one of those golden English mornings that crop up now and then in January. The air's brim-full of yellow light, the grey grass goes back to being green, the trees preen themselves, glowing, as if they were not naked. Chilly midwinter spring.

Abishag woke first and prised apart Felix's bedroom curtains. A ray of light, falling on the wreckage of last night's late supper, turned it to a Dutch still life.

Felix woke to the spectacle, admired it, and then pulled himself up on the pillows, which he arranged about him like a throne. The remarkable morning light made the bed look rather stagey.

It was not a moment for love. It was a moment for talk. They understood this, but for a full minute he was so comfortable with his hand resting (pushingly) on hers, she was so comfortable lying against his throne with her cheek on his shoulder, that they said nothing.

Slowly, slowly the light turned from yellow to white. The still life looked more and more like simple squalor, the motes dancing in the beam became just dust. Yet it was sweet to be alive, and curled up naked in bed.

At last, lazily, they began to speak.

'So what were you up to yesterday? Why did you go to London?'

Felix examined the ceiling. 'What was I... I've been... Was it? Yes I think it was. I did the most horrible thing I've ever done.'

'How smug you sound,' she said sleepily. 'Like a cat. Anyway, I bet it wasn't.'

'No, I think it was... I'm a purveyor to cemeteries, I like cemeteries, I caper on the edge doing beastly things. Dangling people over, pushing them in – but never quite this before . D' y' know who Kenneth Pocock is? Or rather, was?'

'Er. A politician. A Tory M.P. In the government. Defence?'

'Foreign Office. Minister of State for Contracting, which means getting foreign governments to buy British arms. The national gun-runner, in fact.'

'Pocock... I can picture him. Barrow-boy made good. Always in the tabloids with his arm round a teenaged blonde.'

'That's the one. Good at his job, though. And the voters don't mind a rogue or two in government. It assures them that politics is human.'

'Wrongly.'

'Yes, wrongly... Pocock's blondes don't matter. But he has, had, another failing. Or affliction. A mania for foreign military women. Blonde, brunette, bald, it didn't matter. Something about females in uniform drove him berserk. He leered, insinuated, groped, pinched. Even Russians weren't safe from him, and they're built like tractors. He'd been warned and warned, but it seemed insoluble.'

'Gaol. Problem solved.'

'Yes yes yes. But the government doesn't want a by-election just now. And they can't endure a scandal. Above all, not an Incident. When the Foreign Secretary 'phoned me two days ago he sounded positively teary. "What d'y'want done?" I asked, warily. "We don't care, we simply need these predations stopped!" cried Benjy, and rang off. Quite a merry chap, Benjy, he only gets vague and pompous when he's very upset. So I got to work at once and the next morning, that's to say yesterday morning, Pocock received a note at his office in the Commons. On vulgar thick paper – wait a sec, I have it here.'

Culpepper leaned from bed, over the wreckage of supper, to finger his jacket, hanging on a chair. He produced from its breast pocket an unappetising wodge of paper-pretending-to-be-parchment. Margot, who was too comfortable in the pillows to sit up, held it over her head. Once unfolded it proved too thick for the morning light to shine through. Its edges were artistically rough. The ink was pink, the implement a felt-tipped pen, the hand swoopy.

> *i Snežana am burn 1994 in Bulgaria but now i verk as seenyor sheff in Eddies buggers en Mitcham hih stret. i sie you in papers & think you vary fin jentilman of exclusiv cloths. If you like meat blond girl with 34D brar for fun no strengs cum to the kwen's mir Wimbildon kumon at 5 toomoro & i in my Eddies buggers uniform will be so yo will find me eesee!*

Abishag made a disgusted sound, folded the paper, handed it back. 'It's crap. No one would swallow *that.*'

'Pocock did. And quite rightly because it's not crap, every word's true. Wimbledon Common's a well-known haunt, well-known I mean to men like him. In the woods round the Queen's Mere the ground's so soggy the grass grows high, dense, unmowable. Impregnable to the lenses of *paparazzi.* There are strategic park benches. It's a recognised spot for quick flings by public figures.'

'Why do you always know such loathsome facts?'

'It's all true about Snežana too. The name means *snow-white,* isn't that touching? She was born in Bulgaria when she says she was, and as of last week did indeed flip hamburgers in smoking grease. And for all I know did fancy Pocock something rotten. He looks, that is he looked, quite virile. With his brash oversized Davidoff smouldering away, and his smirk and his *parvenu* chalk stripes. Beaming out of the society pages in the *Daily Smell.* Don't you think?'

'No. But I dare say Snežana might. *Did* she write that very offensive note?'

'I suppose she might have, last week, if I'd asked nicely and offered her a tenner. Now she can't.'

'Why not?'

'Dead. Killed in the line of duty.'

'Hot oil?'

'Oh, hamburgers were just her day job. Two days a week for the visa. Her real vocation was peddling. Peddling very bad stuff. Stuff so adulterated no decent dealer would retail it. Stuff that should've been flushed down the loo. But since there's always bad stuff entering the system, the industry needs to recoup its investment, and that's where people like Snežana come in.'

'It must have paid well.'

'It did. However, it was Snežana's bad luck to supply a certain fourth-former, who found bad smack didn't agree with her, and lay in an alley behind a pub overnight, masked in her own vomit, her friends having panicked and run away.

'Then she lay on a ventilator from breakfast-time until dusk. Then she died.

'Which wouldn't have been a problem except that she turned out to be the daughter of a Detective-Inspector.

'Detectives feel strongly about bad drugs. They value purity, nothing less than 98%, thank you very much. They're natural connoisseurs, getting the pick of what the plods confiscate. Even some of the superior stuff seized at airports, which has to be shared with politicians, ends up at Scotland Yard. The idea of his daughter dying from injected brick dust and floor cleaner drove this Inspector wild. He tracked down Snežana and soon she was in Putney Vale... Putney Vale! Have you ever been there?'

'I avoid south London.'

'Ridiculous snob. You've missed the most marvellously dreadful place... You know that long low line of hills across England – the Weald, the Downs?'

'I like the Downs.'

'That's because you think of them as charming and English, benign, sweet. But like everything that *exists*, reality makes them terrible. Everything real is so huge. Every real thing is an abyss beneath your tiny bubble of brain. A reminder of yet more unfathomable abysses... D'y' know how much rain falls on England?'

'Much too much. Yesterday was disgusting.'

'A hundred and twenty billion tons. Or two thousand tons per person. Imagine a cube of water thirty miles high. That's your birthday present from the heavens.'

'It feels about that, yes.'

'My little one, you're only being frivolous because you know that if you're serious you'll get scared... *Everything real is terrible.* The Weald's a colossal block of unporous chalk. Whatever falls on its north face runs off, down to where the chalk tucks itself under the river-mud of the Thames. Even in a drought, Putney Vale stays boggy.'

'Huh! I've remembered the name. Putney Vale's a Victorian cemetery!'

'It is. A horror of a place. They should never have started burying people there. Dig a hole and it begins to fill with water. After a few minutes it's a pool. Pump it with a roaring great machine, and still the coffin splashes when it reaches the bottom. If the graveside prayers take too long, granny comes floating back up, riding on her two thousand tons.'

'I'll make a mental note not to be buried there... I take it Snežana was?'

'No. There's a crematorium at Putney Vale too. Snežana's battered remains were scheduled to be burned and scattered. But Seb and I did pause this afternoon, *en route* to the chapel, to contemplate an actual burial. It wasn't raining in London, hasn't rained there for a fortnight, but sure enough, the deceased came bobbing up to within a few inches of the brim. Seb whispered: "If I got on top, would it sink?"'

'Ah. Delightful animal high spirits.'

'Animal high spirits are more useful than you imagine. More useful than cleverness... Despite Seb, I remained troubled by the wateriness of Putney Vale. How tiny and frail we are! How enormous the elements, how hungry the liquid mud beneath our feet, how—'

'You're *en route* to the chapel.'

'Ah yes, on, on... We went wandering up a shallow hill, on a gravel path between gravestones, boggling at the dullness of modern inscriptions – no poetry! And at the dampness of the grass.

'At the summit was the funeral chapel. A small, formidable Victorian affair, not unlike a stripy cowshed. Two crows shared a wooden bench outside. Water chuckled somewhere beneath our feet. Otherwise there was absolute solitude, abandonment, silence. At the door was a damp blackboard on an easel. It read: *3:30 Mildred McGarroch. 4:30 Snežana Gaydaiski.* It was the right place.

'I sent Seb off to look for Pocock. As you'll have grasped, soggy Wimbledon Common abuts soggy Putney Vale. The Queen's Mere is just over the fence from the cemetery.'

'Which is why you chose it.'

'Which is why I chose it. Seb's job was to find Pocock. His story was that this saucy foreign girl had retreated from the damp into a nice brick building up there, just beyond the trees, and promised him, Seb, a blow-job later if he, Seb, would bring Pocock up now. Would he, Pocock, like him, Seb, to show him, Pocock, the way?'

'A bit thin.'

'True. But it's the animal emptiness of Seb's face that inspires trust. He *is* useful, you know. You shouldn't sneer at him as much as you do.'

'Humph.'

'I entered. The interior was pure gospel-of-Balmoral: dark wood, brass knobs, carved animals, encaustic tiles, marble slabs with Gothic lettering. Rather good. It was deserted, but a printed notice on a door carved in linen-fold, looking like the door of a cupboard, said CREMATORIUM THIS WAY PLEASE. I went through and in the twinkling of an eye tumbled from the 1860s into the 1970s. They tacked the crematorium chapel on to the side of the original building – it was like any other.'

'I've never been in one.'

'Oh? Well, the *décor*'s meant to be soothing. Magnolia walls. One black stand holding one mixed bouquet faded to light grey. Rows of padded chairs, dull-blue upholstery, facing what might be an altar, except that it's turned round, narrow-end on, and has rollers set in its top. This is the dais where the coffin lies. At the end of the service the vicar pushes a button in his lectern: the rollers turn and the dead person slides away through the blue velveteen curtain behind, into eternity.'

'It sounds foul.'

'It is. And in that funny way of modern architecture, it even managed to stink. Of idleness, banality, mouldy hymn-books, flowers past their best. And the dampness that flows forever off the Weald.

'I arrived just in time to see shambling council employees, teenagers in overalls, manhandling on to the dais a very lonely-looking coffin. It sported a wretched bunch of petunias, evidently nicked from the baskets that hang on the eaves of a certain sort of pub. Also, there was a seedy organist, sitting vacantly on his stool. Also an equally seedy-looking clergymen, of the sort known in the trade as *crem cowboys* – they hover about the crem all day, collecting fees from the disorganised bereaved who haven't brought a vicar. This one had a yellow hairpiece. Blue face, rusty black gown. A limp and a lisp. An Anabaptist whisky-priest, I should think. His face had the crusted look of long motionlessness. Since performing Mrs McGarroch's funeral he'd clearly just hung about, peering into the stale air, waiting for Snežana's funeral, which would be the final show of the day.

'It was too much of a crowd for my taste. I cleared them out. I gestured for the minister, opened the linen-fold door, told him to bugger off for twenty minutes; he shrugged, burped, obeyed. The teenagers didn't need cash: I produced two joints and jerked my head. They vanished. Then I got the organist into a corner. I told him I wanted the thrill of playing at a funeral, it was my lifelong ambition, I was funny that way. Eventually I forced fifty quid on him to play truant and let me do his job for him. Not much resistance there either. He slipped away and doubtless settled down in a pub.

'Alone with Snežana! I tidied her petunias, sighed over the indignity of death, perched on the organ-stool, stretched my fingers, tugged out some stops, slapped back others, and started to play.'

Abishag was incredulous. 'I didn't know you could play the organ.'

'I hardly ever do. Especially not here. Our Chapel organ's a fright... But then they're all awful things, pipe organs. Not musical instruments at all.'

'Well—'

'They're really not. Consider your actual musical instrument.'

'I'm considering.'

'It produces a thread of sound, doesn't it? That is, a note; which starts to decay; it runs down as time runs on. But your organ defies time as well as melody. It defies finitude. It's an industrial noise-maker. It pumps out a three-dimensional wodge, cramming and polluting the air for as long as the organist wants. Often, a horrifically long time. Here's a thought: might there be a pipe-organ in hell? Playing one intolerable everlasting sugary chord while the damned rant and beg for it to cease?'

'This isn't sensible.'

'Exactly. An organist doesn't try to make sense. If there's a tune at all, it's overlain by farts and trills and blaring flourishes and fatuous chords. Like a compost heap: fresh grass-cuttings on the surface, rot and blind worms beneath. The organist stuffs in whatever crosses his promiscuous little mind. His fingers fiddle away on the manuals and out comes some windy hymn. But meanwhile he's stamping on the pedal-boards so that, muddled in, is oochy-koochy, or a raucous Broadway number, perhaps a snatch of juke-box, *doity-doit doity-doit*—'

'Who taught you the organ, Felix?'

'My Great-Uncle Wilfred. An archdeacon. A thoroughly sinister fellow. I used to go and stay with him in Devon, to get away from my mother. He taught me to twiddle, so he could pocket the organist's fee as well as the vicar's – he certainly didn't give it to me.'

'Tsk.'

'It's all right, I more than made up for it by stealing his cigars... He liked to have a mere boy in the organ-loft, so that at the end of weddings be could dash up, push me off the stool, and take over. It was always Great-Uncle who played the couple out. They'd be processing to the west door, with their friends throwing rose-petals, while Wilfred smirked and bounced about on the keys. Bathing them in tawdry Edwardiana. Music-hall tunes... Dirty-minded brutes, the Edwardians, weren't they? All their songs are about the same thing.'

'Didn't the couple notice?'

'Subliminally. They were probably disposed to adultery from that moment without knowing why. Great-Uncle, you see, resented having to read them that stuff in the Prayer Book about fidelity and procreation. He wanted to cancel it out. Unsettle the marriage before it began. The two young 'uns went off into their united life with *The voice that breath'd o'er Eden* on the surface of the compost-heap. But underneath was *Hello, Hello, Who's Yer Lady Friend?* or *The Boy I Love Is Up In The Gallery.*'

'Ick.'

'Oh don't blame Uncle. It's all organs are good for. Defiling the air, sliming the mind. That's what all low culture's good for. Kitsch is stupidity made into art, and *mit der Dummheit kämpfen Götter selbst vergebens.*'

'Um.'

'Schiller. Against stupidity the gods themselves struggle in vain. *Dummheit* is what blights earthly life. Even if there isn't kitsch in hell, the fiends certainly use it *here*. Nothing's more morally corrosive on half-educated brains than pap. There's something *seriously devilish* about cheap tunes, gross paintings, wally-cladding, romantic novelettes, soap oper – what is it?'

'Nothing.'

'You started. Guiltily. Now your feet have gone cold.'

'Nothing.'

'Hm... Let me warm your feet. Don't you think there's something vaguely lubricious about the very name "pipe organ"?'

'No, I think you're a dirty-minded delayed Edwardian.'

'At least I'm my great-uncle's great-nephew. I still have his technique. Even clever music turns into farts once it's been fed through an organ pipe. I know how to defile my listeners.

'Ken Pocock was coming. As he approached his rendezvous through the bare trees, he'd have heard me mingling *Amazing Grace* with Cole Porter.

In shallow shoals, English soles do it;
Goldfish in the privacy of bowls do it;
Let's do it…

That's what I played, and I knew it would work its way into Pocock's brain, preparing him for what was to come. He is – was – just the sort of gad-about cad-about-town who goes to West End musicals.'

'So he can pose afterwards on Shaftesbury Avenue. Affably waggling his corona at the *Daily Smell* photographer.'

'Exactly. That—'

'Arm-and-arm with one of the chorus.'

'Yes, and—'

'With her bright fixed artificial smile. Waggling her artificial body-parts.'

'Darling. You're so class-conscious.'

'*I'm* class-conscious!' Margot sat up in bed, genuinely scandalised. 'But *you* are—'

'Anyway, anyway,' and he pushed her back down on to his shoulder. 'That's Pocock's *métier*. Every Tory government needs one profligate junior minister. To remind people of the good old days before the war.'

'May I remind you,' muttered Margot, trying to get comfortable again, 'that you were born in 1978?'

'That doesn't stop me being nostalgic for 1914… Anyway, I knew Pocock would know his show-tunes. And sure enough, I heard someone behind me humming along to Cole Porter. I struck a chord and turned. There they were. Seb looking pleased with himself. Our victim likewise.

'He was even vulgarer than his photos. Loud double-breasted suit, dark blue with pale blue chalk-stripes. Astrakhan lapels on his overcoat. Ludicrous paisley silk scarf round his neck, matching silk square tucked in his breast pocket. Doughy Cockney face, coarsely handsome. All-year Jamaica tan. It takes many, many dinners at the Ivy to achieve quite such an offensive prosperous sheen.

'Actually, *sheen's* the word. Silk tie, enamelled teeth, oily hair slicked over his skull with virile energy: they not only shone, they had exactly the *same* shine. This wasn't just a man who'd adopted certain manners. You couldn't pull him to bits to analyse this and that. He wasn't an assemblage, a work of art, but an organic unity, a work of nature. Philandering was simply what Ken Pocock was for. What he *was*.

'Don't look so disapproving. Isn't it fatuous to criticise species? We have to admire the evolutionary adaptations of Pocock's soul as we have to admire the protective slime of the hagfish. The rasping teeth of the lamprey. The slender insinuation of the tapeworm. I'd been hired to sort him out, and I would. But I found myself regretting the destruction of such a perfect type.'

'This is a pose. What about *Seb's* beastly rutting? You've never admired that. You sneer at it.'

'Oh that's different, that's morbid. It's something Seb was trained to do at Charterhouse as a way of impressing other boys.'

'In shallow schools English souls do it.'

'Ho ho. Listen, Abishag, I'll do the jokes if you don't mind. Your role is to say *ooh* and *aah*....

'Pocock's glittering nastiness wasn't dimmed even in that dingy room. He looked about cheerfully, unabashed at being summoned to a mortuary chapel to couple with a stranger. That's what life was like for him. A busy fellow, a jobbing statesman, has to squeeze his adventures into spare moments, often in funny places. Taxi-cabs, 'phone boxes. On his desk, under his desk, in cleaning closets down side-corridors of the House of Commons. In the cockpits of fighter jets and the lavatories of airliners. Wherever the cares of state placed him, he was ready for a few minutes' recreation. He looked about the emptyish chapel appraisingly, searching for quiet corners. The trumpet has sounded, the war-horse reared.

'"Afternoon, all," said he: layers and layers of West End varnish on a base of Limehouse Reach. "I'm looking for a young filly named, er, Snez-something. This lad tells me she's hereabouts. Anyone seen her?"

'I smiled an ambiguous smile, got off my organ stool, approached the coffin. Even when I laid my hand on it he paid no attention. I can't imagine he'd ever given death a thought. The dead don't vote or shag. "She'll be wearing a fast-food uni – ugh!" He'd had a nasty surprise. Seb and I had lifted off the lid. I'd unscrewed it earlier, I forgot to say, using the screwdriver I always carry in my pocket.

'Pocock recoiled, whipping out his silk hankie and clapping it to his jowls.'

'Not very gallant.'

'No. Although I admit she wasn't looking her best. Presumably in her distant Bulgarian village she'd been thought a beauty. Y'know, as a virgin of thirteen. Lugging home steaming milk in pails against a backdrop of gilded coniferous mountain. Early frost reddening her cheeks, wholesome breath hanging before in a white aura. "Snežana, Snežana," say the village wise-women as she goes past, "you are too fine to stay here and lose your teeth before you are thirty. Run away! Go to Frankfurt or London or New York where everyone is a rich man, make something of yourself."

'And after all it had come to this, she *had* lost her teeth before she was thirty. Lost them down her throat.

'You'd hardly guess it. The undertakers had fixed those cadmium lips in a gentle frown of resignation. They'd done what they could with truncheon marks and police boot prints, caking her with grease and powder like a pantomime dame.'

'Oh.'

'Yes, scientifically speaking it was impressive. You'd never guess how she'd died. I've no fault to find with the paintwork.

'But after *that*, bad taste had taken over. The bad taste of moneyed crime.

'To begin with, the coffin itself was too massive for Snežana's painfully slight corpse. Enough mahogany to encase a grand piano. Almost heavy as a piano, too. Lined with hot-pink pseudo-satin, which brought out the tone of her cheeks – greenish, despite the layers of make-up. Then they'd dressed her in a sluttish cocktail dress which might have done for a hen night in Tooting Bec. Moreover, the stench of formaldehyde clashed with the natural scent of Snežana, living and dead, and indeed with Pocock's cologne – half a pint of Jermyn Street. More over-varnishing.

'Still, humanity's humanity. I was disappointed by his *Ugh*. His face looked very ugly, twisted with disgust, when Seb kicked him hard in the back of the legs and down he went. It still wore a moon-calf look of revulsion as I kneed it....

'You know I always have a pair of plastic handcuffs in my kit? We got these on his wrists, twisted behind his back. We stuffed his hideous silk hanky into his mouth, heaving him into the coffin face-down on top of Snežana. He's a pint-sized satyr. I mean he was. Seb held him in place while I got the lid back on and screwed it down. Then Seb, who has a sentimental side, gathered up the flowers, which had spilled on the floor and got trampled. He made them look as well as they could, and replaced them on top. Then he gathered up the Minister's umbrella and briefcase, got them out of sight. We were done.

'So much for the Minister for State Contracting. He'd been the work of a minute.

'I straightened my tie and settled back down at the organ. I played more loudly than before to drown out the faint clatter of heels: Pocock had evidently grasped where he was, and was hammering on the inside of the lid.

'It was nearly showtime. The teenagers reappeared, obviously baked. A mourner shuffled into the chapel. Another, another, two more.

'Finally the sordid cleric bustled back in and took his place. He simpered, tittered, then remembered it was funeral not wedding, and adopted a sickly smile of consolation. About four-thirty he performed a pantomime of consulting his watch. This took a moment: his hands shook and he seemed to find the numbers intellectually taxing. At last he was sure. He sighed. He nodded to me. I sounded a chord. Glancing with what I think was meant to be melting concern about the chapel, he launched into his rigmarole.

'"So here we all are," he began, unctuously – shame his hairpiece wasn't on straight. Anyway, "all" was a bit strong. No family, of course: they were far away, beyond the Great Balkan. There were, let's see, four women in their twenties, presumably workmates of the deceased. One had her work uniform on beneath her overcoat, and I thought how much Mr Pocock M.P. would have appreciated that sweaty soiled nylon blouse, with tangerine stripes and glaring lettering: EDDIES BURGER'S MITCHAM.

'Then there were a couple of obvious policemen. You can spot them in mufti even more easily than clergymen. The older one, with a fury-purple face, was presumably the father of the dead schoolgirl, here to suck revenge to the dregs.

'There was an old lady, hard to place, not the landlady type. Perhaps she was one of those ghouls who attend funerals at random.

'Finally there was Seb, trying to catch the eye of the least-unthinkable of the four burger-flipperettes.

'A measly congregation. And a measly rite. The minister trotted through the ritual words, eager to get home. No one seemed to attend – and to be fair, no attention was necessary, an ecumenical cremation service isn't a pretty thing, obvious committee-work, says nothing in particular, offends nothing but the English language.

'No one seemed to object to the underlying swell of mood-music, rung from the harmonium by your humble and obedient servant. I suppose they're all used to music in films telling them what to feel and think so that they don't have to follow the dialogue.

'My playing wasn't very loud, just enough to distract from the drumming of Pocock's feet. Organ clamour smothers thought—'

'What did you play?'

'How sweet of you to ask.'

'I try to take your work seriously.'

'Margot… I played a mishmash of mawkish hymns. That was on top, you understand. Underneath, deeper into the compost, Pocock would've heard *Smoke Gets in your Eyes*.

'The crem cowboy's tones became melting. He was reaching an end. I pulled out the Dulciana stop and made a tremendous *tremulo* swell on the keyboard: *Nearer my God to Thee, nearer to Thee!* But meanwhile my feet were stamping out more Cole Porter: *I ain't up to my baby tonight cause it's too darn hot.* A witty song. But once it's been fed through the industrial processes of pipes, it's pap. Bach, Flanders and Swann, Schubert: everything's mashed, and comes out the same.

'The crapulous Baptist was done. He pressed a button, the blue plush curtain parted a little, the rollers turned, the coffin slid toward the gap.

'And here's a remarkable thing. As it rolled, that heavy coffin began to *sway*. To rock about. Almost to leap, like an egg wanting to hatch. Pocock must have made a superhuman effort. There may even have been (naturally I can't be sure) a barely audible gurgle.

'One of the burger-girls glanced about her, trying to catch someone else's eye. She was clearly struggling with the thought *Snežana doesn't seem to be quite dead.'*

'Phew. You were running a risk.'

'Not really. I was sure they'd mind their own business.'

'They were witnessing the assassination of a Minister of the Crown. It *was* their business.'

'No matter. My music was now rising to a stupefying crescendo, *Mmyyyyah, mmmmmmmya'a'ya'a'yah*, and I don't think the congregation would have stirred even if the coffin-lid had creaked open in best Transylvanian fashion. They just sat. Pocock vanished unhatched through the vulgar drapes under the eyes of the congregation. Musak gave them their cue. Their faces stayed blank and sentimental, they didn't move. The pipes made morons of them all. I'd succeeded. The curtains closed.'

'Ooh. Aah.'

'Thank you. I let my racket die away into some saccharine mawdlings, witterings, a snatch of Fauré's *In Paradiso*. Everyone filed out. The policemen went last, doggedly grinning, stomping on their enormous feet – I mixed a strand of *These Boots are Made for Walking* into my aural compost, hoping it might play havoc with them later, in some hidden nook of their police psychologies. The overalled teenagers wandered off; the crem cowboy reeled from his lectern and was gone. Only Seb remained.

'*Did, diddily dah-dah, did* DAH. I stood. It had been quite a show.

'Seb and I strolled round the back of the crematorium, to the business end. No magnolia paint or velveteen *there*. Everything functional, workshoplike. The holy of holies was a concrete cell with a gurney, a plastic chair bearing a day-old copy of *The Daily Smell*, a mop and bucket, and three tall steel ovens standing side by side. One was working: there was a faint hum, it was warm to the touch. I lifted a heavy metal plate covering an inch-thick circle of glass, a peep-hole, presumably so the teenaged louts could check when their patients were done. I peered through it into the long low chamber.

'D'y'know, what I beheld was rather beautiful? Swirling glory, orange and red-gold. My idea of the surface of the sun. And in the midst of it a goddess floated – Mildred McGarroch. The gas, you see, flares out from burners beneath as well as above. The wooden coffin vanishes in a puff, leaving the corpse hovering in mid-flame. She was black but comely. In a strange way I could at the same time see her form, and her bones within. If in life she was fat, the fat had already bubbled away. What hung there was a flawless female figure, a platonic ideal.

'I'm told the human body, more resilient than it looks – more lovely than it looks! – endures in the kiln for more than an hour. Then, all at once, it collapses into coarse ash. During that hour it reveals itself to anyone who can get at the peep-hole, and what it reveals is elemental splendour. I'd expected a glimpse of hell, but it was more like the fiery paradise that Dante—'

'And where,' asked Abishag briskly, not liking this line of thought before breakfast, 'was Mr Pocock, M.P?'

'Him? Ah. Elsewhere. Nowhere in particular.

'You see, like any decent spectacle, a cremation's *composed*. That is, fake. Theatre moves us because it's designed to move us. Actual fist-fights are much less entertaining and brutal than staged fights. A coffin can't really trundle straight from a chapel, through a curtain, into a furnace-mouth. Think of the blast of heat! But *because* it's a spectacular exit, *because* the organ's banging away, it's theatre. You suspend your disbelief. Certainly Pocock did.'

'He'd have been a cool customer if he didn't.'

'I suppose so. Anyway, he believed. He panicked and wobbled. But *of course* he wasn't going straight into the fire. If he'd only thought he'd have guessed he was bound for a storage-room. That's what lies on the far side of the blue curtain. Not inferno, just limbo.

'Seb and I went past the ovens, through a creaky door, into a yet more banal room. Limbo: the place coffins are stacked after funerals, to be incinerated without ceremony some time later. The next day, if the funeral's too near going-home time. And sure enough, there on a gurney was our pretentious mahogany coffin, tagged with a cardboard slip: SNEŽANA GAYDAISKI.

'Out came my adjustable screwdriver. Six screws. We lifted the lid—'

'Oh!'

'Yes.'

'Was this mercy?'

'Well—'

'Mercy's unusual in hitmen, isn't it? Unprofessional.'

'It was... intelligent moderation. Since I'd probably burned out Pocock's foible, there was no need to burn the rest of him. If he disappeared there'd be lurid speculation in the papers and eventually a by-election, which would be almost as irritating as a scandal. I mean, for the government. Not for Pocock.'

'Is that the only reason?'

'If you press me, no. I wanted to see. If my necromancy had worked this time...'

'Your what?'

Culpepper sat up and arranged his elbows on the pillows, which began to resemble a lectern. 'The first play I ever saw was *Lear*. I was eight. It was very bad for me. Remember when Edgar leads his blind father to what he pretends is Dover Cliff, and lets him jump over? It cures the old man's despair, but that's not why Edgar does it, and it's not why I itched to do the same. To break a man and thus remake him! It's Godlike. And I—'

'Occasionally I wonder what it is you want to do with me.'

'Ah.'

'Get on with your story.'

'No, I want to savour this moment. I want you to understand me. Don't you realise what I am? Hitman indeed! Trivial girl. I'm a thaumaturge, a magus, an adept. A demiurge – I've got beyond nature, beyond evil and good,' although the moment he said that there was a pause in the bed while both thought *Can anyone do that?* and Felix thought *What is the nature of my work?* and Margot thought *What is my nature? What have I been imitating?* Felix coughed. 'Anyway, I've got beyond Edgar, beyond Dr Frankenstein. I've even got beyond Ovid – my metamorphoses happen in the real world, not just on paper. D'y'remember how he begins?'

'Frankenstein?'

'Ovid.'

'Um. *My mind prompts me to speak of forms transmogrified—*'

'No, say it in magic.'

'*Animus fert dicere formas mutatas in nova corpora,*' recited Abishag dutifully (thinking *There's bound to be a hint of the tutorial when you go to bed with your tutor*).

'Exactly: that's the motto of my work. That's what I did to Pocock. *In nova corpora.* We lifted the lid and looked on – what we'd done – the process of my miracle...'

'How was he?'

'Unspeakable. Beblubbered, beshat, bepissed, blind, reeking. It was the soup the larva turns into, hidden in the chrysalis. Wreckage at the bottom of Dover Cliff... We scooped him out and dumped him on the concrete floor.

'Then I looked, last among the human race until all is made new, into the face of Snežana. Her mortuary makeup had been knocked off, her tight-lipped smile had come unstuck so her gummy cavern of mouth showed, one eye had come open. She looked, no doubt, much as the police had left her. She'd done stout service for her adopted country. I sighed, pressed the eye shut, and for the second time screwed down her lid.

'Seb prodded Pocock disgustedly with his foot. He made a noise like a squashed frog. Can we say *him*? Perhaps *it*. It wasn't a man. The face wasn't a face, and not just because it was caked over with Miss Gaydaiski's – it didn't work as a face, it was mindless, a clump of external organs in runny putty, no expression. Eyes terrible, sightless, they seemed to drift about in the goo. Mouth a mass of gore, from chewing through the silk scarf and its own lips. Tongue lolling over chin. Trickle of blood from each nostril: two straight double lines dried across its left cheek. Matching what was left of the chalk-stripe suit. When I undid the handcuffs the arms flopped like disembowelled guts—'

'You'd destroyed him.'

'Not at all. Listen: take any post-natal blob of gristle and skin. Drop it into a world of chattering adults. In a few years it's formed itself into a talking person and built itself a mind. Why? Because life's so keen on organising itself. The universe runs after form. The very air is grammatical, it aches to complicate lumps of matter, that's why it swarms with spores. Leave out a mess of damp flour, it ferments into dough. Drop a severed finger, soon it's thronged, a republic of crawlers and burrowers. Metamorphosis—'

'You do go on, don't you?'

'Metamorphosis is easy. The tricky bit's breaking the tenacious form that already exists. Smash that and, if life remains at all, it's sure to reassemble itself as another body, *nova corpora*. Dissolve a creeping caterpillar, it coagulates as a luminous butterfly. Shatter Daphne and there's no difficulty about turning her into a shapely tree – just give her a treeward shove at the moment of dissolution. Boil down a politician into biological pulp, and in due course he'll become—'

'What?'

'Well, a politician.'

'Ha!'

'Of a different sort.'

'*Ha!*'

'You underestimate me. Who was it said *If your eye offends, scrape it out?* That's what I did for Ken Pocock, who wouldn't do it for himself. I gouged out his offensive part. Just enough, let's say 88%. Cut too much, the taproot dies, the man can't come back. Too little, the old villain grows back in his old shape. I left enough life force to rearrange itself into a cleaner form. A new creature. A more subdued politico. Moth rather than butterfly.'

'*Moth?* He'll be permanently deranged.'

'Not him. Not over a little thing like this. Pocock doesn't have much to complain about.'

'But he will complain. To the police.'

'Not him. Who'd believe such a phantasmagoria? I'm not sure there's even a word for what I did to him.'

'Hmph.'

'Don't worry. I went through his unclean pockets and filched the only physical evidence. Snežana's note. This, in fact. Here, I make a present of it to you. Look at it whenever you are tempted to say *amor vincit omnia*, forgetting that it's only the *forms* of love that overthrow order.'

Here Abishag, who was thinking about last night, and romance paperbacks, trash art, love by a cheap formula, and commandeering Felix's role, again looked guilty.

And again was observed. 'Do you have something you want to say? You seem *furtive*. No...? Well, to finish. It wasn't much fun touching the mess that had been Pocock, but we got it under its armpits and dragged it out of limbo, past the ovens, out of the crem, into the world.

'Light was failing. Rainclouds were thickening. The grass was already soaked with the depressing enormity that comes off the Weald, millennium after millennium. As we dragged the thing along its showy clothes got soaked. We lugged it past numberless Victorian statues: drooping seraphim, sobbing lions, putti with fat fists clutched to flabby breasts, obelisks. We reached the fence separating Putney Vale Cemetery from Wimbledon Common. We heaved it up, got our breath back, let it drop. It formed a damp splodge of limbs in the high grass.

'I bent low to address it through the wire fence. Dusk is full of mystic harmonies. Surely at that moment in some shire a brisk old woman, cycling down a shady lane to Evensong, feels a curious jolt. Dismounting, kneeling, she confronts the ruin of a toad jerking beneath her tyre. That's what Pocock was, flopping about in the dank, darkling grass.

'"Pocock," I said, and the head turned. Not like a man's head turning at his name; like a mole starting at footfall. "This message has been brought to you by Central Office." Clearly the creature hadn't heard of Central Office. Of the Conservative Party, of England, even of Pocock. But words are words. I'm sure these ones bit into its brainstem. When it becomes human again it'll hear, and never be free of them. "The message is to leave military women alone. No more uniforms. Or next time you'll stay in the box. Got it? *Smoke gets in your eyes*".'

'"Next time"! You're not certain your enchantment *took*?'

'I may, hmm, have erred on the side of gentleness. Eighty-eight percent's a deep enough cut for normal people. Perhaps politicians and actors require a little move. The coffin going into the furnace, the wood beginning to char. Only *then* turn the tap and draw them out. Margot, Margot, you have the knack of making me doubt myself.'

'Sorry.'

'Seb and I went away content. We had tea in a pub on the Common, then took a cab to Paddington. Meanwhile I've no doubt that manhood grew upon the thing as it lay. It would've crawled into the Queen's Mere and splashed itself. Dragged itself through the twilit woods, horrifying whatever foxes were abroad. Reached the Kingston Road. Lifted a sodden arm. Got its own taxi.'

'He – it – couldn't—'

'Nah. You know how undergraduates manage. Even when they're legless, their reptilian cortex takes them home and drops them into bed. The final human skill, after everything else is lost. Pocock will've made it back to Notting Hill, which is where he has his bachelor love-pad. Had.

It'll never serve as a love-pad again.

'About now he'll be waking up. What is it that wakes? A blob. Which will soon remember how to stand, walk, make duplicitous speeches in the House of Commons. But *not* how to molest American she-generals. The rogue Pocock's dead. Him I slew. The tabloid celebrity, the capering satyr-statesman: obliterated. Another being will wear those loud clothes.'

'He'll get new clothes. Quieter.'

'A good point. He will. But listen: the worst is yet to come for him.'

'It *is*?'

'Oh yes. Pocock's experience yesterday was just experience – *outside* the mind, clean. We can get over experience, even torture. It's *art* that overthrows, because that gets inside. What'll stop Pocock being Pocock? *Kitsch*, the soul-slayer. Whenever he gets improperly close to a woman he'll hear *Too Darn Hot* playing in his head.'

'He *will* go mad,' said Margot, aghast for the Minister, and troubled all over again about Florian.

'I don't think so.... He'll have *wanted* to go mad, trussed up in that satin box. Just as he'll have longed for a fatal stroke. But death and insanity don't come for the asking.'

'He'll be impotent for life.'

'For the life of this parliament. Which is all that matters. He'll be deselected before the next election.'

'But he'll *live*?'

'Oh yes. And govern. I've torn him apart, but he'll do as a Minister. Man killed, job secure… So much for me. I'm fragrant with self-congratulation. Whereas *you* reek of bad conscience. *I've* been reforming the morals of Her Majesty's government, while *you've* clearly been up to mischief.' He took her in his arms, disarranging his pillows. 'Now I'm going to make love to you, and after we've finished you're going to confess.'

Abishag, knowing he wouldn't be pleased at what she'd done, tried to put off the evil moment, humming *Too darn hot*.

'Oh that doesn't work for *me*,' and it didn't.

v.

But who could have guessed how enraged he'd be afterward, when she'd confessed?

'You dared do *what*? To *whom*?'

'To Lucinda,' muttered Margot, quite unlike herself, cringing, 'Crompe.' (*Whom you've never of, so don't snarl.*)

'Who?'

'Second year geographer.' (*Pedantic, egotistical, deranged round the edges. Bit like you.*) 'Has rooms in Abbadon Court. Gamine. Dreary.' (*Bookish. Damn you. Why are you so cross?*) 'You wouldn't know her.'

'No one'll know her if you don't stop this boy before – reckless, reckless, *idiot* child, can't you see what you've done? You've delivered her into inescapable bad art.' He was roaring now. '*Into hell. You understand that, don't you?*'

She shook her head, biting her lower lip. He stopped shouting, put down the pillow with which he seemed to be about to beat her, and smoothed it as he tried, with insulting patience, to explain.

'It doesn't matter what this highbrow boy's pretence *is*. It's *his*. And *she* enters. Into his fiction. Out of fact. She'll be suborned to whatshisname's imagination. She becomes his *possession*. She is *possessed*, she passes out of the daylight… Oh, get dressed. And try to grasp: you've immured Lucinda thingummy in a box.'

You put Pocock in a box, thought Margot, scared, slipping out of bed – and then remembered herself. *I do not get afraid. I am Urania.* 'You put Pocock in a box,' she muttered, glancing about for bits of underwear.

'He' (growled Culpepper) 'was' (karate-chopping the pillow) 'a mass rapist. Almost. *And* I let him out.' Margot was footling with her stockings. 'But what's this Lucinda done to deserve annihilation?'

'But Florian doesn't want to annihilate,' she said in a small voice, still sulky but increasingly afraid (she'd never heard him like this before), 'it's only a ploy. For sex,' at which he struck his forehead so hard it might really have hurt.

'"Only sex"? Haven't you heard that eros is the one human thing that comes to us from before the Fall? From beyond the limits of the world?' Margot was getting into her bra, which always looks like shrugging.

'This isn't,' she murmured, to show herself not wholly crushed, 'what your Great-Uncle Wilfred said.'

'*Wilfred?* That rusty conduit of original sin? He knew nothing. Like you.'

For the first time since childhood, Margot had misbuttoned her shirt, and was furiously starting over.

'Listen. Before the worlds were made' – he uttered this in a belligerent rush, as if shy about saying so much – 'the infinite found itself fancying the finite, I can't think why, and invented sex to give us a picture, no, hint, of how fiercely illimitable mind can crave this or that corner of limited matter. *Why* do you think it's baited with sweetness to make us faint? And set about with fire, and peril, and despair? *Why?*'

'I don't know,' said Margot humbly, zipping up her skirt.

'You don't know. Yet you unleashed it on this little sociologist.'

'Geographer.'

Something else struck him. 'What did you say this Magdalene boy, Fabian—'

'—Florian—'

'—is writing about?'

'John Wesley.'

'*Welsey?*' howled Felix, falling backward amidst the pillows, apparently in despair. '*Wesley?* Have you no notion who—' He bit back what he had to say.

'I'm remorseful, Felix.' She was tying her shoes.

'No you're not,' he said to the ceiling, with exasperation, 'you're just frightened. As you ought to be. I go away for one day, you steal my methods and—'

'I feel like the magician's apprentice. Running amok with his book while he's gone.'

This infuriated him all over again. 'Apprentice?' he bellowed, sitting up to pound the pillow in his lap, as if it were a pulpit. 'You're the chit in the bikini! Striking a pose as I pull a rabbit out of a hat! You've *never* been asked to participate! Now go and intercept—'

'—Florian—'

'—before he incinerates that pitiful creature… *John Wesley!* No, don't talk – out! Stop him! Run!'

vi.

And she did try. But it's one of the paradoxes of Cambridge, a small town bent inward on itself, with only one large street to speak of and one stagnant river closing off its alleys, that it's hard to find people. So her next hour was farcical.

First she hurtled into Magdalene College (the Porter would have liked to stop her but didn't dare, not with that look on her face). She asked for Florian Marsh's rooms, was directed, hammered on his door. Nothing.

She went to Hall. Breakfast was over and she was sent to the café where Magdalene sluggards go.

There she was told Florian had just left, gone to buy flowers in the market.

(*This is madness,* said a tormenting voice within Abishag's head, *you've delivered the Crompe into hell, you're only pretending to run about and save her.*)

A woman selling flowers said that yes he'd been ever so nice and had bought a lovely bunch of larkspur and winter-jasmine, was it a funeral he was going to? He looked oh sadder than sad but such a nice young gent and if—

Abishag didn't wait to hear. Flowers sounded like business, so Abishag went straight back to Wygefortis', where Clinker, the youngest and least repulsive of the porters swore 'No Lady Margot no one carrying yellow blooms nor purple neither hadn't been through the Lodge no-how in the last hour and that's for sure.'

Nonetheless she went quickly into Abaddon Court and stood by the fountain looking up at the first floor. Lucinda's curtains were open; her peevish profile was visible, bent over her desk. So she was still all right.

Abishag considered going in to warn her. No, ridiculous: what did she have to say, really? She considered waiting here, to ambush Florian when he appeared with his bouquet. But no, that was impossible too – she was conspicuous; a light rain was starting up; besides, if she tackled him in sight of his goal he'd make a noise, Lucinda would come to the window, the scene would be unthinkably ugly.

(*What's unthinkable,* said the tormenting voice, *doesn't necessarily not happen, that's one reason thinking's so pointless.*)

There was nothing for it but to retreat toward Magdalene, hoping to catch Florian *en route.*

But she (beginning to despair) reached his rooms again without seeing him.

There was a pad pinned to his door. *Do not visit L.,* she wrote, *come and see me first. Mff.*

Now what? It was nine-thirty. At colleges less languid than Wygy's the day was already underway. A tall boy with a strong nose on a flat pleasing face – the nose of an important, full-grown man – floated up the staircase. He was dressing-gowned, with a towel over his shoulder. He put his hand on the opposite door, but his eyes drifted over her note, and his brows lifted.

'Have you,' she demanded, 'seen Florian Marsh?'

Such sweaty fervour! said the tall boy's eyes, *and for a swot. Wouldn't I do as well?* But he'd been decently-bred, and what he said, in a faint accent she couldn't place, was: 'He left. I'm afraid. Ten minutes ago.'

'D'y'know where to?'

'Just for a walk, he said – been up all night. Don't know why, he's not the all-nighter sort.' He didn't leer or wink, being polite, but his voice insinuated that he himself was cast of different metal. 'I'm Róbert Zseni, by the way. We have the same lecture at twelve. I can pass on a message.'

'It's urgent.'

'So I see, um—'

'Margot.'

'Margot. He sometimes forgets to read his door; better leave your note on his desk. In case he comes back before noon. He never locks his room.'

Zseni swung open Florian's door for her. Within, it was dismal: a bed that hadn't been slept in, a goatish smell, a fug of weary cigarette-smoke; not like a young man's squalor at all. On the desk was a litter of iPad, coffee pot, mug, ashtray, the graveyard larkspurs wilting in a glass jar (the stupid boy had forgotten to add water), and a dozen scattered paperbacks, evidently Hope Mordaunt's travelling library. *What the Duke Says I Do, The Heartist's Model, A Groom of One's Own, Sense and Sensuality.* The lurid hues of her covers contrasted with the morose brown of seven thick, solid volumes standing at attention at the back of the desk: *The Works of John Wesley* volumes XVIII-XXIV.

While Abishag groped for a piece of paper, Zseni picked up the novelettes, one after another, speechless. *Pirate Sins*: a ball-gowned brunette drumming feeble fists against the gigantic chest of a gigolo with tricorne, eye-patch and a parrot balanced on his bare shoulder; Port Royal burning to cinders in the background. *Spoil of a Pagan Emperor*: a slave girl in clean elasticated chiton and silver crucifix swooning against a centurion, his pectoral muscles neatly tattooed with a Nativity. *For the Love of Hamysh McMullett*: a Jacobite laird with (indeed) a mullet dyed platinum, mini-kilt of orange tartan spandex, claymore, and nothing else, pressing into bright purple heather a oval-faced temptress – both of them ignoring the snarling redcoats, also toothsome, hurrying down the glen with bayonets fixed.

'Who are all these baby-oiled woofters?' gasped Zseni. 'Is Florian taking a walk on the wild side?'

'What?' said Abishag without hearing. She had sunk into Florian's chair, and was despairingly reading his iPad. He had indeed been composing a story.

A *Sinful Salvation*,
by Désirée Fuseaux

CHAPTER THE FIRST

*O*n *a sultry spring morning in the year 1754, the beauteous Selina Huntingdon, foundress and patroness of the evangelical sect called The Countess of Huntingdon's Connexion, stood erect but heaving with her lush lips faintly parted in the drawing-room of her mansion in Spa Fields, pressing her splendid bejewelled hand to her fichu, staring in desperation at the black-coated form of Mr Welsey, her own Mr Wesley.*

'Sir,' she cried distractedly, 'no more words!' and with a vehement gesture tore every stitch from herself until

Abishag flicked on angrily, screen after screen. She read very quickly. She was staggered. Florian had struck her as a youth of quiet tastes. Apparently that wasn't so.

'Pray beat me further, Sir!' cried the Countess of Huntingdon, harshly. He, advancing, wiping a fleck of gore from his eye –

Some pages followed of rather good conversation with 'Dr Johnson of Fleet Street'.
Then they were back at Spa Fields.

Her splendid eyes glittered at the sight of the birch. 'My Lady,' growled Mr Wesley, 'I must preach to a Congregation of eight thousand Mechanicals in Hoxton in an hour, and have no Leisure for your Importunities'

– and Abishag grew a little desperate, thinking of the girl she had thrust down into such a cage.
There was a chortle; she looked up. Róbert Zseni, whose existence she'd forgotten, had settled himself on Florian's unused bed with *Wicked Trojan Kisses*, and was rocking back and forth as he read, legs crossed, one hand behind his head, very happy, very boyish.

'Enjoying yourself?' said Margot, bitterly.

'Gigantically! Listen to this:

> *Within Cassandra's bruised heart happed a whimsical lurch at her brief glimpse of the limber Grecian, and 'Ye have I never prophesied, tall stranger' whispered she to herself apart...*

Oh Marsh, Marsh, Marsh, where did you find it all? What are you up to?'

Margot's mouth closed to a slit. But she could hardly order Zseni out of his friend's room if she was lingering herself.

And she was going to linger. Florian must come back after his walk, to collect his disgusting story and ghastly flowers. She'd be here. She'd appeal to his better nature, menace him – meanwhile, *If I'm going to sit here listening to this clown enjoy* Trojan Kisses, *I may as well do my duty with* Sinful Salvation. *See exactly what Florian means to do. I'll wipe it when I hear him at the door. Destruction's nine-tenths of the law. Tap* SELECT ALL; *black-on-white text becomes white-on-black;* DELETE; *a half-second's work.*

So she read on, her face growing blacker and blacker. Zseni read on too, now and then innocently guffawing.

vii.

'Yes! I'm busy, actually!'

'Luce it's me! Florian! Let me in!'

'Go away! You can't come in!'

'Just a mo!'

'No, not a mo!'

'Are you saying "Just for a mo"?'

'*No!* I'm saying "No"! It's ten in the morning, in point of fact! I'm working! Anyway I detest you!'

'You divest me?'

It's exhausting to quarrel through a door. Lucinda flung it furiously open.

'I said I detest – you,' but did she, entirely?

He looked sleepless. Doubtless this was (as the literature said, her sort of literature) from passion unchecked, rampant, and unassuaged. He looked sleepless and slightly damp, from exertion, not drizzle, because it was a fine winter day. There was a fuzz of droplets along his monobrow. Wholesome desire stirred in Lucinda, and also a less wholesome craving: to ascend out of this overpowering world, and spend an hour in the high thin brittle heaven of art. She was ahead of schedule this morning, she'd finished her notes on Markov chain geostatistics, and – 'Oh come in,' she said, disgustedly.

There was, now that he was close (he kissed her clumsily) an odd air to him. *In point of fact* (as she loved to say) an odd smell. But she was in a hurry now and in no mood to analyse. She waved off the kiss briskly and pointed at her iPad.

'Turn it on. We'll start where we left off last night. No, no we won't, as it happens. We've had enough of the Vicomte de Saint-Saleté. You've spoilt him. Let's get something new. Find the next one in the queue.' Meanwhile she'd lugged out her famous lacquered basket and thrown open the lid.

Chiffon, dimity, drugget, organza. how she exalted over them! *Moiré*, lawn linen so cool under the hot hands of a hero, rasping calico, foulard bound to come loose in a passionate embrace, cambric to get twisted between a heroine's legs. Shantung! Taffeta! The witch's arms grubbed through the varied textures and her ideas grew a little giddy, although you'd not have guessed it from her usual severe look. Softest of soft porn, secret of the ages! Cosmos reduced to boxed fabric, as physics vainly strives to do. Hydrogen, helium, beryllium, boron, pah! – say rather hessian, fustian, bobbinet, buckram. The love that moves shot silk and other cloths! Incantation fixed and irrefragable. Costuming!

Florian, who'd been tapping away at her iPad, now meekly handed it to her. Hither and thither ran the nymph's swift thoughts; her eyes ran over the opening paragraph with expert speed: 'When are we?' A *sultry spring morning in 1754*, that can be done, the lilac-sprigged polonaise of tulle would do (she pulled it out), *Selina Huntingdon, foundress and patroness,* etcetera etcetera, *erect but heaving,* yes yes, that type, *drawing-room, mansion, splendid bejewelled hand, fichu,* she had a *crêpe* fichu (*here*), *staring in desperation at the black-coated form of,* yes, she had one of those as well, russell cord – she dug it from her basket, not particularly clerical with its gold frogging but it would serve.

She flung it savagely at her lover. 'This. And the lisle stockings. No, I said lisle not worsted, you're not a coachman. And this'll do for preaching-bands. No, not in here. Go out on to the staircase and change. And get a move on.'

It was part of her method to have her heroes enter her room (with the blink of her eye she transformed it into a Georgian drawing-room, all gilt and sage-green panelling) already in character. She herself became Lady Huntingdon the instant she donned her polonaise. A noblewoman, as usual. High in the esteem of Society, sultry, erect but heaving. Foundress of something-or-other yet desperate. A subtle role. Doubtless she'd develop it in a page or two – 'Enter, idiot!' she called harshly; Florian sidled back through the door in his black and white and struck an unctuous, expectant pose.

Lucinda prepared for a long speech. The conventions of novelettes call for a talkative opening scene: laborious exposition, laborious innuendo. But no, it seemed Désirée Fuseaux had tweaked the formula. 'Sir,' cried Lucinda distractedly and to her own surprise, 'no more words!' and with a vehement gesture—

viii.

Whether Count Róbert Zseni de Mérföldkő is a likeable buffoon or simply a buffoon depends on your own mood, for he never changes his. That morning Abishag found his merry tittering and rolling-about intolerable. And when, every so often, he read out a particularly choice passage from *Trojan Kisses*, her irritation approached the shrieking-point.

For she was puckering her brow, straining to concentrate. What exactly was Florian doing with his romance, this cruel *ragoût* he'd concocted of his usual dry reading and Hope's pulp? What she'd recommended to him was mere sexual manipulation. *A Sinful Salvation* wasn't that.

What, for instance, was the point of this speech, ten pages long, made by John Wesley? Wesley was standing motionless in the midst of the drawing-room at Spa Fields – nay,

> *the elegantly and commodiously appointed drawing-room furnished in the style* néoclassique *said to be the latest mode in Paris.*

Why was he

> *standing and staring sightlessly, a pillar of black, motionless, addressing without regarding her his cowering bloodied*

mistress Lady Huntingdon, a twisted figure in pink silk who wriggled about his feet amidst the wreckage of a porcelain mantel-clock, awaiting his good pleasure

– eh? It seemed his pleasure was to talk. What on earth was he talking *about*?

> 'At Thrupp last Tuesday, your Ladyship, the work was evenly and gradually carried on. After I had preached for two hours they entered into the very being of my words and it was torment to them. One, and another, and another sank to the earth; they dropped on every side as thunderstruck. A stout young woman fell and writhed crying with loud and dismal shrieks, I am in the belly of hell. The unclean spirit did tear her and she uttered blasphemies. Indecent expressions. Her face was scarlet, then black – these are, as it chances, my Lady, my favourite colours. Are they yours? There was a froth about her jaw. I would have liked to feel her pulse but could not come close because of the multitude carried away in violent fits all about her. Would you care for me to repeat some of her indecencies to you, Madam?'
>
> 'Oh John, please not—' She turned aside her splendid head.
>
> 'Calling out, you understand, or so she reported, from the very belly. Valuable intelligence.'

Wesley was an Oxford don, reflected Margot, before they threw him out, and this is what dons are like. They convince, then stand aside and watch the paroxysms.

> 'At Trull we called up the Power of might upon us and he gloried in possession. My only word to them was Ye are his. A well-dressed woman of about your advanced years, Madam, suddenly shouted out in utmost vehemence, even as in the agonies of death. The thousand contortions of her body shewed how the dogs of hell were gnawing her heart. She cried I am the devil's now, I will be his, I must, I will, I will be damned *and shrieked till her strength was quite gone, then lay as one dead until about four o'clock in the morning.'*

'*Do not send me thither, Sir.*'

'*Be silent. In Brill the vicar dared preach against me, dared name me a demoniac. I defied him. The next morning he was seized and lay squealing* Those hobgoblins; do not you see them? There, there! The room is full of them. See that hobgoblin at the bed's feet! *and so died in despair.*'

'*I do not care to see them, John.*'

'*Strumpet. Last autumn in our Love-Feasts and Watch-Nights in Looe the power was upon them to wound. A dozen, a score of times, they sang through our hymn* Ah! lovely appearance of death. *Again and again they chanted:*

> With solemn delight I survey
>> The corpse, when the spirit is fled,
> In love with the beautiful Clay,
>> And longing – '

'*Longing to join it in bed,*' whispered Lady Huntingdon; she was initiate with the secret paths of Wesley verse.

'*Longing to lie in its stead! With beauteous deliquescent flesh! How the grave summoned them, how they yearned! Night after night many women were seized with a strong pain and constrained to roar aloud like slaughtered bulls, groaning and trembling exceedingly until they reached a pinnacle of blessed suffering, yea, 'til their bodies were convulsed, and then fell back, waxed cold and benumbed, insensible we found to pin-pricks, their hands so clinched they could not be unfolded.*

No, thought Margot, Florian's Wesley wasn't merely chilly the way all dons are chilly. This was something else.

'*Do not mock me, John,*' moaned the Countess. '*You are a good man. Your power is godly.*'

'*I preach as I do, being* feromenos, "borne along", *I know not how. I do not love God, your Ladyship, I never did. I have never believed in the Christian sense of the word. I am employed. I want all the world to come to on* ouk oida, "*I know not what.*" *I have no more fear than love, but of falling into nothing.*'

Margot shook her head. This wasn't right.

> 'Once in Bare, a place in Lancashire, toward dawn the Circuit Superintendent caused me to be woken and come down and behold. There was shouting through the Society Room as of a dozen women being put to the sword. How dreadful and pleasing was the sight. I stood over them, with my arms held before, and spoke no word. Like this.'

Róbert Zseni was snorting, covering his large clean-cut face with his innocent dirty paperback.

> 'At Grike in Cumberland, your Ladyship, immense scandal has been given by those who lately heard me and were buffeted of Satan in an unusual manner, being seized by such a spirit of laughter as they could in no wise resist. One of those has since killed his own child, by a blow upon the head. The Power was mighty in that place.'
> There was a tremble in her splendid vermilion lip.
> 'At Box once when I spoke of Perdition and the whole hall was screaming in utmost distress, it was reported to me that there had been two deaths in my audience. Two females, my Lady, gone to see if it what I said was so. I persevered with my message but that night there were no more.'
> The Countess quailed before him, her hands twisting convulsively at the Mechlin lace of her ensanguined bodice. 'What do you

– here was costume drama with a vengeance! (Zseni was kicking his legs in the air with glee.)

> 'What do you want of me, John?' she cried brokenly. 'What?'
> 'I wish, Madam, to devour you. A pox on your patronage, a pox on whippings. I am bard, oracle and magus of this age. I am the love-god, Man and Woman both, desired by all because neuter. What have I to do with this embrace or that? I hold all the people in my arms, I tear them to gory shreds, they chant of love before me: Stamp it on our face and heart—'

It was the password, and the counter-sign 'Rend our sinful forms apart' came whimpering from Selina's lips against her will.

'You are quite subdued to our common hymnody, my Countess, are you not?' and she thrilled excruciatingly at his contempt. 'What does Plato say in the Ion? *"By means of inspired persons the inspiration spreads to others. As the worshipping Corybantes are not in their senses when they dance, so the poets are not in their senses, they are seized with the Bacchic transport, and possessed."'*

'Only Love to us be given,' sobbed Selina, her forehead grinding against her Turkey rug, 'Lord we ask no other heaven.'

'Even so.' He placed his buckled clerical shoe on her nape, quite lightly. 'I require you also to enter the temple of Eros I have built with my words. The house of fire. Do you understand? To enter. The poetry that falls from me in the pulpit like tongues of fire. I desire you to come in, relish and endure. I want from you what I had from the humble folk of Wales. I went into Wales in the spring, your Ladyship, and when I

'Oh God, Margot, listen to this:

> *'Great Troy is aflame,' Cassandra cried fierily, 'as oft I have foretold, nay its very lofty towers are atremble, yet your heart is aflame, O Prince, with vilest passions, and your mind is not on aught but your throbbing virility'*

– O God!'

Zseni should not have laughed at this sentence. *Throb* (with its cognates) ranks as a special, a sacral term in historical romances. It is the creative Word, or rather discreative Word, bringing a close to a story that has been creeping toward *throb* since its first page. *Throb* is deployed like a nuclear bomb at the end of a long ground war. It is the single maraschino cherry atop the swirl of whipped cream cresting the last pinnacle of banana ice-cream: the final, the supreme expression. It cannot be outdone; once uttered it cannot be repeated or retracted. No novelette long survives the appearance of *throbbing*, and for addicts like Lucinda the word is enough to trigger harsh-shallow-swift breathing, and dilation of blood vessels. It is the last trump, signalling that the fictional world has entered upon its delectable death-rattle.

But Zseni was ignorant of this, and *throb* merely made him fall off the bed.

Abishag broke off her reading to bend her eyes down on him and say: 'Silly brute.'

Yet in that instant (it's odd how the mind works) she understood. She understood the goat smell in the room; and why Florian had cast himself as John Wesley in the spectral world of the romance; and even the gruesome flowers. *Of course* there was no water in the jar. They were an offering but not to Lucinda, they were a votive of thanks, or rather they were like the sprinkle of incense on the burning thigh-fat of the sacrifice itself.

In the course of last night Florian the sweet-minded baby-intellectual had called into himself the force of night, the *brute*. He'd written what was wilfully unclean to encompass the murder of another mind. He'd left the wreckage of the rite on his altar-desk: flowers he'd despatched to the upside-down place of death. They were fading into Persephone's hand, they were forming there fresh and new, the fell goddess was smiling over them, bowing her head under its heavy obsidian crown.

And of course, of course, Florian had already gone back to St Wygefortis, the wicked story preceding him, emailed ahead, to complete the immolation – Zseni looked up in surprise as Abishag dashed from the room, not pausing to slam.

Of course you're sure to be too late, said her tormenting voice, but she hoped and she ran, so wildly that people on Magdalene Street turned to look at her. *She is irretrievably lost.* Cannoning through a gaggle of gowned choirboys, knocking a briefcase from the hand of some dotard, she rounded the corner of Jesus Lane just as Florian, dull-voiced, was coming to the end of his long speech. (Lucinda, wild-eyed, had folded her hands over her throat and backed against the wall.)

> '*I went into Wales in the spring, your Ladyship, and when I opened my doctrine to them they screamed all together as loud as they could. At Splott a vehement noise arose, none could tell whence, and shot like lightning through the whole congregation. The terror and confusion were inexpressible. You might imagine a city taken by storm. As you shall see presently. The people rushed upon each other with the utmost violence, the benches were broken in pieces. Their persons lay here and there and cried aloud, writhing; yea, throbbing—*'

ix.

Margot stands gasping in Abaddon Court, looking up. And the windows of Lucinda's rooms, blank with drawn curtains, gaze back down into her own blank eyes.

Lucinda never draws her curtains by day. She likes to be seen sitting primly at her desk, fiddling with equations, and publicly interfering with isobars. So *he* must be there: the damage is being done.

Margot considers bursting in, and finds she simply doesn't dare.

So that's that. She may as well creep away. She's far too ashamed to report her failure to Culpepper. She goes back to her room without speaking to a soul, makes sure to shut the door gently, so her neighbours won't know she's back. *Felix was less cruel*, remarks the voice as she locks the door and tumbles backward on to her bed, *he unscrewed the lid.*

x.

Bong, bong, bong, bong, bong: six, seven, eight, chimed the bells of the Round Church, and Great St Mary's, and St Bene't's. *Bong, bong, bong*; and on *twelve* Little St Mary's took up the prolonged clatter of the Angelus. *Ding-ding-ding; ding-ding-ding*: hard silvery music pulsing through pale still chilly air. Panicky rooks, like black smoke, burst out of this sand-coloured tower and that. In libraries white faces looked up, peered at watches, nodded, began to ponder lunch.

There was stillness in Abaddon Court. Margot had long since gone away. Lucinda's beige curtains remained drawn.

If you looked through them you'd have made out in the dimness the apparent *débris* of a massacre. The furniture was flung about, the bed smashed, the bedclothes draped over toppled shelves or hanging from the jags of the overhead light. The lining of one curtain was shredded and bore the confused glossy prints of a hand wet perhaps with vomit. There was a trail of what was certainly blood leading across the carpet from a mess of broken glass to the upended table, and a thicker smear of blood down the standing mirror.

Florian lay prone, face down, legs under the bed, his parsonical coat hunched over the back of his head. Lucinda seemed to have been flung against the wall. She was propped like a broken doll, left hand grasping, piercing the bare skin above her left knee; her right arm was flung over her head, fixed, fingernails dug into the plaster behind her. Her eyes (one blackened) were open, but it would be hard to say if she could see, or whether that was meant to be a grin, or if she could even speak: there was something about her that suggested human language was at an end.

But this is a mistake, for after some minutes she lifted her exhausted head and muttered 'F-F-F.' A lull. 'Fu-fu-fu,' she croaked, mechanically, uncertainly, as if some dial were being set to the right language. '*Fuseaux*,' she managed at last in a voice of terrible peace, her own voice as to tone but with each syllable oddly separate. 'Means *ski-pants*. One of your nicknames.' Florian opened his eyes, focused on some point a quarter of a mile beyond the wall. 'For me.' Florian shook his head, puzzled or pained, and she added, hastily 'Me. Luce. Not Selina. She has – gone now. Gone back.'

Florian's mouth (also gory; bitten through the skin below the bottom lip) moved as if he were chewing. Puke and pink dribble ran over his chin. He wiped it cautiously away with his palm but said nothing, merely releasing a noise with a slight hiss to it, like the memory of a giggle. Mr Wesley did not giggle, so presumably Florian too had returned.

Now Lucinda was flexing her fingers. There was a hunk of black curly hair, his, poking through the knuckles of her left hand; she tried to toss the lock aside but her hand was apparently too sticky, she had to rub it harshly against the tulle of her ruined dress. 'I knew. It was really you.'

'Me,' he said with terrible effort. 'No'; he raised his head from the soiled carpet and shook it, then seemed unable to stop shaking it. 'No, not, not.'

'Oh I know it wasn't you just now,' said Lucinda, harshly but almost with briskness. She was reviving wonderfully. In a moment she would be able to stand. 'That was the real Mr Wesley, in point of fact. And all the words you got us to say. *They* weren't you either.'

Florian's head-wobbling became more pronounced. 'No. No.'

'To be entirely precise, they were *his*. You copied them all from him. You put us both in *his* mind.' The composed rancour with which she said this made Florian whimper; his head-shaking stopped and he bent his neck back, trying to fix his eyes on her. 'And Mr W. got them from. From.' Here her voice became lower than a whisper, no sound came out as she mouthed 'The Manager' but Florian seemed to understand, and the saying was enough to make another bubble of vomit spill over his chin. She leaned forward and his head flinched back. 'But I mean that it was you who summoned Mr W. You let him script us. *You are Désirée Fuseaux!*'

Then Florian really did manage a hellish giggle – *not* (he explained to himself decades afterward, reflecting on that afternoon in his donnish way) the sort he imagined devils might utter; rather the sound the damned possibly make in access of despair, when the devils have just done something new *to* them.

It was exhausting to shake and giggle so much. After a while his face sank back to the carpet and he went to sleep. His belly-noises were quite unlike his normal snores.

Lucinda put her own face on an angle to look into his. *Yes,* she thought, *there's some good damage here. When at last he goes staggering back to Magdalene in his torn costume he'll terrify passers-by. But it's just physical. To be perfectly accurate. Collateral. Fleeting. He's had his fun, now he's free.* She traced his monobrow for the last time. *You've paid soul for soul. Back to your frigid habits of mind, little Florian.* She could see his whole life dribbling down a crack in the ground before her. He'd dwindle into getting a First, dwindle into being a don, fidget his life away with eighteenth-century footnotes. No doubt he would give up the Methodistical carry-on as a topic altogether too thrilling. He'd settle on mercantile returns to the Board of Trade. Game-law enforcement. Canal maintenance in the first years of George III – some speciality of that sort. This excellent hair would grizzle and recede; he would at last become himself.

Lucinda shrugged. *Mortals.* Last night she had wielded powers from another age, uttering words from beyond herself; she could not imagine returning to a small individual life. So there was nothing to decide now. The choice had been made in her as she convulsed – as she lay ranting in the lowest fold of that black unspeakable gulf out in space, as it seemed to her; like the well-dressed woman of Trull whom Cerberus tore, who shrieked *I will be his* and sprawled dead 'til morning at the prophet's feet. Lucinda was content.

She found, on the second attempt, that she was able to stand. She propped open her suitcase on the wreck of her bed and filled it with socks, underwear, black ski-pants, black T-shirts. (She was rolling forward over her preordained route like a tram. She resembled, in fact, a character in a bustling story, a story controlled by someone outside her own space and time.) There: packed already. She'd be at Heathrow by two if she went by cab. She'd empty her accounts at an airport cashpoint and pay the driver. It didn't matter about money, she knew there'd soon be much more.

She was about to go when she spotted the big dressing-up basket, turned over in a corner. With a final human spasm of disgust she tugged it open. *Ridiculous toys.* She buried her arms in it, pulled open her window, and tossed what she held into the air.

Doublets and hoop-skirts, breeches, frock-coats and chemises, scabbards, busbies and Viking helmets: the whole equipment went clattering and fluttering until the basket was empty. The court was a storm of cheap costuming. And so quickly did she fly down the stairs (administering a great kick to Florian as she went, just short of cracking a rib) that she was out the door and across the court before the last bits had finished floating to the ground.

A certain sort of undergraduate runs away from College every term. But Lucinda was never one for romantic folly. It was not a gesture. She meant never to come back to St Wygefortis'; it was far too puny; she was loosing herself on the world.

Lint the porter read the look in her eyes as she went striding furiously through the Lodge with her single case. 'We'll not be seein' 'er again and none too soon if you ask me,' he told whoever would listen. But who ever attends to Lint?

xi.

THE ~~MERRIE MONTH~~ DARLING BUDS OF MÆNADS

by ~~Lucinda~~ Lulu Crompe

CHAPTER I. A ~~MISERABLE~~ TRAGIC END

The flowery meads athwart Cithæron, lofty mount of Bœotia, rippled with winsome breezes from off the peak, which sportively set bands of shadow to chase each other across the glades. Even so, mayhap, youths from the royal citadel of Thebes had chased fair maidens through these same grasses in the first vernal stirring of the year. But now, in high summer, now in *Hekatombaion,* ~~merry~~ month of ~~bloody~~ gory sacrifice and sacred orgy, the oleander and pine bowed bosky heads over a solitary figure, a man young howbeit full-grown, who dashed across the broad clearing with no

sportive ~~mean~~ mien, glancing ever over his *chiton*-hung
shoulder with apprehension and it may be, dread. Yet he was

'I'm sorry, ma'm. Ma'm. Ma'm, can you *hear* me? The cap'ain has not
yet turned off de fasten-*seat-belt* sign. You'll have to close up your laptop
and put your tray in an upright – *ma'm?*'
'In point of fact,' says Lucinda without looking up, still tapping –

may be, ~~dread~~. terror. Yet he was, withal,

'– we have levelled off, so the sign's about to go off.'
'Ma'm, can you please, *please*—'
Ping.
'There.'
'*Well.*'
'Go. I said, Go.'
'Lordie, Lordie,' mutters the stewardess, waddling away down the
fuselage, 'dare's always *one*, dare's always one and even dough I done draw
the long straw and gets Business *I* gets dat *one*. Four hours and ten minutes
to J.F.K. and I have to have de *one*. Lordie have *mercy*', &c &c.

he was, withal, of royal bearing and goodly form, with
bewitching gold-flecked hazel eyes below a single well-drawn
eyebrow, ~~and a splendid muscular breast down which a finger
might a~~ and a wide brow that hinted at deep, and as it might
be impious thoughts, thoughts mocking and belitting the
mysterious Powers.
    To his peril!
    For Pentheus – such was the young king's name – had not
yet gained the shady shelter of the further wood when the
~~fearful~~ frightful view-halloo was raised in shrill, rapturous
female tones: 'He's there! The lion-cub!'
    The youthful King of Thebes glanced back in despair. Once
they had sighted him hardly could he hope to outrun such fell
pursuers, for there was an unnatural swiftness to them, as also
an unnatural strength.
    Yea, here they were, streaming out of the woods behind
him! A rabble of passing beautiful women, their locks
becomingly loose and streaming, their loose pale gowns

whipped out behind, bright breasts heaving with the chase, bright fillets bound about every temple. Each running foot was bare, each pair of eyes sparkled with divine inebriation, and each right hand bore a wand of fennel impaling a pine-cone, wound about with vine-leaves: the dread thyrsus, upon which no man may lawfully look.

And yet he, even he, Pentheus had dared to steal up the ~~valleys~~ vales of Cithæron to spy on the Bacchic rites. What madness! What had prompted him?

Was it not love?

Aye, was it not wild, destructive love for the wondrous Lycaste in her fine black chiton? Lycaste, wise student of the mysteries of nature? Lycaste who nonetheless had gone forth to revel on the mountainside with all the women of Thebes at the summoning of the new god Dionysus, magus of the age?

Alack, the fierce women had seen him! And came on amain. Without hope yet without pause Pentheus tore on, on toward the dim light beyond the broad clearing, beneath the further trees. And as he ran he heard them raise behind him the cry '*Evoë, evoë!*', proper formula of the bacchanal. '*Bacchus!*', they howled, '*Bromios!*' They were calling the Power upon them, the Power who glories in possession and sometimes appeared to them, standing over them with his arms held before, speaking no word, smiling his weird androgynous smile, the cause of holy frenzy though himself serene. They entered the being of his words and knew his joyous torment, his power to wound; they fell about groaning like slaughtered bulls, and rose trembling, lithe as panthers. How they burned with desire for him! Princesses of the house of Cadmus, serving-women from the palace, artisans' wives from the town, she-peasants from the farms, drab and crone, nymph and matron, all! '*Evoë!*': Pentheus heard the same shout from two score gaping mouths. All of them his Theban people, his subjects, his very kin!

He would appeal to them!

No!

Too late! Like bounding beasts of predation, a dozen Mænads had cut across the glade in front of him, barring him from the woods. They stood ranged before him, ~~scarcely~~ scarce panting, and he swung back at bay, to face the whole mob.

All of them, all of them!

Amongst the chortling rushing throng he made out his mother, Agavë, coming on with the swiftness of a hunting-hound, his aunts Ino and Autonoë, usually so cool, so respectable, dishevelled as from ravishment. With them were many a fair one he had possessed in his mad years of conquest, then flung aside. Callichore, Ereutho, Calyce, Ocynoë – all the frolicsome *belles* of Theban High Society: a score of faces he knew yet did not know, so glowing were their cheeks, so supernaturally bright their eyes, washed clean of human recognition. How had they been so changed? What watch-nights and love-feasts they had been keeping on the mountain!

Stumbling, the wretched king found himself on his knees. It was the same Greek sun he had always known above, the same lucid blue, the usual meadow about him; yet all was impossibly different. 'Mother! Dear mother! Relent!' he cried, knowing it was useless.

'Hist! The mountain lion roars!' shouted Queen Agavë, pointing her thyrsus, then with dreadful skill flinging it, as if 'twere a very javelin. Full in his monobrow it struck him, and for an instant he could not see, only hear his parent's feral shriek of triumph: 'First blood to me! O sisters, Bacchus aids me in the hunt! The prey is ours! *Evoë!* On!'

A foot had caught Pentheus in the throat and he sprawled in the grass. He opened his eyes and behold, it was the most terrible and alluring of all the Bacchantes standing over him, silver-footed Lycaste herself, his lost belovèd, puissant and thoughtless in her ecstasy as any animal.

Yet was she in sooth wholly thoughtless? Had traces of their passages of *amour* been altogether dashed from the tablet of her heart? Was it not love unavowed, breaking through her beastly hunger, that made her breast to heave, daubing a little with pallor the roses in her cheeks? Did her passion not answer him even now? He flung a forearm over his perspiring face. 'What is it,' he wondered in his final hopelessness, 'about your wild Bacchic unreserve that beguiles me so? What have you that no wanton Theban beauty ever yet possessed? Why am I stirred as never in my years of rule?'

Then he thought no more, for their hands were upon him, frantic to right his blasphemy against the god.

Dire it was yet wonderful, this breaking up of his body! Chaotic and yet shaped of order, for the Power of might was on them, directing them and giving euphoric strength.

Ino it was who tugged at his curly hair. A hundred fingernails peeled the flesh from his flanks. But it was Autonoë who put her buskined foot on his shapely chest, seized him about the left wrist, and pulled, straining, her ferocious grunts like those of any wild creature.

Pentheus' face was a mask of perfect anguish. 'Unhand me, you brute!' And so she did.

The royal blood, spraying from his stump, lashed the women like a hot liquid whip, splashing in mouths gaping with rhapsodic laughter. Their blinded eyes rolled up in divine frenzy so only the whites showed. Never, in any luxurious folly of love, had they known such convulsive spasm of pleasure, never such perfect rapture, as in this throbbing flesh.

They had triumphed over him, the insolent historian prince, the young mountain-lion! Now his right arm was off, both arms, one leg prised off above the knee. Yea, the other too! His mother had his head locked between her elbows, tugging; an instant more and she would have it off.

But slim Lycaste had thought for but one trophy. Between the thighs the angry Mænad reached, elegant hands splayed as the talons of an eagle, lovely nails clogged with black blood. And Pentheus threw back his head, uttering a throttled howl as his neck-muscles gave way above the collar bone: 'I am unmanned!'

CHAPTER 2. A ~~GLAD~~ GLADSOME BEGINNING.

Not thus had King Pentheus first seemed to Lycaste two

springs afore the fatal day, when first she came to Thebes, to
study at the city's famed philosophic schools.

Well she recalled that primal morning in the *palæstra*
when she had seen, comely in his royal vesture, the blooming
monarch

'*What?*' She is furiously aware that someone is leaning over her, talking.
'I been saying, ma'm: salmon or *beef*?'

'Beef. Stop. Come back. Have you cooked it yet? No matter. Bring it to
me anyway. That's all. *Go.*'

'Sweet Jesus have mercy on me, three hours and fifty-one minutes to
New York... Where da devil do they *find* dem?'

xii.

```
103500/02/14/13/CBA/ccJH&GS >>>>
RAW TRANSCRIPT NOT FOR CIRCULATION>>>>
***CHECKED BM/PA

live 10:35:04EST Feb/14/2013
CREDITS ROLL 3'44''

10:38:58EST Feb/14/2013
VOICEOVER: Welcome to The Murgatroyd Report! With BEULAH
MURGATROYD!

[AUD.: Applause up
[AUD.: Applause dim

BM: Good morning America. Thank you thank

[AUD.: Applause fade out

Yes. Yes. Welcome to our Valentine's Day special, coming
to you live from NEW YORK CITY, the most romantic town in
America.
```

[AUD.: Applause

Yes! You're you're great. [Laughing.] Thank you, New York,
I love you too.

[AUD.: Whooping, applause

This this Valentine's morning I have with me one of the
most controversial erotic writers in our country today.
It was just four short weeks ago that this young British
woman published her first novel online and in that time
it has gone just gone stellar. She has been lauded as
the newest most challenging voice of feminism. Says one
Princeton professor Never before has the popular light
novel spoken so radically nor been so authentic to women's
real frenzy. But she has stirred unease even downright
questioning amongst mainstream feminists while roiling
just a BUNCH of conservative opinion-makers. Big time! I
mean, Tuesday she was characterized on the floor of the
House of Representatives as I'm think I'm going to read
Congressman Nuckles' words out to get them right

[AUD.: Scattered laughter

as a a hellhag pornographer in

[AUD.: Laughter up

in league with unAmerican powers of the night.

[AUD.: Scattered laughter

That first novel The Darling Buds which quote turns the
bodice-ripper into the body-ripper unquote has sold three
million that's three MILLION copies online and has already
been optioned by Paramount Pictures for 2.3 million
dollars.

[AUD.: Scattered applause

And she tells me there's more where that came from!

[AUD.: Scattered laughter

I think she's going to share with us about her latest project this morning. So let's have big Valentine's Day welcome for Ms Lulu Crompe!

[AUD.: Applause up
[AUD.: Applause down

BM: Welcome, Lulu.
LC: Thank you.
BM: So we're here in New York and I took your book on the plane over from from LA -
LC: Uh-huh.
BM: With this really in-your-face cover art and blood and stuff, and this, this off-the-wall title, MAIND, MAH-ENID, whatever

[AUD.: Scattered laughter

and I said to myself, Beulah, I guess this must be to do with Mae West. But then I read it and it was like wow this is just out there this is like nothing else. So I'd want you just to to explain really just who the heck these girls ARE.
LC: Maenads?
BM: Maenads, yeah.
LC: Well, Beulah, in ancient Greece women were oppressed and and their search for self-discovery was totally disrespected and denied and and
BM: I hear you.
LC: Then this new religion came along. This new god, Dionysus, who preached self-affirmation to them and filled them with with this healing mania and and it was just just a new beginning for them so
BM: Wow. Yeah.
LC: So the women because it was only women you know would

come to him and the established priests said No this is
mad this wild new god, but they they
BM: They were empowered. I I can empa I empathize with
that.
LC: Yes, in point of fact. They were. Full of the Power.
The words of the god dug down into them, tapping this this
source, this energy. This special sort of of love.
BM: That that motivates me. Just where I am now.
LC: So they'd just run out of the city, throw down their
kettles or spindles or
BM: Or whatever. No homemaking for THESE homemakers today,
no sir!

[AUD: Scattered laughter.

LC: Out, up to the mountain. They'd be together up there
together for days and nights. Dancing wildly, singing
hymns, again and again, dozens of times, till they fell.
BM: Freeing themselves. Sisters loosing the inner, the the
LC: Looking for. Finding finding
BM: DISCOVERING themselves.
LC: Finding wild animals. Which they'd tear to pieces. And
men too if the men came to spy on them.
BM: My.
LC: It was called sparagmos as it happens. Sparagmos. It's
very very erotic. And it was was a miracle. The maenads
were so strong. Their fingers were so so they'd just be
able
BM: But this sparag, sporog, whatever, SHEESH. You have
this scene of it in your first chapter and I have to I have
to I felt Where's the romance there? It is this is this
building and affirming or whatever or is it what?
LC: Actually it is, you see. These girls were getting
intimate for the first time, they were -
BM: OK, OK, I can relate. Their inner spirits were
reaching, reaching out. They were connecting.
LC: The man wasn't treating them as objects NOW, he was
was
BM: They were in charge. Strong women.

LC: Totally. So he became the object for them. He was. And
after sparagmos for these women came omophagia.
BM: Homophobia? Now I just need, I have to say for a
modern woman's there's no place for for
LC: Omophagia. What they tore they'd eat and
BM: Wow. Eat it. Some WEIRD diet choices going down there.
Wow. It's just the right moment for for I guess for
commercial break! Lulu Crompe! We'll be back with more of
this challenging stuff in one minute!

[AUD.: Loud applause

– but there is no applause in the Junior Combination Room of St Wygy's;
where a hundred undergraduates, hearing that Lucinda, the deserter, is to
make her *debut* on *The Murgatroyd Report*, have assembled to jeer at the
screen. Margot and Ollie sit grimly in the back row. Everyone else hoots
at Lucinda, then hoots even more joyously at the advertisement. This, in
accord with American sensibilities, so prim about genitals, is unreticent
about the tracts behind. 'Love candy but know it doesn't love you?' A
platinum blonde, clutching a gigantic heart of chocolates bound with a
pink ribbon, stares moodily at the camera. 'Afraid chronic heartburn will
spoil your special festive meal this Valentine season?' The blonde becomes
tragically apprehensive. 'Before your blow-out, fuel up on Belchaway—' The
undergraduates grow so raucous they drown out the ad, and do not quieten
down until the blonde, now grinning with satiety, and dangling the flaccid
ribbon from her finger, fades into a resumption of the main event.

** COMMERCIAL BREAK 3'44''
live 10:47:14EST Feb/14/2013

BM: I'm here live in New York with Lulu Crompe whose
online novel The Darling Buds of Maenads has sold let me
check this yes twelve thousand copies. Is that right Erik?
Twelve THOUSAND copies since we've been on air -
LC: Thank you. Thank you.

[AUD.: Scattered applause.

[AUD.: Boo.

So you've got millions of readers out there, and in the
last few minutes you've got twelve thousand more, and
I have to ask: are you worried at all about how they're
they're going to take it?
LC: Take it?
BM: I mean it's not like a mainstream women's romance, is
it? And there are
LC: It's new, it's
BM: Yeah, but what I mean what I'm saying is aren't you
worried about the copy-cat violence?
LC: Um no because -
BM: Well let's hear, let's hear from your biggest critic
on that point. Representative Randy Nuckles, Republican
of North Dakota, has just phoned in to the studio from
Bismarck - will you, Erik, Erik? Will you put him on?
Congressman?
RN: How you doing, Beulah? Just want to say I'm a great
fan of yours.
BM: Yeah, great, thank you. Now I have with me Ms Lulu
Crompe, and I understand you're co-sponsoring a bill to
have her book um um
RN: Burned by the public hangman, Beulah, that's the
language. We still have a hangman out here and even if
crazed judicial activism stands in the way of capital
punishment as such, we sure as heck are going to use him
to do SOME freaking good, cleaning up this great big state
of ours.
BM: Wow, wow, that's really - but do you think that's an
appropriate response, Congressmen, to a novel?
RN: A novel? I'll tell you what it is, Beulah, it's an
incitement to cannibalism. In my district alone there have
been two cases of women, women who have read Darling Buds,
going out -
LC: I need to stop you right there, Congressman. I mean,
the point is, it's fiction, yeah? Art. And and what
can fiction have to do to do with what people actually
actually.

BM: Yeah, yeah. I hear you.
RN: Miss Crompe, I have to tell you, you just git. Git
back on that airplane and git back to Europe where this
sort of devil-worshipping -
BM: Congressman -
RN: This sort of soft-on-Satan so-called art -
LC: Silence, worm. What I'm saying is, this is affirming
stuff. Women have to look in this story, it's just a story
but it's not, because they say, Yeah girl that's who I am,
that's where I'm at.

[AUD: Scattered applause

I have to meet me where I am.

[AUD: Applause up

BM: So so

[AUD: Applause down

BM: So what's your response to that, Congressman?
RN: Guh. Guh.
BM: Congressman? Are you all right?
RN: Guh.
BM: All right, I hope you feel better soon Congressman.
Scary stuff. Let's move on. Let's have Lulu Crompe tell us
um um about the movie version of her book.
LC: Well Paramount loved it but but.
BM: But there are already problems with with its ratings,
right?
LC: So unfair, Beulah. Before it's been shot, before it's
even scripted. There's been lots of negativity coming at
us. But we're fighting it.
BM: You're a fighter! That's great. You're still in
process, your energy is your passion. I celebrate your
excellence right there.
LC: Yeah. The power's with me.
BM: And you're already you tell me you're already working

on your next book.
LC: Yes, I am. It's -
BM: Tell us about that.
LC: It's set in Mississippi before the Civil War, and it's
about a young woman from Boston, she inherits a plantation
from a great-uncle so she goes down there to to run it.
BM: A-huh. A-huh.
LC: But it's economically challenged, it's overgrown.
So she's she's looking for her integrity, she's saying
she's asking herself how can I hold together, you know,
my strong physical desires, because they are strong, I'm
really upfront about that, and my this girl's need to get
this this cotton worked, to make the place rich again.
BM: And failure's not an option.
LC: That's it! She has the plantation, it's a family
place from way back. And she has this body of labor, but
it hasn't been used properly I mean really worked by her
great uncle
BM: Who's deceased.
LC: That's it. He had substance issues, alcohol, tobacco
products, and he he just let them you know, he wasn't
proactive about getting them out of the cabins. So she
feels alienated, alienated from her labor force, she has
to has to really own it. And part of that is acknowledging
the pain of who she is, and learning to pass on that pain.
Use it. Make it productive, positive. Harvest her anger,
make it pay.
BM: Great. Great. And and what's it called, this new book?
LC: The Touch of your Listful Whips.
BM: Wistful - wow that's - that's another tongue-twister
right there.

[AUD.: Loud laughter

But not in the Senior Combination Room of St Wygy's: there is no
laughter there.

The Master, never well-informed, has been roused from his siesta to
come and see the reputation of his College being dragged in the mire.
He is not pleased to find a score of Fellows already sitting about the

television, all tittering – all, that is, except Jake Osgood, who watches with professional seriousness, for he too is author of dross, and aspires one day to sink this far.

'An *American* television programme,' murmurs the Master to himself, ponderously. He's never at his sharpest in the early afternoon, before he's metabolised his Chablis. 'An interview. With, it would seem, a social worker.' He addesses his Fellows. 'Who is this creature? *Is* she a Wygian? *Is* she an undergraduate here?'

'She *was*, Master,' they tell him, 'In a manner of speaking', 'Vanished in the first week of term', 'I think we can now properly send her down', 'Dignity of College', 'Writing a *women's novel*,' 'Quite.'

'Let's not expel our bacchante,' says the lazy voice of Felix Culpepper, 'let's lure her back – ask her to lecture on literature, perhaps – then stone her to death with port bottles. Thus the dignity of College is preserved.'

The Master's brain is still fuddled.

'Bacchantes? What's all this she's saying about bacchantes? What are you teaching your classicists, Culpepper?'

'Nothing to do with me, Master,' Culpepper says smoothly. He's reclining in the best armchair, long legs stretched out selfishly so the other dons have to step high to get at the chocolate digestives. 'I never had the pleasure of meeting Miss Crompe. She is, was, reading geography.'

Blackhall, the geography Fellow, is flustered. 'But she was a *good* student, Master. No sign of writing, or *anything* like that.'

'Nonsense. You say she was here until four weeks ago? She must already have composed this filth. You ought to have known.'

'Not necessarily, Master,' purrs Culpepper. 'In contemporary culture four weeks is a long time. Cyclic velocity of late capitalism.' (The Master, a Marxist theorist, says 'Ah!', and the more adventurous intellectuals say 'Quite' and 'So to speak.') 'People write at the speed of typing, Master. Publish online in a couple of minutes. Famous by nightfall. Hollywood rings in the morning. *Mænads* will be in cinemas before Easter. Before Long Vac it'll have been supplanted by something even more vicious. I don't think we need worry.' If he felt guilty about Margot applying his methods to Lucinda, well, that was four weeks ago; a long time.

'Have you *read* it?'

'I took a deep breath, Master, and plunged in my head. As into a lavatory bowl – in some Midland suburb, you understand, well-scrubbed, fuming with industrial-floral scent. A few pages were all I could stand. That's enough. Velocity, you know.'

At that moment, in the studio in New York, Lucinda does indeed appear to be enjoying the onward rush of late capitalism. She's smilingly cocking her head to hear the breathless blather of another commercial break ('Don't let bleeding rectal ulcers be a pain in the butt. Let Fundaklenz...') above the sudden stampede of technicians into the studio, scolding the audience for being too quiet, turning up lights, wheeling cameras back and forth, and padding powder on the suddenly drawn, sweaty features of Miss Murgatroyd, whom Erik, the director, is haranguing: 'Emote, darling, emote *less*.' His marvellously-manicured fingers gesture like a perverse fisherman boasting of his measly catch, a minnow, a minnow not of age, scarcely a catch at all. 'Less,' he pleads. Beulah Murgatroyd – shrinking from Erik, shrinking from the cosmetician, from Lulu most of all – says nothing. Lulu leans far forward to lay a hand on her sleeve.

'It's going well,' she says, 'we all think so,' and her hostess is still blinking at that *all*, trying to get her television face back on, as the light on the camera turns red.


```
** COMMERCIAL BREAK 3'44''
live 10:57:14EST Feb/2/2013


BM: Um. Um. Yes. I'm here in in New York with Lulu
Crompe controversial author of Maenads the most the most
challenging debut novel I've read and that means EVER.
LC: Thank you Beulah. I'm a great fan of yours too.
BM: Yeah, great. But let's get back to you for a moment. I
understand that until last month you were studying at at a
British school? At Cambridge college?
LC: I was. Actually. But then I had this idea for, for a
whole a whole new sort of women's writing. I left to fulfil
that that mission. There was this morning when, when
BM: It was your AHA moment.
LC: Not so much AHA as Venite in nocte puellae.
BM: Your subconscious speaks to you in Spanish? That's
- that's, I don't know what that is but it's [laughing
nervously].

[AUD.: Slight laughter
  LC: It it is.
```

BM: Anyhow, you just, you just quit college? I'm going to
take you up there and and. I'm just going to put it to you
you know, right up. Are you, are you saying that's right?
Aren't there people out there who are going to say, Hey
girl, what the? Aren't they going to say I question your
priorities, I question your morality?
LC: Well, Beulah, it's the the you know the role of the
artist. You don't choose it. It comes and and just chooses
you and that's who you have to be
BM: [Nodding] Yeah I've been there, I see where you're
coming from.
LC: So a voice said, the States is where they're going to
click, it's where it'll make a difference. You go there.
So I wrote Maenads on the plane
BM: On the PLANE?
LC: Yeah it's not the best place, they keep coming
and interrupting you. But you know, you get into your
own place when you create. Your fiction, any art taken
seriously is out of the world, down to a
BM: These are deep thoughts. You seem to have a lot of
things going on inside.
LC: My real name is Legion because we are so many.
BM: Er. Wow. That's quite a - that didn't even sound like
your voice. And okay, that isn't even like your smile now.
It's

[AUD.: An isolated shriek.

xiii.

*Dear Oliver. Naturally you haven't written for days and why
should you, I don't expect you to trouble yourself about an
abandoned hag divorcée like your old mother.*

*I am due to write to ask if you are working hard not like last
term. Being careful of yourself and your things. Keeping early
hours, and keeping away from girls, no good can come of such
things as I know all too well. But don't bother lying to me.*

Ollie's blood wasn't curdled, it took more than this. His mother had sounded acid since daddy left, and he read on comfortably.

I have been much bothered, no one worries about interrupting me they just plunge in with distracting news, in this case a tidbit from cousin Julia Mordaunt. Her second daughter Hope, the one who visited you in Cambridge last month (and you said was all right but you never tell me the whole truth do you) has hanged herself in the shed behind their knot garden, ghastly affair, the box topiary is in a state but as she's forever falling out with her gardener and not talking to him there's no point in telling her, I tried it once (about the boating-pond) and she was rude flatly rude to my face.

Of course the Mordaunts are a crazed lot, the wonder is they all haven't done away with themselves especially when you see what their place looks like in winter, the National Trust won't take it off their hands because it would never do for weddings. Perhaps now that Hope's enlivened it they'll be able to hire it out for the occasional Society exorcism. (That was meant as a joke, Oliver, to show that my spirit isn't broken yet.)

Julia vexes me further by sending me this book, which I think I might have been spared. She says, but Julia being Julia who can be sure if she's got this right, Hope borrowed from someone at Cambridge called Abishag (not a likely name is it) and would I etcetera? Here it is, and if you know where to return it well and good. It was apparently Hope's constant study over her last few weeks, so is no doubt wholesome reading of the sort modern universities

'You look awful.' He looked up, blinking, and there above him, to his extreme regret, was Margot, precisely the last person he wanted to see. 'Ollie, *are* you all right…? Do you need something from Mrs Oathouse?' He managed to shake his head. 'Well, do you – what's this? Oh, my Osgood. *Sandcastles in a Sandstorm.* Nice to get it back. I suppose. And – y'want me to read this letter…? Ollie? All right.'

Since he was leaning forward with his hand over his eyes, he couldn't see her read, but he heard her breathing grow more harsh. Then that stopped, and when he took away his hand and looked up she was silently gone, and the bright empty unclean sky looked one notch wetter.

xiv.

Although brilliant, Margot lived at a much lower moral level than Ollie, and her first impulse was *gauche*: she'd void her pain by passing it along, like the momentum of a Newton's Cradle. Osgood slays (*click*) Hope scarifies (*click*) Lady Mordaunt embitters (*click*) Mrs Vane-Powell grieves Ollie crushes Margot disowns Felix…She found Felix crossing Megiddo Court and got in front of him, holding the letter in one hand and *Sandcastles in a Sandstorm* in the other, stolidly blocking the way to his staircase. A fine rain was beginning to mist the air and blur the buildings. Felix, who disliked getting wet, looked impatient.

'Yes?'

'I've killed somebody,' she said heavily. 'I used your methods and I killed.'

'Did you indeed? Was that interesting?' (She recognised this breezy sadism. It was dissimulated self-pity.)

'A schoolgirl. An preposterous visiting schoolgirl.'

'The company you keep. And you a venerable twenty-year-old. When was this fell deed wrought?'

'Four weeks ago. The evening you were in London with Seb—'

'Converting,' said Felix, brightening, 'the deplorable Pocock to righteousness. Oh yes'; and this was true. Four weeks is a long time in politics. Kenneth Pocock had already become famous for unsmiling rectitude, and disagreeable devotion to duty. He'd shopped his own press secretary for fiddling her expenses, then forgone his own salary as restitution to the taxpayer. The Prime Minister had nervously promoted him to be Minister for Censorship and Moral Resourcing at the Home Office. Pocock was now just as popular in the right-wing qualities (as "the Cato of the modern world", as "the Randy Nuckles of the Old World") as he'd been, four long weeks before, in the tabloids. '*Pocock*,' said Felix contentedly: 'one of my masterworks.'

'And it was the same night I, you know, set up Lucinda—'

'Ho ho, so it was. You *were* a busy magician's apprentice. Consigning the appalling Lulu to the underworld!' He'd long got over his irritation. 'We saw her yesterday on telly in the Combination Room. I could feel this black aura radiating from the screen. The Master—'

'I need to tell you about it.'

'About what? The Crompe's aura?'

'The schoolgirl.'

'Let's go in, then, out of the murk.'

'No.'

'Very well, tell,' and he kept up a patient-enough demeanour, standing in the hazy damp, while she confessed.

Afterward, he laughed. '"Whenever you feel like a love story read five pages of Osgood": *excellent* voodoo! His gibberish would make her feel bleak, bleakness would make her nostalgic for girly pulp, she'd have to go back to him. An inescapable spiral.'

'Felix—'

'Don't try it again, mind. My methods are copyright. Even when I'm away. I can't have you flailing about with my weaponry, slaughtering and damning left and right.'

'Felix—'

'Also, make sure Jake Osgood doesn't hear about it, he's insufferable when he's chalked up a death. Oh yes, don't flatter yourself, he annihilates readers all the time. It doesn't take *you* to market his poison. Grieving parents rarely mention their brat's last book to reporters or policemen, why should they? But they send Osgood letters of reproach. Which he brings in to breakfast. "Read this, Culpepper. After you've passed the marmalade. My insupportable truth strikes again, you see. My irresistible words, what a curse." Whereas it's *my* power, of course, make-believe, not pessimism, that—'

'Felix.'

'You've heard that Pocock wants a Royal Commission into nihilist non-fiction and teenage suicide? That would mean Osgood being subpœnaed to give evidence at Westminster. When he gets back he'll be so full of himself life won't be...' He brooded for moment, then added somberly: 'I think it's time I dealt with him', and it struck Margot that a Newton's Cradle goes back as well as forth. Seb suborns Felix abandons Margot inflicts Osgood tortures Hope (the outermost ball-bearing); but then, after a tiny stillness, throttles Hope crushes Margot maddens Felix punishes Osgood...

Felix, however, had fallen away from the question of Jake Osgood and the salvation of the young. He was back with his main idea, which was that he detested getting wet. 'Enough chit-chat. Come inside.'

'But she was *human*.'

'Who was? Oh, the schoolgirl. Why d'y'say that?' He crossly shook some water from the fringe of his hair. 'How can you possibly know? You say you were only with her a few hours. No doubt she had eyes, legs, a head, but so does a gingerbread man. Humanity's rare.'

'Felix, I'm in distress. I've murdered a child. *Explain why you don't care*' – she said this so emphatically that undergraduates hurrying across Megiddo glanced round at this interesting lovers' quarrel. Even the dull chemist Ebbe, whose rooms were just above them, found it necessary to appear blinking at his window.

Culpepper filled his lungs and said all at once: 'The world's crammed deep as the quark and as high as the Oort cloud with entrancing things and tedious humans so that I've never seen why I should particularly care about *them*, every species being a perfect example of itself while each man's so blurred and fifth-rate it's hard to guess what the point was before the point was lost, and although it's true other things don't talk most humans don't talk either, not proper language. And *things* come in such enormous numbers, just a smidgeon short of infinity, there's such glory to attend to it dazzles my eyes – don't you understand? I have to sing in numbers just to ward off the burning brilliance of the smidgeon-less-than-infinity things I know are out there. You tell me that this one girl – Helen?'

'Hope. Hope Mordaunt.'

'Hope spent, what? the last five years of her allotted eighteen nibbling away at lubricious trash. A maggot in compost. This insect came to your attention, so you conjured her with her own dross: *pouf!* She vanishes. That's excellent, that arrests my attention. *I* have forgiven *you* your burglarious misuse of *my* power. But don't expect me to be interested in *her*. It's too much to ask. Too little.'

He had never said as much about himself before, and Margot was silent for a long quarter-minute.

'Speaking of arresting females. I've lunched. I've given up cigars for Lent. Come and share my siesta.'

Another pause. 'Do you love me *at all*, Felix?'

'In my own elaborate fashion. Yes.'

'In your – no, I can't keep up with your tomfoolery. Describe what you mean.'

He drew breath. 'On a mountain beyond Älvdalen named Fulufjället there's a certain mangy-looking spruce known as Old Tjikko. It was a pine-cone ten thousand years ago, about the time humans were perverted by the vice known as art, and started painting cave-walls. I love that tree, I'm utterly in earnest about my delight in it. Its ten thousand years go off in my imagination like fireworks. So do you.'

'I don't just want to stir your imagination.'

'I've explained, I think, that I'm *enraptured* by the universe. Don't trivialise my passion. Utterly in love with it, adoring, dazzled. Or think of Osgood – he belittles it, and kills his readers.'

'You kill too.'

'Yes, but I'm the opposite of Osgood. I'm full of wonder. I arouse people to the stupendous glory. Sometimes that finishes them off.'

'And I arouse you.'

'You're a part of the universe I particularly notice. I compare you to the Challenger Deep, seven miles below the surface, paved with algæ enclosed in geometric silica, jewel-cases complex as stained-glass windows. You fascinate me like that volcano on Mars that's bigger than France. You make me as irrationally happy as an irrational number, digits chattering on and on into infinity. This seems rather a lot to say.'

'Possibly. But it's not love.'

'I've just had an intuition: characters in Hope's paperbacks make precisely that remark *all the time*.'

'Sneering's not an answer. The thing is, you tear people apart in your peep show of a mind. You tear the world into a trillion little thrills. They stand forever amidst the tumbling confetti, hypnotised. That's not quite the same as wonder. Your thrills can't do any work.' He stirred, but didn't speak. 'You love only yourself, and that not much.' He shrugged. 'Wouldn't it be a miracle if mind – mind! – bothered itself with this or that lump, this *person*, this blob of, as it happens, that and that and that, and that and *that*, on and on into infinity?'

'A perversity, Margot. Rather than a miracle.'

Her face became older. 'Is that really all you have to say about Hope?'

'What hope?'

'Hope Mordaunt, whom I killed.'

'It is. I've come to the end of her. Whereas you, my splendid sidekick—' He'd never bestowed that title before.

'No.'

'No…?'

But she had already turned away from him, from his bed, and was walking back across Megiddo, shaking her sad head, repeating over her shoulder, 'No.'

xv.

Considered as a love story, this has been a melancholy wretched abortion. It ends not with a *dot dot dot* of bare toes bounding through yielding carpets to waiting sheets, to a warm tumble of legs, vaguely realised; but with a series of perfectly explicit bed-scenes, as follows.

The scenes all take place at ten on Friday evening, the fifteenth of February, one day past Valentine's Day, two days into Lent. Everyone's doing the default thing people like this do do in bed. They're reading themselves to sleep.

৶

On nights of perturbation and solitude, Felix Culpepper often turns to The Song of Songs which is Solomon's.

He rests against his propped thighs a massive nineteenth-century lectern Bible, inherited from Great-Uncle Wilfrid, with steel-engravings and brass clasps, and turns its brittle pages softly mouthing phrases to himself aloud.

> *I opened to my beloved;*
> > *but my beloved had withdrawn himself,*
> > > *and was gone:*
> > *my soul failed when he spake:*

> *I sought him,*
> > *but I could not find him;*
> *I called him,*
> > *but he gave me no answer.*

Tonight Culpepper's soul is resisting comfort. What's needed is a flanking attack *via* the body. He reaches to his bedside table for his bottle of Noyau de Poissy, a liqueur he fancies not so much for its taste as for its exquisite shade of amber, and for its scent, apricot-kernel, so like cyanide.

৶

Mr Kenneth Pocock, M.P., sits dead upright against his single pillow, pyjamas buttoned as far as his Adam's apple, reviewing the draft of a White

Paper on the censorship of popular philosophy.

> *17.3 To support their goal-orientated criteria on pre-publication protocols, your Sub-Committee developed a broad scheme of structured targets to be actuated by accredited research work evidenced in the demographic distribution of under-20 self-harm.*

Wormwood! In an instant Pocock's face has blackened with congealed blood. The words *under-20* and *work* have, between them, undone him. A volcanic vent has torn apart the bedrock, dousing his mind with magma. *Work oh yes indeed I should think it is industrial pounding of sooty hips grinding under-20s thud of bedsteads in N22 and E7 – agh! Aagh!* But these seismic shocks have also shattered the dam that stands on the far side of his mind; which collapses in a roar of organ music, *give me fever when you kiss me, what a lovely way to burn – no. No.* Frigid waters crash back and forth until his mental landscape is a fathom deep; a tremendous column of steams hisses up from the drowned crater; and the great statesman leans forward in bed, hand grasped to temple, spent.

The moment passes. There are drops of sweat on the paper, his starched pyjamas are creased. But stalwart Mr Pocock, drawing a trembling breath, is already scoring out the racy passage with the red pencil Whitehall allows only to ministers. *Tone down and recast!* he writes severely in the margin, *Remember this may be read aloud in the House.*

Never has there been a minister so assiduous as to innuendo, so severely cautious about the delicacy of the Commons. He's the despair of his under-secretaries, the desolating conscience of the Home Office, the hope of his Party.

ଙ

Margot lies prone beneath her Rothko, forcing herself to re-read *Sandcastles in a Sandstorm*, and what is worse, to read Hope Mordaunt's annotations. *Since I exposed that toddler to Osgood, I ought to remind myself what he's like.* She's reached Chapter Fifteen, 'More Self-Unhelp.'

Unmake the world cruelty by cruelty.

Relationships are the occasion for agony.
Agony is valuable because it registers as blips on the
radar screens of our non-existent minds.

– maxims that must seem comic to everyone; except to lonely teenaged girls, his prey. By Chapter Fifteen, Hope's marginalia (*True!?!?!* and ~~Florian~~ and *I know just what he means*), having touched the limits of language, dwindles to an occasional ❦ or ☹. She must have received with perfect clarity Osgood's tidings: there is no cheer, no comfort, only pain to be navigated on the way to more pain.

The nothing noths and so must you. ◆

⁊ᴀ

Tucked away in Magdalene College behind bolted windows, Florian Marsh leafs through *The Journal of Eighteenth-Century Civil Engineering*. Soon his hand will emerge from the covers to turn off his light, and he'll lie pleasantly, dreaming of footnotes. '*JECCE*, xli, 3 (June 2011), 74': doesn't that have a solid feel?

It was inevitable that Florian would rebound into swothood. His moment of necromancy, casting himself as heresiarch, casting his girlfriend into the depths: that was the extreme point of his short bedevillment. He's already swung back. For the laws of Newton's Cradle apply to such matters. He's neatly passed on his infernal momentum to Lucinda, buying his own self free with another self.

Yet he's not quite unaltered. Florian is no longer merely Yampton's star pupil. There's been a change. It came during the brief scene at Girton (not recorded here, being too pitiful, too ugly) in which he accepted Hope's romantic paperbacks, but rejected romantic her.

What killed her has made him. In those ten minutes his mind grew a cyst of nastiness that'll stand him in good stead for the rest of his career.

⁊ᴀ

Eight time zones backward, in the extreme West of the world, it is still afternoon, but Lucinda Crompe is also in or on bed, sitting up with a laptop, composing *Jack and Jill the Bodice-Rippers*, her next novel. It seems there's no way to turn off the air-conditioning in her hotel room and despite the sunshine, despite the extra duvet she's had sent up from the lobby, she's pinched with cold.

Her unopenable windows take in a vista of subtropical degradation: stunted glass towers, dusty palms, a freeway clogged with idling open cars, and neon advertisements, merging into the vapid electric glare of the sky. The greasy abyss overhanging the low buildings is the Pacific.

She began *Jack* yesterday before dawn, sold the rights to Paramount beside the swimming pool at breakfast, and needs to have the manuscript with a lawyer first thing tomorrow, for if the Motion Picture Association of America can be induced to refuse to rate it before it's even cast, actors' fees come down by half.

It's a period piece. She's cramming in whatever she can think of, Goya horrors, Fuseli, Poe, warmed-over Byatt. Her best model would be *Les 120 journées de Sodome*, but that she dares not think of; it's too close to – to W. (She dreads letting his name form in her mind.)

She shudders, partly with cold, and glances about (*unhand me, you brute*). But the bleakly clean hotel room is empty. The only movement is the innocuous shaking of light from the swimming pool on her ceiling. There'll be no visits before sunset; sunset, when she puts aside her own work, and resumes reading *The Journals*, drowning herself in his experiments, making herself drunk with the cold record of delirium. Until then she's being left alone to slog away.

Even so, how hard it is to mould dirt out of the vacant air of California! … A synonym for *gut* – not *eviscerate*, she used that a paragraph back. *Draw*? It'll do. *Drawing him, Jill, her breast yet heaving with unwonted pallor, laughed abruptly at the agonised pulsing of –* .

No, *pulsing* is no good. *Fluttering*? Drab. *Frenetic*, no, *ecstatic fluttering*? Too butterflyish. Did it *pound*? Devil take it. Did it *pitterpat*? *Tremble*?

ॐ

> *I have compared thee, O my love,*
> > *to a company of horses in Pharaoh's chariots.*
> *As the apple tree among the trees of the wood,*
> > *so is my beloved…*

ॐ

Only healthy-minded Róbert Zseni, across the landing from Florian Marsh, Róbert the only child, Róbert the mother's darling, is exempt from this general misery. He lies on his back, chipper as ever, curtains open to the night, right ankle propped on left knee, left hand on pillow cradling head, other hand holding aloft (of all possible books) Pope's *Iliad*.

It's unguessable how influence will work. *Wicked Trojan Kisses* put Róbert in mind of the real thing, and for the last four weeks he's had a splendid time with Pope. He reads a hundred lines; then the book slides from his hand, closing itself on his bedside rug; his lamp goes out; off he floats into unspotted sleep, rosily smiling. (There's often an aggravating sense of elves watching over Róbert, kissing his cheek, smoothing his linen.)

He's particularly enjoying Pope this bedtime, now and then laughing aloud as is his custom.

> '...*Not thus I lov'd thee, when from Sparta's shore*
> *My forced, my willing, heav'nly prize I bore,*
> *When first entranc'd in Cranæ's isle I lay,*
> *Mix'd with thy soul, and all dissolv'd away!*'

ॐ

> *17.5 In developing a legislative framework consistent with*
> *such firm guide-lines*

'Oh God, oh God', whimpers Pocock, striking out the wildly inflammatory word *firm*, twitching with physical anguish, 'I can't bear it. Will my torture never end? Can there ever be phrases dry enough to be safe? When, when?'

ॐ

Or does it *tremble*? Is the right word *vibrate*? Does it *palpitate*? Or *thump*?

ॐ

> *Thus having spoke, th' enamour'd Phrygian boy*
> *Rush'd to the bed, impatient for the joy.*
> *Him Helen follow'd slow with bashful charms,*
> *And*

– for even Homer throbs –

clasp'd the blooming hero

୫ఎ

Stay me with flagons,
            comfort me with apples:
                        for I am sick of love.

Who sees with equal eye, as God of all,
A Hero perish, or a Sparrow fall,

Atoms or Systems into ruin hurl'd,
And now a Bubble burst, and now a World.

POPE

Lætare

1. The Playwright's Green Room

FELIX CULPEPPER LAY across his armchair, legs crossed over the arm, reading with sulky disgust *Proceedings of the Academy of British Metaphysics* while blowing bubbles from a mother-of-pearl pipe.

The disgust, the bubbles and the journal had the same cause, which was Lent. Felix had semi-lapsed in childhood and his brain was a muddle: a fantastic paganism of his own gave way, now and then, to anxious orthodoxy. But even during his infidel phases he couldn't shake off the habits of his clerical ancestors. True, the reverend Culpeppers had always been a bit vague as to doctrine: genteelly disconcerted by the Evangelical Revival, startled by the Tractarian revolt, pained by the outward ooze of the Broad Church, they didn't like to see any idea pressed to an extreme. And as to morals, they were perfectly easy-going with themselves; even, as far as propriety allowed, easy-going with their rural flocks (always excepting Great-Uncle Wilfred, the tyrannical Archdeacon of Totnes). However, they did hold, mildly but stubbornly, with Lent. And Felix couldn't get out of his head the principle that it was only decent to shoulder some small austerity each spring.

This year it was his after-lunch cigars. It was Culpepper's custom to smoke middling cigars whenever he felt proper, but also every day an excellent one, a Hoyo de Monterrey, La Habana: just one, but it was important, for it marked the reliably happy interval between luncheon and siesta. He was never more nearly-human than in the twenty minutes it took to burn through his short fat toro.

But not just now. Abstinence is harsh when it's mere sterile practice without theoretical application, and Lent was never a gracious time for Culpepper. This year he was surly during the hour after lunch, and indulged a morbid impulse to irritate himself more than he was already irritated. That was why he made himself read academic journals, which he despised. In the same spirit, he'd unearthed this extravagant bubble-pipe, spotted in a French antique shop years ago. For suds he employed a sterling silver fingerbowl, inherited from a great-grandfather, and a shampoo from Trumper's of Mayfair; and thus blew preposterously expensive soap bubbles in mockery of his vanished smoke rings.

What was the excuse for his crossness? Today, the ninth of March, was gorgeous. The blossom was out on Christ's Pieces, spreading itself below Culpepper's bedroom window. Tomorrow was Lætare Sunday, the recess Lent takes from Lent two weeks before Lent ends, a premonition of Easter. It was physically warm too, a premonition of summer: from Megiddo Court rose the sound of self-consciously languid youth on the lawn.

For all this, shadows were darkening over Culpepper's face. It was not just a question of doing without his supreme tobacco. Just as he'd given up his daily Habana, Margot had given up him. She usually helped him take his siesta, and without her the cigar would have lost some of it savour even if it had existed.

Morosely he sketched an article: 'Parameters for measurement of diminished sense-data in ontological non-veridicals.' *If the number of yetis in the world were divided by zero, would* – there came a knock on his oak, which he ignored: w*ould the resulting impossible number be greater than the set of impossible* – he heard the door opening nonetheless, and sat up sharply. Only Margot (and his wretched sister Gertrude, who was unlikely to be in Cambridge) dared enter without being summoned. By the time the inner door was tapped he had got the harrowed look out of his face, at least he hoped so; he'd put down the bubble-pipe as unbefitting his grandeur, and after a moment's thought had slid the journal down the side of his armchair.

'Enter!' Surely his voice was just as ringing and arrogant as three weeks ago, before the Margotian frost began?

She entered; but what a wan business she made of entering! It was if every step was an ambivalence; as if it was natural for her to go to his sofa and not his bed (as she did), and sit looking at him (which she did too), not familiarly, not socially, but rather as if she were stagnated in a posture of hesitation.

This is what it had been like for four weeks. She hadn't formally broken with Felix, so had no need to treat him politely; but she wouldn't come to him any more. He was left perpetually dangling, he was made to live in the dock, waiting for the jury to come back. His nerves could bear it no longer.

She seemed to think so too. Didn't she have a decisive air to her, after a month of hesitation?

He tried rearranging his legs, he tried coughing, but his dismay remained obvious.

Yet when she did break the unendurable seventeen seconds of silence, it was only to point at the journal he had secreted and murmur, gravely, 'You're reading philosophy?'

Nothing she'd said over the last four weeks had been easy or smooth-edged. But this inconsequential, fatuous remark seemed easier than most of her remarks, and he resolved to assert himself. He picked up his metaphysical *Proceedings* as if seeing it for the first time, pulled it open at the middle pages, made a witty pretence of turning it ninety degrees as to ogle a centrefold, tut-tutted, then suddenly chucked it as hard as he could. This wasn't much of a success: being unbound, and printed on the thin crackly paper beloved of academics, *British Metaphysics* merely fluttered upward, executed a skittish curtsy in the air, and swooned to the carpet three feet short of the bin. But at least Culpepper was a man again; he scowled at it theatrically, then took up his bubble-pipe.

'Lavatory-fodder,' he pronounced. Margot folded unusually white knuckles in her lap and waited. 'Ever been given a bubbsy to dandle, Abishag?' Puff, bubble, bubble. 'Disgusting creatures…'

'Good to eat, though. Don't y'think? Not fried, not roasted, the flesh's too delicate. A *daube*: stewed without first browning the meat. With apricots to bring out—'

'Don't be whimsical, I've something important to say. Infants are so stupid the only game they understand is peek-a-boo. And what are philosophers, eh? Eh? I'll tell you.' Bubble-bubble. 'They're simply men stuck at the baby stage. They're perfectly content cooing and giggling all day long because something exists yet doesn't exist. There, not there, there, not there. Mind or matter or morality or meaning: they get it to hide its face, then peek out through its fingers, and that pleases them.'

'Bejasus an' bless their innocent 'earts ter be sure,' said Abishag in Oirish.

'Ye – es,' said Culpepper, who never liked being unsure if he was being taken seriously. Puff.

'Of course what you say is probably true of the run of philosophers. But – but then. There's always.'

She paused, and a sensitive barometer would have detected the air in Culpepper's sitting room tick up many millibars. For it seemed she might be on the verge of pronouncing the name *Jake Osgood*; a name that had been taboo since the start of their quarrel – if quarrel is what it was – for after all Osgood was the rub.

The tacit prohibition was doubly awkward, because Osgood was an amusing topic, not out of the way at all. Osgood was prominent; St Wygy's was proud of him; Cambridge, even, was proud of him, proud of his ill-tempered academic monographs, prouder still of his popular bestsellers he pumped out, one a term and one every Long Vac. *Your Life is a Waste, Why We Don't Need the Cosmos, The Case for Universal Suicide, In Praise of Nothing*. They were even proud of his television interviews. It was a standard journalistic ploy, when gingering-up stories about school 'bus crashes or fires in orphanages, to invite the smirking "renowned Cambridge nihilist philosopher" into the studio. He'd run well-chewed nails through ill-cut hair, rub his soft palms over his chaotic wide-nostrilled lipless face, and explain why such disasters were *a good thing*. If the studio was very lucky it would have the parents in too, so he could tell them in person why the death of their child was merely a discontinued narrative: "No worse than coming to the end of a particular meat pie".

Even last week, when Osgood had been interrogated by a committee at Westminster, Margot and Felix had not mentioned him to each other. But now 'There's always Osgood,' said Margot, and Culpepper's face promptly thickened with blood. 'Philosophers are harmless elderly babies. *Except* for one vicious farting urchin who's four years old. That's why he gets all the publicity, four year olds are so interesting,' and oh how that publicity rankled with Culpepper, who'd been Osgood's contemporary. ("*No. He was mine.*") They still visited each other's rooms to sneer. It was unequal sneering. No One Must Know that Felix was hired assassin to the Establishment; certainly Osgood mustn't know; officially, he was just an obscure Latinist. Whereas Osgood, although his academic speciality was just as dusty – some nuance of solipsism – got quoted by *Time* magazine and *Rolling Stone*. He was boggled at in the streets. He notched up occasional death threats. She'd heard Osgood say, on one of his hostile friendly visits: 'I long to govern the world by blasphemy, Culps. Each new thing I uttered would be so excessively monstrous it couldn't be gainsaid or endured; and people would have to obey... Don't let this idea frighten you.' And: 'Y'know, Culps – *Culps*, my dear,' (this was to her) 'is what we called this funny fellow at school. Or *Padre*. That was during his religious period in the fourth form. Y'know, Culps, at some point in the twentieth or twenty-first century you ought probably to have done something. Too late now, of course. Eh?' And Felix would have somehow to smile.

Now, too, he did manage to smile at the forbidden name. 'A four year-old. That's very good...' Then, with sudden rage: 'College ought to stop him humiliating us all. Why can't we carry him into Aceldama, strip him naked, torture him with his own books. Do you think it's possible to *kill* a man with paper-cuts? A million or so? We ought to find out.'

'But doesn't the Master think...?'

'Oh yes yes yes, Osgood's protected. But not because of his so-called work. Just because gets on the telly. The telly! Think of that!'

'Yes, I gather he's on television *a lot*,' she said stupidly; but her eyes did not have a stupid expression, nor did her voice sound quite as if she were chattering haphazardly. If Culpepper had been less full of himself, he'd have observed her tense fingers; he might have sniffed the norepinephrine surging in her cortex; he would have been more wary.

'On *popular television*.' He thrust the pipe back between his teeth.

'But y'know, Felix, his work's *not* nothing. I turned the pages of Universal Suicide. So original in –'

'Original! Blah! Osgood's a cheap warmed-over version of Hegesias – Peisithanatos they called him, the death-persuader – a foul philosopher twenty-three centuries back. The Greeks were sensible, they didn't argue, they simply suppressed him.'

'Yes, but Dr Osgood –'

'And even dear old Hegesias,' declared Culpepper, attempting desolating remoteness, 'wasn't original. He'd been got at by Buddhist missionaries from India. It's always the identical dreary Asiatic whining.'

'Well I thought it was hard to see round Osgood's argument against the existence – '

'Ha! Ha! Silly bint ...' exclaimed Culpepper, taking fire. 'Remember Johnson's remark, when Boswell said the denial of matter couldn't be refuted? Johnson kicked a stone and sent it flying: "I refute it *thus!*" That's what I have to say to wee Jakie Osgood. I refute him –' the contents of his chest broke through his bubble pipe, as when a bagpipe is squeezed under a Scotsman's armpit. An eruption of bubbles, tiny to middling, rose above him in an inverted triangle. 'Thus,' he finished, feebly, breathless. '*Thus.*'

'But does—'

'Sceptics.' He got his voice back. 'Can explain everything only if you accept their definition of "everything". Paranoid lunatics explain "everything". Ask a dirty old woman in a provincial madhouse why she's there. Because she's Marilyn Monroe. Everyone denies it – that shows they're part of a conspiracy. No one bothers to dispute her identity with her because they're afraid of being convinced. There! Refute her with argument! You can't. Her idea covers the data, covers all possible data. Whatever you say is grist to her monotonous mania. Her system, or refusal to accept a system, is a perfect impenetrable sphere. It's immune to chipping. But it's *puny*.'

Here Abishag performed a pretty charade. She was an ingenuous girl trying to follow a hard argument, scrunching her brows, squeezing her lips, giving her chin a tight wiggle; being an aristocrat, it didn't matter to her what Felix, a competitive bourgeois, thought of her mind.

Culpepper eyed this performance. He understood that Abishag was only pretending to be dim, something he would never dare do himself. She was exploiting her unfair class-advantage. He was outflanked, then, not just by Osgood, but by this piece of fluff from Debrett's. His mood blackened further, and his voice dropped. 'Y'know what's happening to us now, sitting here, little girl?' (*Growing older*, thought Abishag.) 'I don't mean us, I mean the planet.'

'We're spinning round the sun?'

'*No* – I mean yes, yes we are, but that's a slight motion, sluggish. What matters is that we're whipping round the Galactic Centre at half a million miles per hour. Us and our sun and the whole galaxy: three hundred billion other suns, and all their uncountable flocks of planets. And what *is* the Galactic Centre?'

'It *sounds* like a hypermarket.'

'It is *not* a hypermarket. It's infinite darkness. Virtually infinite darkness, virtually infinite weight. You can't speak of it – imagination fails, of course, but even arithmetic doesn't function properly.' Margot's face pretended to strain at such *hard* ideas, which irked Culpepper beyond any self-control. '*Bint*. If we scrunched this planet to black hole density it would sit in my palm – a grape the weight of Earth. Drop this grape into an abyss, and another, and another – fast as thinking, half a dozen worlds a second, click-click-click, cl'-cl'-click. After eight thousand years you'd have accumulated the mass of the Galactic Centre. Which is merely absurd. Number's stopped working. The Centre's without quality. Light and time vanish over the lip of that abyss and cannot return. The galaxy's a line of foam on the edge of that ocean. A rim of bubbles... It's not that Osgood's *mistaken* in calling the universe bad, he's insane to try to call it anything. The fuckwit ought to be quiet like the rest of us and boggle.'

'You're never particularly quiet, Felix.'

'No, don't you see,' he gushed in a real rage, 'not just quiet – still in the mind. The only sane response to such sensational truths is to stop trying to account for them. Stop chattering. The mind should crouch in front of illimitable light until—'

'This doesn't sound like you.' Which was true; the black mood had broken down some of his usual reserve.

'Until – ah! – it breaks open with brightness and floats off the floor. Into ecstasy.'

'*I think you sound like this because you're craving tobacco.*' (*I think you sound like this because of your clerical ancestors.*)

'Ecstasy,' he continued grimly, 'doesn't prove anything, yet it's the only adult reaction. Not that scientists notice, they're almost invariably stupid. Nearly as babyish as philosophers. But their driest studies – astral physics, genetics – produce the raw material for rapture.'

'Stronger than cigars?'

He ignored this asininity. 'Y'know, if I'm ever fool enough to write fiction, I'll not try to out-sensationalise the cosmos, I'll just cram in as many facts as I can. Tricked out with a dribble of narrative. *Facts* will be the entertainment.'

'Oh goodie – a novel about genes and black holes.'

'All right, here's a girly fact just for you. Y'know there's a diamond hung above our heads? In the tail of Serpens. A planet weighing three hundred Earths. A haze of oxygen on the surface, then solid diamond to the core. Ten million septillion carats.'

'Bit flashy, if you ask me. I wouldn't be seen dead—'

'This knowledge falls the necessary trillions of miles through space and pierces my head with a shaft of perfect silver joy. That joy is not in my mind, Abishag, I scarcely exist, my personality's a glint on the surface of a consciousness that's like a grain of rice, my intellect's a sham and my body will soon be *pâté* for worms. Yet my mind's large enough to receive the light of the diamond planet. Our thoughts cannot get round the girth of that splendour. We can't cloak it. Everything we understand may be as deluded as Osgood says – nevertheless we can't doubt the glory. And he can't account for *that*. I refute him with my diamond planet.' And he mimed Dr Johnson's famous gesture.

'But,' said Abishag heavily, *faux*-thickly, 'you can't *really* kick it, can you? Not like a stone.'

Felix's teeth tensed on the stem of his pipe. 'I don't need a *planet.*

Osgood's system is tinier than this bubble.' He extended a finger: a bubble adhered to it, quaking, like a perched butterfly. 'This fleck of soapy water, this terrifying wonder, has no possible function. It's only a few microns thick, invisibly thin in fact: we only see its iridescence. Yet it contains' – he flicked it into non-existence – 'contained all mathematics, because it knew how to calculate the smallest area capable of covering its volume of air; it anticipated all science, because it engineered a perfect sphere; it implied all art, glowing with every colour; its movement—'

'Well then,' said Abishag's most dulcet voice, mocking, tempting him, 'you need only to get Osgood to confront a thrilling bubble, and you *could* refute him *thus.*'

A furious pillar of bubbles went straight up into the air. She'd overshot. Culpepper was too enraged even to be indiscreet. He simply glared.

She burbled away as if she hadn't noticed. 'Do it, Felix. I think you *should*. He'd be so terrified he'd stop popping up on *Newsnight*. And publishing stupid articles. And essays in *The Observer*. And depressing bestsellers. He'd give all that a rest.'

'You once sneered at my "thrills", you said they did no "work". You think I'm *innocuous*, don't you?' The clerical qualities were quite gone from his voice.

'Poor Felix, I think you and Osgood are deadly in quite different ways. You don't overlap.'

'Ha!' (*Condescending little bitch.*)

'So no, if you press me. I don't think your bubbles could really *get* to him. To *Peisithanatos redux*... Could they?'

Culpepper sucked, frowned, puffed orbs of filmy soap. This was a new low for him: to be, not ridiculed, but *patronised* by his own adolescent creation.

Nothing more for nearly a whole minute. Then an extraordinary dark light flushed his face, as happens on occasion in the faces of jealous men. '*Yes you silly tot, my bubbles could*. As a matter of brute fact *they could.*'

'Do it, then. Do it now.'

Culpepper considered. He pictured his rival in his loathsome rooms in Sheol Court. Then he glanced out of the window into Megiddo. 'Not now, no. But very soon.'

'When?'

'It depends.'

'On what?'

'On the weather. On whether it rains this afternoon. Yes, exactly on that. Let the gods decide...'

Evasion! said Abishag's grin. Which was going too far. Felix dropped his pipe into the fingerbowl with a rattle and a sullen little splash. 'Enough. I've work to do. Well, sleep to do. Solitary sleep. Off you go. Supervision over.' He meant it.

2. *The Box Office*

It's never reckless to hope for rain in England. It pelted down that afternoon, a burst of summery wet just after tea, brief but heavy.

And at ten came a hammering on Abishag's door. Culpepper: not in his usual linens, but in black polo-neck, trousers, boots all black, a huge black backpack carried lightly on one shoulder, the costume of a boy heading off to spend summer Inter-railing about Europe. Leering and impetuous like a boy, too.

'You,' he snapped, 'come with me. Now. Put on something dark.'

'Um – are we going to convert Osgood?'

'That's a word for it.'

He was boisterously impatient, she rather shy. The night was remarkably warm and close, moonless, and with enough cloud to blot out the stars. College seemed to be full of people whispering, subdued by the heavy weather. The two of them didn't speak until they'd crossed broad cobbled Gehenna Court, with the uncouth bulk of the tower Acheron on their right, and passed into the arched passageway leading to Sheol, where Osgood had his set on the first floor.

Culpepper had turned cautious. He'd peeled off and stood away from her, behind her, in the archway, gazing, and spoke under his breath. 'W'd'y'see?'

3. *A Masque*

She looked, and sighed.

Sheol, she reflected, was definitely the least impressive of St Wygy's courts. The archway and north range were Tudor brick, a trifle fussy and sombre, perhaps, but good enough; the east range, which fronted Emmanuel Road, and the low south range, where the rooms looked over into gloomy Aceldama, were ragstone, Restoration work, of no particular style, although the slate mansard roofs were fine. It was the west range that was the eyesore. Linden-Bowyers, who was Master of St Wygefortis' College in the early 'Twenties, had torn down a run of inoffensive Gothic and put up, *épater le bourgeois*, a Bauhaus slab of middling-grey cement and aluminium tubing. It was in its day the most *avant-garde* building in Cambridge, and the wretched thing was listed Grade I; there was no getting rid of it, and its mechanical bulk dominated the whole court by day.

Happily, it was a College tradition to keep Sheol in almost rural darkness by night. Indeed there was always something countrified about the court, dating perhaps from the centuries when the College vegetable-garden had been here. The thick stand of ancient beeches here, in the north-east corner, for instance, blocking the archway into Gehenna: stand on this spot, peer through the trunks, ignore the frightful west range, and you might be looking into the court of an old-fashioned country inn. The sort of innyard where English drama began, in fact.

And how theatrical Osgood was! He had the south-west corner, the best set of rooms in College if you didn't mind nasty architecture, which of course he didn't. A fine sitting-room looked over Aceldama, a bedroom commanded the Master's Garden; yet, as usual, there he was in that tiny chamber hanging over Sheol, with scarlet curtains pulled back and overhead light blaring. Its two windows were tall, nearly reaching the level of the floor. Osgood liked the world to watch him crank out world-denying prose and consort with hobgoblins: volumes of Stirner and Steiner, Heidegger, de Man and Hume, carpet to ceiling. The rooms near his had their lights off; Osgood's box blazed away like a Punch and Judy stage.

'W'd'y'see?' repeated Culpepper impatiently from behind her.

Margot shook herself and concentrated.

'Er. It's very quiet,' she whispered back. 'Two or three people sitting on the grass.'

'Yes, but Osgood.'

'Are we going to surprise him? One window ajar, about six inches. Door shut. He's at his desk, back to us, banging away at his keyboard. And smoking. Tapping furiously. No, he's pausing; he's lighting another cigarette. He's back to work—'

'Good. Wait – how did he light that cigarette?'

'With the stub of the last one.'

'Excellent. Chain-smoking. As he often does. Filthy habit. Not like my elegant diurnal cigar. How different Osgood is from me.' A sigh. 'Twenty-two days 'til Easter. Twenty-two days 'til my next smoke.' He sidled out of the archway, took her elbow, and pulled her into the clump of beeches. 'Filthy and dangerous. Know how many Britons die each year pulling on jumpers with cigarettes in their mouths? A hundred and seventy-nine. More than are killed by cocaine. Or even by Osgood's scribbles.'

'Is that true?'

'Yes, but look again. What's *outside* his room?' He was keeping himself out of sight, behind the enormous bole of one of the trees.

She leaned forward. 'Um, nothing. Just the court. No, all right, first the flower bed, with a trellis of wisteria rising to the second floor. Then the path, *then* the grass of the court.'

'Excellent. How wide's the flower bed, would you say?'

'A good six feet.'

'Precisely. Too wide to jump.'

'Yes...'

'And it's rained. Which is why we're here.'

Abishag thought for a moment. '*Because* the rain will make the flowerbed damp enough to show footprints.'

Culpepper, out of sight behind the tree, sounded genuinely pleased. 'Amazing child. Yes.'

'So it'll seem certain no one climbed the trellis and came in the window. To surprise and refute Osgood.'

'Yes.'

'*Are* we going to climb the trellis and refute Osgood?'

'No. I doubt it would support me. And the mud, my darling, the trampled *Gladiolus aquamontanus*, the snapped *Dahlia cuspidata*.'

'We're going through the door?'

'Locked. Always locked. He locks himself into that vile puny room where his vile puny mind pours out bad prose in the sight of all men. Then back to his cold bed for spiteful dreams.'

'We're *throwing* something in?'

'Close. In a way. The opposite of the truth. Wait. Watch me. And *try not to scream*.'

Abishag, astounded by the insult in this last remark, watched her lover go on all fours and slink across the grass, an intenser shadow in the melting grey gloom, disappearing.

The warm sky pressed down. Here and there came dull voices from undergraduates enervated by the unseasonal heat. *Why am I here?* thought Margot, pettishly. *I'm doing nothing.* Her eyes were getting used to the dimness, and she could make out Felix again, a black-on-grey silhouette.

Beneath Osgood's window he dropped his pack, pushed it into position with his foot, and lay with his head on it pillow-wise. *It's disgusting how comfortable he always has to make himself.* Out of his pocket came the mother-of-pearl pipe and a canister, evidently full of suds. For after swirling his pipe in it, he blew one perfect, enormous bubble. It caught what light there was, shimmering like the thinnest possible molten silver, wobbling upward curvaceously, vanishing into upper darkness. *Oh bravo, Felix!* she thought bitterly. Another, another. *I do wish, so so wish, I could calibrate my mockery.*

He had his range, like an artilleryman. The next few went exactly where he commanded: over the path and herbaceous border, up to the first floor, in through the half-open window to the monster's den.

A bubble; another bubble. Another. They were regular and homogenous now, and they made her sick. *Felix's productions are usually more entertaining than this. There're no jokes, no violence. Not even dialogue. It's a fustian masque, antemasque, an acting out of a philosophical position with* bubbles. *Not even interesting bubbles. Why no variety in size? Siamese twins? Trinities? Four-leafed clovers? Forty-four. Forty-five.*

An identical bubble slid through the window each second and a half.

I'm not *going to count them – that way lies madness. Forty-six, -seven, -eight – no… This is industrial tedium. Watching bolts rattle off a conveyor belt. Worse. Liturgical tedium. Breathing out a thousand filmy anathemas, in the hope that the demon will change his mind on the thousand-and-oneth. Refute him* thus. *Thousand-and-first I mean.*

Boredom and the heavy night were nearly putting her to sleep. She sat on the dense grass under the beech, resting chin on knees, witnessing the inanity of her man. *Is he evil? Is he good? What am I training in? Not that he trains me. God I'm sleepy. But if he would—*

'Gaarrrr!' How embarrassing. She *had* screamed.

4. Le Théâtre du Grand-Guignol

Three things had happened virtually at once. There'd been an amazing scarlet burst of light, rendering the court for an instant clear as with lightning or camera-flash; there'd been a dull gentle boom, swelling at once into a dry rushing roar; and there'd been a simply hideous shriek from inside Osgood's room. Her mind had slammed shut, and out had come the scream, a noise she'd hardly uttered through all her confident twenty years.

Uncountable shrieks and oaths answered her from every direction: wordless shouts of amazement, cries of horror, then energetic yells of 'Fire!'

Culpepper's dark form rolled straight back across the lawn into the cover of the beeches. He shot behind a trunk, then stood.

The quiet night had been shattered. All about was a confusion of dark bodies dashing across the court toward Osgood's window – already a swirling glory of gold and red. Flames, almost solid-seeming as water, poured and tumbled over the sill. Grey smoke, dense-looking as plaster of Paris, clambered the wall. Most terribly, in the midst of the burning twitched a black figure, vestigial, scrawny as a cricket, grasping a burning curtain – only for an instant before it dropped, pulling down curtain and all. In that instant Margot thought it had screeched 'Save me!'

Raving noise. Fire alarms somewhere-everywhere. Bells. Shouts from every direction. A siren, distant sirens, sirens approaching. People running. Atrocious brightness radiating out across the lawn disastrously red, half a compass-wheel, hellish. *Well, fairground-hellish, perhaps.* (Paralysis was past. Margot's mind was reviving.) She glanced down. *Good God, I'm holding Felix's hand. That's not often allowed.* She glanced backward. Two grotesque fire shadows stretched out behind them, through the beeches and up the wall. *We're like giants.* She coughed, to test her voice. Tolerable.

'Felix. What just happened?'

'Events,' he said airily, not bothering to whisper any more. 'Events, events, events. The final event, I suppose, ought to be this. Emptying my pack.' Without making a fuss of it, he opened his bag's mouth, embraced it, and squeezed. Then he shook it, sniffed. 'Do you still smell it?' He shook some more, then popped the deflated thing behind a tree, and sat down.

'What?' she muttered.

'Did you smell the murder weapon?' He pulled her down beside him. Was it bravado that made him speak so normally? Sheol Court was thronging with rushing, swaying people, it heaved; what if someone was eavesdropping?

'Did I – *what?*' she said, at his volume.

'Did you smell it, Abishag, as it fled joyously upward into the stratosphere, there to gnaw away ozone and improve the English summer?'

'*What...?* Yes. A bit sweet. Oily. Cheesy.'

'Exactly.'

'Camembert. A Camembert left in your backpack from a picnic last autumn.'

'Daft child. Who ever died of Camembert? It was methane.'

'But methane smells of rotten eggs.'

'Untrue. Chemical companies put the eggy smell in so people'll notice leaks. This batch was ninety-nine point nine nine nine something *per cent* pure. I borrowed, well, stole two plastic tanks of it from the university labs this afternoon. Innocuous stuff, methane. Not toxic, lighter than air – less controversial than air if it comes to that. Osgood called breathing "an autonomous mechanism for torturing consciousness". Did you ever read that? Although he denied consciousness as well. *And* denied the validity of logical utterances, such as denials. *Vacuous* man. If I'd been on the philosophy faculty—'

'But what about the gas?'

'The methane? Well it's friendly stuff, easy to use, doesn't want to make trouble. I went into my bathroom and unscrewed the tanks under a rubbish bag until they stopped hissing. Then I tied the bag shut round a bit of rubber hose, sealed the hose with a wooden peg, and stuffed this simple apparatus into my backpack.' Boys were now throwing buckets of water into Osgood's window now. They'd formed a chain-gang from the gardener's shed, where there was evidently a tap. Back and forth the iron buckets went, casting weird swaying geometric shadows on the grass. The sirens were getting close. 'See how the hose sticks out? I sucked on it while blowing my bubbles.' He was groping through the flaps of the backpack. 'The one bad thing about methane is the aftertaste. *Where's* my hipflask? Not that pocket. Not that pocket either... Well, there's another thing about methane, bad or good as you decide: it's explosive once there's more than one part to twenty parts air. Aha! My hipflask. Cheers!' He swilled out his mouth, spat on the ruddy grass, then swigged a huge dram. 'Better. My dear? Would you?'

'Thank you. Cheers.' She drank a little unsteadily, coughing on the spirit. She handed the flask back and adjusted her voice. 'So you bubbled away until it ignited—'

'No even that. It happened sooner than I thought – I *imagine* it was because Jake loved bursting things. Ideas, logic, coherence, poke, boom. Spying a bubble he couldn't resist touching his burning fag-end to it. Rainbow-hued beauty, grrr, poke. Not a big enough boom to kill him. But with the methane already in the room from burst bubbles, and his greasy hair, not to mention his own mess, evil books, papers, polyester upholstery, gauze curtaining, he created a firestorm. An excellent instant pyre. Look! Cambridgeshire's finest at last. *Tarantara!'*

Across the lawn trotted the fire brigade: antique warriors in preposterous helmets and rubber armour. The crowd parted to let them through – the bucket-passers relented; some vulgar girl applauded. As they ran past, their broad East Anglian faces seemed to Margot impossibly red, gilded by the blaze, flushed with heat and exertion and the strain of looking heroic in noisy wellington boots. Riding the air between them was a pale undulating serpent with a bronze head. The fire-hose! Someone bellowed, the serpent stiffened. When it was stiff as post, the head fireman twisted its head as if breaking its neck, and it spat a column of gushing whiteness through the window, crashing and tinkling, throwing up before it a theatrical pall of smoke.

The water fell into the fire and at once – so it seemed to Margot –

5. A Carnival

– the whole scene was transformed for the second time that night. It was like the moment in an old-fashioned opera house when a lever's pulled and mountains glide away, the sun's doused, the raked hillside sinks, tables judder in with their candles lit, an immense drape flutters over the backdrop, flaps of mock-lath and woodwork rise like the sails of windsurfers, someone cues the moon, the orchestra changes key, the less jaded portion of the audience gasps. The bandits' cave has become a tavern in the town.

Even so, in an instant the silent nocturnal court had turned into a roaring chamber of Hades, with a panicky mob of shadows lit by catastrophic crimson; and now, in the twinkling of an eye, the fire was gone, normal electric lights started coming back, everyone stopped shouting.

The crowd sighed, it ran its hands across its hair, and even smiled, and suddenly the scene changed and the mood turned festive, drunken, lurid and coarse. The cataclysm had become a county fair. Margot wouldn't have believed any atmosphere could alter so quickly.

Felix showed no impulse to leave the scene of the crime. He and Margot stayed for hours. Everyone did. Two hundred people milled about Sheol Court. At first they maintained a certain decorum, chatting in hushed voices, cameras kept in pockets. Culpepper's hipflask was one among many, but people swigged discreetly. (An ambulance crew came sprinting across the lawn, then came out slowly, shaking their heads. More highly-socialised people managed to sigh or shake their heads in turn.)

The difficulty of remaining sombre was that the great College officers appeared, and instead of setting an example, capered about the lawn. The thought of dining on High Table with an empty seat where Osgood used to sit made them feel like boys again. And then there was the physical damage! Now the police were rigging up floodlighting in the dim court, the west range of Sheol looked particularly grisly. (Culpepper, abashed at the thought of visiting arson upon his own college, murmured to Abishag 'I wouldn't have done it, you know, if he'd lived on Megiddo or Abbadon.' She squeezed his hand, a little absently.) The Master and the Home Bursar stood with folded arms and exultant faces, eyeing the pear-shaped black mark that began at Osgood's study – a sopping shell of charred wood – and stretched to the roofline. 'What a shame,' remarked Sir Trotsky with fine frankness, 'it couldn't have burned five minutes longer. Just to make sure.'

'Oh, don't worry. Water damage'll have done the trick, Master,' said bluff old Sir Rory. 'D'y'know, I believe fire departments must be paid a retainer by architects. Sly rogues.' On cue there came a terrible rumpus from another staircase, well away from the flames, where firemen were running amok with axes, flinging smashed timbers from the windows. 'They're never happier than when flooding a basement. We'll have the bally thing down by Easter!' cried Sir Rory, rubbing his hands.

'When something else goes up, won't we have to name it the Osgood Building?'

'Not a bit of it, Master! We'll name it after you. Oh, I suppose we can stack the bathrooms in the corner, on the site of his rooms, and call it the Osgood Block. So undergraduates can piss in his mouth.'

By now the fire-hose was off. Policemen could be seen pottering about, their thoughts so obvious they might as well have been displayed above their heads in thought-balloons. 'Now then, now then, what do we have here?' 'Door locked from inside. Shut until the firemen kicked it in.' 'Damp flowerbed outside the window, sir, definitely clean of footprints.' 'Window-frame's clear of fingerprints, Inspector.' So no possibility of foul play?' 'None at all, sir.' 'Very good, very good.' 'Airtight.' 'Can they take the remains away now?' 'I can't see why not. Any chance of a cuppa?'

Out came the corpse, covered with a white sheet. As it swayed across the court its cindered right arm fell free and lolled against the ground.

'Incredible clumsiness,' said the finicky. 'The fatal hand, the hand that wrote such evil,' said the romantics, as if books were still composed with goose quills. 'How desiccated,' said the practical; 'are there going to be drinks?'

Drinks! Once the body had gone, the mob in Sheol Court felt no need to preserve funereal dignity now. It was constituting itself as an informal garden party. This was a great night in the history of St Wygefortis' College; they began to glance toward the Master.

Who was saying: 'Really, I think we might...' A flunky murmured behind him. 'What is that? The Vice-Chancellor has arrived. Interfering bumpkin. I'd better see him in private. Rory, would you kindly go and rouse the butler, and ask him to bring out a good deal of the second-best hock and the third-best claret?'

So trestles went up, decently covered with white cloths, silver buckets, and trays of glasses. The Bauhaus wing was gone! Osgood was gone! The floodlighting was switched off; the clouds were found to have dispersed: it was a starry wonderful night after all. People brought candles from their rooms. Tristan Bolswood had dug up a copy of *Why We Don't Need the Cosmos* and sat cross-legged in a circle of undergraduates, reading passages in comic voices. They drank to the cosmos. They guffawed. Seb Hawicke Trocliffe was seen to light a joint from a patch of embers the firemen had missed.

Naturally Mrs Oathouse was waddling about by now, dispensing handfuls of mephedrone: 'Take the edge off your trauma. Trust Nursie, you need a little something.' The wake was turning rowdy. Someone had fetched a guitar. Someone was improvising bongo-drums with the metal ice-buckets; people clashed empty wine-bottles together. There was enough wreckage on the lawn to build a small bonfire; with so much soot about already the grown-ups didn't seem to mind. They didn't even object when Ollie appeared from Beelzebub, the College library, with armfuls of books. 'Osgood's complete works!' he roared, and the mob was soon dancing about the bonfire chucking them in one by one, in time to the barbaric music. There were so many, not all of them could have been by Osgood; but no one at Wygy's is seriously averse to book-burning, and besides, the swirling silhouettes of the dancers, going round and around the flames, were too fine to spoil. From the top floor of the east range of Sheol, the rooms of the physicist Screwgrave, where the more nervous Fellows had assembled for a discreet party of their own, the lawn, with its fiery gold centre and long black tapering radiant shadows, resembled a negative sunflower.

A television crew appeared, coarsening the mix still further. The media gazed at the denizens of St Wygy's as at a freakshow; the freakshow gazed back at the media, amazed at such unaccustomed accents, such make-up, such portentous voices. Journalism, as ever, honed in on the least stable cases. 'So, Home Bursar, how would you describe the feeling of Cambridge tonight?' The reporter shoved a huge microphone into Sir Rory's good-natured face, and Sir Rory, who had just put his seventh glass of Bordeaux behind his back, blinked.

'The feeling? I would – dear me, I'm awfully sorry, I'm not laughing, it's this smoke, got in my eye I think. There, that's better. What were you asking about? Feelings, yes. It's – oh dear. Oh ho, ha. Apologies, apologies. Perhaps you should talk to someone else. Oh ho!'

'Fucking hell. Okay, Peter,' growled Frank Flute the journalist to Quine the cameraman, 'there's a mingy one over there, at least she won't keep tittering. Excuse me! Excuse me, madam. I'm reporting for *The Truth as of Now*. May I ask if you work here?'

'Oy'm the Felloo in Sociology,' whined Nikkie the horse-faced sex-starved Brummie. Screwgrave couldn't abide her and she was standing about at a loose end.

'And could you tell me your impressions of your late colleague, Professor Osgood?'

'Oy kwoyt loiked 'im, 'e was always positive abart things. Well no 'e wasn't, but 'e wasn't negativistic, not really. Well I mane ee was, but in a positive woy. There was always something really life-affirmen abart the woy he pointed out the pointlessness of everythen at lunch.'

'Really?' said Flute.

'No – there's wasn't, I suppose. Not really.' Mephedrone never brought out the best in her.

'Thank you, thank you, that was great. Okay Peter, let's try...'

''Old on, can I gid ert me tellyfowun number? The'er moy be a geezer ert the'er who wants ter cum an' console me fer ar sad loss. Eet's—'

The television crew fled, Nikki in pursuit.

Margot, from beneath the beech trees, was watching the carnival with growing repulsion. 'Felix,' she said. (Felix was lying on his back on the grass as he liked to do, turning his glass of claret round and round in the mingled starlight and firelight.) 'Felix. Horse-faced Nikkie is prostituting herself on television.'

'That's nice... But she'd have better luck on the radio.'

'Although even then—'

'Yes, even then. Really she ought to learn a few indecent expressions in Braille,' he murmured, although clearly his mind was far away, 'and hang about homes for the congenitally deaf and blind.'

'*Now* the broadcast zanies are talking to Woolly.' (Who was saying: 'Well in a very special sense, poor Osgood *was* a believer. He was always denying things, and to deny is a sort of movement of the spirit, is it not? A *pilgrimage*, indeed.')

'That's nice too. No one's ever listened to Woolly.' (Who was telling the camera, wistfully: 'All thoughts attest to thought, and so all thoughts, by which I mean all our rich, diverse mental experience, all we bring to share with others on this journey – for what is life but a journey? – in a sense *mean the same thing*.')

'College is suddenly a vulgar circus. Whose doing is it?' It suited Margot's subtle, shifty purposes to seem shocked, and mildly disapproving.

'Mine. But my conscience is clear. Pure. Well, 99.999% pure. Perhaps trace elements of malice were involved.' ('But what about Professor Osgood's practical proposals, Reverend? Contraceptives in the drinking water? Poisoning school lunches by lot? Machines to be installed on trains, dispensing razor-blades to those depressed by their commute?' 'Some of his ideas were indeed challenging; but to challenge *is*, in a very special sense...')

'Trace elements.'

'Heresiarchs, Abishag, are burned as a matter of public hygiene.'

'Ugh.'

'Think of the happy youths, the happy happy youths who were fated to read the books Osgood was going to write, and hang themselves. Now they're free to live to ninety!'

This was exactly what she was thinking, but what she said was: 'Think of the nip of the flames.'

'He *yearned* for the stake. He strained to provoke it. All his outrageous hatred. You could boil down Osgood's whole *œuvre* to one phrase: *Come and get me.*'

('...mere dogmatic orthodoxy, but to trust, as Jake did, in *nothing*,' bleats Woolly, 'is, properly understood—' Even television tires of fatuity in the end; besides, the dons up in Screwgrave's rooms were dropping walnuts on them, trying to hit Woolly in mid-pate and wake up his ideas. 'Thank you, Reverend, we have to go back to the studio.' Frank Flute positions himself where he's always happiest, directly in front of the camera. At home there are television screens in every room, even the loo, and he's always playing back his own broadcasts. He likes to think of himself as his audience; he longs to throw an affectionate arm round the camera and peer into the lens, his eyes soft with love; to reach in – which Quine would never allow – and touch that lovely cool curve, as if to tweak his own adorable nose.) 'I'm speaking to you tonight from St Wygefortis', Cambridge, a college shocked and in mourning. Behind me grief-struck students are consoling each other by reading aloud from the works of the dead professor, a man his colleagues are calling, and I quote, "really positive." This is Frank Flute reporting live on what police are describing as a truly, truly tragic accident. Over to you, Tom.'

'Thank you, Frank,' artificially-prematurely-grey Tom Snout told the million tragic people who watch television at midnight, lavishing on them his level-three statesmanlike-frown. (This was no slight on the University: level-two was for small wars, level-one only for death and divorce in the Royal Family.) 'Just to recap on that headline: controversial Cambridge philosopher Jake Osgood, whose testimony before a Parliamentary committee last week caused, and I quote, existential mayhem, passed away tonight in a fire police speculate was caused' – here came one of the cheap, heavy, pauses beloved of television; 'by a dropped cigarette. Next up:' in a flash Snout was doing his level-one prurient eyebrow; a well-filled bicycle-short filled the screen. The Phœbus-like eye of the free press, roving over the planet, lighted on California. 'Schools that reward top exam results with liposuction: sexist or sexy?'

6. A Planetarium

'His death was caused,' murmured Felix, gazing up the starry sky, 'by *joie de vivre*. Joy claims its victims as certainly as lust, and fear, and the itch for power.' Sheol Court was emptying out at last; the bonfire had fallen into embers, the wine was gone; Screwgrave and his cronies had drawn his curtains, and were merrily thrashing each other with clothes-brushes; the young revellers had formed smaller parties of two or three, or four, and slipped away. Soon Margot and Felix too would retire to Felix's bed. Meanwhile they were lying together on the grass, fingers muddled together. It was quiet enough for him to murmur.

'Not by a clumsy cigarette?'

'*And* that. But fundamentally, it was joy that incinerated the jeerer against joy. The night sky tramples the blind beneath its beams. Why must light pierce darkness? Why must I burn Osgood?'

'There are so many answers.' *Of which the best is: simply to prove you're not, we're not the same as him.*

'I know you think my bubbles fey. But contemplate Cassiopeia, on the nor-northeast horizon – d'y'see, behind the tower? If I had my pocket telescope on me I'd show you the supreme bubble: the Bubble Nebula. A wobbly ball of gas so wide it takes light six years to cross it and red, O so red Abishag... Who was it called a tulip "a thin clear bubble of blood"? Browning? The Bubble Nebula's a blinding ruby-red blown film. See it, and your heart tries to climb through your ribs... *That* was the fiery bubble that slew him. Not mine. The thrill of it exploded him. He was a victim of the nebulæ.'

Margot, who'd grasped this idea already, had stopped attending. Indeed Culpepper wasn't listening to himself, he was waiting for Great St Mary's to chime twelve, and filling in the time.

Meanwhile she too was voluble by default, filling silences the way rain-water fills ruts, without any particular end in view. 'My mother was born the day of the moon landing. D'y'know that Nixon was sure it was going to fail? That his astronauts would be stranded up there and die?'

'Yes, I knew that.'

'On her thirtieth birthday she declared, the selfish slapper, "Thank God they came back, it would have *ruined* my day for the rest of my life." But *I've* often thought how interesting it would be if they had stayed. Then whenever we saw the moon we'd know we were looking into an airless open tomb.' *That's my vocation, then. Sidekick to an artisan of superior graves.*

'A whited sepulchre in fact.'

'Yes. There would be Buzz Aldrin and Neil Armstrong, lying dead in their space-suits. Never aging a day.' *Somebody has to do it.*

'They'd disintegrate if their suits were torn,' objected nitpicking Culpepper.

'They *wouldn't* be torn. They'd stay uncorrupt. And bit by bit the moon would come to seem sepulchral. Moonlight would always be ominous. I don't think you'd be rabbiting on about the fatal glory of the galaxies if the night sky were embellished with mummified cadavers.'

'Hmph,' said Culpepper, still listening for chimes.

'Like a brace of skulls hung on a Christmas tree.'

For all this loose talk, she was thinking: *Night is glorious, though – every night. Clarifying fire in darkness. This night especially.* And she was wondering how it must have been in the good old days, on the good old nights,

7. A Liturgical Spectacle

after an evening burning of a heretic. When the screaming had died away, while the grease still bubbled on the stakes, as the choir processed back across the piazza singing *Te Deums*, was the crowd hushed and troubled? That's as Woolly would imagine it.

Or resentful and frightened? That's what a Whig historian would assume.

Or sated and serene? That's how the pious would like to think.

And it was all nonsense. The people would have been stirred, they would have been raucous! She shut her eyes and (with another clatter of stage machinery) she saw it before her – grilled sausages are hawked, and joked about, tumblers and dwarves bound, wheeled stalls of ribbons are rolled out, wine-sellers appear. Lovers murmur to each, their ardour whetted. Mothers look down with shining eyes at their children, who are playing at inquisitions on the cobbles. (Here Margot moved her hand to Felix's quiet chest.) Life has been crudely vindicated against its slanderers. The mob is justly happy.

Perhaps we'd prefer humanity to be more patient with erring oddities, but (thought Margot) *it isn't, it's simply too fierce and sure to care about free play for its enemy. Perhaps the crooked pedant himself, as he felt the verdict of normality licking against his skin, almost enjoyed—*

'Abishag, listen: midnight! That means it's tomorrow! Lætare Sunday! Only twenty-one days 'til the permanent return of after-lunch cigars!'

Xochiquetzal

i.

THE CAREFUL GOOD taste of Felix Culpepper's sitting-room is relieved by his enormous ashtray. This is a pseudo-Aztec affair: a turquoise life-sized death's-head fixed upright in a black earthenware bowl.

Against the rules, I, Margot ffontaines-Laigh, am going to record why it's there. I'm doing this, one, because I loathe it and want to abuse it; two, because although the October sky is already threadbare, Michaelmas Term hasn't begun; I've come up to College early, find it empty, and am at a loose end. Three, I suppose, because I want the thrill of writing up (something my sinister ex-lover has utterly forbidden) one of his misdeeds. And this one is perhaps, it's hard to be sure, the nastiest of the lot.

And four, because Felix is safely away. I'm told he's at the brainless Seb's place in Cornwall, with his other minions Ollie and Tristan. No doubt they're committing another job, another necessary crime; I hardly care. Although I've just locked my door to be on the safe side. He likes to surprise, but not to be surprised; and he would be surprised (I'm not sure what he'd do) if he found me chronicling the Affair of the Aztec Ashtray.

Let's get the object fixed in your mind.

If you're ever allowed into St Wygefortis' College, which seems unlikely, if you walk across Megiddo Court, ascend staircase II, turn left at the second landing, knock on the oak, are ignored, press through to the second door nonetheless, and are summoned with a lordly, impatient shout, you'll find yourself in Dr Culpepper's set.

Here, unless you are stupid, or very grand indeed, you'll be impressed. Through a door on the left is his bedroom, of semi-happy memory, with an indifferent view west across the narrow no-man's-land, Christ's Pieces, which is just straggling trees and bad grass, to the lumpish backside of Christ's.

But the view east from his sitting-room, over Megiddo Court, is good; and the interior is extremely fine. It affects Baroque, more or less. The walls are covered in green damask. Dutch landscapes hang from the picture-rail on red silk cords. A pair of moss-eaten garden statues flank the fireplace, which Felix, in defiance of College regulations, uses: they represent God-knows-what, but have glorious allegorical breasts and the ruin of floral headgear. On the mantle is a silver-gilt *Daphnis and Chloe*, fake I think. No one piece of furniture is particularly splendid, but the effect's lovely, particularly at night, since Felix keeps the electricity off and lights his rooms with gas-lamps; so much for another College rule. (His small Murano chandelier, of polychrome parakeets eating polychrome guavas, good as a stunt, is only lit at Christmas.)

I've said the dear boy's good taste is 'careful'; perhaps it's fairer to say 'carefully careless'. He's astute enough to notice that when the *bourgeoisie* come up in the world, decking themselves out with things created for their betters, they make their houses even more nervous than before. To do him justice, he's massaged out that upper-middle-class tautness. He *manages* a devil-may-care air. You wouldn't guess his father was a jobbing solicitor. Nothing's reverently arrayed: a gilt bust of Louis XIV is used for straw hats. There's scuffed leather upholstery. There's even a bad charcoal sketch, of me, on an easel: at least there was when I last saw his rooms, two months ago. It may have been abolished. And nothing was overly clean; although that owed a lot to the Elmsgall, his slovenly bedder, rather than to swagger.

In short, the room's not excessive. It couldn't set anyone's teeth on edge; there's no need to blunt the effect with tourist tat.

But did he *choose* to do that? Perhaps at the core of a man, if he's domestic, is not his soul but his sitting-room, the self-expressing temple for the worship of himself. The pith of that room's the low table where he drinks and smokes; and in the midst of the table's an ornament that gives the game away. Felix's holy-of-holies is occupied by this sad knick-knack: a geometric curve of coarse, dead-black, featureless pottery called (he tells me) *barro negro*, holding the Aztec fake with its rubbishy plastic lustre.

Aztec? Aztec? Weren't the Mixtecs of Oaxaca the ones who did the enamelled skulls? Anyway, it's not really a fake of anything in particular, it's a pretentious *pastiche*: exotic artifacts recalled in the light of Duchamp, Koons, Hurst, and pranksters of that stripe. No one would think it a real skull. And the mosaic that covers it is clearly not turquoise, lignite and agate, but plastic squares from Taiwan. Also, it's not sombre and satanic, like real Pre-Columbian works. There are shards of mirror encrusted about its fixed grin, and flecks of camp gilding where the hair should be, as if it's trying to be not as ugly but as tawdry as it can.

Its excuse for existing is that when Felix smokes his after-lunch cigar, he taps ash through its eye sockets. For the next twenty-three-and-a-half hours it's ignored. God knows how the Elmsgall cleaned it out.

I'm being stupid: of course, she *didn't*. The ash must have built up since March. What'll happen when it starts spilling out? Will Felix throw his Mexican bauble away? No, because it's been (as the lower orders say when they monogram their towels) *personalised*. Across the forehead Felix has painted in gold

> *My cranium's the cosmic vault: your world*
> *rides cranial blood, and in brain-cum is swirled*

– a quotation from the mercifully small corpus of Brockland Croke, the neo-Imagist poet. Do I mean neo-Projectivist? No matter. Croke's a revival of something or-other no one had thought to revive before; which is what it takes to get labelled 'audacious' in *The New York Review of Books*.

Now here's the embarrassing truth. While the *kitsch* skull is a joke, the *kitsch* verse is only a semi-joke. There was a time, in Lent Term in fact, just before the Easter vac, when Felix took Brockland Croke seriously. For a while Croke bode large in Felix's inner life; such as it is.

Bode is exactly the verb. Like most dons, Felix isn't much of a reader: just dead Latin and not too much even of that. He doesn't read contemporary poetry. Nobody does. Poets write only to dazzle or insult other poets; or to appear, unread even by the editors, in highbrow journals, where their short irregular lines create blobby white space, upon which the intellectual eye, weary of dense prose, rests gratefully. Felix, flicking through *The New York Review*, rested on the blank area around a poem by Croke. He paused; unhappily read a line. Then more. Then the whole thing, greedily. Then he went to Heffers and bought all four of Croke's slim volumes. The boding began.

I did my best to mock him out of it. 'Why, Felix, if English poets can have pretty names like Wordsworth, Byron, Tennyson and Auden, must North Americans be called Gary Snyder, Hilda Doolittle, Snodgrass, and Croke?'

'Oh don't try to be æsthetic. Not about America. Listen to this: *I must harrow to your marrow: Soul's a bird and I'm the scarecrow*… Isn't that just awful?'

'Yes. It is.'

And it was. I'd quit Felix's bed after the Affair of the Magician's Apprentice in mid-February. *Quit* makes me sound more decisive than I was. It wasn't technically a break-up. I simply couldn't decide whether he was a villain or not; thus whether I was a mass-murderer's journeyman or not; and until I knew what he was and what I was, I couldn't picture what we were. The little of his power I'd usurped had worked only ill. For three weeks we simply lapsed, and I'd sit staring at him from sofa, not bed. In early March he sorted out Jake Osgood, the Philosophy Fellow whose books incited people to kill themselves. (Even in my present defiant mood I daren't write about Osgood and the Affair of the Bubble Nebula.) The damage, then, was reversed; I could imagine Felix as hero, myself as hero's help; we drifted together again.

But I suppose every hero requires a nemesis. Jason needs Medea, Holmes needs Moriarty. Even comic-book supermen must be given monstrous rivals to fight, KRUNCH! KER-BAM! If you work your wonders *without* an antagonist – if you're incomparably clever Œdipus or Hamlet, or the Pied Piper, or Jehovah in the Old Testament – who's to say you're not yourself the monster? The removal of Osgood left a cavity in Felix, until, a few days later, he chanced on Croke, and the boding began.

I understand that well enough now, in autumn, now I'm turning into Felix; I didn't understand in March. 'My boyfriend's getting weird': I was simply discontented. How many grains of the Croke annoyance outweigh the vast but finite heft of being in love? What was to be done when he *imitated* Croke? One day I received verses titled *Fractures*, a reproach which I'll fish out now from behind my Rothko, and staple in place between these sheets. Here:

> *Margot grew tired of flesh, and learned to love*
> > *invisible bone.*
> *So, making love, my skeleton would move*
> *at pleasures deeper than the hands' or eyes'*
> > *with audible moan.*

> *'What is this keening from my cranium*
> > *and upper thigh?'*
> *She would not say, but at her lips the brim*
> *of her own crisp and flowering white within*
> > *bent in reply.*

I want to be fair. Not even in the depth of his madness did Felix think Croke's work *good*. He'd merely been infected with it. Croke had entered tapewormwise, and couldn't be washed out. But why, you may ask? Why, even if Felix is prone to obsessions (as he is), become obsessed with *Brockland Croke*? Why with this precious academic versifier, State Laureate by decree of Arizona's deluded authorities? Why with a man whose feathery nest at a remote university must surely be less well-furnished than Felix's own?

The answer is: havoc.

Let's consider Croke's third collection, *Innards*, which sold 120 copies (110 of them, no doubt, to university libraries). *Innards* contains a dozen narrative poems, describing a dozen young people. First we're told about their appearance, then their character, then their inner thoughts, then the howls and pleas they utter as they're killed, then the squelches as they're eviscerated, the pops and cracks as they're dismembered, finally the look of their cadavers after a month lying in the outdoors.

With Osgood departed from us, Felix was the only bookish person in the world with the habit of homicide. That gave him a certain authority; it also made him morbid. Any specialty narrows the mind. Judges can't be trusted to decide, only juries of laymen. I, the jury, found Croke guilty of being a bore. But by mid-March, Felix had reached the point of frenzy. He was beyond imitating Croke's poems, beyond evaluating them, even beyond reading them. He was reading things *into* them, the way Baconians find anagrams in Shakespeare. He was convinced that they recorded Croke's literal murders.

'Listen to this: *Ribs twist against the grain of sternum Five, six, seven times. Then out.* That *must* record something he's experienced.'

'Or seen on telly. A police drama. I'm told they're graphic.'

'No this is *reality*. I taste it. The tang.'

'Perhaps. But since we can't find out what goes on in Arizona, or greatly care, I suggest—'

'You're not listening. I *know* what's going on. His poems describe carnage he's perpetrating himself. Have you read *The Man Who was Thursday*?' He found it on his shelves and started leafing. 'Philosophical policemen go to tea parties disguised as Decadent poets. To detect anarchist sentiment among the artists before it can flower into terrorist action... Here! "We were only just in time to prevent the assassination at Hartlepool, and that was entirely due to the fact that our Mr. Wilks (a smart young fellow) thoroughly understood a triolet." ' He slammed it shut. '*Exactly.*'

'Yes,' I said as I generally say, 'Felix,' wondering how much more I could bear.

However the frenzy, indeed the whole Crokesque period, came to a sudden end shortly afterwards. And I ended it.

ii.

One annoying thing about this story is that Felix Culpepper might seem its guiding intellect. Which is perfectly untrue.

I have a science of faces of which he knows nothing (humanity being almost invisible to him). Science itself has not caught up with me, neither has painting. No novelist seems to possess this lore; indeed most novels assume *There's no art To find the mind's construction in the face* – people are so contiguous they make fundamental mistakes about each other – which is what gets the stories going. Whereas what we call mankind is a zoo of species, drastically divergent.

Most children understand this. My science formed in my head from studying my mother's men-friends. They came and went at a steady pace, and I was familiar with the usual drama of arrival and departure, but in between they were as different as squidworms, seahorses and clams, with nothing in common but my mother, the mindless rockpool through which they passed.

Most adults put this dangerous knowledge out of their minds, but not me. I cannot forget, and neither can you once you've read the field-guide. Here it is.

Two species concern us, both clumsily called human. They have two entirely distinct faces: those looked out of, those looked at.

The first species has a CASEMENT face, which exists to carry eyes, nose and ears. Of course just as an architect, providing casements so his clients can look out, defines his style with sashes, sills, shutters, louvres, so the self incidentally portrays itself in cartilage and skin; and although the attempt's usually botched, the charm of a CASEMENT face is that it's pretty much oblivious to being looked at; almost like a sunset, or a tree in blossom.

The second species, DISPLAY, has, when fully-developed, a metallic sheen. The face is usually attractive; not always; but grows disgusting the longer you look. Say a man becomes besotted with a made-to-be-looked-at DISPLAY. He marries her, and is unhappy – not, as his friends assume, because it's easy for the beautiful to be unfaithful, but because such features grow creepy viewed morning after morning over breakfast.

We subdivide the DISPLAYS into two subspecies.

Usually such faces are meant to looked at by *other people*: this is the SHOPWINDOW face. The touch of eyebeams isn't immaterial. The features of a beautiful woman are burnished by having eyes run across them. Her features become more perfect by being regarded, also more inhuman; and if this goes on long enough we have an actress or a model. When you meet such a person you're astonished something breathing the same air and drinking the same sémillon can be so utterly alien.

But then there are DISPLAY faces dehumanised by being looked at too much *by themselves*. You'll have been in a hall of mirrors at a fun-fair? A pavilion of distorting, enlarging, shrinking looking-glasses? The French call it a palace of ices (which is a good phrase), or LABYRINTHE DE MIROIRS. A LABYRINTHE visage is both actor and audience; the same eye is subject and object. And this is simply an abomination, like incest or suicide or child-sacrifice: an outward impulse folded back on its own flesh.

There's no absolute divide between CASEMENT and SHOPWINDOW faces; there are lots of hybrid, intermediate stages. You'll have been to a hill village on the verge of becoming self-conscious. It's still lovely, as a by-product of being sturdily built; the actual rot hasn't begun, the busloads of tourists, shops selling sweatshirts instead of bread; but the dew's been shaken off the rose, and you know it can't come back. A CASEMENT can decay through various stages and become a SHOPWINDOW; a SHOPWINDOW can tire of being a sex symbol and become normal.

But a LABYRINTHE DE MIROIRS face is quite disjunctive. It can never develop into anything else, it stays put. While a SHOPWINDOW often has a hunted look (we all know the sort of woman who keeps glancing about to make sure men still desire her), a LABYRINTHE is essentially oblivious. It's a face blind to every sight but one, every viewer but one. When social convention requires it to be pointed outward, its purported gaze is as disquieting as the purported gaze of a portrait, or an open-eyed corpse.

A LABYRINTHE or narcissist is dying from the inside out. In paintings Narcissus is a pretty youth preening over a mountain pool, but that's not what Ovid says; Ovid understood the science of faces, and knew Narcissus couldn't stay pretty, but must moan and shiver and dribble with lust until dementia killed him. He starved to death, he died of thirst hanging over the waters; and death didn't cure him. His corpse bred *narcissi*, which is to say daffodils, garish flowers often mistaken for onions at the bulb stage. Daffodils are full of lycorine, the tincture of LABYRINTHE-ness. The symptoms of lycorine are melancholy, stomach cramps, hyper-salivation, anorexia and tremors: in other words, it turns you into Narcissus. No doubt the chemical inspired the myth. Lycorine is one of the fatal toxins concocted by the mind for its own use.

Of course a LABYRINTHE will die for real: his face then moves on. But is that *it*? Are we certain death's a cure-all? I know we're all supposed to think so. But what if there's truth in the old idea of the beatific vision: the supreme pleasure of eternity will be to see the divine face, looking back? Mightn't there be a matching maleficent vision for those predestined to be damned this way?

That's why the Narcissus story is more frightful than people think. He wasn't ruined by an external curse, but by what he was from birth, that is, an ice-palace, a LABYRINTHE. Ovid gives him this obscene truth to whisper to his watery self: *Lovely kid, what hurts is that it's not mountains separating us, not oceans nor not a bolted barbican;* exigua prohibemur aqua, *it's just the teensiest scrap of water that thwarts our fuck.* That teensy scrap is simply the boundary of the reflection, or in other words the boundary between Narcissus and the universe. Narcissus wishes the surface of the pool weren't there. He wants to abolish the meniscus and be all in all: to obliterate the cosmos until his four eyeballs meld, one comely torso be submerged in the other, so that Narcissus can be all in all. Well, what if self-lovers get what they crave? Wouldn't that be the final atrocity of the Pit?

I do not normally apply my science of faces to those I know; one does not want to regard friends on track to hell; but I did once, by accident. The insight broke up affairs and precipitated the Croke crisis; Felix playing a bit part.

iii.

The other annoying thing about this story is that Sebastian Hawick Trocliffe might seem to be the protagonist. Which is nonsense. Seb isn't the protagonist of tying his own shoelaces. His shoes surely wriggle across the floor each morning (what am I saying? Afternoon. Early evening, if he's been on a particular bender) to butt gently against his toes. He's the last word in grinning inertia. He can't possibly be the hero of anything. None of the events I'm about to record would have happened if I, I, Margot ffontaines-Laigh, Dr Culpepper's official squeeze and semi-official sidekick, hadn't spied on Seb one afternoon.

I didn't mean to. His door was ajar. I pushed it open. His back was to me and he didn't move. He was standing in front of the floor-length looking-glass he keeps propped up in his sitting-room, *looking*.

The glass is a recent development. Seb was unkempt and careless when he arrived at St Wygy's, exactly a year ago; in those days Ollie was the vain one, although in his case self-love was almost entirely centred on his curls.

Since the Affair of the Dictator's Brat, Ollie's become more serious, cut his hair short, and passed on his narcissism to Seb; partly in the physical form of unwanted hair products (never safe in male hands), and partly according to the spiritual law that states the quantity of fatuity in the world must remain constant.

Anyway, now it's Seb who fusses about windburn and combs.

It was curious to see him in the very act of fussing. I waited for him to turn, but he didn't. I waited to see how long it would take. Seconds ticked away into minutes. After a minute I couldn't speak, it would have been too embarrassing. But neither could I steal away. I was paralysed, as before horrors. His gaze was too intense for him to notice me, any more than he could notice you, hovering as it were over his right shoulder and gazing into the glass with him, even if the conventions of narrative allowed him to see you. His face hovered in the cold dead flat mineral glass, and I had to regard it.

ॐ

I was witnessing Seb at the moaning stage. He's sure to achieve dribbling and convulsing before he's done. If I ever need to dispose of him (and it's crossed my mind) I'll feed him curry made with chopped daffodil bulbs, and it won't be cruel; I'll merely be hurrying on the process of chronic lycorine poisoning he's already inflicting on himself.

Seb stuck out his chest, explored the line of his flank, smoothed his long yellow hair with one hand, thumbed his lower lip with the other, enjoyed his stubble with the back of his hand, felt the edge of his excellent teeth with a knuckle, caressed a temple, fingered an ear. At last he uttered a sigh, profound as the sigh God breathed over complete unfallen Creation, seeing it was good. I stole away under cover of that noise, like a mystic heavy with an apparition of Tartarus, like Dante creeping out of Malebolge, like a spy bearing news of idolatry to a Grand Inquisitor.

iv.

I didn't mean Seb any harm. Human beings can only be mad in one direction at a time; my idea was that news of Seb's lunacy might shake Felix out of his own.

I found myself mounting staircase II of Megiddo Court. I knocked at the inner door; the grunt not quite hostile enough to send me away.

He was, as I expected, miserably prone on his sofa, turning the pages of *Just Blood*, Brookland Croke's fourth, final, most revolting collection of poems. I watched for a second or two.

'Hawicke Troscliffe's clinically unhinged. Did y'know?'

'Ah.'

'It's not just shamelessness, all public schoolboys are shameless. He's brazen-faced.' (This is as much as Felix would understand of my science.) 'Bestial. Demon-fodder. His monotonous lechery's just a front. An excuse to spend hours in front of his glass, keeping his weaponry polished.'

'Ah-huh.' He didn't look up.

'After he bombs at Tripos he'll sink and sink and end as a porn star.'

'Hm?' Felix turned a page.

'The first day on set he'll wave at the camera: "Hi mummy!"'

'Ah.' But then Felix did put down his book, and lifted his face to mine. 'Shamelessness. Brazen-faced.'

'Yes. We're discussing Seb. I'm telling you about Seb. You look stoned. When will this stop?'

He said 'Ah,' and I gave up. I'm not sure he heard me go. To make it clear to myself how little I cared, I went to Beelzebub, the College library, found a book, and opened it.

A quarter of an hour later I heard a voice, his voice, *singing*. Going to the library window I beheld the Fellow and Tutor in Latin prancing (or gambolling) across Limbo, the shapeless flagged area beyond Beelzebub and the kitchens. 'Brazen-faced, brazen-faced,' he was chanting, waggling *Just Blood* like a thyrsus. 'Shameless, shameless. Pliable, pliable.'

So Felix's gloomy spell was over. Good. But why was he dancing that way, and not me-wards, to celebrate his restored sanity?

I watched him tripping under the tower of Lethe. *I* am Culpepper's assistant in mayhem, *I* am his Watson. What business did he have vanishing into Erebus, the covered bridge crossing Willow Walk into Abaddon, where dwells, of all insignificant people, Sebastian? How dare Felix recruit that flyspeck, especially as I'd just reported him deranged and damned?

I'm not being peevish. It's a matter of decency. Watson's role as *aide-de-camp* was usurped against all reason. Which is why now, six months later, in autumn, I have taken upon myself Watson's other function, with paper, behind a locked door.

v.

Brockland Croke (this is how I picture him) has a textbook SHOPWINDOW face. It is squareish, attractively jowly, heavily tanned, blue-eyed, intellectually chinned, with rippling waves of fine white hair. It is pleased to be looked at. It is smirking (I should think; if Felix had sent me I would not have to guess). A smirk is its factory setting. Its lips move sleepily and moistly, which also seems normal.

More unusually, the face floats, unattached. It's a nightmare head, Orpheus chanting verses without a body, floating in a halo of pagan silver light. Above, below and behind is impenetrable black.

Then we notice the microphone sharing Croke's nimbus. As our irises dilate we make out the short bulky body perched on a barstool. It's a poetry reading, then, in one of those arty cafés endemic to university towns.

'*Sheer off your tendons with a bread knife, baby,*' recites Croke. *Face Peel*, the second of his collections, lies open on his knees, but only as a stage prop. He knows his small *œuvre* by heart (if that's the organ he uses) but has learned over the years that if the punters see you finger your books, the paper becomes precious, a tertiary relic of the Muse, and they're more inclined to buy signed copies afterwards.

Meanwhile his eyes roam the dingy cabaret tables. It's not much of a house. There are five tragic spinsters in a body, of a certain age, doubtless with sheaves of manuscript to show him afterwards if they dare, if they dare. There are two intense loners in their late twenties with masturbation complexions, always a toss-up whether they'll merely top themselves or "go postal", thank God no one ever "goes postal" in arts cafés, the game's too meagre. Who else? A gaggle of teenage girls overwrought with veganism ("We went to this *reading* last night and it was *totally* real"). One hardcore ex-hippie, grey hair in a ponytail, gnarly thighs in cycling shorts, present because he digs the scene, poetry is counter-culture and fucks with The Man. One of Croke's students, making her presence visible and even *nodding*, impudent lazy troll, bet she's hoping to soften her failing grade. Fat chance, fat baby. Of course Jamie the Stalker, the thoroughly innocuous stalker who always comes to Croke's readings. And finally there's the truculent arts columnist from *The Tucson Voice*, who as always is making it clear she has to be here, is bound for better things in Manhattan one day *pretty soon*, and meanwhile can digest fraudulent old Croke perfectly well thank you while composing her review on her

BlackBerry *with her thumb*.

The shameful thing is that Croke digs the scene too. He loves readings. He doesn't mind that the audience is pathetic, he doesn't mind spending an hour selling six copies at $14.95 of which only six lousy bucks come back to him in royalties. It's not ears or minds or moolah he desires, it's eyes. He adores the sensation of hopeless gazing: his mouth, his hooded eyes, his nostrils (which he flares to mark a cæsura). He's giving audience. He gives him what he wants.

What's this? A latecomer? No one comes late to poetry readings. And it's a type Croke can't place: *A boy, tall boy, expensive haircut, red trousers – red trousers in Tucson! Everyone here wears cowboy duds, apart from us culture-vultures in sweaters woven from granola. Who who* who *are* you?

This boy settles at the back table, leers at a waitress while making hand signals for a tankard, a large tankard, peers through the gloaming at the other devotees to see if there's anyone to ogle, finds there isn't, glances (glances!) at Croke himself, then goes back to the waitress's bottom.

'*Mangunk to earthgunk,*' says Croke; snort for cæsura; '*dust to dust; adjust.*' Annoyed. intrigued, he's trying to make eye contact. Not a thing. Ah well, this is the last poem:

> '*You know you wanted it, know you craved this thrust*
> *of bayonet, 'cause, babe, your blood's just rust.*

That's it, y'all! Thank you,' and amidst a dry rustle of applause (the faint, self-satisfied applause peculiar to small-scale *Kultur*), Croke descends from his barstool throne. His subjects leap up, nails out, wanting a piece of him. Jamie the Stalker, hunched sideways in his lonely chair, raises tortured eyes in a hopeless CASEMENT face, his you've-never-loved-me-have-you stare. The arts columnist makes heavy weather of pushing SEND. The waitress brings tisanes. Croke walks through them all and stands over the back table.

Languidly the boy turns from eyeing the girl and raises a clear, smug, blithe, unsoulful face (*Gee, you could be British*) to the great man. 'Hi.'

(*British! Ker*-ching!) 'Why, hal-*lo.*'

'You're Professor Croke? Wow. Sorry I missed some of it. It was, y'know, don't know what. It said things. You're a poetic poet.'

'*Moi? Toi* is obviously a *cognoscente*. May I buy *toi* an *autre bier*?' Being Canadian, Croke has superstitions about the erotic power of even the worst French.

The boy drains his tankard and smiles. Croke sits with his back to his fans. Baffled of their prey, they drift away and do whatever people of that stratum do. Meanwhile Croke fixes his gaze on Seb, SHOPWINDOW beholding LABYRINTHE, never a happy arrangement, neither face can possibly get what it needs.

vi.

The *quantity* of America is so gigantic it becomes, in the end, a *quality*. Almost every instant, almost every frame, is dull, and the superlative roads make the shoddiness all the more painful, whether it's hard grey towers seen at a distance; or seedy streets, nearly Third World in close-up; or off-white plastic, spray-on-brick suburbs, which might have gone up last week and may be shipped further west tomorrow. The European tourist has to damp down sensibility. At least that's what this thirteen year old girl did. How else to endure roadsides that are straggles of shrub and scrawny aspen? This was the summer Mama, in New York, ran away with a film-person, of course a SHOPWINDOW, who was too stoned to drive but needed to get his 1955 Thunderbird to L.A. "yesterday." From the back seat I saw everything: empty arable counties, huge untidy crops, castleless hilltops, nameless creeks, numberless spireless hamlets selling nothing but petrol, forests that are all hemlock, ranges that are all scree. He goaded Mama to drive faster, faster, which sped the affair through the usual stages; we abandoned him and flew home at the Nevada state line, and his biopic of Rutherford Hayes never got made. The faculty America demands is memory. This is daydream landscape, vivid and unreal, only to be seen in retrospect. Its millions of tedious snapshots fall together in the mind and reveal something sublime.

It's not like this in Asia. Asia's as vast as America, but it has to be comprehended by renunciation: by sheering away the huge finities until one sits cross-legged, solitary in a thicket of bamboo, lost in the eternity of a single plucked lotus in your lap. (At least that's what I did in my year off. Once or twice.) The typical Asian arts are austere: one calligraphic twist of brush on rice paper, and there's the canyon of the Yangzte, there are the pine-buffs of Hokkaido, here's the Deccan plateau or the Empty Quarter.

But the supreme American artform is the road movie. Even roadside events that would seem explosive in Europe – a cloven mountain, a blasted plateau, twelve-pointed roadkill, a concrete statue thirty feet high of a goldfish or a garlic-bulb – iterate themselves, blur, fall into irregular rhythm, sink at last into a background hum. This is a continent designed to be seen at seventy miles an hour day after day while listening to commercial radio.

However, if we'd been suspended in the sky above southern Arizona at ten on Friday evening, 15th March 2013, following an open-topped Jeep Wrangler winding its way up into the dry coniferous mountains called the Catalinas, what we would have heard is Bach.

We'd have seen white hair blowing about in the driver's seat; yellow hair whipping out behind the passenger; and in the back seat a huge canvas bag. ('Got my guitar in it'; a lie; it contained gels and unguents.) And we'd have heard *Amore traditore*, a secular cantata.

Croke was full of strong, simple, half-civilised ideas. He believed in Bach as seduction music just as he believed in French. He was also convinced that altitude lowers resistance. That was part of the charm of his remote mountain log-cabin. 'Ya'll understand when I say cabin, it's just four bedrooms, a Jacuzzi, an artesian well and a 38-inch plasma screen in the rumpus room.' Although its greatest charm was simply how far it was from anywhere. '*Anywhere*. It's so deep in the Catalinas no one can hear you scream. Of course *I* do most of the screamin'. After a readin', I'm pretty riled up. Another beer?'

Seb had not heard of Bach. He liked the Jeep and liked the sensation of warm night wind lifting his hair (although after two days of American airports he was running low on moisturiser, and unsure about anything whistling on his skin). They'd risen out of the desert by now. The scruffiness of cactuses and mesquite trees had given way to slovenly stands of juniper and oak. Not that the citified Seb grasped these details.

He thought he'd better make a remark. 'Empty out here,' he bawled above the racket of the Jeep. 'Peaceful.'

'Bless Patsy! That's just what it's *not*. Arizona's plumb crazy. At the university they smoke ganja and do yoga and make themselves freakish-uptight. Tuscson townies are software billionaires retired at thirty to turn cognac-drunk and get ab-*dook*-ted by flying saucers. The Mayor was nominated by the nightclub owners' collective. For five years there's been a local mass-murderer on the loose, they call him The Faulty Toaster, 'cos he slices and burns studmuffins. And the mall shootin's are to die for. On the Res—'

'Ganja?' shouted carefree Seb, who hadn't listened to much of this speech and why should he? 'You wouldn't happen to have...?'

The poet tittered. 'In good time, purdy one. *Not* in an open Jeep out here in the *boon*docks. The only mountainy-folk here'bouts who don't believe

Jesus is comin' soon are looking out for Elvis. Or they're Californians who've drifted east and think extreme-West-weird gets respectable if you cut it with Wild-West-survivialist.' His cod Southern accent was turning fantastical. 'See that ornery ole fortress yonder, other side of the canyon? He'll be following us with his telescopic sight, just in case we turn out to be the Is-*lame*-ic invasion at layust. He won't mind your beer, but a toke? *Quel effronterie!* There's like to be a l'il red dot back of your neck this very second.'

This made Seb think of sunscreen and he asked 'Is it going to be hot up here tomorrow?'

The poet smirked in a way I wouldn't have liked were I in a Jeep with him. 'We goin' well beyond hot, precious,' and indeed they were twisting up toward the timberline, the beginning of cool air and continuous conifers. 'My place is at eight thousand feet, it gets snowed in every year. Tonight's balmy, but don't you go 'suming you'll wake up to sunshine tomorrow.'

Then the poet laughed, driving even more quickly round the curves of the boringly perfect road (built, as it happens, by the forced labour of men interned for their Japanese descent). A moonlit fir flashed by, another another another another, a ragged hundred, two thousand, three, a million, two million, five million, ten million, twenty-five. Sooner or later this is going to amount to an effect, although not for the expendable Sebastian.

vii.

Croke turned off the mountain road, paused to unlock heavy iron gates, paused to close them again, then bounced down a dirt driveway. After ten minutes he stopped, turned off his headlights, turned off his engine, turned off Bach, let the brake go, and floated bumpily home. Seb, who had been dozing, roused himself.

It was one in the morning. The moon was down, and the sky was such a mass of galaxies that the gables and chimneys of Croke's house were negatively clear, a starless cut-out. The stillness was rather terrible.

'Let's have a drink on the porch,' whispered Croke. Invisibly Seb shrugged. Invisibly he went round the side of the house, mounted the steps, found a rocking chair. In the background there was some bother with keys, a burglar alarm, creaking boards, gasp of an opened fridge, the metallic clatter of ice-cubes. Seb was almost asleep again when he felt a cool hand on his shoulder and a freezing glass pressed into his hand.

Croke had brought a tray and a kerosene lantern. 'Whisky, honeybun. Well, bourbon. I know you Britishers have yo' doubts 'bout it. But on a warm nights it's' – then he says something I can't make out and shan't guess. I'm transcribing the dialogue from a recording, you understand, and don't want to dilute veracity by making anything up. Everything out loud is verbatim, every action is as reported by Seb: you're reading the purest journalism.

It was easy to catch voices in the bar and in the Jeep. It was like listening to a radio play. However, the machine stayed in Seb's huge canvas bag, and even on such a still night I have trouble picking up what was said ten yards away on the porch.

But frankly, from the scraps I *can* make out of that conversation or monologue, I don't think we're missing much. (The cries of nocturnal hunting birds, on the other hand, are remarkably clear. I wish I could transcribe their baleful music.)

'The artist,' says Croke, predictably, 'cannot be bound by… Exp-*here*-ience, gruesome most of all! That's what frees… Beyond evil, beyond good… *L'art pour l'art*, as Gautier… *La mort pour l'art*; that's what's really necessary… was enraged by the reach of my pedagogy, pederasty per-*haps*.' Here the great poet quite distinctly burps. Then he chants. '*Peddy-weddy, goggy, goggy; rasty rasty rasty*. Nasty. But nice. Smidgeonette more?' Glugging. 'I see myself, precious, as the perfection of the work of Poe, of Mr Edgar Allen Poe.'

Every so often Seb says 'Oh?', but evil of this sort is over his head, even when he's properly awake. (Slow creak of his rocking-chair. Screech owls. Nightjars going *peent-peent*.)

After a while Croke talks dirty. 'I used to want to stretch upward towards… come across some angelic youth tryin' to dirty himself… a stalacmite meetin' a stalactite. Sodomite and sodomtite, so to… *Calcium*,' I make out that word clearly enough: 'you'll have seen in caves, every so often a drip gets lucky and finds a column rising in exactly the… pillar. Pillar of the community. But no longer… tastes different, quite quite… Pillar of salt. City of the Plain. That's me, calcium. Milky. Inescapable.'

As he rambles, his Dixiecrat accent thins out. I presume it was just part of his apparatus for battening on Americans, who believe writers ought to be decayed sozzled Southern gentry, not Winnipeg burgher stock. Croke sounds more and more Canadian, also muddier and muddier.

Eventually he's got himself sufficiently drunk or unhallowed to murmur

'Come try out my jac-*ooze*-ee.'

More blurred noises, feet, hiss, the start of a loud continuous bubble. Suddenly the voices are so clear and loud, despite the water pipes, they might be few feet off, and I find myself *there*, witnessing what occurred an ocean and a continent away, seven months ago, *here, now*: 'Yeah, incredibly. Just want to sleep,' murmured Seb. (I'm muddling my tenses.) Splash. Bubble-bubble-bubble.

'It's *not* sleep you feel, honeychild,' says Croke. 'It's par-*awl*-ysis.' His voice is tense and luxurious. He seems to splash noisily closer. 'Awful-truth moment. Uncle Brocky's been deeply, deeply wicked. He's put drugs in your drinkypooh. D'you wanna know why? 'Cause he's The Faulty Toaster.' You'll have guessed this; what comes as a shock is not the news, but how intellectually vain Croke sounds about it. 'Brocky's art is not just a matter of paper, he does all he says he does.' Slosh, slosh. 'You'll be my eleventh. By dawn you'll be lying in the wood with my other ten. But I'll have seen the real me re *fleek*-ted in your eyes as they fade to black. And *first*—'

'Dr Culpepper! Can you come now? This fat bastard's got his hand on my knee.'

Felix came round the corner of the porch, recorder in hand. 'You all right, Seb? Careful not to drink or eat anything? Good. Get out, then.'

Loud watery noises. '*You* all right?'

'*No*. It was suffocating in that bag. And bumpy. And your cosmetics reek.'

Croke's mouth was swinging so wide his flawless teeth glittered in the starlight, which danced and flickered on the churning waters of the pool and on his wet pelt. I'm informed. 'Argh,' he certainly said.

'Croke, Croke, Croke. There you are... Y'know, you'd still be all right if I hadn't heard you read your stuff aloud. Well, all-rightish. My original idea was to chain you up with these' (he produced two pairs of handcuffs from his pocket; I hear the clanking) 'and leave you for the police. With my recorder propped on a table, playing your confession over and over. The State of Arizona could've had the fun of trying you, electrocuting you, gassing. Psychoanalysing you on television. Whatever they do out here to mass-murderers.'

'Lethal injection?' offers the literal Seb, muffled as from towelling his hair.

'Bah! Injections! Soft-on-Satan! We're ratcheting up the penalty. Seb, left hand.'

Croke was too staggered to resist or even stand, and the Englishmen soon had his arms stretched out, each wrist handcuffed to the wooden rail running around the Jacuzzi.

'There. Seb, d'y'know how to turn the bubbles off?' An abrupt silence. 'Thanks. Go and get dressed.' A pause on the tape of three and a half seconds, during which I can hear Croke breathing.

'Look, I don't know anything aboot—' he says at last, his Southern drawl entirely gone.

But Felix wasn't conversational. 'Be quiet. I'm your judge, Croke. The trial's over. You need to understand the sentence. Your—'

'What I said before – it was a joke about—' He's violently cut off. Furious choking, struggling, liquid flailing.

Felix pulled Croke's head out of the water. '*Silence*, you prosy fraud. Interrupt again, I'll hold you under for a minute.' He made himself comfortable. 'You're a poet who despises poetry. You think it essentially opaque. It was amusing to confess, wasn't it? To advertise your crimes in print – quite safely. But your trash reached me. I thoroughly understood. Obviously I couldn't denounce you; no court entertains evidence in verse. So I came here, with a student who happened to be sufficiently… the word given me was *brazen-faced.*'

(There! there! Pause the machine. Did you catch it? The one moment in The Affair of the Sadist Poet where yours-truly, the protagonist, gets a look-in. Entirely uncredited, you notice.)

Distraught noises, and I think the word *Drown*.

'Not at all… A good solid oaken tub, isn't it? Here's the thermostat.' Croke released a sort of strangled whine. 'I see it's marked up to 112 Fahrenheit, with the last ten degrees shaded red to show they're a bit *ouch*. But I prise loose the dial. Twist the thermostat round to, I should think, 135, which frankly is *oww*. A bit more, 220 or so, which is *flay.*' There's a crescendo of farmyard noise from Croke, who has apparently left not just poetry but language itself behind. 'Now I turn on the tap so you don't steam dry. A tad more? About right. Spilling over the brim now, but when things get cooking it'll be close to equilibrium. Good night. Sweet dreams. Seb!' he shouted above Croke's ruckus. 'Seb!' – very loudly, since Croke continues to disgrace himself with moans and squeals. 'Seb? Where are you?'

Seb appeared, mildly shamefaced.

'Let's go. What've you been doing?'

'Looking round the house. I found … this groovy mirror. Sun-shaped. On the ceiling over the master bed.'

Felix can be heard to sigh theatrically above Croke, whose outcries are dwindling into the aural background. Our heroes are walking away. Seb sounds jaunty, as is generally the way with self-infatuated DISPLAY faces, until lycorine build-up undoes them in middle age. 'Great house. Make a good shag-pad. Fires in every bedroom...' Thus, chatting pleasantly, they get in Croke's Jeep and drive away.

For an hour they worked their way out of the Catalina Mountains on a dirt track, down craggy valleys and up rugged ranges, heading north and a little east, Felix driving.

'Stop!' said Seb. 'I hear something.'

They pulled over, got out, and found themselves on a sort of natural balcony, a shelf hanging over the endless rolling expanse of mountain forest. The far wall of the valley had battlements so high that, even now in March, there were traces of snow. Its peaks were flushed pink. The sky was beginning to pale behind them; the stars were dimming, there was a fresh pine-scented breeze. The universe was quickening. But below in the valley all was still black. From a point on the dark hills opposite they heard a scream, silvery with distance but clear. It was (Felix told me) quite unlike the unmanly snivels and yaps with which Croke had farewelled them. This was a cry of such perfect agony it seemed clean of personality. It was a noise bereft of moral flaw, distilling and expiating our species' illimitable, elemental suffering. It was almost noble.

It was repeated once more. Then nothing, nothing.

🐉

'And then nothing, nothing,' said Felix.

'Zilch,' explained witty Sebastian. 'Not another peep. Are there bigger plates than these?'

'Scullery. Drying rack. Y'know, Abishag,' Felix said, 'I think that was the uncanniest moment of my uncanny life. Those excruciated cries, jabbing upward! They weren't so unlike the jagged radiance of ten thousand fading stars stabbing down. Do you follow? No? Perhaps you had to be—'

'Play her the recording,' shouted Seb from the scullery.

'Oh yes. I held up my machine to try to catch Croke's last croak – listen... Recorded, it's not really so interesting.'

viii.

'No,' I agreed dourly, having heard chirrups from his machine, 'not so interesting. More bubbly would be nice, though.'

This was six days later, Palm Sunday, the twenty-fourth of March, about noon. I'd just been summoned to Felix's overdecorated rooms. The two travellers, or 'adventurers' as I'm sure they'd have wanted me to call them (or even 'conquerors'), were dirty, unshaven, unironed, uncouth, and in roaring spirits. They'd just come from Stansted by cab – had missed dinner last night changing planes – had lost a connection in Madrid or was it Paris, everything was shut, they'd hammered on a delicatessen window at the airport until someone relented – they'd finished two bottles in the taxi and got their driver to swill from the third. I didn't follow their silly story closely. Now we were having an impromptu picnic of Champagne, bread rolls, salmon, *pâté*, smoked oysters, a cold duck, *bresaola*, tarts, cheese and grapes. Both boys were talking with their mouths full and shouting each other down. Their luggage was flung above everywhere, and there was a big brown cardboard box on Felix's desk which I eyed, wondering if Felix had had the decency to feel shame at desertion, and bring me a guilt offering.

(What a pitiful delusion.)

'Well, when we were sure there was nothing else to hear we drove on—'

'Culpepper got us lost twice.' That *Culpepper* was nice.

'Seb buggered up navigating. We reached an ex-mining town called Oracle in the end and we decided' (that *we* was good, too) 'to spend the night. Well, morning. The sun was already up. We woke at dusk when it was too late to find the way back up the mountain.'

'So we found a steakhouse instead full of cowpokes—'

'Costumed retirees from Seattle, Seb. Let's not fool ourselves.'

'Men who drank like cowpokes. They introduced to us to *chicha* which is made from maize and so revolting you have to drink more to take the taste away.'

'And they taught us line-dancing. No, tried to teach us because line-dancing and *chicha*—'

'—cancel each other out!' One has to ask: if Seb Hawick Trocliffe can finish them for you, how good can your sentences be?

'And got drunk, and went back to our hotel, but this time I was up by ten, and kicked Seb until he woke up. And we found our way back to friend Brockland's pad up the dirt track. Where we found – d'y'want some oysters?'

'Thank you, Felix, no.'

'Then I'll finish them. There was a column of steam going up, but I turned the Jacuzzi off and after a few minutes we could look in… You've made chicken stock? The tub was at the slightly overdone stage of stock-making. A raft of yellowish fat and grey fibrous meat on top, tangled up with slithers of bone. And strands of thin white hair—'

'With lots of Croke-soup bubbling below,' I murmured, thinking of the meniscus well and truly abolished, true Croke united with his evil reflection.

'Actually,' said Seb through a *foie gras* sandwich, 'I wished we'd stayed to watch.'

'Not for two days. Tedious. Well, we waited for it to cool, then we shovelled—'

'Who's this *we*, white man? *I* shovelled the bones and goo.'

'My associate,' (*associate!*) 'I admit did much of the actual heaving.'

'Over my shoulder and into the woods. Splat. Splat. Splatter-tat-tat. Meanwhile Culpepper sat holding Brockland's skull as if it was – who's the geezer they tried to make us read about for A levels?'

'Yorick, Sebastian.'

'No, that doesn't sound right.'

'Hamlet.'

'Yeah, think that's it. Anyway, Culpepper'd—'

'I'd leant over the tub. Fished it out, rinsed it off, caressed it. Fell in love.' I thought of Narcissus over *his* pool, feigning to notice the other boy, the enemy fated to kill him. Felix's self-obsession sometimes disguises itself as other sorts of love.

'When the tub was tolerably clear we pulled the plug and let the Poet Laureate of Arizona gurgle away.'

'Then we—'

'—filled it with up with fresh water and boiled it and swilled it clean. Looked—'

'—like new. Not that I'd want to sit in it, mind. Am I opening another? Abishag?'

'Thank you, Sebastian, yes please.'

'Oops! Sorry.'

'Don't worry, Sebastian. Bubbly doesn't stain much. So was that it? Is that the end of your story?'

'Ah, well,' sighed Felix, 'not quite.'

'In fact this was the point when everything went, y'know, pear-shaped,' said Seb, duck leg in one hand, roll in the other.

'My fault.'

'Nah… I got Croke's wine and beer out of his kitchen and loaded up the Jeep. When I got back I found Culpepper still mooning over his skull. Would anyone mind if I polished off the last tart?'

'No,' I said severely, 'I would not mind.'

'It was the most *beautiful* thing, Abishag. Utterly pure. Boiled free of evil flesh, thoughts, poetry. Cleaner than cleanliness. Hyper-baptised. It vindicated my vocation. You understand? I *had* to bring it home as a trophy. It was too wonderful to leave.'

Too wonderful. I suspect Felix, the only remaining killer in the republic of letters, simply fancied his reflection from the other side of death. 'Really.'

'The trouble was airports. In America they x-ray bags. Wouldn't the bloke staring at the screen yell when he saw Professor Croke grinning back at him! We'd be for it. What we were to do?'

'Chuck the skull, Felix, into the depths of the forest. Drive away. *That's* was what you were to do.'

'Unthinkable. How could I leave the most self-regarding poet of his generation staring up at the pine-needles?' His affection for Croke was of a curious sort.

'Plus being pissed on by deer,' added jolly Seb. 'Can we move to red for the cheese?'

'In the scullery. Not the Rioja or the Sangiovese. There should be a decent claret.'

'What did you do, Felix?'

'Since we couldn't fly, we drove. Took the Jeep and headed south. At Mexican airports, you see, they probably don't bother with x-rays.'

'Is this all right?' asked Seb, flourishing a Saint-Émilion that was too good for him.

'Yes. Decant it. We took turns, drove for three hours, and at dusk crossed through a fourteen-foot steel wall into Mexico.'

'But by the time we reached – reached – what was the hellhole called, Culpepper?'

'Cananea. *Horse-meat* in Apache. A grid of orange dust.'

'Yeah. The last flight had gone—'

'—so we—'

'—we went on the most awesome bender,' exulted Seb, splashing wine about. 'And there were these women who…' There followed an anecdote I shan't disgust you with. 'So then it was Wednesday afternoon and the next flight was Thursday evening so we thought—'

'*I* thought,' murmured the Holmes of his generation, carving out a little intellectual credit from his bogus Watson.

'*Culpepper* said: "It's Mexico, the land of death"—'

'—*a tierra de los muertos*—'

'—so why not *gussy up* the dead?'

'And thus make absolutely sure about getting it through security. Clever, yes?'

'Possibly, Felix.'

'So we found an artisan with no teeth named Francisquito, and had him turn Brockland into an artifact. Would you like to see him?'

'Um, possibly,' I said, but it was too late, the silly children were tearing open the big cardboard box with little whoops. Out he came.

He was beyond expectation.

'We didn't know what to call him,' said Seb, who was dandling the thing on his lap. 'I mean, he couldn't be "Croke" now that he was an Aztec god, could he?'

'Francisquito was a shocking pagan,' said Felix, taking the thing from Seb. 'He knew the whole pantheon. Explained it at length. Begged us to choose wisely. Took it very seriously.'

'We tried out Micky – Micky—'

'Mictlantecuhtli. The Aztec Pluto.'

'Or Tlazo, Tlaza—'

'Tlazolteotl. Imagine what that sounded like in a mouth with no teeth. Tlazolteotl's like Silenus. In charge of drunkenness, filth, *pulque* hangovers.'

'Is *pulque* the white sticky stuff we tried at the bar above the garage?'

'Yes.'

'Fucking horrible firewater. Worse than whatsit, *chicha*. Anyway, we eventually decided to give it a sex-change' (I wasn't getting used to this *we*) 'and call it Zokky-quait, Zochy-guet – *what* is it, Culpepper?'

'Xochiquetzal. The infernal Aphrodite. She has a retinue of—'

'Birds and butterflies! That's it.'

'Our artisan said the *conquistador* priests had appropriated Xochiquetzal as the Virgin of Ocotlán. "But we do not care what they say. We remember. We like her the way she was, *señor.*"'

'Xochiquetzal's the goddess of sex, excess—'

Whores, obviously. And artisans who make luxury items—'

'Patroness, then,' I offered, tartly, 'of the North American way of life,' and was ignored by Felix, who plunged on:

'Such as gilded skulls. Or, I suppose, poetry published in thin expensive paperbacks by Faber & Faber. All in all, more suitable for Croke than Tlazolteotl or Mictlantecuhtli.'

'Francisquito was pleased with our choice,' put in courteous Seb.

'He was. When he brought us the finished product, yesterday morning, our last day in the dusty town of Horse-Meat, he told us he'd been up all night before it, praying. He'd even sacrificed cockroaches to it.'

'Ah,' I said, staring with redoubled distaste. 'Not butterflies?'

'Cananea's not a butterfly sort of town.' Felix held it as if he would kiss its no-lips. 'A glorious metamorphosis, of course. This head, that used to ooze appalling High Art, is now delightful folk-art. But I wasn't quite satisfied. I didn't want *merely* the goddess of sadist poetry. This is meant to commemorate the *particular* Crokean genius. D'you see? So I borrowed a brush from Francisquito, and added a few lines from the works of the great man.' *My cranium's the cosmic vault.* 'Then we drove the Jeep into the desert and lit it on fire. The *Policía Federal* will find it and trace it to Croke. It'll add colour to the suicide theory. There's already been a rather touching obit in *American Poetry.*'

'How nice.'

'We thumbed a ride back to Cananea. And so to airports, aeroplanes. Francisquito had given us an export certificate – REPRODUCTION FOLK-ART – so we didn't have to be secretive after all. I showed Xochiquetzal off at Stansted. The officer said "Very striking, sir, but I don't think my wife would let us get one." Do *you* like her, Abishag?'

I stared at her, reigning from her new home at the centre of the coffee table. Xochiquetzal did not look back, but neither did she look away. She was beyond LABYRINTHE; she had the most perfect YORICK face. She sustained none of the usual traffic between faces. No eyes, no actual face indeed; an insolent stare nonetheless. *Explain me*, she said. Also: *Do you like me the way I was, señorita?* I could think of nothing to say.

'Time to christen her,' said Felix. 'So to speak.' He produced his humidor (in arrant breach of his Lent penance). 'Seb?' Seb took a cigar. 'Abishag?' I shook my head stiffly, sticking to my wine.

'*Do* you like Xochiquetzal?'

'She – it's very surprising.'

'Actually, this is all prelude. Even Xochiquetzal. The truly astonishing thing happened while we were waiting for Francisquito to finish work. *Didn't it, Seb?*' He glanced at that gormless blond. 'Seb fell in love.'

I was in a dreadful new universe. By definition a LABYRINTHE DE

MIROIRS cannot fall in love (except with the obvious person). I gaped and put down my glass. When I looked at Seb, I found him blushing, grinning feebly, soppy about the eyes, head down, fidgeting with his cigar.

'Tell her about Benita.'

Seb cleared his throat. Felix puffed and fiddled, making a meal of lighting up, as he always does.

※

Something important had happened before he got his cigar to belch smoke. I'd resolved to break with him for good, which I duly did later that afternoon. It was to do with the way he said '*Didn't it, Seb?*' His tone was unendurable, avuncular, Falstaffian, pagan. The man was a leader-astray, parasitic on men who lead further astray, like Osgood and Croke. Well, he needn't look far; henceforth *I* would be his Moriarty. I'd out-pagan him.

I have no doubts about this decision. Or rather I had no doubts then; and it's the March me I'm trying to get on paper.

> *Margot grew tired of me, and now my bones*
> *   stand on a frame.*
> *Love's not enough for her, and love, like blood*
> *titrated, boiled in phials, gets given*
> *   a technical name.*

Now in October, after the defeats of summer, I am, quite frankly, weakening. I fear I'm about to take Felix back (if he doesn't find this paper and do whatever he'd do if he knew himself betrayed). But in March! –

※

'It's true, Abishag,' said Sebastian, flushed. 'I'm smitten as ever was.'

'Despite Francisquito's hecatomb of crushed cockroaches? Despite the goddess of whoredom and luxury? Despite Croke's verse?'

'Despite all that.' Sebastian sounded, damn it, not implausible as a lover. 'No clouds of butterflies for me. I've turned mono. You know, not not-stereo. The not-fucking-around word.'

'Monogamous.'

'That's it,' said Seb with a luminous smile, proud to be in command of such a term; and indeed he was, to my certain knowledge, faithful to his Mexican for nearly a fortnight, after which she faded from mind, and he went back to his usual ways.

Not that he was the same boy. The husband blameless for forty years who errs once with his secretary is not the same man afterwards. There are many virginities to be lost; some are terrible losses. Seb has committed monogamy. A fissure's opened in his shallowness. He's no longer just Narcissus. Xochiquetzal does not entirely prevail.

'And what's she like, your belovèd?' I said, to break up his luminous smile.

'She's posh. Well, by local standards. She's the grand-daughter of the mayor of – of—'

'Cananea,' put in narcissistic Felix, who'd got his cigar burning at last, and would be silent and amused until he finished it.

'That. And Benita speaks – oh!' He lit up. 'I'm *not* an ineducated blockhead, Margot, whatever you say, they *do* speak Spanish in what you call Latin America.' Felix had the ill-grace to laugh at this. 'But Benita talks English too, as good as an American. She understands me. I say something and a bit later she says it too. In fact everything she says sounds like me. So I feel there's nothing between us. I mean, y'know, nothing *separating* us. She may as well be inside me. Even when I'm not there. Because I'm here. D'y'see? It's sort of hard to talk about.'

I saw. Just the teensiest scrap of water. 'But what's this echo of a female *like*?'

'She's sweet.'

'That means *thick*. Is she good-looking?'

'*Nice* – well, decent-looking. I'd call her face interesting—'

'That's like the Chinese curse "May you live in interesting times". It means *ugly*.' It means CASEMENT.

'You're being a shit. Look, here she is,' and he opened his iPad. Benita was the wallpaper. (What human *souvenirs* these two strange boys had chosen to bring back from their North American jaunt!)

'Ah.' I saw. 'I see.'

I saw, and I lost my temper. I turned nasty. I *am* nasty; my most basic principle is never to let this show. Benita's soul (I thought) must be stowed in her stilettos: they're the human-looking bit. From the ankle to the parabola beneath her breasts she's a cyborg engineered to resemble a twelve year old boy; above that one enters the realm of nightmare. My eyes can't free themselves from her breasts, which might grind themselves into my eye-sockets – not literally, they're far too far apart. Is this unnatural language? Well they're not a phenomenon in nature, they jut apart like guns on a battleship turret. If I slapped them, would the silicon reverberate? Or bounce like vulcanised rubber? Or swish like brandy in a hipflask? I want to hold them down and let them boing back into place... What bribes the mayor of Cananea must have solicited to pay for such surgery on his ugly grand-daughter, what drug cartels he must have courted! Her unremarkable plain face, caked over with make-up, is almost invisible in her glare of bosom. She can scarcely walk on those shoes, it must be an effort to stand, but if she does take them off to run, won't her breasts punch her in the chin – left right, left right?

If I'd said any of this, imbecile Seb would have thought me jealous, which would have exasperated me past bearing. So what I did say, sourly, coarsely, grossly, violating my basic principle, was: 'You've heard of zombie ants? A spore infects an ant, takes over its brain, gives it convulsions, makes it tumble from the nest. The fungus devours the soft living bits, leaving only its shell. After a few days a fruiting-body bursts out upwards of its head. Which is exactly the significance of blonde hair in our species.' The hair of the grand-daughter of the Mayor of Cananea was dyed the shade of a lemon. 'It spews forth more spores which—'

'This is rubbish.'

'It's not. It's called *Ophiocordyceps unilateralis* and lives—'

'No, I mean it's rubbish about Benita.' He gave a curious sniff, took back his iPad, and gave it a long sentimental stare. 'Beauty,' he mused, abstracting for the first time in his life, 'is in the eye of the beholder.'

'Which suggests something about your eye. Pocket-mirror boy.'

'Benita's full of y'know, the inside sort of prettiness. Not like me. Stuff you can't see.'

'Spiritual beauty?'

'Yes – that's what I was thinking of.'

'And that too,' laughed Felix, ashing his cigar into the poet's wonderful cranium but obviously thinking of himself, 'is in the eye of the beholder.'

Quintember

'NEVER.'

'Sure as I'm standing here. And the *other* young fellow, not the blond one, the one that's not so big-built round the shoulder so to speak, I always notice him too 'cause he's got a sort of shiny fireman's helmet with wings to it over his red hair. And wing things tied to the back of his feet and a sort of snaky stick.'

'A *what* d'y'say?'

'Stick with snakes, Gladys. Like a curtain rod with doodlies going up and down it. But the snakes don't give me the pip being metal, it's the owl that I draw the line at. I said to Alfie, "What're you going to do about the owl?" "What's wrong now?" says Alfie, not looking up from the sports page, selfish bugger. "What owl?" he says. "The owl next door," I says, "if you think I'm—"'

'The *what*, Val? I never.'

'It's the tall girl what has it, the one with the helmet right down over her face so you can't see her. It sits on her shoulder. Alfred says, "She's like a pirate with a parrot," silly bugger. "Pirates, owls, pigeons," I say, "I don't care what they are." I says: "I don't know what Westley Bottom Road's coming to and if you're not going to do something about it—"'

'What did he say to *that*?'

'Nothing, Gladys. Not a thing. But I can tell he's not happy 'cause he says he never sees hide nor hair of me any more, me having to spend so much time upstairs in the spare room keeping an eye on next door. Haven't I, Mr Brownlow?'

'Well then, Miss Squint, well then,' said Mr Brownlow the shopkeeper, as he generally did, leaning his large body over his counter, turning his bland gaze indifferently from big-boned Val, with her querulous overmuch of orange perm and severe nose, to Gladys Drybble, wide-eyed, hamster-like, ingenuous. 'Who's rightly to say?'

'And anyway,' continued Val in her high nasal whine, 'Alfie has his own bone to pick with number 29. There's one of them, a cripple, anyhow he's got a nasty limp or pretends he has, he's set up an anvil in the stables, bangs away at all hours he does, early mornings even in the all-together never mind the chill, so that Alfie's budgies—'

'Good morning, then. Good morning, Val, Mr Brownlow... Gladys.' The three of them started like guilty things, looked about and only then down, as people generally did when Bess Elmsgall spoke. 'What's this about banging in the mornings?'

'Oh. Oh, Mrs Elmsgall. Well I never. We're *ever* so pleased to run into you. Aren't we, Val? Val's been telling us about the new people. At number 29, you know. It's *ever* so interesting.'

'Half a pound of suet, Mr Brownlow, if you'd be so good. At number 29? The big Seacome house?'

'Yes, where Madge and Ernie were renting the gatehouse and keeping an eye,' babbled Gladys, loose-fleshed, chaotically shaped, waggling her head so that her fine hair, dyed blue, was pierced and pierced by the morning sun, 'but it's been empty since March 'cause *they've* gone to Brighton where Madge's second girl is, married for the *second* time and three nippers to look after, *not* all of them by either husband says Val and one of them not quite right in the head—'

'Steady, Gladys.'

'But you did say that, Val. *And* you said—'

'Will that be all, Mrs Elmsgall?'

'No, Mr Brownlow. I've quite a list. A pound of marzipan.'

'Well then. Pound of marzipan.'

'And oh, Mrs Elmsgall, now it's been taken by awful students. Number 29 has. One of those communes you read about in the *Daily Maul*. And they never go out, isn't that right Val, they just walk about the house and gardens all day. *In the nuddy*, says Val.'

'Hush, Gladys. Mrs Elmsgall don't want to hear your nonsense.'

'It's never non—'

'*Gladys.*'

'But it's *true* Val, isn't it? Every word. There're a dozen of them and—'

'A pound of marzipan, Mrs Elmsgall. And what else will you be having?'

'That will do for now, after all, I think, Mr Brownlow. I find after all I had better be getting on. I am expected at St Wygefortis' College. A special luncheon.'

'Well then, Mrs Elmsgall. That'll be two quid and ten pee.'

'Two pounds ten. Thank you. And good morning to you, Val. I'm sorry you have trying neighbours. Perhaps you'd best ignore them. I hope to see you at the Baptist Ladies' League on Friday evening. Gladys.' And she was gone.

'Oh, what an old *cow* she is.'

'Ladies, ladies.'

'*You* needn't laugh, Mr Brownlow. We've all had it up to *here* with Bess bleedin' high-and-mighty Elmsgall and I don't mind who hears it. Just 'cause she works at one of the colleges in Cambridge she gives herself the airs of a ruddy duchess – but come on, Val. Tell us more about your commune.'

'Really, I'm not sure there's much more to tell.'

'Oh but you said—'

'And I hope you won't go passing on what I've said to everyone, Gladys. We needn't go on about it, need we? Westley Waterless has always been a respectable village and I don't want people to think we've gone all modern. Alfie would get the wind up.'

'Beg pardon I'm sure.'

'Well, I must be getting on, too. Alfie has to have his dinner on the table on the dot or he gets bilious. Ta-ra.'

'...Oh, that Valerie Squint. If it's not one thing with her it's another. Worry worry worry. That brother of hers. I tell you, Mr Brownlow—'

ii.

Elizabeth Elmsgall walked as briskly as her stumpy legs could manage out of Brownlow's, before she had to hear what those women would say about her. Down Church Lane she stomped, past the factory farm standing windowless with its feet in the mud, to the crossing with Westley Bottom Road and the 'bus shelter.

In any English village, be it never so picturesque, half-timbered, Regency-fronted, flinty, or hung with begonias, the 'bus shelter will be an unnerving spot. It will be full of dripping silence. There will be shadowy dilapidation, and obsolete notices taped to softening wood, curled up with damp; loathsome sexual offers and telephone numbers in marker pen; lost umbrellas, apple cores, the tang of human urine. But the Westley Waterless shelter is far worse than the run: it gives itself the air of a wayside gibbet.

Today, as usual, Mrs Elmsgall was absurdly early for the 'bus into Cambridge. She scrambled up on to the bench and enthroned herself, feet not quite touching the ground.

It would be hard to know whether she was annoyed or pleased at having to wait. Her face was a russet apple, somewhat rotten and brown-purple; the mouth was particularly irregular and cruel, a caving-in of liquifying flesh rather a natural orifice; its tiny eyes were mere pits of putrefaction, nothing to do with light; its expression was blank and lifeless as her burnt-umber shoes, or her Key-West-lime handbag. Although it was a warm noon, the first day of July, almost hot, she had on her *faux*-fur collar and her almost-tweed crimson suit. She sat in this get-up in the 'bus shelter and endured without sign the scrutiny of Westley Waterless through half a dozen net curtains.

Westley Waterless is a wretched huddle of houses along two streets, one of them a dead end. It's too close to Cambridge to be properly rustic, too far out to appeal to dons; anyway, it is nearly devoid of decent houses. That is to say, there are some nineteenth-century brick semis in Church Lane; where there's also one low cottage with a thatched roof, which has been prettified beyond recognition by a retired dentist (a foreigner, as they say in the village, meaning that thirty years ago he arrived from Little Wratting, nine miles away and more, over the county line in Suffolk. Westley is so inbred, it has such peculiar customs, and ways of speaking – as we have seen – that no incomer ever becomes local). Otherwise the village consists of mean bungalows from the era of Clement Attlee. Except, of course, for the Seacome house, of evil report.

Hastings Seacome was a retired late Victorian broker with either a very queasy conscience, or a superstitious dread of rustics. Perhaps he was simply as unwelcome in Westley Waterless as the dentist is today. In any case, when he had finished building The Rise, his heap of a house, he put an eight-foot wall about it.

That expanse of brick still manages to dominate the village. The grisly wall is now mossy, and cracked all the way about. There's a ten-foot section which has collapsed altogether, so that only a shaky wooden palisade separates the rank expanse that used to be The Rise's cucumber-beds from the semi, number 31 Westley Bottom Road, where Val Squint dwells mirthlessly with her brother Alfred. Yet for all this, the wall seems to block in the village, which feels pent, cut off from the landscape.

The landscape is, in any case, flat, soggy and meagre: drained fen, muddled chalk and clay. It grows oblongs of beige barley, and strips of vomit-coloured oats. Nothing shields it from the North Sea and the wide northern plains of the Continent. Photographed in a unfriendly way, it would have the look of Russia rather than England.

This first of July it looked like Russia in stupefied summer, Russia after the hay has been cut, Russia of hamlets mouldering on the suffocating steppe. It might come as a surprise to see the horizon broken not by an onion-dome, but by the stunted flint turret of St. Mary-the-Less.

The parish church would have been square in front of Mrs Elmsgall if she had lifted her eyes a little to take it in. But she saw nothing of this world. She stared sightlessly at her orange shoes. When the single bell of Mary-the-Less suddenly tolled, eleven cracked strokes, she did not start.

Nor did she appear to hear a bird nearby: a robin, singing out of sexual starvation, sexual starvation, sexual starvation, not from joy. One grating note repeated again and again. The robin bounced from ivy-throttled beech-bough to wooden 'bus-shelter roof; it hopped through rotting tabloid newsprint and the glossy pornography that gets flung from the upper windows of school 'buses. It did not seem to notice Mrs Elmsgall, who could be silent even when she moved, despite those squat limbs and rolling hips. And when she was still, she was still as a mossy rock; birds would come within reach of her fingernails, which was a mistake. Her stillness was not of this world. She'd been standing in Brownlow's for fully five minutes, for instance, before anyone noticed her. She'd overheard all the report of those idiot hags.

Idiot hags. Maleficium. Spawn, mudfilth, Bess said to herself, although her carbuncular visage, pointed at the mud below her feet, showed no sign of vehemence. *Gladys Drybble manifestation of Nuit. Val Squint: blast her. Mulier habens pythonem in Ændor.* It's grand what big words pop into your head if you just sit quiet-like. So Bess Elmsgall always found. *Brownlow the grocer too I consign. O Count Astarot, I compound him. Ahriman! But I'll tell him who ought to know about it. He'll come running. Obeah, Wanga.* Her toad face did not twitch. She was an unadorned vessel of baked dirt, about to bear to St Wygefortis' a pestilence, a plague of heathenry.

As far as she could manage, Bess Elmsgall had served the night since her girlhood. An unprofitable servant she had been up to now. What had she to offer her masters? In the village nothing but spite and petty calumny. At St Wygefortis' a few smashed vases, none of them genuine Ming; ink occasionally poured into rare books; bruised furniture. Now at last she'd come into her own. *There is a woman that hath a familiar spirit at Endor.* She had it in her, possibly, to corrupt a whole college.

Bess was full of deceit about trifles as about greater matters. For example: it was true that there was a special luncheon today at Wygefortis'. It was quite untrue that she would be helping to serve it, despite what she hoped to make those gossips think. Only once or twice had she been roped in for a College dinner, at the last moment, when no one could be found less repellent or less clumsy; and after each occasion Chyld, the butler, had sworn never to employ her again. She was, in fact, simply a bedder, and moreover the most unpopular bedder in College. It was for that reason she 'did' the rooms of Dr Culpepper, who was likewise unpopular.

A superior young man, murmured Bess Elmsgall, to herself, with malice. And so he was, although not for any reason that could be understood by what she thought of as her masters; who (so it seemed to her) were moving in her mind, moving her to divulge, to tell—

But her 'bus had come.

iii.

'*Fff!* Ooo. *Arrh.* Look at him then. Who'd've thought? Jus' like...'

'Hm? What was that, Bess?'

'Do beg pardon Dr Culpepper, sir. Only talking to myself.' But Culpepper had caught the frightened hiss of her breath.

Felix Culpepper was full of self-pity. He was always abroad in July. This year he'd been made to stay in Cambridge to finish his *Quincentennial History* of College, now very overdue; and to top up his sufferings, had been drafted to coach idiot classicists, the ones kept back for summer retakes. He was bored, he was morose; he was slouched deep in his armchair, one long leg flung unhappily over another, bony knees stuck high in the air. He was trying, for the fifth time, to get through an essay by Harry, his stupidest pupil.

St Wygefortis' is notoriously the stupidest college in Cambridge, he told himself, picking at the scab, *the classicists here are the stupidest undergraduates, and of them all, Harry, Harry, Harry...*

While Culpepper had been thinking this he had, in a dim sort of way, been watching Bess, with her huge bottom stuck high in the air, overshadowing her curt legs. She was scrubbing his hearth, and he was wondering, as he often did, how could she be so long about it, yet leave it muckier than before. 'Oh God, oh God, even the doings of my warty little bedder are more arresting than Harry's thoughts on Petronius.' He put down the unreadable essay and stepped over to his fireplace.

Which was adorned with postcards. Now, in high summer, his students had fanned out over Europe, and beyond, and their postcards were flowing back, a trifle derisive. Culpepper, sucking up mockery, took bittersweet satisfaction in taping views of fjords and volcanoes over his blue and white tiles. Postcards from Venice, and he was stuck in Cambridge. Aswan, and he was stuck in Cambridge. Lake Van. The Crimea. They had gone everywhere, across Rajasthan and through Amazonia. Margot ffontaines-Laigh had gone too, the one known as Abishag; Culpepper's cleverest student, whom he had tutored and got into Cambridge, his *inamorata*, his *nemesis* ('My *objet du désir*'), his morbid obsession ('My destiny'); his professional assistant in assassination; gone, after a term of snubbing him, of posing as his enemy; gone into nothingness, too, in that she'd renounced and forbidden the very name *Abishag*; gone, refusing to tell him whither; sending no postcard.

'Do you like one of them, Bess?'

'*No!* That is… Who is it, sir, if I may be so bold?' Bess, who was short-sighted, had wiggled forward on her knees and was bending very close, but she was curiously careful not to touch what she saw. Her fat head and thin curls were in his way. Culpepper casually reached past her and pulled the postcard off its tile, uncovering a sleepy blue barge towed past a motionless blue windmill. *Elysium,* thought Culpepper as he always did when he looked at his Delftware; *the terrestrial paradise. Oh to be able to flee into a blue-white tile, to be hidden under tin-glaze, to be at rest.*

It wasn't a particularly exotic postcard. It had only come from Potsdam, and showed a statue in Frederick the Great's pleasure gardens, which had apparently appealed to Tristan Bolswood – that rather Prussian youth. A slender white marble male was heaving aloft a squealing female, even more slender, even nuder, in front of a calm *parterre*. He glanced at the back and read aloud, very Germanly: 'DIE ENTFÜHRUNG DER PROSERPINA DUCH PLUTO UM 1750.' Culpepper's German accent was one of the myriad paltry things of which he was vain.

The Elmsgall was duly flabbergasted, as one is by blasts of German.

Hmm; why should a bit of Baroque garden décor *stagger Bess? Of course she's a Baptist, it might just be the bare flesh. Bare stone. Cooped up in marble.* What he said was: 'It's Pluto, Bess. Hades.'

'Who's he, then?'

'He's king of the underworld—'

'He's *Lord Satan*?' Bess voice came trembling. She was apparently unable to rise from her knees. Her brown face was nearly white with awe behind its purple carbuncles and black hairs.

'Good God no. Nothing so serious. Just the classical god of death. This shows him – er – kidnapping his niece, Proserpine.'

'And does he have a puppy with two extra heads?'

'Yes, Cerberus, who – good heavens, Bess, do you need to sit down? Let me help you up… There. Do you need brandy?' No, no, a Dissenter. 'Sweet tea?' He got her to her feet; the postcard slipped to the hearth; Mrs Elmsgall dropped into a chair.

'No thanking you kindly sir. Right as rain in a tick.'

'But what's the matter?'

'Just the shock, sir. Seeing him in a photo. When I was thinking he was made up. In our village so to speak. They've seen him there.'

Mad, of course. Anabaptist. 'Hades resides in your village, Bess?'

'Oh I know it's not really him. His beard's not real, I hear tell. But he has a little pointy crown just like that. And he's got a Jack Russell, with two toy dog heads sewn on to its collar, cruel I call it. And he goes about with not a stitch on, just like him on the card, excepting his crown of course.'

'Mrs Elmsgall. You're saying there's an eccentric in your village who pretends to be Hades?'

'Oh it's not just him, sir. Eleven others. All staying together in the big house. They do say. You see, three months back the tenants moved far off, Sussex way (but they were only in the gatehouse, the big house being in a right state). Then these young people moved in. Students by the look.'

'By the way they're dressed, you mean?'

'That's it, sir, they're not. They don't wear nothing. Not proper clothes as you might say. There's a tall girl with a long flowing thing on, hardly a dress at all, more like a bedsheet, and anyway she has a bird sitting on her shoulder all day long and that wouldn't do if it were a decent dress would it? Dirty I call it. And one of them, a proud-looking girl, has on something like a bridal gown, ever so many pleats, *and* a sort of veil over her head. But the rest of them are naked as ever was. Of course they hardly ever leave the house and there's a big garden but still we're a decent village, we don't hold with...' On she goes, regurgitating things she might have overheard from Gladys and Val, things she might have picked up from other rumour-mongers; also things it is hard to see she could, mortally speaking, know. 'And they lie around in the evenings on beds. The big front room looks like a mattress shop. They lie about propped up on elbows two to a bed to have their supper and it don't bear thinking of what they get up to. Eight boys and four girls. *And* the Jack Russell with the two stuffed heads bobbing round its collar. *And* the owl. And the other girl, the one who's always giggling, has white pigeons following her about on long pink ribbons, pecking. Nasty. They don't even speak English among themselves, sir, it's Gypsy maybe. Or Polish. One of them wicked foreign things. I says to myself they're just bonkers, that's what they are, hippies like, and they couldn't fit them in at the county loony bin and that's why they're here. But then I saw your card with the spitting image of the boy with the stuck-on beard and so I came over all funny. Ever so sorry I'm sure sir.'

Felix stood in his bay window, staring out over his unsatisfactory view: Megiddo Court empty for summer, torn up in squares where the gardeners were relaying the turf. 'It can only be,' he murmured. 'It must be. Who else but she? Who else would think of... or dare? And if so...' He swivelled. 'Bess, may I have the address of this extraordinary household?'

'Oh sir, I hardly like to say.'

'Come, Mrs Elmsgall.'

'It being a private house and all.' He produced a five pound note and, rather than handing it to her, pinched it under his brass Ganesh on the edge of his desk. The money dangled in mid-air, out of jurisdiction: *secundum* (mused Felix) *principem potestatis æris, according to the prince of the power of the air.*

'It's a very small village, sir. It might get back to people that I've been speaking out of turn.'

He added a second fiver, a second and final one, all that was needed, although Bess tried to inflate her bribe to fifteen pounds: 'Anyways sir, what harm are they doing? That we know of?'

iv.

Yes, what harm were they doing?

What harm *had* Abishag, no, *Margot*, been doing? She'd broken with

Felix at the end of Lent Term, over the Affair of the Sadist Poet. He'd expected easy forgiveness, but when College reassembled in May, she was still calling him "Dr Culpepper", politely and distantly. 'Come back to your rooms, Dr Culpepper? But I believe our supervision isn't 'til Thursday.'

He'd ground his teeth and given up, unable to prevail against her coolness. Her way of waging war was to ignore him, expending the charm that had enraptured him on the whole University. That was her tactic. Felix held, as an article of faith, that she was doing all this to enrage and humiliate him. After all, she did enrage and humiliate him.

But was it a tactic? As Easter Term progressed, it looked distressingly as if she'd put Culpepper behind her. She appeared to have fixed on a University career, not as mistress to the Latin Fellow of Wygy's, but as Muse and arbiter of her generation of undergraduates. It was Margot ffontaines-Laigh who set the fashion; Margot who decided who was fashionable; Margot who made and broke student politicians, who decreed the extravagant parties, who condemned this don or that to boycott and abuse, or handed him a clutch of disciples.

Easter Term 2013 was the 500th anniversary of the founding, in shameful circumstances, of St Wygefortis' College, and Margot took charge of celebrations. The Master was in awe of her. He repeated her commands to Governing Body – 'Lady Margot, the Chair of Festivities, thinks a garden party *vieux chapeau*, and I *rather think...*' 'The undergraduate committee is set on a spectacle on the night of the Anniversary Banquet, and *it would seem...*' Governing Body shook its head and obeyed.

This was particularly remarkable because the Master, Sir Trotsky Plantagenet, was such a swollen toad of vanity. He descended from Henry VI's little-known bastard son, begotten when the saintly king was assaulted in the Tower by a Claustral Prioress, sent by his Yorkist captors to procure an apoplexy. In the course of the twentieth century these Plantagenets became Advanced. So, what with smug Marxism and royal blood, Sir Trotsky was not easily flustered by patrician manners; he might have been expected to take a ffontaines-Laigh in his stride. But that spring Margot's prestige stood so high even Sir Trotsky deferred. ('Besides,' as the knowing bedders told each other, 'he fancies her something rotten.')

Behind Chapel there's a small square court named Cocytus, paved with pale cobblestones. No one had dared burn anything in Cocytus since the bonfires for the Glorious Revolution. But Margot at the zenith of her authority had smiled down even Woolly, the bewildered and stammering chaplain, and an immense amount of firewood was heaped up just short of Chapel's south wall.

The night of the Anniversary Banquet was a typical May evening in Cambridge: which is to say the rain was cold and heavy. Nonetheless, the entire Fellowship was lined along the east and west ranges of the court, gowned and hooded and mortar-boarded, each holding an umbrella over a candelabrum, because Margot had commanded spectators to bring candelabra. Even Culpepper hadn't dared absent himself. He had stood there, as cold and enchanted as everyone else, in the strange shaking firelight.

She had appointed as White general the Chancellor of the University, who happens to be the Duke of Edinburgh. He, in the tropical uniform of an Admiral of the Fleet, stalked up and down beside his bonfire on the south side of Cocytus Court, consulting his advisors. He seemed in perfect earnest about the game and indifferent, despite his thin tunic, to flakes of sleet hissing into the flames.

An order was muttered to the White herald, who cried: 'His Grace the Duke of Northumberland: three paces forward. Rook to Queen's Knight four. Check.' There had been uncertainty about who should play the rooks. Margot had resolved that they were to be, if not exactly castles, *proprietors* of castles, with cardboard models of their property as headgear. Such was the fashion to obey Margot that the owners of Blenheim, Longleat, Castle Howard, Castle Goring and St Michael's Mount vied to be invited. So now the Duke of Northumberland in coronation robes, with a cardboard Alnwick Castle swaying above him in place of coronet, stepped forward over three pale squares, one of them marked black with ash.

Check! A fanfare from the upper room in Cocytus reserved for the trumpeters.

The other windows were crowded with undergraduates, obedient to Margot's command to wear black tie, keep their lights off, and be silent. She herself, clad in the much-taken-in uniform of an S.S. *Gruppenführer*, lolled on a black-canopied throne on the north side of the court, consulting nobody. She surveyed the board, then spoke to her Black herald, who announced through his megaphone: 'His Majesty King Oyo Rukidi IV: one pace to the fore, if you would, and slay that pawn. King takes King's Bishop's Pawn.' The reigning Omukama of Toro shuffled shyly forward: he was a nervous and untalented second-year economist, in loose black robe with a gold border wider than his head, and huge matching bonnet. He bopped with his sceptre a White schoolboy in ermine, who collapsed in ghastly spasms. The kettle-drums and cymbals sounded for a death; the undergraduates dangling from the windows forgot their orders and whooped. Lackeys appeared and carried the pawn off the board and into the antechapel, which was serving as Valhalla for the White battle-dead; the two White bishops (Norfolk and St Germans), in matching cream copes, were standing about it drinking brandy Alexanders. The dead Blacks, in the Master's Lodgings, drank Guinness, and Culpepper observed through the open window the monophysite Archbishop of Gondar making himself sick-drunk.

Margot's chessmen were a mixed bag. The exiled King and Queen of the Hellenes, there by special command of Uncle Philip, were delightful, but the Abyssinian prelate was not delightful; neither were the four knights. Sir Trotsky and the drunken Fellow in Psychology, Sir Wayne Scuff, were White; she had recruited two old Wygians, politicians from corners of the Commonwealth, as the Black. All four were tricked out in helms borrowed from the Fitzwilliam Museum, with coloured plumes. Sir Trotsky and Sir Wayne kept their visors up, leering and waggling and rattling the shining cuisses on their aged thighs. The Black knights, being dubious politicians, did not see the humour of the game, and took its mock-warfare seriously, especially Sir Erskine Sandman, disgraced ex-Prime Minister of Barbados, now a rather embarrassing Honorary Fellow.

White won, as Margot had courteously intended all along. The Omukama of Toro was borne away on a bier with mock solemnity; in Chapel the choir sang a truncated requiem; then broke into a *Te Deum* as fireworks ruptured the sky above Cambridge with a dozen unnatural shades.

Sir Erskine, however, burst into tears and flung his helm clattering on the flags. This was regarded as such bad form the Chancellor declined to stay for whisky and cigars, and was motored back to Windsor. 'Remember that blighter from our Caribbean tour in '87. Can't hold his booze. *And* a bad sport. Damn fine game, though, girlie,' at which Margot curtsied so low it seemed impossible she could rise again without someone grabbing her elbow. But she did rise, and immediately took to bed one of her pawns, a very tall Kenyan ('Scrawny even for the Kisii,' muttered Culpepper to himself), a classicist ('An uninteresting classicist'), Odingo Nyachae.

So Margot's chess was counted a triumph, despite the weather, despite the royal snub, despite the death of the Fellow in Spanish (who caught a chill and couldn't shake it off), and despite the ruin of a Jacobean stained-glass rose window, which succumbed either to the heat of a bonfire or to the noisy celebrations after the game. Woolly was persuaded to say 'In a special sense an *empty* window is much more affirmative of the spiritual message we wish to share,' and that was that.

Sir Trotsky, who was angling for a K.C.B., had a plaque placed in Cocytus boasting of the only literal chess match in history: HIC PRIMUM IN SÆCULIS .... INCOMPARABILI DUX DE EDIMBURGUM ... GLORIA. For he had by now utterly lost his head. He boasted of the peculiar glamour of Lady Margot to other Heads of House, and did not notice their eyebrows rise. He became ardently compliant; she became recklessly proud. There was wild donnish talk of Madame de Pompadour, Zenobia and the Kérouaille.

Inevitably came disaster and reaction. All at once, toward the end of Easter Term, Margot was no longer welcome at the Master's Lodgings. She, who had been immune from work, found herself facing Penal Collections, which is to say she was formally reprimanded by a panel of dons; of whom Felix Culpepper was chief.

If Culpepper had been great-souled, he would not have relished the occasion of her Penal Collection. But he wasn't great-souled. 'Lady Margot, you have completed only three of the ten essays I set. Instead it seems to us that you have wasted the whole term perpetuating pagan stunts.'

'May I smoke, Dr Culpepper?'

'You may not,' said Felix, who was himself lighting an unscheduled cigar to make a point. 'Stunts, I was saying. Tomfoolery injurious to College's reputation. Your chess game was gross. It was a splurge, an apostasy, a hint of human sacrifice – it stank of the Colosseum.' He blew a smoke-ring. 'Then you sank further. Was it kind to make Mr Leigh sacrifice flowers in Styx?' Culpepper recalled how Woolly had looked, in a surplice wet to the knees, wading through the sluggish waters of that brook, with the south wall of College lowering over him; chanting as he pulled petals off a marigold and cast them here and there: 'Zeus!' (pluck), 'He loves me; Jesus!' (pluck), 'He loves me not; Xochiquetzal!' (pluck), 'She loves me; Krishna ....'

'The Chaplain said it was the most meaningful inter-faith liturgy he'd ever performed.'

'For which you repaid him with your agitation. Against calling Easter Term "Easter Term"—'

'The Master accepted our case.'

'He bowed to your whim out of courtesy. If that is how we should categorise his motivation this term.'

Gudrun von Spluffe, Tutor in German, coughed at this, wriggled in her chair, and said in her strange turtle voice: 'But you not satisfied were, yes? You on-pressed.'

'You might,' said Culpepper, 'have spared us bother about days of the week.'

'Zat I also zink. To Vednezday und Friday vat objection zere is?'

'Woden's Day, Frigg. The stink of Wagner and Himmler and Jung. Ick!'

'Vat is "Ick"?' Culpepper explained the word and the Spluffe bridled. 'Zese Götter—' She spoke so loudly Sir Wayne woke from his post-breakfast snooze, chortled, belched, wet his lips, resumed his repose.

'In any case,' continued Culpepper, more softly, 'you badgered the poor Master about the week. And right through this term College has been forced to adopt those Manx names.'

'The ancient religion of Man is very pure.'

'How zey are?' asked pedantic von Spluffe. 'Altogether ick to me zey seemed. Jecroon Sunday is – no, Jedoon—'

'Jedoonee. Jedoonee, Jelune, Jemayrt, Jecrean, Jerdrein, Jeheiney, Jesarn. Beautiful British pagan names.'

Felix put his head on an angle, trying to gauge the sincerity in Margot's face. What, really, was this militant heathenness about? *Whom* was it about? He wanted to think it was about himself; for it was true that he was becoming more orthodox under the weight of his murders. Was that all?

He on-pressed. 'Lady Margot, the days of the week were grim enough. But you made College a laughing-stock with the campaign over "July" and "August"—'

'They're vile too, Felix. Dr Culpepper. Nero renamed his birth-month Neronius; if such vanity's ridiculous for April, why is it tolerable for Quintember and Sextember? Those horrid self-divinising emperors, Julius and Augustus, had no right to impose themselves on the sacred republican calendar. It's a small step from their interference in religious matters to the final tyranny of Constantine. I was erasing a blasphemy.'

'You were being a silly child. What right has one Cambridge college to amend months? Or terms, or weeks? Or creeds? You merely got us mocked in the House of Commons. Your were trying to out-Crompe Lucinda Crompe, race her back into heathen darkness' – which produced a sucking-in of cheeks, because Miss Crompe's name remained *taboo* at St Wygyfortis' College. 'Then let's move on.'

'Zen! Your taurobolium!'

'Yes. *Your taurobolium.*'

Her taurobolium! Margot got permission to dig a pit to the west of College, in Christ's Pieces, and raise above it a brick stage with a platform of planks pierced with holes. Dons who wished to undo their baptism were invited to lie in this ditch at dawn, oak-crowned, robed in their doctoral gowns, while a bullock was slain above them. Surely such hot inebriating blood on face, tongue and bald-spot would render them venerable, inerrant, perhaps immortal?

The response was painful. Even Sir Erskine welched. He was besotted with Margot, but the Barbadian courts had just convicted him *in absentia* of embezzlement; he was afraid there'd be press photographers about; he dared not risk enraging his devout compatriots lest they press for extradition. He would not be de-baptised, even in hope of being bedded afterward. Margot flayed his cowardice with her tongue. He staggered away mouthing, and never saw her again.

The Master of Wygefortis' was infatuated enough to submit; and a half-dozen Fellows from various colleges consented to join him in the pit. But what Fellows! What shabby shambling dribbling oddities! And what difficulties they raised. Any don cranky enough for a taurobolium is cranky enough for pacifism and veganism. Margot could not make these sorry figures bend their principles. They would abjure the Galilæan Deity only if no animals were harmed.

Word got about. The energy dribbled out of her revolution. She found herself standing in rainy half-light at dawn on the first of June, soggily dressed as priestess of the Great Mother, supervising a choir that couldn't stop giggling as it offered its hymn. Before her on the platform were three boys stripped to the waist. She flicked her hand at them impatiently, and they, with great blows of their sledgehammers, immolated a pyramid of pineapple, coconut, watermelon and pumpkin. The effusion gushed down into the muddy trough where seven elderly academics wallowed, whimpering, in fruity unction, vegetarian ecstasy.

Culpepper had got up early to watch this fiasco from his bedroom window. He was in his best dressing-gown, smoking one of his best cigars, humming snatches of a Mozart Mass. *My God, look at them! Look at the Master! They're having to help Kane of St John's out of the hole – I think he's given himself a heart-attack... Poor Professor del Zeugma! Pumpkin seeds in his eyes by the look of it... Everyone's turning hilarious. Look, the choir's doing a can-can... Abishag's storming off, fists at her side... Well, what can she have expected? Even parody religion requires real blood. My poor wicked ex-darling, you have undone yourself!*

And indeed Margot ffontaines-Laigh promptly went out of fashion. It was no longer the thing to be her friend. Her following shrank to a hard core.

The Master of Wygefortis', now universally known as Juicy, was not part of that hard core. He had been humiliated by the pomobolium, and blamed 'that ffontaines-Laigh moppet' for his various sufferings:

First, the obnoxious new nickname.

Secondly, the shame of having to back down. Overnight his college ceased to be Cambridge's neo-pagan institution. It dropped Roman dates and Manx days of the week from its notices and correspondence; Vernal Term went back to being Easter Term; College Grace was restored before meals, the invocation of Ceres suppressed; Woolly was commanded to remove his *louche* statue of Antinoüs from Chapel (where he'd been burning joss sticks to it, chanting passages from *Dorian Gray* before it, tricking it out on Jemayrts, its sacred day, with silk underwear, and otherwise misbehaving). The other Heads of House made merry over these things, and Sir Trotsky Plantagenet was mortified.

Thirdly, most insidiously: he found himself personally haunted. He hadn't expected that. His family being Advanced, he'd been reared in pristine atheism and was left, of course, unbaptised. So he didn't need to be de-baptised, and had approached the ceremony in Christ's Pieces light-heartedly, as an antic imposed by young Lady Margot, with herself as prize.

But as he stalked home that morning to the Master's Lodge, his D.Litt. gown dripping with coconut milk, a hunk of melon stuck in his hood, he detected a certain overpowering smell. At that moment it seemed the least of his burdens, for there were ribald crowds of undergraduates taking snapshots, and a television crew from Thailand; and at the gates of College he was met by a bedraggled party of pagan graduate students, slightly behind the trend, who wanted to garland him. (He'd snatched the wreath from their hands, trampled it, and rusticated the lot of them.) But even once he reached the sanctuary of Tartarus, his Lodgings, the smell remained. *It's pineapple juice, unmistakably. No – pineapple syrup.* Sir Trotsky tossed his robes out of his study window to lie in the rain. He stood long under his shower. Yet somehow the sacreligious stink still polluted him. *Damn her. The scent of cheap tinned Filipino chunks. Horribly strong. Damn her to eternity. Made from concentrate and sugared. Damn.*

If Sir Trotsky had a soul, it was his body. For decades his intellect had been an overfed muddle. His conscience was stillborn. His passions were asleep: when he was libidinous it was only because there was nothing else to do. His pomposity, indeed his entire personality, had faded and hardened to a carapace, through which, if anyone looked closely one could see the inner blankness. No one did look, because he possessed (for no reason at all) a stately figure, accentuated by a firm paunch, copious billowing snow-white mane, Stoic-philosopher jawline, benevolent eyes, fine long hands. These were all people noticed about him, all he loved of himself: they had *become him*. It was cruel but it was inevitable that the curse should fasten *there*.

The days dragged by and the pineapple-syrup stench, if anything, grew stronger. In private Juicy was like Lady Macbeth, obsessively rubbing at his tainted skin. In public he was Macbeth himself, facing the ghost of Banquo on High Table. He could not make out the Fellowship at all: *Do these bloody swine notice or not?* Sometimes he was sure: *They're teasing, they pretend not to, I'm going to confront them.* But then he'd tug his lip and lose conviction: *After all, they're* always *aloof. Snuffly. Twitchy. Damn, damn, damn. Perhaps it's nothing...*

In the last days of every Easter Term, High Table develops a particular atmosphere. *We've got to keep up appearances,* each Fellow says to himself. *Moloch's still full.* (*Moloch* is what they call Hall at St Wygy's.) *The undergraduates are still watching.* Oloroso with the cucumber soup; Montrachet with the turbot. *But very soon they'll be gone – Then: transport! – I can let myself go – I'll eat in bed – Wear frilly knickers over my trousers* – Griotte-Chambertin twenty years old, Margot's age, with the saddle of venison. *Summer in four days! I'll be able to talk aloud to Engelbert – Poo-poo – F.R. Leavis* (these are all imaginary friends). Thus the Fellowship gloats on its coming solitude, when each can slither further down the slope. Not one gives thought to the madhouse awaiting them at the bottom. None but the careworn Master.

He nodded at Chyld the butler. Chyld, an ancient hunchback, hobbled over to a brass gong and struck it, on the second attempt, with a silver mallet. Everyone in Moloch struggled to his feet. Woolly intoned a long Latin thanksgiving, recently restored. Then the Master and Fellows of St Wygefortis' College filed out to Caïna, the Senior Combination Room, for dessert. The undergraduates – dull Scholars, duller Commoners – stood with heads faintly bowed over the long tables, parodying reverence.

'Juicy looks like death,' murmured Tristan to Seb, dullest of them all.

'His vibrator got stuck and he had to sit on it right through dinner,' Seb speculated.

'It's a theory.'

Margot, who for the last week had sat a few places away from everyone else in Moloch, stood like a statue, remote, graceful, untroubled, her finger marking her place in the *Anthologia Græca*.

The dons sank into their leather armchairs in Caïna. No one ever got used to Chyld's curvature. He was so bent he could only speak to a seated man by twisting his head sideways, as if to kiss cheeks. 'Inniskillin Vidal 2008, Master?' he hissed in Juicy's ear, spraying spittle up the lobe. Juicy winced, then nodded. It was the wine they allowed themselves in the last week of each term.

'Delightful stuff,' the Fellows told each other, 'Strong nose of orange rind', sip sip sip, 'Peach', 'Peach? No no, Wybrants, a nectarine cultivar I think you'll find', '*Thank you*, Home Bursar, I stand corrected', '(Oh dear, another squabble coming)', '*I* would say a Carolina Belle peach, grown on a south-facing slope, bedded in slightly too much bone meal', 'Humph!' snarled the Home Bursar. 'In a special sense, are not all fruits nectarines,' offered Woolly, drawing everyone's contempt on himself, 'and at the same time not?' 'But Granny Smiths! Let us at least agree on Granny Smiths!', sip, 'Yes, Screwgrave, yes!', '*And* white lilac', '*And* pineapple of course, distinctly pineapple—'

The Master started. He half rose from his chair. It was in his mind to cry *Which of you have done this?* Instead he managed to gasp, with blackened face, 'Damn damn damn Margot ffontaines-Laigh. That little harlot.'

'Yes, Master,' '*Ja, mein Meister*', 'Quite, Master,' said the Combination Room, not quite following Juicy's line of reasoning but grateful for his firm hand on the tiller. Culpepper crossed his legs and waited.

'Might we *send her down*, Master?' asked Sir Wayne Scuff, slavering bile. He had not enjoyed being a knight in Margot's game of chess. She'd sacrificed him for a pawn: that sort of thing smarts.

'*Yes*,' said Juicy decisively (and there was a small stir of excitement: 'A sending-down', 'Our first sending-down since the Crompe!', '*Ja, bitte*'). Culpepper caught Chyld's eye and waggled his empty glass. 'No. Better not. It'd get into the papers. We've had enough of that this term.' There was a downward shiver of disappointment. Even Chyld was nettled, and with shaking hands poured ice-wine into Culpepper's lap. 'But anything else...'

'Might we give her – Penal Collections?'

'No.' No one ever gets these at Wygy's. 'Well, yes. Yes. I can't see why not.'

The Fellows pulled themselves up in their armchairs again, smacking their lips. This was better than nothing. Felix uncrossed his legs and brushed his groin.

This humiliation was inflicted on her the next day. It culminated with a speech by Culpepper, in a more-in-sorrow-than-in-anger manner that would have mortified a woman less proud than Margot. 'I think I speak for my colleagues' (Dr von Spluffe pinched her grey mouth tighter than might be thought possible; the line was thin as a hair. Sir Wayne farted happily in his sleep) 'when I say that we hope for better. You must be more ductile next term, Lady Margot; more yielding, more obliging. Over the summer I would like you to translate the first five books of Tacitus, four hundred lines of Nonnus...' On he went. It was an appalling list.

When he had finished his moppet had risen, bowed to the drunkard and the Boche, nodded to Culpepper, and retired from the room. An hour later, when he went looking for her, to make up, she was gone. She left no address; she was not in London; until he had heard Mrs Elmsgall's tattle, Felix had had no clue where she might be. But he knew now, and she could escape him no longer.

v.

Culpepper does not often invite our pity. But we ought to appreciate how painfully he was in two minds that sultry evening, as he drove out toward Westley Waterless.

This is just, said one of his minds, an undergraduate prank. *I need only be donnish to frighten them off. Anyway, I love her. Prank, caper, escapade – those are the words. Lark.*

But *I've been lured out*, said the other mind, *by an eerie crone. To behold a profanity hounded from this island fourteen centuries ago. I was deliberately enticed. Something expects me to be allured by this blasphemy. And I am allured, curse it. I'll perhaps be* expected. *Also, she may understand what she is doing. Also, I am in love with her.*

Tugged between these two attitudes, both insincere, Culpepper could barely manage the long straight road, bending now and then for no reason as it wittered over the long flat land. He was so bemused he nearly crashed his Land Rover (a rust-red Series III, carefully kept muddy), which is to say nearly crushed smaller, flimsier vehicles beneath his tyres.

The flatness of Cambridgeshire is nearly absolute. Sky fills the stage; land shrinks, it has no speaking part, it forms the footlights. But despite the immense vault of cloudy air, despite the high watery light, despite the remote wisps of foliage like trickles of smoke, this is landscape that feels heavy, formed as it is of mud sinking under its own weight. *We're at the sump of the world*, said the more excitable of Culpepper's two minds;

there's a spiritual law of gravity, it added insanely, *we'll never again be able to ascend a hill.* His milder mind snorted: *Rubbish, this is just East Anglia, low but nice, cosy.* But: *It's not cosy, it's gothic. People think it's jagged mountain ranges that are gothic, fir-forests, broken turrets. But it's these flats. This landscape does nothing, anything could happen on it, anything at all. Regard that*— Mild Felix: *You may as well shut up.* Excitable Felix: *Silence won't help you any more than emptiness.*

After half an hour of this, Culpepper pulled over to brood on his map. Westley Waterless is a straggling little village. Only one pub was marked, lowering beside a twist in the road from Cambridge. The Seacome house was at the other side of the village, on the road to Great Bradley, Haverhill, and the wide world beyond, with its park and its wall stretching halfway back to the tavern. Culpepper's idea was to leave his car on the near side of the village, beside the pub, and creep up on the big house on foot.

It's hard to say why he needed to surprise Margot and her commune. It was also hard to say how he might hope to ambush what he was afraid of by walking up to it.

But that word let the cat out of the bag. He was *afraid*, formlessly afraid.

He reached Westley Waterless. THE DIRTY SWAN said the signboard, over a clumsy painting of a half-grown bird muddying itself in a puddle of beer trickling from a bottle: REGINALD SQUAT, PROPRIETOR. For ten minutes Culpepper simply sat in his Land Rover, staring at the cygnet and dithering. What with inarticulate terror, and the East Anglian purple-grey evening light, and the shadows streaming away before him across parched Siberian flatness, and perhaps love, Culpepper felt a terrible thirst. He strove; he fell. (*I can spare fifteen minutes.*)

The Dirty Swan is not a prosperous inn. Without it is muddy white, within muddy yellow. The bumpkin behind the bar, presumably Reginald Squat, answered Culpepper with a grunt, and drew a pint of thin liquid with such an oily meniscus it made Culpepper think of a swirling alluvial creek contaminated by motorboats. The only other drinker was a stout yokel, also mud-coloured, who regarded him with frank silent disdain.

Culpepper, feeling shy, let his eyes wander and dilate in the gloom. A tall jar of pickled toads reared up on the bar beside the crisps; an inexpertly-stuffed swan took form nailed to the wall above. The glass case over his head held not the usual sailors' knots, but a variety of nooses ('AMERICAN 13-PLY SLIP-KNOT: SAN QUENTIN, 1ST MAY 1942'. 'LONG-DROP, PENTONVILLE GAOL, 23RD NOVEMBER 1910'. 'LEATHER HALTER: TOMBSTONE, ARIZONA, 28TH MARCH 1891'.) As quickly as he could, he finished his beer, which lay on his stomach like cold gruel, and asked the way to the Seacome house, not because he didn't know, but because he hoped a human voice, even his own, would take the edge off that sepulchral place. This was a mistake. The other guest made a little moan. The publican looked away, down at his grubby floor, then, without meeting Culpepper's face, pointed vaguely out the pub door. Culpepper nervously went to the loo on the way out, and found a potted mandrake where you'd expect the condom dispenser. A curiosity? A love philtre?

Dusk had closed in during those ten minutes in the pub. The sky was not dark, but it was dingy. Colour had leached out of the world. It was like wearing sunglasses inside: nothing was invisible, everything was deadened.

In short, it was a clumsy and uncertain Culpepper who struck down Westley Bottom Road. This was, he found, a mere straggling country lane, much potholed. (A solitary robin advertised casual sex. A faint breeze tried to form indecent words in the beech leaves.) After a 'bus shelter, which made him shiver for no reason, and a short run of ugly bungalows, and the silent intersection with Church Lane, there was nothing on his right but fields, fields half-heartedly ploughed, furry with weeds, sown as it might be with torpid parsnips waiting for frost. On his left was a long brick wall which in its time must have had pretensions. There'd been marble coping, now mostly broken off, with an ornamental urn every twenty paces. The urns were ivy-choked; here and there one had toppled over and lay in the uncut grassy bank that rose between road and wall. On one urn Culpepper made out a satyr with immense glaring eyes which seemed to blame him that its horns were smashed, its revels ended. There was a lot of rubbish in the grass. The village evidently treated the wall as an informal dump. The park that lay beyond seemed to be hopelessly overgrown. Untended oaks slumped over the wall, full of dead branches, choked with vines, almost leafless even now in July.

It's all very well, Culpepper thought, *to call these details local colour – extremely* brown *local colour. The fact is, everything feels* laid out. *Like a gruesome welcome mat. Expected, expected, expected*: he couldn't get that word out of his head. Anxiety, that most boring of mental faculties, rang its changes. *This evening is ominous; it's sinister; it's ominously sinister, ominous to a sinister degree...*

It's our mettle that's being tested now, not Culpepper's. Why was he jittery on Westley Bottom Road? Are we tempted to look for supernatural explanations, which is to say no explanation at all? This is a moment to resist credulity and prove ourselves rational. (Worse temptations lie ahead.) We don't need spooks to account for his low spirits, any more than we need them to account for Bess Elmsgall's sense, nine hours before, of being told things in that 'bus shelter. Cambridgeshire is a forbidding county, Westley Waterless a grisly village, dusk a menacing hour. Culpepper had drunk ill-kept ale. He had not drunk his usual gin and wine. Worse still, he had missed dinner: Wygefortis' dines unfashionably early, at seven, and it was now getting on for nine. He was a man of the robust well-fed sort, whose equanimity is at the mercy of stomach; delay a meal and such men are promptly hag-ridden. That's enough to account for his disquiet. Everything predisposed him.

After about three hundred yards the wall was broken by elaborate *art nouveau* ironwork gates, monogramed *HS* for Hastings Seacome the guilty capitalist. In the dying light Culpepper could make out a small stone gatehouse, heavily shuttered, on one side of the gates; on the other a stone post engraved THE RISE in Gothic lettering. *Vain boast,* thought Culpepper, *the ground beyond these gates barely goes up. The house may be at an elevation of five feet. Yet that's a matter of awe on these alluvial flats. The Rise is higher than absolute lowness. Seacome was as proud of it as an abbot with a llamery perched on a snowy Himalaya. Proud –.* But here he shook himself, annoyed. He was dawdling, fantasising, flinching. He must get on.

The gates were rusty, loose on their hinges, and unchained. He pressed them, slid through sideways, pulled them creaking behind him, and gingerly made his way up the unkempt drive.

The villa came into view, a florid Edwardian nightmare gone to seed. Culpepper made out striped brick chimneys, gingerbread eaves, broken shingles, tiles dreary with moss, pointy windows, and a turret, no, two turrets, one topped by a weather-vane.

Yet he hardly noticed the house, so appalled he was by a sudden stench. Not rot, not a carcass: a smoky smell that seemed, he couldn't say why, ancient and incongruous. Burned meat with something else on top of it, sweet, clinging, nauseous, like honey spilled on a stove.

The gloaming had reached that point when shapes turn incorporeal as smoke, while the shade beneath them was solid as black marble. The gables looked like grey froth on the immense solidity of the empty porch. The silence was thickening, too, filling the foreground of his mind.

In front of the porch was the wreck of a flowerbed, a circle of black churned earth monotonously laid out with spiky white plants. Their glaring six-petalled flowers seemed to suck in all the remaining light.

Asphodel. And that mangy shrub's a laurel. This, I imagine, is meant to be their herm: it had begun life as a garden sundial, but had been tricked out with a crude plaster bust and plasticine genitals. Before the herm stood a metal barbecue, smokeless, exhausted, and daubed with gold paint. In its ash Culpepper made out something pitifully biological. A charred paw.

He had one of those moments when we notice how noisy our bodies are: ducts spurting and hoovering, gut busy as a factory, blood spraying as from a fireman's hose, heart pounding like a newspaper press, printing lies.

He turned from the flowerbed (thundering and swishing) to the blind facade of The Rise. Its windows had white gauze pinned over their insides, and the stained-glass panel above the door was blocked with a plywood pediment painted white. The lightless house seemed not so much empty as condemned, awaiting demolition. *What a lot of nervous fidgeting! Hush!* He forced himself to stand still, stop thinking, stop imagining, attend.

The silence was not absolute. There was a faint sound: human; distant; musical. Not singing, chanting. Not English. From behind the house. It ceased. A long pause, during which he was disgusted to be able to hear his heart.

It resumed. He recognised it: ἰκοίμαν ποτὶ Κύπρον – a chorus from Euripides! *O to come unto Cyprus, isle of Aphrodite…*

Rapidly (*If I don't run forward I might run away*) he turned from the porch, and ran round the side of the house. There was a muddle of shrubbery to his right, and on his left a bewildering array of conservatories, bow windows, wooden battlements – the rambling house was more huge than he'd supposed. The second turret was attached to a separate wing, sticking out at right angles from the main block; he trotted about it, along a dank gravel path where overgrown rhododendra pressed him against peeling clapboards. It was so dark that when he finally rounded the house into a diffuse blaze of firelight he flinched, gasped, and pulled up sharply.

No, not a bonfire. Just a dozen faintly swaying clumps of flame; torches, in fact. They were grouped in a circle in a wide alley of poplars that ran away behind the house, some fifty yards off. That was the first thing he grasped. Next that the torchlight fell on naked ruddy flesh, white draperies, glittering metal. Then, that there were a dozen people facing inward, lifting their burning swaying torches high above their heads.

The evening had become very still, with no breeze to gutter the flames. The tongues of fire swayed because the people were shuffling back and forth as they sang, in time to their chant, nearly dancing.

The Greek verses stopped, the shuffle stopped. A guitar strummed thrice out in the shadows. Then they began to sway and sing, this time in English. But what English!

> *Let's fly to Cyprus, Venusland!*
> *Where the psychic powers erotic*
> *soothe the mental and neurotic.*
> *Let's go run along the strand*
> *at Paphos, where a single river,*
> *with its hundred mouths aquiver,*
> *sucks the rich and rainless sand.*
> *Hear me Bacchus, Mænad-master!*
> *Bear me, moaning, to the vaster*
> *mountain of Olympus. And*
> *there I'll faint at gods until*
> *you roll me down the Muses' hill,*
> *where grace revives on every hand*
> *desire. For I desire desiring.*
> *I obey your law requiring*
> *orgy rite of Mænad—*

'PROFANATION!' – an immense shout. '*Profanation!*' – louder, shriller, enraged. 'An intruder!'

The darkness (it was absolute night now) was crammed with rushing lights coming at him, brouhaha, dashing silhouettes, cries, hoots, fluttering wings, chaos, all thrusting straight at Felix, who to his shame – the moment would come back to him often in the future, a sudden pang – blundered backwards with a sort of sob, tripped, and sprawled on the unmown lawn. He shut his eyes.

He forced himself to open them, and blinked in the fiery glare above and over him.

It seemed his mind had dropped into an abyss of perfect gibberish. Reared up in the confused, shifting light between him and the furious indigo sky was Pallas Athena. He beheld frigid wisdom, eternally young, tall, severe, dreadful in beauty. Everything about her seemed designed to crush him: her majestic peaked helm; her great Gorgon-masked bronze shield; her snowy chiton. She leaned on her eight-foot spear, she flashed her gilt gorget, she looked down her long perfect nose at Culpepper lying under her feet.

And a Jack Russell with two false heads was sniffing his shoes.

None of this struck Culpepper as remotely funny. He tried to form the thought: *They're play-acting. It's only Abishag. Margot.* But the words flew out of his head, leaving him as terrified as before.

The owl on her right shoulder had its eyes shut against the torchlight. It opened them on him, and exclaimed contemptuously '*Hoo?*'

'Γλαῦκ᾽ εἰς Ἀθήνας,' groaned Felix, whose head was swimming. *Owls to Athens.* He'd never fainted, and wondered if this plummeting-backward-rapidly-through-space sensation was the start of a faint. Spinning behind himself over a cliff... He heard, so clearly it seemed to come from every direction at once, or even from within the anarchy inside his skull, a dark, masterful voice. Was this death?

'Felix, you oaf. How in the blazes did you find us? And what d'y'mean by interrupting evensong?' Athena addressed him. *No*, Margot ffontaines-Laigh was speaking, her voice as always low and bassoon-like. The firelit heads that ringed his vision, like hours marked on a clockface, were human. White folds, bare shoulders, a metal hat on Ares, bacchante ivy in the hair of Dionysus, more metal on Athena who was just, just his darling Margot. He felt himself grinning feebly, he even heard himself tittering, so that Athena stomped her spear on the grass in vexation.

'*Hoo?*'

The goggling idiot eyes of her bronze Gorgon swelled at him, as if to petrify.

vi.

'There was a gent. Like,' mumbled Alfred through his toad-in-the-hole. Alfred never spoke at supper, he only chewed, and his sister looked at him in surprise.

'A what?'

'One of those pree-verted gents. What you get at the University.'

'Here in Waterless? Tell us another.'

'It was. Earlier this evening. *And* asking the way to the Seacome place. Mucky doings I shouldn't think.'

His words excited Val, although you wouldn't guess it from her staid boiled-porridge features. An adult recruit for the commune! The fearful sinful things she might be forced to behold tomorrow, when the sun would come up and she would put her head through the rickety palisade, rioted in her imagination. Palpable thrills passed through her stout figure. Her spine was an electric eel in spasm. Very slightly she wet her undergarments.

Her brother was wrought of finer clay. Alfred's was an essentially literary mind. His waking hours were devoted to the Singles columns of the popular press. Although he'd never had the courage to reply, still less to post his own advertisement (dreading his sister as he did), these studies had formed him intellectually. Lechery could not touch him until framed according to the conventions of his chosen genre, which were strict and obscure as the rules of dactylic hexameter. *WM, 35, educ.,* Alfred fluently murmured to himself, imagining the transgressions of Culpepper, *DF, F, seeks walk on small-town wild side. GF a plus. No em-att.*

For some minutes number 31 was a happy home. Val, clearing away the toad and bringing out stewed prunes, passed without jolt from *voyeuse* to censor, from gross fleshy pleasure to ecstasy of the spirit. What riches she'd bear to the next meeting of the Baptist Ladies' League! Its vigilance and severity made it the terror of the district, but the sad fact is, there's precious little in that bleak corner of England to begrudge, little to terrorise; puritanism is starved of matter. Often the League had to content itself passing resolutions against what it had watched on telly. *How grateful the Ladies'll be when I tell 'em!*

Curiously enough, Val had held back news of the goings-on at number 29, for fear the Ladies might manage to shut them down. *Just wish I'd not told that blathermouth Gladys Drybble. Only did it because she has a camera with a tellyscopy thing. Brownlow don't matter, he never says nothing to no-one.* But a social scandal was a different matter. When they heard of an interloper from the University visiting a student commune by night, the Ladies could be relied on to invent details more dreadful than any reality.

Phra-na, phra-na, thought Alfred to himself, finishing his seconds of prunes.

Val pictured the Ladies' next meeting. *I'll wear my apricot twinset. And the porcelain brooch with the view of Skegness. I'll wait until the President's about to make her report, then I'll stand up, all sudden and serious. 'Mrs Elmsgall and ladies,' I'll say, 'allow me to gracefully interrupt if you would be so very good. I bear tidings of exceeding heaviness. It will pain you to hear that the worldly-wise of Cambridge itself are coming out to Westley Waterless as to a resort of vice...' With my hand on my bosom, like this. Other side of my bosom. Not covering Skegness.*

What a salty, blood-flecked, crackling titbit they'd have to work on! Fit to be mouthed for a month or more, worried, softened with spittle. *And to think it was her own Alfie who had heard…* Suddenly her eyes narrowed.

''Ere, our Alf. Where did you come across this gent of yours?'

As the eyes of the rabbit when a stoat rears over the edge of the furrow flit wildly, here and there, hopeless, so were Alfred's eyes.

His sister read the signs. 'Alfie Squint, you've been in the *Swan*! You have been abasing yourself with the liquor of uncleanness in that unrighteous place. You have backslidden beyond hope of remission. Profanity!'

The Squints have been Dissenters since Oliver's day. Chapel-talk comes easily to them. 'I wrestled mightily with Apollyon, sister, but my strength—'

'Fiddle-di-sticks! You *lusted* after the bondage of Moab. Alfred Squint, if I've told you once I've told you a thousand times.'

vii.

In the end, the gods were very English about it all, and asked Felix in for a drink.

But they weren't like that at first. When they pulled him to his feet, they had been angry, and he had been afraid.

'O Athena!' said Zeus in gruff, passable Greek: 'know you this mortal? Is he not a blasphemer worthy to be flung from the Tarpeian Rock?'

'Yes and yes,' growled Margot, 'but don't be ridiculous [καταγέλαστος], there are no cliffs in Cambridgeshire.'

'We could put him to the torment of Tantalus,' suggested Hades, naked but for his black infernal crown. 'You know, hang him upside down beside a decanter of sherry and let him die of thirst. That might be fun [ἀπόλαυσμα], don't you think?'

It dawned on Culpepper that not only was Hades a boy of twenty in false whiskers, he was a boy he recognised: Benge, a third-year classicist from Trinity Hall. And look, it was Tristan! Tristan Bolswood of his own College, of his own coterie, with a panther skin, a vine-leaf chaplet and a sprig of muscat grapes. And even Ollie Vane-Powell, his own dear Ollie! In tunic and dyed curls, lugging a smith's hammer. Hermes, with his snaky curtain-rod, winged helm and winged sandals from some expensive theatrical outfitters, was that titled Hungarian reading history at Pembroke College – Count Róbert something; what was the rest of it? Zseni de Mérföldkő. Ares and Poseidon were likewise Cambridge undergraduates, though behind the dark beards he couldn't put a name to the faces. Zeus, whose beard and hair were cotton wool, was a burly rugby Blue from Oxford: he'd seem him play at Twickenham. And that lovely girl masquerading as Hera, with the regal set to her breasts, robed, crowned with the *polos*, matronly haughty, was a creature from Robinson, or perhaps Girton; he'd taught her last term.

It was in fact the usual crew – it was precisely the hard core of disciples who remained to Margot when she dropped out of vogue in June; them, and a few recruits. The usual crew! Felix had to stop himself giggling weakly with relief. How could he have felt such a frenzy of terror a moment before? And how was he to keep his eyes off Aphrodite, a girl he'd never seen before, who ran her violet eyes over him, and was intoxicatingly beautiful, and gloriously honey all over? He'd no word for the colour of her, it swam and glowed on her curves, it scintillated in the torchlight, it made his own skin flush – although out of the corner of his eye he felt a chilling look from Artemis, another stranger, lissom, with long, long legs coming out of a short hunting-dress, a buckskin quiver and businesslike bow. He sensed antagonism between the Huntress and the goddess of Love.

They were all of an age, just as he'd expected before panic shut down his brain. *They're virtually children and I am an adult. At least I'm a don.* He was on his feet now, and had stopped gaping. *I'm a don. They clearly feel young and unsure of themselves.*

Not Odingo, though, not the willowy aristocratic Kenyan, playing Apollo in a gold peruke pricked about with laurel leaves, and nothing else. He continued to smile at his rival with the benign half-smile of pure reason, which is an extremely blank, malicious look. 'Immortals! I shall flay him,' he announced in Greek, 'as I flayed the pesky Marsyas.'

'You bloody Swiss boarding-school degenerate,' barked Margot in English, 'you can't open a packet of nuts without asking me for help. How could you get a man's skin off? Oh, come inside everyone. We need a drink. You,' she added scornfully to her other lover, 'may as well come too. Walk.'

So they trooped off toward the house: Cerberus dashing gaily ahead; next Athena, stomping along with spear and ægis grasped in her fists; Apollo swaying beside and above her, holding her torch and his; then the rest of the pantheon, two by two, nude or semi-nude, toting the impedimenta of deity, trident, grapes, the caduceus which cut no ice with Gladys. Last came Felix Culpepper the man, feeling rather shy and silly, and watching the weird wobbling shadows the torchlight threw on the thick dim grass.

Either it was the gods' custom to keep silence after their evening Mysteries, or Margot's temper damped their talkativeness. There was no moon; the mansion before them was enormous, very dark, and uninviting.

They filed into it through a door that creaked and wailed on its hinges; then for a while the only noise was the creaking of floorboards.

Culpepper looked about in disquiet. The whole gigantic edifice was clearly on the point of dissolving. Doors dangled at odd angles, ceilings sagged, walls were streaked with water-stains or festooned with dangling strips of paper. There was no furniture except for broken-down sofas, and chests of drawers mottled with mildew. Off right and left Culpepper had an impression of dark staircases soaring off into musty vacancy, landings untouched by human feet for decades and deep in dust, crazy galleries dangling by a plank. Occasionally a stairwell was blocked off with plastic tape. In places the cobwebs were so dense the top half of the passageway was invisible, a grey blur. Everywhere the ruckus of footfall set off scuttling behind the wainscoting. They passed a ballroom with its folding doors stuck half-open. Their passing made its bagged chandelier tinkle.

Culpepper had gone back to being in two minds. Was this all just a scheme to improve their Greek over summer? Was it conscious evil-doing? *Equivocal, equivocal,* he thought. *Why, for instance, am I taking their* clobber *seriously? I can't think of it as mere costume.* Their helmets looked workmanlike, the owl looked sacramental. *More importantly, what do* they *feel about it?*

He tried to read the attitude of the gods from their gait and set of shoulder; for despite his self-absorption, Culpepper was used to living among the young as a sort of zookeeper, and was skilled, in a contemptuous way, at gauging their moods. Were they bored with their charade yet, or not? *Was* it a charade for them, one more obedience to the whims of Margot? They'd been at this game for more than a fortnight, if the Elmsgall was to be believed. Were they sulky, zealous, brisk? Were they ripe for mutiny?

They reached the forequarters of the house and the few rooms that seemed to be inhabited. Candles were lit, the remaining torches doused in metal buckets. The goddesses went off in one direction, the gods in another, and for a moment Culpepper was alone on a threadbare circle of carpet. He could hear clatter as equipment was shed. He poked his head into various rooms: a scullery; a sort of gym, with sunbed and weights; a forlorn windowless chamber with a shelf of books, a plaster bust of Homer, and a table of irregular Greek verbs taped to the door; a grubby drawing-room evidently doing service for banquets, with satin-draped mattresses arranged in a square beneath an unfinished mock-Pompeian wall painting. *Pretty much*, he thought, *like any student digs*; and the thought made him irrationally confident.

'This way, Dr Culpepper,' said Margot, reappearing; she was over her rage, or had changed tack. She steered or pushed him into a small room and shut him in. It was a parlour at the very front of the house, with a few chairs, a low table, a filthy, empty bookcase, and windows wide open on the circular flowerbed. The night air was warm and close.

He could hear her through the door, shooing her disciples kitchenward. *How horribly hungry I am.*

The door opened. She entered with a lit candle; set it on the rickety table; stared at him inscrutably; sniffed; and set about divesting herself of the trappings of godhead. That is: she propped her shield against the rusty hearth; plunged her spear head-down into a pot of desiccated soil, with a few dry twigs left from its dead plant; deposited her owl on the bookcase, soothing it with expert strokes (it fell asleep at once, its head twisted backward); shook out her chiton; sat down opposite him; doffed her helmet, placing her foot on it, and folded her arms, belligerently. Then with a visible effort she remembered to fold her hands in her pleated lap in a mock-girlish way, and assumed an air of pained politeness, as to an elderly intruder; a carnal uncle, say, breaking in on a Bible Study.

Culpepper admired this pose for a little while, and then said –.

Let's admit at once that it wasn't a successful conversation. Perhaps neither party had worked out a cogent attitude. Margot, despite her subdued shock and irritation, was a gentlewoman and couldn't help feeling that she was a hostess, obliged to put her guest at ease: that, at least, was the impression she gave. Culpepper, despite his damped-down anxiety and amusement, knew himself to have acted badly by barging in on her eccentric house party. Neither could get out of their minds the last time they had spoken, an age ago, three weeks back, at the Penal Collection. Neither could quite resist querulous flirtation. Moreover, there seemed be some current in the room, indefinably flagitious – it's embarrassing to mention so vague a sensation, but the fact is it got stronger and stronger and finally wrecked the conversation. Which went like this.

'Έξιτη Ατηεναια!' Culpepper had assembled some pretty lines from Callimachus as they'd trekked through Mr Seacome's pile: 'Come forth, Athena, Sacker of Cities, golden-helmeted, who rejoicest in the din of horse and—'

'Yes, yes,' Athena interrupted in English, 'I thought you'd say that. It's interesting to see you, Felix, but you mustn't chatter. Interesting, I mean, in a way... Anyway it's a sensation to be speaking a barbarian tongue again to a worldling. We immortals let ourselves use English until after breakfast, then—'

There was a timid knock at the door. '*Δεῦρο!*' she snapped, and the rugby-playing king of heaven and earth sidled in with a tray: glasses, a bottle, a bowl of pastries. She pointed at the table, caused him to glug the bottle into the glasses, and then flicked him out of the room with her finger. She drank at once so there'd be no nonsense about clinking or toasting.

Another unhappy pause.

'Do you not like retsina, Felix? You seem to be toying with it.'

'Er – yes. But that stench coming in the window.... What is it?'

'Seared meat. We had a holocaust this morning. We sacrificed a tom-cat and interpreted its entrails.'

'Oh,' and shrugging, helped himself to a pastry.

'Yes, "Oh." Can't you grasp that we're not just dressing up and polishing our Attic? We're doing the religion. Tristan has paid his parents' char in Holland Park to pray to us each dawn.'

'Ahm.' Culpepper, famished, was making a mess of the filo.

'We can't, you see, very well worship each other. Tristan, Dionysus that is, tries to guess her prayers, and either grants or denies them. Odingo, Apollo to you, attempts to inspire a pythoness in Tunbridge Wells.'

Culpepper, who couldn't discern Margot's tone, tried to sound neutral. He finished his second pastry. 'Is the pythoness a char too?'

'A barmaid. An established oracle. The regulars ask advice, she retires to the loo, smokes a spliff chanting "Phœbus, Phœbus," then comes out and tells them what to do.'

'Ah... May I finish these?'

'Do. You like them?'

A non-committal noise, although he was wolfing them down.

'On Thursday we definitely changed the weather. Zeus can nearly make thunder. We keep our portfolio above the *Financial Times* average by inspecting guts. But haruspicy's a difficult science. Voles are no good, their livers are too small. Stray cats tend to have diseased organs, their left lobes are often indecipherable. The tabby you're smelling now—'

'I didn't mean that. The *sweet* stench.'

'Ah. Nectar. I admit there's not much to be said for nectar. Nectar's simply hydromel. Mead. Perhaps if the local honey were better... We brew it in the cellar. The mash tun fits under the sunbed. No one enjoys it but the rule is no nice ambrosia until you've drunk up all your nectar. I supervised this batch. With hops, to cut the stickiness. I don't think it smells so bad.' She pouted.

'But ambrosia's all right?'

'Yes, because it's *Amanita muscaria*.'

'No it's not – at least scholarly opinion is—'

'Hush. Pedant. It's clear from Pindar that it *is*. Fly agaric, the elvish toadstool, the red one with white spots. We grow it in the toolshed and parboil it. We have it as pasta sauce, and on toast for breakfast, and we tried stuffing leg of mutton but that wasn't a success. Ambrosia's not a terribly interesting taste, I admit, but it's hallucinogenic. That's the important thing.'

Ah! thought Culpepper crudely, relaxing a little, *that's how they endure it. Undergraduates! They've been off their heads the whole two weeks.* What he said, having finished the pastries, was 'May I smoke?'

'You may not...'

He put his cigar-case away. 'Why is there a sunbed?'

'Æsthetics, Felix. Or verisimilitude. Our appearance matters. We're watched. I don't mean the old trout next door who spies on us.'

'"We are made a spectacle unto the world,"' quoted Culpepper dreamily, '"and to angels, and to men."'

'Yes, we're a spectacle. Spectacles create what is actual. Certain energies might not be released if...' Culpepper shrugged and Margot checked herself. 'Those of us who don't wear clothes looked odd for the first few days – except Odingo. Tanlines, y'know. In particular Aphrodite, whose complexion I noticed you admiring. She began with two leprous bikini stripes whiter than her pigeons.'

'She looks the part now,' said Culpepper crudely. 'An inspirational spectacle.'

'What a coarse beast you are. Even for a mortal. That foul quiver of lips... You're imagining orgies. I'll have you know Hera goes about each night locking doors. Artemis won't even allow rough talk at table. This is a sort of monastery. We've greater adventures on hand than bed-hopping. The experiment's innocent. It's serious.'

'Including that skinny Kenyan of yours? Is his role innocent and serious?'

'Apollo, whose lack of tanline *I* admire, bankrolls us. As it happens.

He's rich. Back in Nairobi his daddy's Minister of Social Welfare. Apollo bought the house and equipped it. We're here until Sextember.'

'Sextember!'

'Which the impious call August. Right through Quintember – yes, Quintember, Quintember, Quintember. You can smirk, you can thunder anathemas, you can fold your arms and toss back your slightly-receding locks, but what we're doing is real. This place is holy as Delphi, aweful as Delos.'

'My dear girl, come off it. We're in rural Cambridgeshire, on a normal Monday evening in the year of grace 2013.'

'We're not in Cambridgeshire, y'know – anyway it's not Monday, it's Jelune. *Kalendæ Quintilæ*, which is to say the first of Quintember, in the second year of the seven hundred and forty-eighth Olympiad. No Augustus or Constantine can distort that truth. Which we can restore.'

'Cant.'

'Can.'

'*Cant.*'

'Prick.'

'I said "cant."'

'When you grind your teeth it is hard to know what rude word you're attempting. You were always rude. I'm relieved to be so far beyond you.'

Culpepper's eyes widened. 'I admit that at the end of term I was severe—'

'Were you? I forget. I'd larger concerns.' At which Culpepper passed over altogether from desire to righteous anger. 'Gnashing is not refutation.'

'Don't try vulgar intellectual intimidation on me, young lady, I taught you the technique. When I came to you, you were a callow schoolgirl, and for this—'

'Don't use that tone. Monotheistic thug. The Quintember experiment is the event of the millennium. It's mere vandalism to track us down and play the heavy don. Attempted vandalism.'

'But I do want to play the heavy don, Abi – Margot. This is nonsense, and has to stop.' Wonderful how his swagger was coming back. Why the devil should he have been awestruck? 'You're fathoms deep in sacrilege. I'm your moral tutor. (Also your lover: that's by the way for the moment.) You're *in statu pupillari*. As are at least nine of your playmates. A word to Juicy about Olympus, and I could get all ten of you sent down for egregious misconduct. As for Artemis and brown-bottomed Aphrodite: where'd you dredge *them* up?'

'Oxford.'

'Aha! Also vulnerable to sending down. A clean sweep.'

'We don't care. We defy your vile old universities. You can't make us leave. It's a free country.'

'Who tells you these things? It's not free, it's riddled with regulation. You're not allowed to have twelve people staying in a house without a permit. You're probably not allowed to have anyone staying in *this* house: if it hasn't been condemned, it should've been. You're certainly not allowed to brew mead without a licence. And I imagine it's illegal to keep a wild owl. Even a mangy barn-owl like that.'

'My owl—'

'I'm here to break up this perverted house party. Dismiss your playfellows. Send them abroad, dispatch them to their mummies, tell them it's time for proper hols. Come back to Cambridge with me. We could have a late supper at Midsummer House.'

Margot looked down her nose. 'Midsummer House. Hols. You take this very lightly, don't you?'

'On the contrary. This is the climax of my career. I've occasionally investigated crime and assassinated people. But to unravel the plots of the underworld! To obliterate an entire pantheon…!'

'Your mockery's childish.'

'Very well then, I'll be forthright. Your twelve gods are feeble. They may as well be killed off. There's nothing here but your self-indulgence.' How Culpepper wished he was sure of this. But he'd got into character, and was sticking to it. 'This is just a comeback from your coconut-bashing farce. I heard the rumour of children dressed or undressed as Greeklings and said: "Aha, Abishag! Just her style."'

'That name's forbidden. Anyway, you're wrong. This is not like my pomobolium. Which I admit was a blunder. Why bother unchristening a few old men? – men already too wicked to be worth tempting? Why lure a single college into a few pagan gestures? Those were puny victories. Why not unbaptise a civilisation?'

This was, clearly, the moment to pulverise her pretensions. Culpepper could not understand why he was instead reverting from anger to dismay. Was it her new manner, her loftiness? 'We make no secret. The world's about to see. Now. This Quintember. What we're doing isn't private. *The Powers are abroad again.* Already the villagers scream at night. You'll hear them begin in a minute. Though this window.' Somehow Culpepper could not bear to look out of the dark window; he couldn't endure what might come through. 'In a few weeks, as we grow stronger, we'll have colonised the dreams of everyone at the second-best university in England. By the time term begins every don will be ours – except, perhaps, for a few obdurate Galilæans. And what Cambridge preaches England will soon confess. Then all nations.' She patronised him with a smile. 'What you think of as the world is coming to an end. Seventeen centuries of darkness are being rent. This is, as men will say, the apocalypse.'

Some wild metaphor is needed to describe the effect of her words on Culpepper. Between astonishment, disgust, rage, jealousy and fear, his body burst upwards like a balloon – a balloon thwacked back and forth between the vast young goddess (she suddenly seemed larger than himself) and the horror of the window.

'You're so ineffectual, Felix, you can't *stop* anything. But perhaps you can go with the flow. You might be useful. Is *that* why you intruded? Your night-sweat may lubricate the terror of others. So go back and explain how frightened you are.'

'What do you mean,' he said, in a low voice he had to fight to keep steady. 'What did you mean that this is – is not Cambridgeshire?'

'The Rise has already ceased to be in England. It's becoming somewhere else.'

Culpepper did not reply. He not speak again that night. His mouth seemed jammed. He'd lost the gift.

'Tell me, little one, why does the Church continue undecayed, century after century? Because of spectacle. She simulates the New Jerusalem. She makes the timeless place locally visible. What are her gold mosaics and processions and sacraments for? Men never believe the unseen. They return from the Church's Mysteries having been – elsewhere. Their citizenship's elsewhere; they pass through earth unarrested; they have diplomatic immunity.' Margot's voice was becoming sterner, calmer, greater, more remote. *This*, thought Culpepper, entirely daunted, *is just how the inviolate goddess of Athens would sound.* 'Meanwhile, where are We? We remain broken statues in museums, standing beside the butterflies they pin on cork. Our words are coruscations in scraps of scrolls, written in languages men think are dead. Not even when the West falls away from the Creed of Nicæa does it return to Us.' How fine she sounded, how serenely enraged. 'Philosophy! In My own city of Athens they invented it, and led men from Us. How right We were to fling Æsop from the rock, to give Socrates hemlock! Nevertheless, *Ἑνικήκαμεν*,' which means *We have conquered* – Culpepper's cowed mind registered that she had stopped speaking English. 'Philosophy is dying. Mortals are once more ready to credit whatever spectacle they are shown. If they see Us again, they will believe. We *retheophanate*. The everlasting *pneuma* comes back to the altar prepared for it: a humble place, but accurate enough. Imposture becomes reality, pseudo-Olympus merges into the everlasting mountain.' The great syllables of her Attic were filling the room to its brim, or perhaps merely filling his brain. Her speech seemed to burst up within him. 'What does place matter? What myth does not speak of places being drawn beyond place? On a particular spot to the south of Troy, Prince Anchises lay down with Love herself. A patch of moss in a wood becomes the throne of eternal desire, from Whom all things spring.' Culpepper had nothing to say in answer, indeed he scarcely heard her, dazed as he was by the brightness of her face. 'Spirit hurries out of flesh. Incarnation is undone. Gods walk on earth, gods of ichor and deathless flesh. We wax in puissance. Half a moon more and every mortal in Cambridge will start seeing Us in visions. Then they will start thinking as We would have them think. We shall possess Our ancient lands. *Ἐνικήκαμεν.*'

No, her face wasn't glowing. It was simply shining in the light pouring into the dingy little room. Everything in it was bright. Her helmet, on which she propped her left foot, was ablaze, he couldn't look at it. The empty bowl of ambrosia *vol-au-vents* cast a shadow on the tabletop. There was a light resting on the ceiling and walls, an ethereal light – no, that was the wrong word too because ether must be thin and tenuous, while this was simply the rich tremendous yellow of natural sunshine.

How could there be sunshine? It must be nine o'clock by now. Dreading to look out the window, he looked, and blinked in the intensity of noon brilliance pouring over the white stone; stone, not wood. A perfect casement of marble framed a perfect rectangle of blue. And such blue! It was the sky of a cloudless summer morning in the South. He reeled to his feet into the light and, grasping the sill (a wide ledge of marble, so warm it felt like firm flesh), lurched half out.

He was on a mountain-top. Below the window was a fall of five or six feet to a lawn thick with flowers: fritillaries, snow-white asphodel, hyacinth. This lawn fell steeply to a line of cypresses, and below the cypresses was a profounder drop, down and down – his eye was baffled by such steepness: umbrella pine and bright black rock, patches of scree golden as sand, and lush grass tumbling over the crags, down and down. The flank of the mountains broke up as it fell. Here it opened into rounded valleys watered, it seemed, with innumerable springs (it was incredible he could see so far), which joined in a rapid brook under glades of ilex. But there it fissured apart, so that water, smashed into whiteness, leapt in cataracts and plunged eternally through the air. A pair of eagles wheeled in one lucid abyss; their majesty and youth stung his eyes, he was too frail to look on them; he dropped his gaze. Beneath them was pasture at the mouth of the canyon, and a line of firs dense as a wall. At last came a sort of stratum or veil of haze, as if the air thickened; and through the veil he could see the lowlands where pale-green predominated over evergreen, black and gold. Then the yellowish coastal plain; and at last, silky, bright, sublime, vibrant with a thousand momentary glitters, the sea. The islands were superb as jewellery. Some were like gentle floating hillocks, some almost as craggy as the mountain itself. The archipelago, purple with distance, reached the horizon.

He threw his eyes up from the sea and lost them again in the sky, the flawless azure. He'd seen skies this blue over the Mediterranean, but never so overwhelming. This looked endless, not in expanse but in tenure. The sky was not blue because the morning happened to be cloudless (and this was undoubtedly morning); it was blue because it was. He didn't doubt that it would be blue for ever. No cloud could tarnish its lustre, no wind could ever worry it, no rain would come from it. No snow would ever fall on this peak, for all its loftiness. And there was a quality to the brightness for which he had no words. It was a sunny sky, yet it was not simply lit by contingent solar fire. Another sort of lumination filled it and came out of it. This was light created differently from the sun's light: a steady white radiance that hovered over the mountain; that seemed to be anchored on the mountain; that perhaps came out of the mountain itself, ineffable.

From this terrible sky his eyes roamed back to the mountain summit. Beneath his window, groves and gardens spilled away from the marble palace and the window: meadows, *allées*, topiary, flowerbeds; here and there a statue; there, perhaps a half-mile off, an immense fountain half visible through a stand of oaks. Everywhere the grass so lush it made him think of the joy of naked feet. Here the ground declined smoothly, and the lawn was taut and smooth over its downward contours as skin over a well-made human body. But just to his left he saw a marble terrace, pure white but undazzling in that calm unvarying light, with a balustrade around it, and a bench hugging the balustrade; and there the fall was unspeakable. It plummeted almost to the coastal plain. Rugged spurs of the mountain fenced in the void on either hand, but directly beneath the balustrade the rock dropped away sheer, only a little less flat than a wall. To look down that cliff, Felix thought, would be like sitting on a beach staring out over motionless ocean; the unimaginable perspective would be too much for his mind to endure. But he knew that it wasn't designed for his mind. The beings who sat on that bench and looked over that balustrade at the doings of men were greater than he: he couldn't pretend not to know that.

Indeed, he couldn't even pretend not to recognise the lie of the land. He'd been down there once, fifteen years ago, knocking about Greece with a backpack. He'd taken the ferry from the Sporades and landed at Iolcus, meaning to hitchhike across the plain of Thessaly and climb. But there'd been this German girl on the ferry, with mad compliant eyes and a stud through her nose. There was a bar in Iolcus they both liked. There was a half-ruined hostel where they had the dorm room to themselves. So he'd dawdled at sea-level, made the girl photograph him with the sacred mountain as backdrop, and passed on to Athens.

Nonetheless he had the names pat. Those peacock-coloured waters were the Thermaic Gulf; behind him was the Pindus, the spine of Hellas; to his left the Bermion, walling in the uplands of Macedon; to his right, marching away south down the coast, were Ossa, towering over the Vale of Tempe, and Pelion. And this, centre of all things, was Olympus.

Had he been looking out for a minute, or an hour, or an unvarying day in which no shadow moved? He forced his fingers to ungrasp the marble ledge, he forced himself to stand and turn; almost we might say he forced his mind to be afraid. For it seemed to him appalling that he was not more appalled. Perhaps it was the scent that had enthralled him and soothed his terror: the smell of pine forests, perfumed flowering trees, sun-warmed grass, and even, blowing up through Olympus' undying vales, salt from the Ægean.

Real terror was with him now. Pallas Athena had resumed her helmet. She stood upright and oblivious, much as she had stood through the centuries in the Parthenon. And either the room had become much larger or Felix had shrunk. He did not reach the bottom of her golden greaves; he was vermin scuttling about the wainscoting of Olympus; he felt (significantly, perhaps) like Alice miniaturised by mushrooms. He scuttled backward out of the room, keeping his eyes fixed on her feet. He spun about.

And then his fear reached a pitch which he would have thought no sane man could bear. For although he was in, or ought to have been in, the grubby dining-room of The Rise, with its preposterous square of mattresses, what he saw was the most enormous chamber he'd ever known.

It was vast as Salisbury Plain. No, not that; but as vast as a rugby pitch? He couldn't say, his sense of scale was overthrown. In any case, it was insupportable: a baleful glory of pale pink slabs, silk hangings of saffron and chryselephantine pillars, stretching away, past an amber fountain and pool open to the sky, to a portico that seemed to overhang the blue chasm. A breeze lifted the silks above his head; the marble room was so airy it seemed to fly. And its lambency was a discernible substance, the type of all light perhaps. The overplus of it was too great for the room to hold. It poured out of the portico: a lucid cascade plummeting from the deathless gods to wash the world with joy.

All this was background to the real horror. What madness to have fled Pallas! Here his suffocation was eleven times worse. For on eleven supper couches lay the eleven immortals, all, it struck him, as vast as mountains. Not one of them glanced at him: he was a flea who defiled the perfection of Olympus too slightly to be detected. A dazzling young boy was drawing wine with a silver pitch from a *krater* in the midst of the couches. Father Zeus extended his crystal cup, his other hand rested on the head of an eagle with the sharpest eyes Felix had ever imagined.

They were expectant. In a moment Athena would repose on the empty supper couch; they would sing the hymn and begin their feast. The thought of the gods singing turned Felix's guts to water. He would endure anything rather than hear such enormous music. He spun about and fled back to the room where he had left Athena. She was approaching but he plunged on, flickering, it seemed, between her ankles. Fleet with despair he leapt up, swarmed over the windowsill, swayed in agony, let himself drop.

He fell. He jarred his legs in landing and sprang away before he could feel the pain. He staggered forward and just caught himself from sprawling. But he didn't fall. He found himself careering downward. With a heroic effort he invoked the miserable circular flowerbed in front of The Rise, and even managed to see it mistily as he sprinted past: pallid flowers in churned-up soil, a fleeting ghost-vision like a bubble of greasy steam against the glaring reality of a field of *narcissi* bobbing in the sun. He had cleared a hedge of laurel with a bound and was running down mountain paths, winding and doubling back on themselves; beneath his feet was a gully. Not so (he squeezed his eyes and shook his head), not so: he was trotting down the puny drive of The Rise. That, that. The Radiance, no it was dark and dank and close, the blazing Radiance was so intense the gully seemed almost black, but it was drowning with columbine which caught the Radiance and glowed. Not so. Night, night: he thrust the mountain out of his brain, he pulled down nocturnes over his eyes. He was not dashing between immense poplars, he was slipping through rusty gates. With an effort he was back within the midnight of Cambridgeshire, jogging beside the decrepit brick wall, beside the grass full of rubbish. Then there was a flash – he had come round a corner out of the mountain path, out of the shadow of a canyon wall. Dazzling upland greensward met him, a shoulder of land turned against the unending blue, crowned with a beech wood and the unmistakable outline of a centaur. It turned its curious bearded head toward him, its olive torso moving, its chestnut flank motionless and warm, but Culpepper cried out against it and with a spasm of will held off the miracle.

Not that it was a miracle. We resist that word; we're not credulous. The man was exhausted, he had a sickly imagination, and a half-baked classical education; he'd worked himself into a state driving out to the village; he was befuddled by lust and bewildered by Margot's insinuating voice. More profoundly, he was weepy for his lost dinner. Finally, he'd consumed on an empty stomach God knows how much fly agaric.

Felix Culpepper was in Westley Waterless the whole time. He never left: we need to cling to this idea. Culpepper himself clutched it as a man flung overboard clutches flotsam. With heroic desperation he refused to see what his disorder showed him. That was not a huge apple tree golden as the Hesperides'; he forced his brain to conceive instead the unlit bulk of the *Dirty Swan*. Beyond the *Swan* was a smaller mass in the general gloom, a glowing thicket of heliotrope in a meadow – no it was not; a car, his red Land Rover. He had the key out now, he was gulping tears, he thrust the key blindly through shining flowers, no, he was scratching the bodywork, he thrust again, scratched again, found the slot, twisted the key, the blessed door opened; the dull *tock* of the door was his happy knell, it drove Olympus away; he was free of radiance, he was in England, clinging to the open door, retching and weeping on a blasted plain, at night, a rapidly-cooling night in July not Quintember, in England, in England, with the sultriness abated and a fine mist settling in.

viii.

At number 31, Alf Squint had been sent to bed without his Horlicks, still in disgrace because of his debauch at the *Swan*. His sister remained in a strop, and since supper had mithered him almost without drawing breath. 'You have lapped up tares,' was her theme, 'and confess yourself unworthy of covenanted mercies.'

The covenanted mercy in question is a malted milk-powder made for Baptists and other people who think cocoa too voluptuous. The Squints had it every night of their lives, and without it Alfred lay sleepless and disquieted.

Noises of celebration came from next door. The undergraduates of number 29 came out after their late supper to dance in the shrubbery (the drizzle had stopped). They were celebrating the rout of Culpepper, who had, said Margot, jumped up in the midst of her harangue, hopped through the window, run off, and would surely never come back.

You might think that Alfred, given over to dirty-mindedness as he was, would relieve his insomnia by stealing from bed and ogling those nude limbs. But that is to underestimate the liberty of the human spirit to spoil itself in its own way. Squint had devoted himself to one variety of erotic pleasure. Raw flesh was incomprehensible. Even a naked goddess could not move him unless she had been configured for a Singles column: *SF, 6000 yrs., v. (virgty endlessly renewed by bathing @ Paphos), sks. GL mortal WM for gd. times. Trojan descent a +. No atheists, satyrs, Titans.*

Anyway, Alfred didn't dare try the experiment and pull back the curtains, not with Val so narked with him. She was sure to be at her station upstairs in the spare room, keeping at eye on them students. It was all very well for her, she was keeping tabs on behalf of the Ladies' League. But if she saw *him* looking out of the window – well, he wouldn't like to think what would happen. No Horlicks for a month.

Thinking such unquiet thoughts he fell into an unquiet sleep, full of evil influences, in which two huge black rocks clashed together and came apart, again and again, with sickening slowness, while he, longing to get through them to the garden on the other side, sucked his thumb-knuckle and whimpered 'Durn't, durn't.'

ix.

Culpepper, too, had been mithered, just as badly as Alfred, by the misfortunes of the evening. But unlike Alfred he'd been a bred a gentleman, of sorts. When, well after midnight, he got back to College, he forced himself to saunter through the Lodge, forced himself to nod at Clinker, least inhuman of the porters, forced himself not to run across Gehenna Court, then Cocytus and Megiddo. Only once on his own staircase did he abandon all sense of shame and bolt up three steps at a time. He thrust himself through his door, lunged at his drinks cabinet, poured himself a finger of whisky, tossed it down, coughed, poured three more fingers, sipped, sighed, fished out a tin of truffled *pâté* and a packet of water-biscuits, and with a chaotic noise collapsed into an armchair.

After an interval of nibbling and sucking he stood, took his tumbler, and went to press his forehead against the bay window that overlooked Megiddo Court.

He could see Harry's lights on, and Harry, dimmest of classicists, playing some computer game, clearly without a thought in his head. *God*, mused Culpepper: *July. Quintember. What a month. No-one in residence but dunderheads resitting failed exams.* Seb, of course: somewhere in College – or more likely, lurking about the women's colleges, sniffing out she-dunderheads – was Seb. *The dimmest of the sociologists, thus the dimmest undergraduate of all. (How's it possible to fail an exam in sociology?) At the dimmest college in Cambridge, dimmer of the two universities. It's appalling to think how far down the scale of evolution Seb comes.* Culpepper, feeling quite disproportionately unhappy, refreshed his glass. *Not that I congratulate myself. Who's here apart from the imbeciles? Dons like me, not fit to go anywhere better. We're the nadir too, the shabbiest, in our shabbiest mode.* More Scotch. *Why in the depths of the Long Vac are we so eccentric, grotesque, unwashed? Because that's the truth about us.*

The maundering mood was unusual for Culpepper. But he indulged it for a quarter of an hour, until the moon rose at last: a terrible waning slither, coming up east-north-east over the tiles of the Library.

ॐ

At length he turned to go to bed.

The lunar glow, falling through his window and over his shoulder, picked out the whiteness of Pluto and Persephone. It was the postcard that had startled Mrs Elmsgall that morning, lying where it had fallen. With a little cry he sprang on it, rent it, scattered the fragments in his empty grate; and covered his face.

No, he would not risk sleep, and meeting whatever was waiting there. He sat wrapped in a duvet on his sofa with a thermos of tea-and-rum, gazing blankly westwards over the ugly public lawn named Christ's Pieces. Greyness ebbed out, colour ebbed in, birds returned to work. At last, a bit before five, the sun came smirking over the craggy roof of Chapel, and harried into motion the second day of Quintember.

x.

July wore on, but slowly, slowly.

It aged another week, becoming more Quintemberish each day.

૪૨

The drought brought out a Mediterranean cast in the Cambridgeshire flats. The fields turned from khaki to gold. Beeches sucked in their sides, pretending to be poplars. Modest East Anglian knolls took on the air of Tuscan crags, casting romantic shadows; the eye looked for charterhouses or walled villages. Everywhere was an even, energising southern light prone to make an Englishman feel tired. Above all the blue of the sky grew deeper and deeper, opening in on itself.

૪૨

Against that backdrop the commune, listless, depressed and dogged, continued its work.

Margot–Athena sat apart with the *New Statesman*, quietly inveigling the minds of the authors toward polytheism. Ares was in the kitchen, poring over a serious newspaper, pushing along the civil war in Syria. But Aphrodite, the playful Oxonian, had a tabloid open before her in the gazebo. Her pigeons strutted back and forth across it, whistling and cooing, occasionally voiding (quite redundantly) on the prose. She was making professional cricketers fall in love with each other's wives.

Tristan–Dionysus was experimenting with wines suitable for drinking in that desolate patch in the day just after breakfast. Ollie–Hephæstus was encouraging Mount Karangetang to erupt and devastate the East Indies. Artemis, the serious Oxonian, was at the chase, creeping about the overgrown acres of the park, spearing fat bunnies.

Poseidon spent each morning at the ruinous ornamental pond behind the shrubbery. He took with him his transcription of that morning's shipping forecast. *Rockall, Malin, Hebrides*, he read: *strong breeze six to high wind seven. Rain.* 'No, no, we're going to pep that up a bit. Let's make it a severe gale nine to violent storm 11, squally showers. And we're sending it back north, into Faeroes.' He doused himself from a jug (wetness was authentic), then violently swept his trident over the mossy sludge at the bottom of the pond. He was driving the spume from Rockall; immense mountains of black water rode before him; his Nereids danced between, shepherding the white crests; his tritons blasted force 11 gusts from their conches. At least, he hoped so. He wouldn't know how obedient the seas had been until tomorrow's shipping report.

Hermes, who was Róbert Zseni, could not be bothered with such indirection. He believed in overt methods; and he believed (in too ingenuous, childlike a way for it to be called vain) in himself. Moreover he had a foreigner's reverence for vernacular verse. Thus he posed flamboyantly in the shrubbery, reciting Swinburne; Hera and Zeus filmed him; the result would be uploaded to YouTube.

> 'And Pan by day and Bacchus by night
> Fleeter of foot than the fleet-foot kid,
> Follows with dancing and fills with delight
> The Mænad and the Bassarid...'

This is what the commune was up to that hot, dismal week.

But how they yawned! And how they bickered! (And how serious ill-will crept up on them, faint and soft at first, as it were mossy, but intractable, like black-green growing over lost architecture in the rainforest: sphagnum, then liana vines, strangler figs, banyans embracing pillar with giant barked spider-legs. It hardly matters what shape you began with, by the time the jungle's finished you'll look like a ziggurat, and be useful only for rituals of human sacrifice.)

'I wish you would go,' said Margot one night that week, perfectly seriously, with hatred, looking up at Odingo, and at the same time opening her arms to him; for free will was one of the things becoming blurred by the upward climb of undergrowth.

❦

Val initiated Gladys into the mysteries of espionage, and Gladys spent hours propping her telescopic lens on the sill of Val's spare room, recording doings at The Rise.

Sometimes the two ladies were more daring. They'd get their bodies atop the loose planks of palisade, that spiritual divide between The Rise and number 31. They'd let themselves fall into the wild grasses of the ancient cucumber bed. They'd creep around the ruined greenhouses, badminton lawns and rockery. Then, stealthy as war correspondents, set up their camera behind a bush, and observe the doings at close range.

This was once Gladys had mastered the tripod. She'd inherited her equipment from the late Mr Drybble, a dedicated bird-watcher because bird-watching kept him out of the house, away from her. He'd died of a chill two winters ago, failing to photograph an Arctic redpoll. Gladys had never missed him 'til now. If only he could come back for one minute to explain the *f*-stop!

§

In the course of that stifling week, Culpepper thought about what he had seen at Westley Waterless.

At first he was merely afraid.

Then he set about steeling himself for action in the ways dons do: elaborating, complicating and decorating his thoughts until they were a mere muddle and could not hurt him. Thus: *Classical myths are charming and dead-dead-dead: that's what I've always assumed. But after all, for millennia these gods were in my ancestors' minds. First with British or Germanic names. Then, for more three centuries, Latin.*

Just consider, he told himself – it was now Wednesday morning, Jecrean, the third of July; he was calming down – *just consider how promiscuously the gods leave traces in the culture I inherit. And culture's a thousand times more complex than language. My conscious mind can't be aware of all of it. There's too much to attend to, it envelops my consciousness. At any moment a remembered god may creep up on me unawares, out of some ancestral brain.*

On the fourth of Quintember he thought: *After all, what's Margot doing but applying Culpepperian methods on a larger scale? It's just homicide by imagination. What I did to Pocock she's doing to England.*

By the afternoon of the fifth, three days before the nones of Quintember, his thinking was such a mess he could say: *Heredity. That's the only reason I was vulnerable. That's the whole story*; and saying this he took a fountain pen, a dandified notebook (bound in cream-coloured leather, marble end-papered, silk-ribboned), emerged from his rooms, and strode off to do battle in the College Library.

⁊ҩ

Hell tugs. Its gravity's more insidious than the traction of earth. In an hour of itch and drought, angrily stomping a foot, you find you're through the crazed mud; it's only about your shins but you're fain at the rich profounder suck; stamp, wriggle, do worse; the soil (around your nipples now) matters less, you're quadrated to a different pole; time works backward too, cause is reversed; the ogrish creature you'll soon be compels your present being; and see, the dry turf is about your brows.

⁊ҩ

By the afternoon of Thursday, Jerdrein, the weather was simply appalling. Cambridgeshire no longer resembled Tuscany, it was more like a tableland in Andalusia. For there are Spanish plateaux dismal and blasted as any Russian steppe: plateaux where the heat is befouling and gritty, where it smothers, and gets into the crannies. There folk become wizened in the womb; are born crushed; live behind shutters, resting their foreheads on rasping fingertips, listening to the cicadas eat up the afternoon. In that blasted quarter there was a stir, once, when the tide of the *Reconquista* washed over and the Moors died; again at the start of the Civil War when the parish was enlivened by an atrocity, its priest perhaps pounded to death with his alabaster statue of the Sacred Heart; once more when Franco's troops came for the atheist postmaster. Apart from that, nothing. What human frolics can hold their own against such torrid stillness?

That's what our county looked like by Thursday. The very sunshine had developed a grey tinge: the fields looked as if they had been sprinkled with glittering cat-litter. Root vegetables despaired of resurrection in autumn and withered in their beds. We sweated but our sweat was nearly all salt, stinging our dazzled eyes, bringing no relief. Our tongues felt as if they'd been licking hot copper, ale could not cleanse them. Even if we doubled the recommended dosage of Zolpidem, our insomnia became steadily more hideous.

⁊ҩ

The East Cambridgeshire Baptist Ladies' League meets at eight in the evening every second Friday – day of ill-omen, day of Frigg who swoops from the ramparts of Valhalla mounted on a distaff, naked but for her sooty cloak.

This particular Friday, the fifth of Quintember, was as harsh as any Baptist Lady might desire. The afternoon had been wanton, sultry and heavy. Towards teatime an abrasive wind sprang up from the north, from the sands of the Wash, awakening smells in the cracked ditches about Westley Waterless. The sun, a baleful ball of rust, had sunk into the flat haze to the west – the moon, a cruel scythe, had gone down too – before the Ladies assembled in Ebenezer Memorial Hall. Hot darkness was triumphant. The power of the hastening night seemed very strong.

The Ladies who drew up their chairs for their League hymn (Charles Wesley's *The smoke of the infernal cave*) were not looking their best. The heat had stained their frocks; it had produced, beneath their clinging hems, curious rashes; and as they sang, they beheld with dismay what it was doing to the platter of sponge fingers upon which they would feast once their solemnities were complete. The raspberry glaze was so moist the flecks of desiccated coconut had stained and sunk, appearing like the first blush of leprosy. '*The servile progeny of Ham, Seize!*' the Ladies sang; but their hearts weren't in it.

There was thin attendance. Many Ladies were bilious or fretful from the weather. Val and Gladys weren't there because the commune had staged another hecatomb that night, with a brace of mallards. The gushing billowing uncertain light of the bonfire was playing merry hell with Gladys's light-meter. Val snarled with disappointment at the thought of filthy shots ruined. They couldn't tear themselves away, not even for the Baptist coven.

Mrs Elmsgall, too, had absented herself. She knew it was dangerous not to be at the Ladies; absentees were *discussed*. But she had business of her own: an errand in the copses about Druidsgrove, the wood at the back of The Rise, an errand she daren't let go, not on such a fine moonless night, not when the pipistrelle was abroad, the scops owl and the timorous yellow-necked mouse.

ॐ

The truth is, Bess Elsmgall's not settled in her own mind. Ever since Monday – that is, ever since she had delivered the message to Dr Culpepper – she's been left entirely alone. She doesn't like it one little bit. *Has* he come out to inspect the young 'uns or not? She can't tell. He just sits shivering in his rooms, ignoring her even when she spills his rubbish bin. Even when she broke one of his little china thingummies he just looked up, shook his head, kept silence. Nor are They speaking to her. Nothing comes into her head. She doesn't think it right, seeing how useful she's made herself. So she's come out for a romp to catch Their attention.

Hunting, in its ignoble or illegal forms, is Mrs Elmsgall's *forte*. Her grandfather Edgar was a champion poacher, and what he didn't teach her of traps and snares isn't worth knowing: of liming of twigs, poisoning of creeks and warrens, filing of ferret-teeth, badger-baiting, nest-robbing, eel-tickling, deer-hobbling.

Tonight it's to be a fox's den. She sniffed it in the copse weeks back, and now she creeps unswervingly along the wall of The Rise, stealthy as a night-animal herself, toward the rank volpine odour. She pauses suddenly, dives sideways into the grasses, fossicks in the darkness, finds the urn with the glaring stump-horned satyr, feels with experienced fingers for his tufted rump, crouches, kisses, chuckles, proceeds. *Requiescete, vulpes! Advenit bona fortuna* – hark to her! Abysmal thoughts are astir in her after all, they bubble forth, she's not abandoned, she's in the vein.

Yes, there's no great difficulty completing her business. When she's done she slumps in the grove with her back against a yew, all in a muck sweat, nursing the slight gash on her left forearm given her by the vixen. After a while she gets up, takes off her purple track suit and orange cloth cap; takes off all her things. That's better. Her wound's caked. She can get on. She gathers up her spoils, and, unerring in the stuffy darkness, plucks rough-stalked meadow grass. When she has enough she begins to order her materials. She works patiently and steadily despite her unwieldy, hairy fingers. She twists the six cubs' heads back and forth 'til they come off the bodies, then plaits the cut grass, poking the strand carefully through each left ear, out each right. Six cubs: a large litter. She knots her necklace together, making sure the heads hang straight. Now she stands and, solemnly, as if crowning herself, lowers her trophy past her wispy hair, past her potato nose, past her many chins, until it rests on the tremendous shelf of her bosom. An owl hoots, astounded. The vixen, which escaped half-throttled, watches from the shadowy depths of Druidsgrove. Who knows what else watches as Mrs Elmsgall, tossing her head to music heard only by herself, begins to dance? A little starlight, exhausted it seems by the nocturnal stickiness, shakes here and there on the leaves as she hops and sways. The surface of the pond in Druidsgrove glitters behind her. Her breasts flop up and down, a half-beat ahead of the unheard rhythm; her buttocks leap and clap a half-beat tardy. Her fingers, sticky with fox-kit gore, slap her thighs. Her immense and dangly lips form, I'm sorry to say, again and again the one name. 'Felix,' she sings as she dances, 'Felix, my Felix.' Her formless monstrous body gleams all over.

Here's the thing: if God is love, the devil is the Second Law of Thermodynamics. Every process in the universe eventually runs down, that's what this law dictates. Order must crumble into lesser order; energy dissipate until it become at last useless warmth, drifting off into space, irrecoverable; until at last the cosmos is a miasma of matter pulverised unimaginably fine, spread unimaginably thin, motionless, perfectly uniform and chilled. Bess, who has never heard of thermodynamics, knows her in bones that the world dwindles. Her one passion is to push it faster down the slope. Therefore she's happy this evening. She's sucked her fingers clean: the blood of the cubs is being converted into bodily vigour, into her dance, which causes her to perspire. The evaporating droplets leave Bess's stench behind in the atmosphere, in the brooding boughs of Druidsgrove, amidst the fungi and mistletoe. But the pure energy she squanders does indeed escape. It joins the nightly flow of energy from the turning earth into the void. Elizabeth Elmsgall is performing the first act of the tragedy of the heat-death of the universe; and (unless the universe be brought to an end and made new) nothing in the world can stop her. Entropy's the very devil.

᪥

Jcheiney, Jcsarn. The nightmares afflicting the University became insupportable. (Dons respond badly to drought.)

᪥

Jedoonee – or as we used to say, Sunday, Sunday of the Christians. The sky had lost its blueness: it was merely off-white. Juicy, emerging from yet another futile bath, and hearing the bells of Little St Mary's, was moved to make a noose for himself. But he'd never had any historical interests as a boy, never pored over pictured scaffolds; he couldn't visualise a hangman's knot, couldn't get it right. Suicide requires a residual *joie de vivre*. There's a pitch of despair below the level of self-destruction. After an hour Juicy reached it. He let the rope tumble from his fingers and stood vacantly at the window of the Master's Lodgings, mouthing he knew not what with cracked lips. He went on existing.

ぬ

Jelune, Monday morning once more: the sixth of Quintember: the sixth day since Culpepper's disaster.

It was early, by his *louche* standards, as he lolled in his rooms in his armchair, in white flannel trousers and pale green linen shirt, drinking coffee. His curtains were still drawn, but shafts of grey-white light stabbed here and there. One shaft picking out his cream-leather notebook on a sideboard – looking well-thumbed, well written-in, no longer virginal. Another shaft rested on the empty spot on the fireplace tiles where he'd torn down the postcard of Pluto, revealing a blue and white barge towed past a blue and white windmill.

Mondays were the day Culpepper's bedder grubbied his floor with her mop. She was so engaged, just like last time. He was looking and looking at her. At last he put down his coffee and murmured: 'Mrs Elmsgall. I've been reading about you. In Beelzebub.'

It was a muted way to begin the counter-attack and ransom England, but it had an electric effect on Bess. '*Reading*, sir?'

'In the College library, yes. Old newspaper files. You've quite a history, haven't you?' He stood, and picked up his notebook. 'Your first husband vanished in er, er, where is it? Here. In 1975. In a snowstorm. And wasn't found for a week, by which time it was hard to say much more than that he had frozen with a terrible expression on his face.'

She seemed inclined to smirk. 'Kelvin always looked like that. Long as I knew him.'

'Your second husband drank lye – by mistake, said the coroner's jury, after deliberating for three hours.'

'You should have seen *their* faces when they came back into the box. And the way they got away afterwards, not wanting to talk, so it seemed.'

'Your only child died by strangulation in its own pyjama cord.'

'Little Noël. The scamp. But why,' she was on her feet now, and her eyes were level, on his stomach, 'why're you so interested in these old stories, if I may make so bold?

'That's it, isn't it? Just old stories. But they relieve my conscience.' He put down his notebook.

'Relief? Of what, sir?' she wanted to know, rolling the *r* sounds.

'I'm about to *do* something to you, Mrs Elmsgall.'

'Oooah,' said Bess saucily, leaning on the shaft of her mop so that the nasty gash on her forearm showed. She was not surprised. She *knew* Friday night's effusion of fox-blood would stir things up. 'To me, sir?'

'Yes, to you. D'you see that crystal cruet there on my desk? I'm going to dash its contents in your face.'

'Oooah' – half-alarmed, half-leering: perhaps splashing counted as foreplay amongst the higher orders. Anyway, Culpepper picked up the cruet and unstopped it.

'You don't recognise this, do you, Bess? You've never seen it before, have you? I borrowed it from Chapel. Well, stole. From the sacristy, where I'm sure you've never been. It contains holy water.'

She howled at that. It wasn't very loud (she seemed to be choked), but it was definitely a howl. She snatched up her big metal bucket full of suds and retreated backwards toward the door, while Culpepper advanced on her with his own puny weapon.

'Aah –', she burbled, '*caput mortuum, Obeah, Wanga*. Don't come near me, sir.'

'What're you afraid this will do to you, Mrs Elmsgall? Will it wet you? Or cleanse away those warts? Or will it burn you? Will it sear your flesh?'

'How can you say such things to a poor old – old—'

'Old what? *What are you?* Are you a woman? Or—'

That's as far he got. She fired the first shot, watered the first shot. She emptied the bucket straight at him. He was soused, so was the carpet. Suds poured out of his hair and blinded him. Before he could get his eyes open he heard her tear out of his set; almost at once there came a tremendous crash on the stairs, aluminium bucket noise mingling not unmusically with a shriller shriek from the Elmsgall, and a crunch of bone. Wet shoes, mediæval stairs, panic.

There was a babble of voices from everyone else on the staircase. When excited, dons sound very like geese. Culpepper didn't bother going to look. He went into his bathroom, got off his wet linen things, donned a dressing-gown, and stood smoking a cigarillo in his bay window until, eventually, he saw the porters come running. Then an ambulance crew. Four groaning paramedics carried that small creature away across the court, ranting. The paramedics were wiping away Bess's soap-bubbles; a foam of spittle kept forming on her moustache. Her eyes were turned right back so the whites showed, but Culpepper thought she noticed him waving bye-bye out the window. Anyway, his wave invigorated her: she writhed so that it was as much as they could do to hold her.

She seems unnaturally strong, mused Culpepper. *But she won't recover. Her hip might but her mind won't. Next week she'll be promoted from hospital to madhouse. Not the usual county madhouse. The Deepdell.* And a spasm of respectful horror rippled through his mind, for the Deepdell is famous in Cambridge. It's where flighty dons and highly-strung undergraduates all go in the end. Step they ever so trippingly, the Deepdell opens its mouth and has them. It's organised like a college, only more so: *She'll feel at home. And have people she understands to prey on. I'll watch my colleagues dragged away in better heart, knowing they go to Mrs Elmsgall.*

As she vanished into the archway that leads from Megiddo to Cocytus, Bess began to shout. Her language was shocking. Languages. Late Latin, Chaldee, Ostrogothic, Aramaic. (He caught his own name in the babble.) *Thank God we're out of term, with no undergraduates about except the imbeciles.* Seb Hawicke Trocliffe was indeed standing staring; but Seb barely understood English, he wasn't a problem. *Indeed, he's so immune he might be useful...*

Culpepper leaned out of the window and waved to Seb, who in the manner of the stupid stared at every point of the compass before he saw him, then waved back merrily, then slowly realised he was being summoned, then grinned inanely, and began sloping across Megiddo.

ଛ

My esquire! thought Culpepper. He pulled himself upright and threw away the little cigar (carefully, so it flew into the hearth in a tiny trail of sparks). *To battle, then!* A week of sophistry had hardened into something like courage. *First blood to me. No more licking of wounds. Am I not more powerful than any of my grunting forefathers? Can I not resist pseudo-supernatural nonsense? Then I ought to resist it. Time to buckle on armour. So to speak.*

He flung open the door to Seb. 'Sit there! Drink this! I need you.'

He went into his bedroom, got out his magic robes, and started to put them on. *I'm not afraid of undergraduates. Nor of mushrooms. Nor even of Margot. And those are my only enemies at The Rise – there's nothing else.*

He dressed for war, then admired himself in the long looking-glass in his bedroom. *Not,* the warrior told himself, twisting sideways to enjoy the swish and sway of his hood, *unworthy of my ancestors.*

xi.

'My ancestors!'

Tribesmen, belligerent but melancholy, tow-haired, dirty-skinned, wing-helmeted, bare-thighed, inclined to chapped lips. Gazing out over the Baltic from their flat, thin, muddy, twisty peninsula, Angeln (which means *bent* and *narrow*: an omen). Fourteen illiterate centuries of this: fourteen centuries of being *Anglii*, Angles, the last of men, a footnote in Tacitus: an undistinguished tribe *fluminibus aut silvis muniuntur*, penned in by creeks and woods.

Then, hearing the legions were gone, clambering into long ships, rowing over the narrow seas. Burning fora, sacking villas, butchering dark squat Britons, mating with widows. Begetting a mongrel race, Angelfolc, Englishry, sad, reserved. Puzzled by missionaries, trodden by Normans, happiest left alone under oaks and willows, blinking up at ash-coloured skies through weak blue eyes.

'My ancestors'! Came at last John, a Cavalier rewarded with the barony of Colepepper. Begat Thomas, second Lord Colepepper, sometime Governor and proprietor of Virginia in the Plantations. Who in old age begat (on his fourteen-year-old French parlourmaid) Charles FitzCulpepper, bred a barrister, who begat Theophilus, who begat Augustus, who begat Augustus FitzCulpepper *junior*, who slyly trimmed his name to *Culpepper*, fixed the pronunciation *culpa*, and begat Arthur, who begat handsome Gerald, who begat Osbert.

England swelled; the Culpeppers too. In the palmy days they were colonial grandees all over the roomy Empire. Osbert Culpepper, barrister at Gray's Inn, became a District Officer in India and Palestine, a judge in Kenya. In Kenya he suffered genetically from cracked lips and hanged a large number of Mau Mau cultists for unspeakable atrocities, of which he never tired of speaking in knighted retirement, in a pale turquoise windy house above a Dorset sea-cliff.

Osbert begat Neville, Winston and Clement. Winston was a grey bewildered chap from infancy, conceived in an air-raid shelter, weaned during the Blitz, raised on Spam and Woolton Pie. The Angelfolc were falling back on their island, *fluminibus aut silvis muniti* once more; socialism reduced them to something like their ancient heathen despair. The flummoxed look never left Winston's face. He went into the Law, a confusing business. By the 'Seventies the Culpeppers, if not precisely decaying, were certainly not rising: sluggishly up and down perhaps, up and down, like the darker-coloured glop in that newly-invented thing the lava lamp. Winston bought one, and liked to sit looking at it by the hour. His curiosity, which might have glorified itself if he'd been governing far up the Brahmaputra, Essequibo or Limpopo, spent itself on the mystery of warm red oil soaring up to an altitude where it must cool and drop away. Such was the British Empire; such was Winston Culpepper. Now that he's senile and immured in a Home it's hard to imagine him anything but old. Yet technically he was once a young man, capable of begetting Agatha, Felix and Gertrude, whose earliest memories are of cynically watching their father sit watching his toy...

Such was Felix's breeding. As a boy, he and his sisters often went down to Dorset to stay with Grandpapa. Agatha thought Osbert creepy but would go anywhere their mother wasn't. Saccharine Gertrude though Grandpapa sweet. Felix liked him *because* he was creepy.

Their creepiest game began with dragging furniture about the drawing-room, building a bench, dock and jury box. Grandpapa would don full regalia: wig, red robe, white bands, black scarf, tippet and girdle. His cook, housekeeper and gardener would be drafted into the game, being just intelligent enough to sit as jury and pronounce 'Guilty, garn, terrible guilty, m'Lord' when nudged. Gertrude, with doll eyes and chubby pleading baby-hands, made an excellent ineffectual barrister for the defence. Agatha would prosecute bitterly. Grandpapa's summings-up were models of vindictive bias. Then Gertrude, pale with half-pretended horror, had to change role. With nervous sheriff fingers she'd settle the ludicrously slight black cap on Grandpapa's enormous wig: a raft of silk on a sea of angry horsehair. 'The sentence of this court,' Grandpapa would pronounce in the mincing, kindly tone traditional (he told them) on such occasions, 'is that you, Felix Osbert Baine Culpepper, having been found guilty of refusing your nice spinach at lunch, be taken from this place to the place of execution, and there be hanged by the neck until your body be dead. And may God have mercy on your soul.'

Sometimes Felix would be brave and stick out his chest, sometimes he would collapse to his knees in the dock and wail for mercy. Sometimes Gertrude would sob stonily, sometimes she would shriek 'Mercy, m'Lud, he's but a youth!' Sometimes Agatha would cry 'Spinach is avenged!' Grandpapa didn't mind, he enjoyed the game every way it was played.

After the trial came the hanging. They staged it in the old stables, using a trapdoor through which hay used to be winched. Grandpapa played, as directed, hangman or chaplain or prison doctor (whose job was to attend to sentimental Gertrude: she always fainted). He did whatever he was asked, but only out of politeness. This part of the game didn't interest him. The spectacular moment when his loved and detested grandson dropped through the trapdoor moved him not at all. His reward was back in the courtroom, where he had been allowed to utter the fatal words.

Those words were like the *Fiat lux!* that got the universe going in the first place. No; they were the words dividing land and water so there might be physical order, so that life might evolve. In Osbert's sentence of condemnation, he divided a monster off from the run of mankind, which was to that extent vindicated, purified and set free.

This was serious play for him. In some occult fashion he was placating the shades of the Kikuyus the Empire had failed to protect from the Mau Mau: the villagers mutilated, dropped down wells in sacks, burned alive, disembowelled.

That is what Sir Osbert might have told himself, if he ever tried to define his pleasure, which he did not. Angelfolc do not enjoy definition. But his grandson, seeing deeper as children do, knew that Grandpapa wouldn't bother with this game again and again if he weren't also cutting off and condemning something in himself.

Mau Mau recruits underwent perfectly hideous ceremonies: ritualised bestiality, coprophagia, torture of infants, incest, consumption of exhumed brains. Self-respect was broken within them. By the time they were fully initiate, they'd cast off what both Africa and Europe regard as humanity. They were capable of anything at all. This is what made them useful to their masters. For there's this to be said for self-conscious evil: it resolves the exasperating divisions within our minds. Doing away with order releases pure energy.

For all his civilisation and his brittle courtesy, Osbert was excited by such power. He was himself human only in a pinched fashion; he could see the point of shedding humanity altogether. Thus he *knew* what the Mau Mau were up to (and Felix knew that he knew). Osbert never wearied of wearing the black cap because it allowed him to divide himself. He was imposing order within, cutting away his own taste for devilry, hanging the beast that paced about inside Sir Osbert Culpepper, M.A., C.B., M.V.O., D.L. (Felix, who was somewhat less human than his grandfather, never hit on any such effective ritual.)

꧁꧂

Such was Felix's spiritual education. It was over by fourteen, when his grandfather died, for Felix never became a real adult, any more than Osbert did. However, his outward and superficial education rolled on and on, culminating at twenty-eight when the Cambridge authorities rightly or wrongly gave him a doctorate in Classics (there being no point in Law now hanging was abolished).

Felix, who'd pursued dead languages in a not-very-lively fashion, knew how trifling his scholarship was. Nor did he have illusions about scholarship itself. His Ph.D. moved him only because of its physical trappings. A Cambridge doctor, as he presents himself in his extravagant or 'festal' form, on such 'red letter days' as Christmas and Whitsun (or when the Vice-Chancellor shall so decree), looks like a man of blood. He has great red scarlet stripes down his black gown, a scarlet hood behind, and a black felt cap of felt with a scarlet tassel.

On the morning his degree was conferred, as he processed through the streets to the Senate House, the newly-made Dr Culpepper felt himself reborn. *Everything until now was nakedness.* What staggered him most about this get-up was not its splendour or its extravagance, but its resemblance to the robes of a red judge, a justice of the high court. *These are clothes that allow me to shed a man's life-blood justly.* The idea dazed him; he passed through the long ceremony in a rapture of bloodlust. He wore his cheery hat like a death's cap. Afterward, on the way back to College, he saw Japanese tourists lift their cameras to snap him, pause, let their cameras drop, mouth Os of dismay, step away. *Scarier than Grandpapa, he murmured to himself. At last*; and he soon had a reputation as the most merciless, sarcastic tutor in the University.

❧

Worthy of my ancestors, reflected Felix Culpepper that brilliant Quintember Monday, standing before his looking-glass, dressed for a red letter day. *In short, I'm possessed with a bewildered passion for retributive justice.* The trick of getting your doctoral cap to the correct killing angle is to do it right once, the first time; he knew this, yet couldn't stop fiddling. *Surely the tassel's too close to my ear? It's a shame I don't believe – although I certainly have the air of a man doomed to relapse into Anglicanism in middle age. Now there's too much forehead. In people without an organising credal scheme, the passion for retribution is unpleasant. But that doesn't stop it clarifying the mind,* and he shrugged the enormous gown so it cascaded back from his shoulders.

Clarity, yes, of a sort. The Mau Mau posed as respectable pagans, adoring En-gai the creator and Olapa who is the moon. Osbert had seen through that. He'd grasped that they were devil-worshippers, victoriously full of evil for its own sake; which both impressed and appalled him. Felix was similarly appalled and impressed by Margot's cod Olympus. He meant to overthrown it, which is why he was sporting the festal robes of a Cambridge Ph.D. He was besotted with it, nonetheless.

Very well, he told himself, turning from the glass, *I am besotted.* Que voulez-vous? *It's the nature of devilry that no one drawn to the tang has any business tampering with it. Yet no one not drawn understands enough to war against it. Therefore such warfare cannot be edifying,* he concluded, sighing, and sallied forth, slamming his door behind him and taking the stairs two at a time.

'Come on, Seb. Bring this.'

'All right. It's heavy.' They clattered down the stairs. 'Where are we going? Somewhere good?'

'No.' *Wasn't there always something spooky about an Inquisitor-General in the old days? Loyal, dogged, clear-headed, necessary as hangman or sewer-sweep, yet somehow... disquieting. Exorcism and inquisition are necessary* – they burst forth into the court, his scarlet glory billowing behind, monstrously red in the tyrannical yellow light, Seb in a dirty T-shirt loping along behind – *necessary, and very ugly.*

xii.

What with their score of naughty projects, their private campaigns of retheophanation, their infidel mischief, the immortals were so preoccupied that the first they all knew of Culpepper's second coming was a crash; then prolonged honking.

Honking! At the very doors of the sanctuary! (Next door, at number 31, the curtains convulsed.)

All divine work was abandoned. There was a general excited dash to the front hall, which betrayed how very bored those young people were.

This thought struck them too. Shamefacedly, the gods pulled themselves together, snatched up whatever bits of equipment lay at hand, so they might face their enemy with cold dignity.

There was no subtlety this time. Culpepper proposed to take Olympus by storm. He'd put his front bumper against the rusty gates, then pushed forward until one gate screeched backwards and the other fell down. Then he'd stamped on the accelerator and come roaring up the drive, scattering gravel *ting ting* against the house. He'd swirled about the Asphodel flowerbed, so that the rear of his Land Rover was thrust aggressively toward the front door. He'd bounded up the steps in his ludicrous, dazzling scarlet. He'd burst open the doors and left them open behind him, so that sunshine streamed in between his legs and over his shoulders. He'd stood in the hall shouting 'Margot!' He was egregious.

Hermes, thinking *This shouldn't be about personalities* and *I am the herald*, gestured as violently as he could with his serpentine wand. *If only my snakes would come to life!* Odingo Nyachae straightened his gold wig; after a moment he remembered Apollo's malign smile of reason. Poseidon came in dripping, Aphrodite was impeccably unflirtatious. (*And as rumpled*, thought Culpepper, *as such a radiant creature can be when there's nothing to rumple*.)

In fact none of the gods looked particularly glamorous. Last night they'd kept one of the great feasts of antiquity, the *Ludi Apollinares*, with corybantic dancing in armour and long drinking from bowls. They'd left off at four, and morale had been low since Hera woke them for lovely ambrosia on toast at the usual hour. Morale had been low, and the curious malice that had been growing on them had been very strong.

Athena leaned wearily on her Gorgon-shield. This time there was not even half-hearted hospitality in her face. 'I cannot imagine why you're back. And,' she said, 'you look bizarre.'

'*I* look bizarre? Good God. Listen, events need to speed up.'

Ares openly yawned.

'I indict you all for sacrilege. What you're doing is obscene. Are you serious about it or not? If it's just truancy, evict me now and I'll have you all sent down before term begins. If you're in earnest, hear me and answer, and I'll leave you in peace. Well?'

There was a pause. Things hung in the balance; whether trivial things or not it's hard to say. But the flashy menace of a don weighed heavily on their undergraduate minds. The pause didn't last long; and although it would have been sensible to fling him out, they succumbed.

'Oh very well,' snapped Margot, 'let's—' She bit her tongue, remembering the proprieties.

Rugger-bugger Zeus coughed, and, managing to speak Attic, pronounced: 'We shall answer you, importunate son of earth. Let the council of the immortals assemble. In twenty minutes. After a... um, break for coffee.'

'No no, if you dare defend yourselves, dare it now,' cried Culpepper, keeping up momentum, shooing them out through the conservatory and outdoors, into the brilliant mid-morning light.

xiii.

'Al, Al!' beseeched Val. 'Come up here now! Do! Come and *look.*'

There's that daft sister of mine yelping agin, Alfred snuffled to himself. He was snipping prostitutes' ads out of the *Sunday Snort* to paste into his secret scrapbook, and had no intention of going upstairs to gawk at dirty student types. His lips rounded out the abbreviations. *Like it means lunch'll be late.* He held a clipping up to the light – *WBDW, 23, offers* – and put it down, puzzled. W *widowed, oh yes,* B *Black, phra.* D. *Garn.* W *woman. But what's that* D *doing, then? What's it mean? Something nasty...* Intellectually thwarted, Alfred stuck the enigmatic piece in the scrapbook and shouted up the stairs for his lunch.

Nothing. His selfish bitch of a sister had gone out and left him.

As the shock wore off, an expression of infantile stealth broke open in Alfred's face. He slipped out of number 31 and, with a good deal of glancing round corners, slinking, flinching, and sucking of dentures, took himself down Westley Bottom Road and into *The Dirty Swan.*

xiv.

'Ζεῦ ἀστράπιε (Lightning-Tossing Zeus)! Day-Maker! All-powerful Father of gods and men!' declared Hermes the divine herald: Róbert Zseni, artless undergraduate of Pembroke College, was letting himself go. 'And you, O sky-dwelling and deathless ones! Twice has this mortal ventured to profane...'

If Hermes sounded stagey, his excuse might be that the setting was theatrical. Culpepper and the gods had trooped into a clearing in the oak wood beyond the swimming pool. Long ago Seacome had built a summer-house here, of which wreckage remained. Its back half had collapsed and its dome was akimbo, but it made an impressive throne for Zeus, who sat on the top step with the canopy over his white silky hair. *(Why do I feel I've seen this place before?* wondered Culpepper. *Why do I feel I have been gravitating toward it all summer?)*

The other gods were enthroned on twelve high-backed chairs, bought by Odingo from Norwich, whitewashed, then tricked out with ivy and gilt. In the centre of this circle stood Culpepper, gathering to himself all the benefit he could from his scarlet. (The trouble was that naked flesh is in the end more impressive, more serious than any robes.)

How ominous this feels, brooded Culpepper, trying to maintain his outward swagger. *How important. If they defeat me, what do they win?* He considered Cambridge: a nest of heretics in the sixteenth century and regicides in the seventeenth, Hanoverian Quislings in the eighteenth, Soviet spies in the twentieth. *Yes, no doubt it's ripe. Whatever's at once pedantic and disloyal finds a home there. How could we resist this new deviancy? The revolution last term at Wygefortis' was abortive. But maybe that was just the prelude. And if the University falls, what of the kingdom?*

It was, he found, impossible to smile at these questions. It was impossible to smile at Hermes' oration, despite his rattling curtain-rod and brass ankle-wings, despite his grammatical mistakes. It was impossible to smile at the majestic bow of Zeus's head as he agreed to hear the suit, for Zeus was, for the moment, all the poets said. When the prime author of things nodded, the noble assembly fell silent; almost one could feel the earth shake, sky holding its breath, distant seas calm with the tension.

But: *The atmosphere's wrong.* Culpepper had hoped to conduct himself as at a Penal Collection. He felt horribly like defendant not plaintiff (*and to how much victory can a prisoner in the dock aspire? That judge, barristers and jury will find against the court, rush from the courtroom, hang themselves?*) But it was more than that. *Hell tugs.*

'Behold,' concluded Hermes, tiring at last, 'the court stands ready to hear you plead. *Hodie! Jelune, ante diem octavum Idus Quintilæ.* That means Monday,' he told Culpepper cockily, sitting down, 'in your barbarous tongue. Eight days before the Ides of Quintember.'

xv.

'*Never!*'

'He's at. The Rise. Now. I tell you. Oh Gladys. My poor insides. I came running. Right over. To fetch you. A tall masterful chap. In one of them University get-ups. All red. He didn't wait to be let in. Smashed. The gates. Shoved through the door. Started yelling and yelling. A name. Such a rude-sounding name it was. Alfred won't stir. Oh my poor. Insides. Come on Gladys. Hurry. Who knows what he'll. Be up to. Before we get back. The young prof fellow I mean. Not Alfred. Bring your camera. Girls with nothing on. Now gents in red gowns! Whatever will the Bappo Ladies say about it? Cripes!'

xvi.

'Farting,' said Culpepper, staring up into the broad circle of blue overhanging the tight circle of tree-tops, 'though harmless, universally offends. Sneezing's treated as a quaint comic foible. People smile, say *Gesundheit*, hand you tissues. Although everyone knows or ought to know that public sneezing can be a form of mass murder. It's how all the epidemics begin. A man who throws a grenade on the Tube can hope to kill a score of innocents; the man crushed beside him, just back from Asia with a curious green rash and a tickle in his throat, will kill billions if he sneezes. With every sneeze, forty thousand droplets erupt on the world, each laden with enough infection to empty a city.'

It was a glorious Sicilian morning; he'd never known such weather in England, and was hot in his doctoral gown. But being himself, if not cold, unnaturally formal, what moved him most was the shape of the clouds. Today they were architectural, they had massive foundations resting on the horizons as on bedrock; their top layers were repetitive and shapely, like crenulations, and painted by the sunlight behind. They comforted him.

'Let us consider this, this *provocation* of yours, philosophically. You think it's farting in the face of your civilisation. If I may put it as politely as that. But I say you're sneezing: passing on exotic fiends, imperilling your species.'

When Culpepper lectured he was two people: Greater Felix, talking and talking and talking; Lesser Felix, creeping about the back of the auditorium watching what people were doing with their hands.

The gods were already restless. Athena was relishing with her little finger the sharp talons of her sleepy owl. Poseidon was irritably dibbling Trinitarian holes in the coarse grass with his trident. Dionysus was going through the brunch of grapes he carried as a prop, picking out deficient specimens. And it was not like last time. They were not merely restless the way the young are restless. There was a smear over the scene which the sun didn't cancel out; there was something growing through them; a degeneration.

Greater Felix continued to bluster; Lesser Felix, who knew his lecture was going badly, was becoming afraid. *All these warnings to them are true – I'm not just deliberately wasting time.* 'It's impossible to go back to a transitional stage. A caterpillar can become a cocoon but a butterfly can't. A heathen worships a shapeless meteorite: it has a certain plausibility because it's inscrutable the way the world's inscrutable. He can develop into a sophisticated heathen, worshipping the more-than-womanly loveliness of Aphrodite,' whose eyes met his. 'But a monotheist can't regress to being a polytheist. It can't be done.' *So what* are *you regressing to, children?*

More than resentment was in the air. Culpepper thought uneasily of Pentheus, torn to pieces for saying less than this, and Ixion, invited to Olympus to explain himself, then endlessly tortured for misbehaviour. How far would these twelve teenyboppers go if riled?

'You, no matter how debauched or misinstructed, are children of a monotheist culture. There's only one direction a monotheist can go if he wants to defect. Not back but down. You are opening the lower depths. You're invoking—'

Apollo made one of those soft finger gestures only Africans know how to make. (Culpepper paused to regard it with envy: *Like tendrils of polyps swaying underwater. I'm elegant enough when I stand still, but my movements have a crude, four-square, flung-about quality.*) 'All this,' debonair Apollo inserted into the pause, folding his fingers, 'is merely gothic.'

'It's a nice point,' said Culpepper roughly, 'whether *any* gothicism could be as creepy as your classicism. Hasn't it occurred to you,' jabbing a crude finger at his rival, 'that the Antique is only charming *because* it's absolutely dead? Antiquity was devilish enough when it was alive: coliseums, human sacrifice, debauchees, despair. "Gothic"! From someone who's been immolating voles and tom-cats!'

It seemed that Culpepper's insults had become too crude to be borne. Athena with a sigh replaced her owl on her left shoulder, and stood up.

xvii.

A single eye caressed her. It caressed them all, like a prurient cyclops. The telescopic lens of a camera twitched back and forth. Behind it in the undergrowth squatted Gladys, making little moaning noises of excitement as she clicked, and Val, gnawing her knuckles 'til the blood came.

They'd been overcome with excitement. They'd got the ladder out of Val's shed and clambered over the palisade separating number 31 from the grounds of The Rise. They'd crawled through bushes, run double across the croquet lawn, wriggled through the scratchy undergrowth of the grove. Now they crouched and swayed on aching haunches, half-demented with the thrill.

The gods, as ever, thought it beneath their dignity to attend to such creatures. Culpepper didn't notice them, because by now he was genuinely afraid.

xviii.

'O Father, eternal judge of god and things – and,' Athena added with distaste, 'men, why is this mortal suffered to insult us with the scourings of his gnarled brain? Too well we know where all philosophy leads. If he has anything to tell us that we do not know, let him tell. If not, let him depart. Or remain to abide your wrath.'

So Pallas Athena argued; and all the divinities of heaven murmured, some saying this, some that, so that a murmuring passed through the grove like a rising gale. *Now I shall see how far their anger can go,* thought Apollo. *I should have tried to make that force 11 veer north-east from Rockall,* thought Poseidon, who had been interrupted in his half-finished work. *It is and it isn't Margot speaking,* thought Culpepper. And the same tendrils thrust up, inexorable through all this diverse thinking.

Zeus, greatest and best, silenced the Olympians all with a nod of his lordly brows, heavy with the grandeur of captaining a college First XV. 'Have you anything specific to tell us, mortal? Be brief.'

'I have!' said Culpepper, glancing at his watch. 'I've spent the last week in our College library. Discovering *most* specific things... What a fearful affair a library is – don't you think?' He took off his cap, produced the cream-coloured notebook from its depths, began leafing through it. 'The decent bits of humanity. Flesh, breasts, flanks, innocence, babies. The worm or the flame gets those. What survives on paper is human libel. Heresy, perversity, cruelty, prosecution, extreme—'

But he'd tried the patience of the gods too far. There was an eruption of heckling, unparliamentary language, booing. Ares rose from his seat. Apollo smiled terribly and crossed his legs.

'Don't you know where you are?' shouted Culpepper above the hubbub. 'Don't you know what Westley Waterless is?' Angry shouts. 'It's the most demon-ridden village in England.' Derisive laughs. 'This isn't a slur on the Quintember experiment. I've been doing some research. Hear me!' He waved his notebook.

Zeus, sighing, made a magnificent gesture for everyone to sit. 'Ten minutes,' said the Thunderer. They were good students underneath it all, they revered facts; they sat.

And Culpepper, who had the right page now, began to speak rapidly and precisely. 'Just outside the walls of this grisly estate is a copse called Druidsgrove with a pool which Ordnance Survey maps mark with a question mark because no one's ever fathomed it. When surveyors try their plummets disappear. They claim without evidence that the mud must suck with unusual vigour.'

'Fair play to the surveyors,' snorted Poseidon. 'I credit the mud.'

'Local legend – I found this in a Latin chronicle – says the pool in Druidsgrove is bottomless. Or rather not bedded on earth, it drains into Styx. The Georgian antiquary Brereton reports that on clear nights when the pool's full of stars it reflects not our sky but the constellations of the Southern Hemisphere. He says that at midsummer the Druids would load a stallion with rocks and drive it into the water to sink and never be seen again. It had gone to be the mount of Æron, god of slaughter.'

'The paganism of ancient Britain,' said Margot, uncertainly, 'was very pure.' Apollo's face was like a looking glass, but it did not reflect the sunny glade: everyone could see him dropping Culpepper, well-weighted, into that pool.

'There are evil tales without limit about Westley Waterless.' He flicked some pages. 'Roger de Beywk, rector from something-or-other to 1472, said to have sold his soul, always recited his Paternoster backwards, hunted with a pack of black mastiffs the terror of the county, impregnated half the village. Defied the archdeacon (whose visitation book I've read). Finally vanished in a lightning storm one All Hallows' Eve on his hundredth birthday.'

'I cannot feel,' sneered Dionysus, 'even an antiquarian thrill.'

'Once de Beywk baptised a baby with water from Druidsgrove. It grew hairs over its body, dreadful fingernails they couldn't keep clipped. One night it vanished, they found the family dog with throat torn out, a smashed window, nothing else; then a wolf began to prey on the local sheep.'

'Might I further point out,' continued Dionysus in a muffled fashion – he'd begun eating his grapes – 'that it'll be lunchtime in twenty-one minutes?'

'Under Jamie Stuart the church tower collapsed one sunset. In the ruins they found the crushed body of a naked woman and a freshly strangled baby, an adder still knotted round its neck.'

'It's pleasing,' remarked Artemis, fiddling angrily with the tip of an arrow, 'to hear of peasants with interesting hobbies.'

'Under the Commonwealth, Matthew Hopkins the Witch-Finder General seized on three old women in Westley Waterless, a village he deemed "unutterably given over to Lucifer." He hanged them from an oak on a slight rise to the east of the village, on this spot in fact, where Seacome was later to dig his swimming pool. That elderly specimen over your head, Mr Nyachae, may be the one. One of the condemned was named um, um Perseverance-unto-Judgement Puyke, a descendant it seems of the demon priest. She left seven grandsons, who watched her kicks subside with apparent relief. Their spawn have populated the district ever since. My bedder's called Mrs Elmsgall, but can you guess her maiden name?'

'This is childish,' growled Hera.

'It was Elizabeth Elmsgall *née* Puyke who lured me here. She lives, lived in Westley Waterless. She heard all about you.'

'A silly coincidence,' said Hera.

'Trifling village gossip,' added Hades.

'That hairy dwarf-woman didn't think it a trifle. She was in awe and dread of your commune. She was, as far as I can make out, *sent* to tell me about it. Because I was thought vulnerable to its allure. I suppose I must seem, from certain low perspectives, ambiguous. You young idiots were prompted to commit mischief, and I was to come along and be suborned by it. Then God knows what was meant to happen.' *God knows what is meant to happen. Can't they feel the tension in the air?*

'This is literally deranged,' said Athena through her teeth.

'Seventeen minutes to lunch,' said Hades. 'I vote—'

'Don't think about the village, think about the house. Does it signify nothing?' Culpepper flourished his notebook. 'It was built by Hastings Totty Seacome, M.P., one of the lurid monsters of the Victorian City of London. Made his fortune importing adulterated beef. Corrupted the entire Metropolitan Police force to cover up the deaths and after that the coppers were so compromised they couldn't touch him. Seacome diversified. He fixed races, manipulated stocks, embezzled from the Liberal Party. He worked with a partner, a crooked banker named Crosby; the two of them reached a plane of financial make-believe not again achieved, I'm told, until the dawning years of the twenty-first century. But their greatest profits came from an opulent emporium opposite Westminster Abbey. Stocked with extremely young countrywomen their agents recruited as parlourmaids. Only when the girls got to London did they discover their mistake. In that brothel they wore demure crisp white dresses, and giggled, blushed, carried milk-pails, whispered shyly of wheat prices for all I know. Anyway they were a cool relief for men bored with urbanity, tired of the raddled whores of Soho.'

Athena sighed so loudly her owl opened its eyes.

'Poor Crosby and Seacome. In the midst of the 1890s a cholera epidemic wiped out most of their stock. The opulence of the house apparently stopped at the fittings, it didn't extend to the drains.'

There was a riding tide of restiveness.

'This – listen, this got them into the papers, and Crosby was terribly murdered. Stripped and nailed in a barrel with twelve-inch red leeches. The best detectives were hired, but the crime was never solved.

'Seacome was frightened. He sold the brothel, now the site of Methodist Central Hall, liquidated his holdings in the City, retired to the shires. An evil whim prompted him to build his pile and lay out his grounds on the edge of this execrable village. On this accursed hillock, in fact. Perhaps he was drawn.'

Hades began to heckle about lunch.

'The police might – I *am* going to finish, Ollie. The police might have pursued and assassinated him. He had many other enemies, notably the parents of his prostitutes. The fate of Crosby was ever before his eyes. But as it happens retribution came from within. Within a few years it was rumoured in the village that Mr Seacome didn't dare leave his house. There was no more tripping to Paris and Baden-Baden. He lived as a recluse—' Hades was disgracing himself. 'As a recluse on the first floor. And then his servants began to glimpse—'

'His servants!' shouted Dionysus who was Tristan Bolswood, a lawyer's brat and a Londoner. 'Suggestible, drooling rustics. What can their evidence be worth?'

'To glimpse young girls at dusk, in lovely white frocks and bonnets, floating out of the trees of the Park. They didn't speak; they just stood about holding milk-pails, with their free arms round each other's waists, looking up at the curtained windows on the first floor. As the light faded only the vague pallour of their clothing could be seen; then nothing. But the village domestics—'

'Who were not so cretinous,' interrupted Tristan, 'that they couldn't have read all about Seacome's waifs in the *Daily Maul*.'

'The village domestics reported that they got closer and closer to the house. One by one they deserted their master, until only a broken-down old ostler, who served as butler, remained in The Rise at night. At last the boy who lit the fires, a squint-eyed goblin of a boy named Edgar Puyke, cycled up one sunny dawn in June 1904 to find every door standing open. The butler lay dead in the library, clutching a candelabrum, with –.'

'Let me guess!' shouted Ollie, rudely; he was horribly hungry. 'With an look of unspeakable dismay disfiguring his face.'

'"With an expression of strange, intense delight fixed across his venerable features." I quote the *Haverhill Chronicle* of 17 June 1904. Perhaps the *Haverhill Chronicle* meant to solace the family of the butler, which was Low Church. Or perhaps Seacome's nocturnal visitors, who had to eliminate the witness, did it in the kindest way they knew.' Athena made a gesture of violent impatience; her familiar hooted. 'In any case, the wicked millionaire himself was found at the top room of the front turret, a sort of dusty attic he had apparently tried to barricade. He died clutching the goat-like legs of a pseudo-Louis Quinze chair, as if to fend something off; his face was bluish-grey, eyes shrunken, fingers wrinkled as from dehydration.'

'Pah!' cried Tristan. 'The symptoms of cholera. I'm not—'

'Exactly. As the *Haverhill Chronicle* points—'

'I'm not listening—'

'Points out, the onset can be sudden, and—'

But by now the gods were riotous. They were all on their feet shouting, except for Zeus, who clung to his dignity and remained on his throne, and Athena, who sneered, and Apollo, who was waiting for worse.

Above the racket, Culpepper shouted: 'Do you apostates know why you're here?' Contemptuous jeers. 'Has Odingo told you? Oh he hasn't?' That quietened them a little. 'You think he just found The Rise. He's the money, after all. He bought it because it was cheap, because it's a wreck, because it's been uninhabited since Seacome's day. That's what you think, isn't it, you boobies? But it was your father,' he roared, rounding on Odingo, who shrugged with contempt, 'wasn't it? *He* told you to come here.' Margot gave Odingo a long look. 'Kipchumba Nyachae, now a minister in the Nairobi government. Who was an *inyanga* before he became a politician. Who rose to power amongst the Kisii because of the ferocity of his curses.'

'One or two of which,' murmured Odingo (everyone was suddenly quieter) 'he has passed on.'

'Tell me, Odingo. "Apollo" if you like. Even before you came to Westley Waterless, why did you come to Wygefortis'? Is that another detail you've not explained to your cronies? With your A-levels and your money, you might have chosen a much better college.' Odingo's shrug was a marvel of elegance. 'Was it, O Apollo, because your father, that pioneer of darkness, chose it for you? Was it because he knew your tutor would be called Culpepper – rather an unusual name?'

Athena gave Apollo an even longer look. She did not like being a means to an end.

But Apollo managed a tremendous smile; and Margot's face went curiously blank. 'Indeed, our family owes the hanging of my great-grandfather, a mighty *inyanga*, to the British Empire. And, I gather, to your forebear. But listen' – and here he sprang up, ignoring Culpepper; his throne crashed backward – 'all of you. Private vendettas are an irrelevance. We're not here to listen to fustian ghost stories. Nor to debate principles. We're not here to listen at all. We are here to act. And to obey.'

His smile was serene and terrible. He gazed at Culpepper, and Culpepper found he could not speak. The menace in the air was suddenly beyond bounds. *This,* he thought in a panic, *isn't a trial, it's a sentencing. My role's got muddled.* He became so alarmed he flung aside his schoolmasterly little notebook, which was making the wrong impression, and groped in his pockets for a cigar. He lit it. There: much more like a Penal Collection. But the gods were standing about in a way that looked more and more like a lynching. *None of us are ourselves.*

Apollo paid Culpepper no attention. He was addressing his colleagues with horrible grace. It came to Culpepper with a double jolt that this was no longer quite Odingo's voice; and that it was using the purest, most resonant Greek.

'How tepidly we have worked, Deathless Ones. We have dabbled in visions. We have prognosticated, almost smiling, from the guts of stray cats.' The other eleven were staring at him with listless, anonymous faces, and tense muscles. They looked literally out of character. They might have been anybody. They might be about to do anything. 'What we require is strong incantation, the puissance of Circe and Hecate. We hanker for richer blood, for thick steaming blood—'

Hysteria and courage can look much the same. Jamming on his doctoral cap, trying to make it look like a death's cap, Culpepper cried: 'I also am not here to debate! I am here to warn and condemn. I pronounce,' and here he lifted both arms above his head, 'anathema upon your gimcrack Olympus. The centuries of light reprove your hankerings. Your project is thwarted, your blasphemy overthrown! Your experiment is ended, and your cursèd house is bound to fall beneath the weight of your perversity! To fall! To fall!'

And he ran. It was not easy in those robes and it was not dignified, but he dashed away through the untended undergrowth of the wood –

xix.

where it occurred to him to pause before the bush in which Gladys was cringing – to bend, and apply the burning tip of his cigar to her protruding lens – and then to run some more, out of the trees, to sprint (although he could hear no sound of pursuit) behind the stables, across the ruinous croquet lawn, between sinister bulging shapes of box that were once topiary, over the cracked ornamental pond with a leap, past the shrubbery, round the perpendicular wing and the conservatory, to the front of the house where the Land Rover sat. He

xx.

vaulted into the driver's seat.

'Did I give. You enough. Time?' he gasped.

'Oh yeah,' said Seb, half-asleep in the seat beside him. Seb had got out the Land Rover just before Felix knocked down the gates with it. His orders had been to stay out of sight until he heard the house empty out, then enter through its open front door with his bag of tools. 'Oodles. It's done. One thingummy bolted with a whatsit to the roof-beam on the first floor and then through a hole I drilled in the corner of the chimney. One round the um. Thingy. Over the front door.'

'Lintel,' said Culpepper, still out of breath.

'And the last chain's hung round the middle of the main staircase. Where the two bits come together and it narrows.'

'There be hanged by the neck until your body be dead,' murmured Culpepper out of pure nostalgia, turning the key.

'And I sawed through a few things until my hand got sore. I had tons of time. Got bored. Looked round the squat. It smells funny. Lunch was half-ready in the kitchen. Hippie food. Brown wholemeal pasta with brown sauce in a pot and brown bread and a brown crunchy salad. Grim. What were you doing in the garden with those naked girls?'

'Talking,' sighed Culpepper, tossing his cigar out the window and turning the key, 'talk, talk, talk, talk-talk. Contentless blather. What does anyone ever do at Cambridge? When what we need is action—'

Bold words. But when he stepped hard on the accelerator there was no action. Tortured gears bellowed, back tyres squealed and began to bury themselves in the gravel; the heavy chains stretching from the Land-Rover through the front door into the house snapped taut. From within came a vague disastrous wooden ripping. Nothing more.

Culpepper chopped up into four-wheel drive. But for a second, for two seconds, for three, nothing happened: the ruckus of the motor increased. His face too was white and strained, the woodwork of the giant house groaned, the very sky seemed to quiver and stretch, as if about to tear from this trial of strength between edifice and engine. The Land Rover wailed for mercy; its front tyres began to lift. The chains rattled and graunched. The house growled to its marrow. Over these sounds Culpepper started shouting poetry as if it were prayer:

> *The cloud-capp'd towers, the gorgeous palaces,*
> *The solemn temples, the great globe itself,*
> *Yea, all which it inherit, shall dissolve*

– and on that word, with what seemed a pentecostal gust of energy, the Land Rover sprang forward, free, amidst the most tremendous orchestral clamour of smashing: a thousand shivered windows, a thousand snapped beams, a thousand toppled bricks, all uttering their death-yell at once. Culpepper braked.

The house did not dissolve so much as erupt. There was in it a latent energy—

(As always, we're resisting supernatural insinuations: torque and gravity had been imprisoned for centuries by trees in Norway, taking in the strength of the sun; when a century ago those trees were felled their power was invested in the house and in its raised, bent and stacked timbers. They sat quietly as the decades went by – many sedate-looking objects in England are simply waiting the right moment to explode – and now their force sprang free.)

The first rupture of roof-beams cascaded backward, bringing down the great central clump of chimneys. These, which stretched four storeys from basement laundry through kitchens to ornate chimney-pots, fell in separate directions, bursting into flower like a tiger breaking from its cage: a fierce orange flower petalled with white teeth and claws. There was a sunburst of roof tiles, joyously piercing walls and floorboards, knocking out struts as they spun to earth. Collapse ran back like a row of dominos. The conservatory burst, a glass grenade: its twisted panes were in a twinkling of an eye a million needles of glass in sun, shredding the foliage, disappointed, however, of flesh or eyeballs. The furthest wing of The Rise groaned, creaked, complained to itself, then noisily grudgingly slumped inward, folding walls against floors, laying its timbers together like a pyramid. Smashed plaster rose as a cloud.

Meanwhile one turret had come soaring overhead and landed in the asphodel bed, peak-downward like a torpedo, just in front of the Land Rover, which shook and reeled, bombarded by hunks of wood, chunks of mortar, ceramic shards. Its back window cracked. A heavy thud produced a dent in the roof just above the driver's seat. A rain of plaster and splinters smothered the windscreen.

The bombardment sank to a patter of kindling. Then stillness. An immense creak. Another smash. Reverberations. Deeper stillness. Indignant bird-noise.

'Disco,' said Seb.

'Chains,' said Culpepper in an uneven voice. They leapt out and unbolted the three chains from the tow-bar, flinging them back into the loose heap or quaking hill of shattered timber, which was all that was left of the front of The Rise. A huge, lazy cloud of heavy white dust was billowing outwards.

Through the cloud and behind the ruination they could see empty rooms torn in half, with swaying floors. As they watched, the side-wing made up its mind. It slithered forward prone on the earth, pulling down its roof over its shame in a final cascade of tiles.

Distantly, from behind the pulverised house, beyond the range of the catastrophe, they could hear divine shouts. A single panic-struck dove squawked up into the blue.

Our heroes got back in. Culpepper released the handbrake. The battered Land Rover slid silently down the incline, through the violated gates, out into the quiet road.

xxi.

'Seb?' said Culpepper, fifteen minutes later. 'Seb? *Seb?* Are you all right?'

'Hey!' bellowed Seb, 'you're up here! You can fly too!'

'We're in my Land Rover, Seb. We're heading back to Cambridge.'

'Wow! So we are! … You've got a flying car!'

Culpepper glanced at him sharply. Seb had his head out of the window, looking down: far down, judging from his posture.

'A car that's also a biplane! With flames coming out its back,' shouted Seb, 'like a backwards dragon… Gosh, it's glorious being your sidekick.'

'Margot's my sidekick. You're just a sort of henchman.'

'That's glorious too… Wa-hey! You almost caught that eagle in your propeller.'

'How high would you say we are, Seb?'

'Awwww… a good thousand feet. Don't you think? There's The Wash over that way… The North Sea behind us… And all these fields. Flat, flat fields, like chess. Not square squares though. The other thing. Wrongboids. And three colours. Light green, dark green, orangey. Funny sort of chess… Look! I can see two rooks coming over the fields.'

They were passing through a dismal hamlet (although not to be compared to Westley Waterless), Six Mile Bottom. Byron used to come to Six Mile Bottom to see his sister and commit incest. Culpepper rather liked the place's raffish atmosphere. Anything went here. But he didn't think the city of Cambridge was ready for such a noisy visionary. He pulled off the main road, and pottered along the lanes that lead through Great Wilbraham. It was drained fen out here: treeless, dusty and desolate in the strong sun.

'Um – how much of the mushroom sauce did you eat?'

'I finished the pot!' cried Seb, still at the top of his voice. 'It seemed a pity to… you know, waste it. Since the house was coming down on top of it. I didn't have dinner last night, because I was at a party at King's… Wow, *look* at them!'

'What?'

'The two rooks. But they're not rooks, they're ogres. They're alive. Thirty foot high.'

'Gog and Magog?'

'Nah, that doesn't sound right… They're big brown shaggy fellows. Greek by the look of it. Oh, they have serpents instead of legs!'

'Ah. Γίγαντες. Earth-born giants. They revolted and fought the gigantomachy. A war against Olympus.'

'Do they pull it down?'

'No, Athena found a herb they couldn't resist. They were slaughtered.'

'Just goes to show… Greek myths aren't true.' He turned on Culpepper his blond idiot face, blank, happy and animal, a little ravaged at the edges by drugs.

'He's consumed the whole commune's midday dose, now he's seeing the unhallowed seed of Uranus,' thought Culpepper, momentarily worried. 'But no, this is how he always looks. He won't be harrowed the way I am. Was. Was last week. Monsters can't find foothold in such an empty mind.' Seb was leaning out of the window again, trying to catch the giants' attention with shouts. 'I have my hipflask of whisky. We'll wash the ambrosia out of his system. The charm of working with subnormals is that you don't have to worry about damaging their minds.'

'All right, Seb, time for a drink. We're pulling over.'

'Landing, eh? Booze for the heroes of the gigantomachy!' He pulled invisible goggles over his eyes, flung about his neck an invisible white silk scarf, and gave Culpepper a cheery thumbs-up over the racket of the propeller.

xxii.

To say that the *Dirty Swan* was not used to having four bare or close-to-bare young ladies, not to mention eight blokes in the altogether or near-as-maybe, float into the parlour bar without an *Excuse me* or *Pardon*, is to say what is inadequate and what is inane. It was a shock surpassing anything Westley Waterless had ever known. It was more staggering than the Viking raid of a thousand and four years before. It was more staggering than the witch-hunt of 1645. It was more staggering even than the collapse of the Seacome place, which had happened an hour before, witnessed only by Val and Gladys. (And Val and Gladys were still wandering about the wreckage, open-mouthed; they had yet to come running through the village spreading the news.)

One instant the *Swan* was as dirty, silent, dim, yellow and empty as usual. The next it was crammed with billowing snowy linen, flashing gilded armour, an owl, flesh. Such flesh, squeezed up so close! Such bright breasts filling the air, splendid rumps crushed against plaster, scrota spilling over bar-stools! Reg the grim publican let fall the pint-glass he was holding and merely gaped, his hand still held out, grasping the immaterial tankard. Alfred's mouth swung open too, his eyes rolled up, and he dropped from his barstool to the floor with a soft thump. No one noticed, and he was fated to lie there forgotten until evening, when he was tripped over in his dark corner, and carried off to hospital with a heart-attack. An extremely mild heart attack: 'Nothing to kill you,' explained the jolly cardiologist, 'a friendly warning shot across the bows.' A hint to give up leching and find a less stimulating hobby if he wanted to live to the next turnip harvest. Which he did.

Meanwhile, the young 'uns were pushing around long-disused tables and chairs, and making themselves at home. 'Might we possibly use some such thing as a 'phone?' asked Margot brightly, focussing such a tremendous smile on Reg, a most unobliging man, that he could think of nothing to do but wordlessly hand his mobile across the bar. 'Thanks awfully. And a dozen pints, please.'

'Eleven,' said Odingo. 'No ale for me. A glass of Dubonnet, my good man.' Reg had never heard of Dubonnet; but nor had he ever seen or heard or imagined a seven-foot black man in a gold wig and nothing else coming into his pub to order anything at all. He found nothing to say.

'Don't be such a pill,' said Margot to Odingo, with the 'phone to her ear; 'Ignore him,' she mouthed brilliantly to Reg; and into the 'phone, 'Hallo, may I order four cabs please? We're at – *where* are we? The *Swan*, Westley Waterless. A spiffing pub, you ought to visit it…. Where are we going?' She addressed the company at large: 'Where are we going?' The ex-gods sounded vague. 'London, I expect,' she told the taxi company, 'or places of that sort. How long? Oh, make it a whole hour then. That's splendid of you. Goodbye.' Reg had placed a pint before her; he'd even found a little paper mat to go under it, a sophistication never before seen in the *Dirty Swan*. 'The darlings say they'll be here in an hour. So there's plenty of time for a spot of luncheon.'

In moments of particular social awkardness, Margot often imitated her grandmother's manner, which she'd despised so much as a child. Only recently had it struck her that her grandmother, who was also a clever woman, must have consciously put it on. It would have been artificial and preposterously dated even in her grandmother's youth. Indeed it was so Edwardian Margot's grandmother possibly copied it from her own grandmother. It worked precisely the way armour works: that is, although shaped to fit the vulnerable person beneath, it was complete in itself, stood by itself, glittered, overawed, and let nothing through. It came with a particularly metallic smile, which Margot now employed to say: 'Chin-chin, all!'

'Chin-chin!' said everyone except Odingo, who said '*Cul sec*' and sniffed. In fact he was catching a whiff of Alfred, lying beshatten, vomit-haired, motionless, unglimpsed, face-down in his corner. But Odingo assumed it was bad beer and made a face.

(Everyone except Odingo was behaving remarkably well. The crash – just an hour ago, but it seemed a century – had left them standing in a circle by the ruined pool, blinking. None of what was in their minds seemed to make sense, or belong there; it dribbled away, it was gone. They looked about at each other, smiled, and went to inspect the fallen house. There was nothing to be salvaged. It was a write-off. All their things were buried beneath its immense wreckage. They had the clothes they stood up in, which is to say three cotton robes, a hunting-tunic and some metal headgear between the twelve of them. 'Only honour remains,' Zeus had pronounced mock-heroically: 'let's find a pub.' He'd been applauded by all except Odingo, who'd petulantly flung the key of Olympus into the debris – it vanished deep, and came to rest beside the invisible chains. Then they'd processed down Westley Bottom Road. Venetian blinds had been fingered apart, vases smashed, eyes covered with parted fingers, husbands slapped for making unseemly noises. In any case, thus they reached the western edge of the village and *The Dirty Swan*.)

After a fortnight of fermented honey, magic mushrooms and shocking wine, it was wonderful to drink beer, even Reg's badly-kept Bass. It was even wonderful to lunch on Reg's fairly honest cheese and pickle, for the gods had not been eating well. Every few days Odingo, their financier, had produced three hundred-pound notes from his wig, where he stowed them in a neat pocket; and it was the duty of Hera, Olympian mother, and Hermes, patron of merchants and thieves (he kept the left-over cash rolled up in his caduceus), to climb into cotton dress and trousers and trek down to Brownlow's village shop for supplies. Brownlow waters his milk. Brownlow adulterates his flour with plaster-dust. Brownlow gets his packaged things cheap from a man in an unmarked van, all past their sell by date. His ciggies are smuggled from Pakistan and his wine comes from God-knows-where, certainly not where it says on the labels, which have amazing spelling mistakes. Brownlow's wine-labels had been a source of grim mirth to the gods. He doesn't make much from such doings: his illegal profits go on bribing health inspectors. But Brownlow's a shopkeeper of the old school: if he's not cheating his customers he can't believe he's doing his job.

Reg is also old school, happy to poison regulars. However, it so happens that he hates Brownlow with such a lifelong hatred he's prepared to drive to a supermarket in Haverhill for vittles, just to spite him. Besides, Brownlow is in cahoots with the Baptist Ladies' League, and the ladies, who disapprove of so much, might start passing Resolutions if they learned he was abetting the riotous pleasures of the *Dirty Swan*.

Therefore the Red Leicester on which the ex-immortals lunched was, by the standards of Westley Waterless, wholesome and delectable. And by the second pint they were feeling more wholesome themselves. The speed of their recovery gave the game away. The house had fallen from them like a chain hacked off a prisoner's leg.

In any case they were very young, and so in awe of the ancient universities of England they might well half-believe a Doctor of Philosophy and college Fellow has the power to throw down houses with his *ex cathedra* voice.

In any case, they hopped down from their Olympian selves, and came home happily to their own characters. They were relieved to be free of the Quintember experiment. Even Margot. But not Odingo.

The Jack Russell, *né* Cerberus, was happiest of all. It gambolled between their legs, beside itself to be shot of the two toy dog-heads that had been stitched to its collar. It had been given the heads to play with, and was joyously gnawing them to threads.

The owl, perhaps, had doubts. Margot had set it on the jar of pickled toads. Every so often it opened its eyes, startled by the clamour of the drinking party, and asked a question. Possibly it missed the stillness of

Olympus. 'What am I am going to do with you, old thing?' ex-Athena asked it, smoothing its temples with her forefinger. She had captured and tamed it herself. 'Will you thrive in the wild? Or have you gone soft?'

'Oh, it'll be swooping on fieldmice by nightfall. You can tell it's still a *manly* owl,' giggled April, ex-Aphrodite, with a roguish glance at its beak. She was an Oxonian undergraduate, clever, light-headed, and out of place amidst these earnest Tabs. 'But what am *I* going to do with *these*?' She pointed to her four doves, tethered by their pink ribbons to a chairleg. 'They really *are* decadent.'

Celia *alias* Artemis was from a different, rather superior Oxford college. She was dreamy, clever, poetic, and also out of place amongst these Cantabrians. Now Celia gave a hard look. 'I don't imagine two weeks even of your company, April, can distort the character of a common pigeon.' *Slut*, she added with a look.

Frump, said April's eyes, but aloud she just said 'Coo' in Cockney to her pets: ''ear that, me lovelies? She hups hand calls you common.'

'Let me throttle 'em with their ribbons, Miss,' suggested Reg shyly, with his eyes closed, 'and I'll turn them into a nice pigeon pie for you.' Reg Squat had never been so conversational in his life; but then he'd never had a bint in the altogether lean across his bar and work her lashes.

'We could make a proper execution of it,' observed young Benge of Trinity Hall, who had been playing Hades. Some of the aura of the Underworld still hung about him. 'If you wouldn't mind opening your case of hangman's nooses, we could make sure those ropes are still supple. One noose would do for all the birds at once.'

'Oh gods, I mean God, let's not have any more killing,' sighed ex-Hera. 'The sacrifices are something I'm not going to miss. It was horrid how the cats fought.'

'It was the rabbits screaming that I hated, *hated*,' gushed April. 'Ollie slit them so slowly.'

Celia rolled her eyes.

Ollie, who had played Hephæstus, was abashed. 'You *can't* get an animal open quickly, not with a stone knife.'

('Gotcha!' shouted Poseidon, who was using his trident on the darts board and had just managed to spear all three rings at once.)

'What I'm not going to miss,' said Tristan, ex-Dionysus, 'is the vintages. *Genuine French Champain.*'

'*Chatoe la Feet*,' recalled the former Hera, shuddering. '*Santa Million.*'

'Sounds like you've been shopping at Mr Brownlow's,' said Reg with an actual grin. No one in Westley had seen Reg grin since last December, when the Baptist Ladies had devoured a Battenberg cake from Brownlow so out of date it had grown invisible, virulent moulds in its buttercream. They'd shrieked, and pounded each other with fists getting at the single lavatory; the losers had fled outside, where harrowing scenes had been enacted behind Bethel Memorial Hall. Mrs Elmsgall, who had been unaffected, informed Brownlow, who said 'Now, then,' although he had a lot of explaining to do later. Val had told Alfred and Alfred had told Reg. Reg had grinned. Now – for the last time in his life, as it happens – he grinned again. 'He's quite the lad.'

Zeus mimed flinging a thunderbolt in the direction of Brownlow's Stores.

'Tell you what,' said Reg. 'From now on, you come here for your booze, and I'll get you something better.'

'Thanks, Reg, but we're leaving Westley today. For good.'

'You are? What about the Seacome place?'

'It collapsed this morning.'

Reg, for whom the gruesome old house on the edge of Westley was one of the facts of life, paled at the news of such a prodigy. '*How did that happen?*' he managed.

The commune was, quite rightly, eager to hasten to resist any hint of the supernatural.

'Nothing out of the ordinary, Reg,' Benge told him.

'After all,' observed Zeus, 'it's been condemned for decades.'

'It was,' suggested Artemis, 'that leaping about last night. The boys,' she told Reg, 'ran all over the house shouting. In armour.'

Prude, said Aphrodite's glance.

'Perhaps we oughtn't to have taken the Corybantic dance upstairs,' admitted Ares, a Peterhouse man who hardly ever spoke.

'The agent did say upstairs was unstable,' murmured Margot.

'True. I hope,' Tristan the lawyer's son said to the frowning Odingo, 'that it won't bugger up your insurance. Best not mention armoured dancing when you fill in the forms.'

'I do not imagine,' said Odingo acidly, in his careful mission-school English, 'that my insurance covers the *Ludi Apollinares*. Any more than it would cover Dr Culpepper's curse.'

No one relished this mention of the anathema. 'Oh, that was just a flourish.'

'Just Culpepper being angular.'

'Meant as an antiquarian joke.'

'Charming in its way.'

'Shows he cares.'

Odingo remained sulky or, as it may be, sad. 'Anyway, it is fortunate that the pater keeps chaotic accounts. Otherwise he would be aggrieved the house I had him buy for us fell down.' There was an ambivalent murmur. 'At least it leaves the summer free. I'm pushing off to Monte. At least, I think I'm going to Monte. Anyone care to come along? Margot?' He pronounced her name with tenderness.

But it seemed that Odingo was to be disposed of as easily as the redundant wildlife – had indeed already been disposed of. In her grandmother mode, Margot was too aristocratic to be embarrassed, even by a betrayal she was committing herself. She simply tossed her hair and tweeted her owl's beak.

Suddenly the cabs were there. Zseni was unscrewing his caduceus, shaking out pound coins and notes, they were pressing them on Reg, who gave them the nooses as a souvenir; Aphrodite presented him with her sacred pigeons and kissed him on the cheek (he'd never been as happy before, will never be happy again); the owl, not liking the look of taxis, escaped over the grey fields, as was no doubt for the best; Odingo, getting into Margot's cab, made a fuss about sharing it with the Jack Russell, but Margot preferred the dog to the man and out he got; 'Here!' said Celia imperiously from the second cab, but April, from the third, merely lowered her gorgeous brow, patting the seat beside her; she prevailed; then her cab driver made a fuss, saying he was a good Muslim and couldn't have an entirely bare woman in his car (sitting by a bare black man, although he didn't dare mention that aspect of the question), so April borrowed Hera's veil and covered with face with it – the cabbie had to be satisfied with the veil and an extra tenner, and grumbled to himself about *sharia* as far as the M25. Reg waved them off, then turned back vaguely looking for Alfred, who seemed to have wandered away; the lead taxi driver, who had never seen London-town before, honked joyously all the way down Westley Bottom Road. Thus the divine glory passed from that place forever.

xxiii.

'"Resolved,"' reads Matron sunnily, ten days later, '"that the East

Cambridgeshire Baptist Ladies' League implore remission of sin, an increase of prevalent grace unto holiness, and the blessing of the Lord in life or death, or permanent vegetative state, upon sister ELIZABETH LOBELIA ELMSGALL, laid aside on a bed of sickness, with whom the League expresses itself Present and Vigilant in Spirit." Isn't that kind of your friends, Bessy? And such a nice card too!'

Which wasn't strictly true. The card reproduced an early nineteenth-century Evangelical woodcut of a wan, bedridden woman, with black nightcap and white nightdress buttoned to the throat; the Recording Angel was seated in the air above, disobligingly jotting down her thoughts.

Matron, who believes in unceasing merciless cheer towards her inmates, holds this image at an oblique angle so that Bess, trussed to the bed, has to see it. Bess growls a curse, rather a vivid curse, in Ancient Egyptian. (As ever, we resist superstition. Mrs Elmsgall spent ten years dusting the shelves of academics; there's no reason why she shouldn't have taken books down, and memorised things along the way.)

'*And* they've sent a bunch of such lovely fresh wildflowers. To remind you of your own dear village.' Val and Gladys took a lot of trouble assembling this bouquet from the wasteland and copses about Waterless. It contains balsamine, hensbane and belladonna, bird's foot trefoil wound around sticks of hemlock, sturdy clumps of poison ivy and creeping-willow, grace-notes of wormwood, all in a ruff of stinging nettle.

Matron believes in intense sensory stimulation for violent cases (it's part of her punitive method), and lowers this bouquet toward Bess – who with a sudden lunge from the neck buries her teeth in it.

Years of torment have left Matron wary, even at her most jovial. She skips backward waggling her fingers, which she kept a good inch beyond gnashing range. Still! – *Dear heaven, that was a near thing!*

Bess has chomped through the stalks. She's shredded noxious flowers like a lawnmower. But instead of closing on bone, her dentures, which she filed to points years back, have mashed the garlic flowers her sister Baptists secreted in the midst of the posy. Their little surprise.

The garlic sends Bess into a frenzy. Her false teeth chatter like castanets, bloodying her lips with a pink froth. Her body quivers stiffly in its bonds, her moans become animal.

Matron's smile remains fixed as she thrusts Mrs Elmsgall back on her pillows and makes the straps snug over shoulder and broken hip. But then Matron's smile is always fixed. 'Let's keep our hap-hap-happy face on, girls,' she invariably trills to her nurses as she bustles along the corridors of the

Deepdell. Her nurses stare after her dourly. 'It's all very fucking well for her,' they tell each other, 'she's Matron already.' By which they mean: *That's why we went into psychiatric nursing, innit? The work's bloody disgusting and the pay's crap but we get a chance at the jackpot.* Their eyes go soft and wistful as they think of it. To be a matron! To have unfettered access to the drug cabinets of an entire asylum!

Matron (she has a luxurious haunch, and a rolling camel eye) thinks so too. *After that,* she murmurs to herself, closing the door on the whimpering Elmsgall, *I think I deserve fifty oral mils of fentanyl. Just to tide me over to elevenses.* Eleven is when the syringe comes out, never a moment before; just as the grating apparatus she uses on her patients' soles never comes out 'til teatime, be she ever so impatient with them. Matron runs an orderly madhouse by her lights. *A pleasure anticipated is a pleasure blurred.*

Two junior nurses, pinched waifs, wait outside the Elmsgall's room, clutching towels and leather straps. Rumpy Matron beams at them. (*Life's just one long orgasm for Matron,* they think.) 'You're giving Bessy her bed-bath? Wonderful. She likes her water nearly boiling, I understand. Make sure she feels every drop. Then do give her gums a massage. That always relaxes these difficult new arrivals. And remember, girls: hap-hap-happy!'

xxiv.

'Well then,' comes the bluff honest voice of Brownlow later that Thursday afternoon. 'I've got some bad news for you, Gladys, and then I've got some good news. I sent your camera away to the photo shop in Dullingham,' which said it would be £40 to fix and offered him £100 for the parts when he told them not to bother, 'and they said nothing doing, it's a write-off. The inny-bit's quite burned through, they said.'

'Oo-ar.'

'But they managed to salvage the film, or most of it. "Mucky stuff," they say. "Queer customers you got there in Waterless," they say, "are you sure we ought to be developing these?" "Listen here, my lad," I say, "none of that. Mrs Gladys Drybble is one of the most respectable ladies in our village and I won't have any of your loose talk about her, see?" So here's the envelope. They charged me four quid' (they gave him the prints for nothing) 'and really I ought to ask you eight for it retail but seeing as you've lost your camera I'll let you have them for a fiver.' The negatives he has stored away, in case something occurs to him.

'Oh Mr Brownlow, you're *ever* so kind.'

'Mind you don't let Alf Squint see them when he comes home. If you take my meaning. Not with his angina and all.' What he means is: *Don't let the dirty bugger get any thrills for free.* Brownlow is disturbed about Alfred, who telephoned that morning from the cardiac ward, cancelling his secret subscription to *Naturist Living.* 'They're enough to get a chap a bit lively.'

'*Never.*'

Gladys doesn't go home. She hurries from the village shop to Val's house, 31 Westley Bottom Road. There she deals out her trove on the kitchen table, slowly, in sequence, like tarot cards.

The two curly perms, the purple and the orange, bend together, rapt; their Nescafé grows cold.

First come two or three tragic blurred studies of a redpoll, taken by the late Mr Drybble the afternoon he caught his death. Then, after eighteen months of disuse, his widow's first shots: long-distance snaps of naked nymphs and youths playing croquet on the lawn.

Lunching in the gazebo.

Strolling through the rose garden. Dozing in the shrubbery.

At this point Gladys gets the hang of focus. Cerberus chases a ball, Aphrodite's ringed doves strut about pecking the grass. Cerberus chases the doves into the trees. Athena's owl chases the doves out of the tree. The gods run about shouting, retrieving doves, Artemis in hitched-up skirt and suede boots, Ares with angry scowl and circular shield on his arm, burly trident-brandishing Poseidon conscientiously pausing to re-wet his torso.

'I *never*,' says Gladys.

Some overexposed snaps from Wednesday, exactly a fortnight ago, when the Olympians held a council. Zeus presides enthroned beneath an oak; the gods make prepared speeches.

'That girl with the owl was always the talker,' says Val.

Now, although each god's skin is a consistent shade, the pictures themselves are becoming whited-out, each frame slightly more overlit than the last.

Hephæstus pallidly crosses the little rectangle in Gladys's hand on his way to the anvil. Faded Hera scatters seed into washed-out green. This photo, meant to capture slender Hermes sunning himself, his winged cap and sandals stowed under a bush so they don't get too hot, records his body as a featureless strip on the barely-tinted snow of the lawn.

Then they come to the climactic day, Monday. There are five or six shots of Felix in his scarlet, squabbling with the gods enthroned in their grove.

'Ooooh,' exclaims Gladys.

'Fancy,' says Val in her most genteel Anabaptistical voice, 'a University gentleman like that in such an immoral place.'

She has a point: the final pictures are downright sinister. One shows the bottom half of red-robed Felix running through the wood, veering toward Gladys as she lurks trembling in the bush.

By now colour is burned away: each photo is a white blur within a painful aureole of orange-red, with shapes dissolved into outlines, swimming through the whiteness.

The last photo we can make out shows, or hints at, Culpepper's ghostly hand, pushing forward his burning cigar-tip – the fire from which all this consuming light flows.

After that picture comes oblong after oblong of perfect glossy white. They are all the same, all nothing. Yet it's these ultimate photographs Gladys lays down most solemnly, as if she were a nihilistic medium.

Val Squint takes an enormous breath. She'd feared dull doings in Westley this summer. 'Nothing to look at out of our spare-room window now the Seacome place's fallen flat. The students packed up and gone. *And* Bess Elmsgall's gone to the bin, ha! *And* Alf's in hospital for his ticker, not that I miss him much. Not to mention his budgies are dead and not needing to be cleaned up.' She'd watched them starve, pretending each one was Alf; grieving to think there'd be no more thrills coming her way. But now: 'These pictures! We can be going over them 'til it's time to start on Christmas cards.'

She releases a trembling sigh. 'Well, Gladys, I'm ever so sorry about your camera, but *do* let's go through them again.'

And they tell over their evangel, images consumed by too perfect an abundance of what enlivened them, spectacles out-spectacled; much like the ecstatic catastrophe of Semele, who asked to see beyond every veil, every feigned name or narrative or attribute of divinity, and behold infinity in Himself.

Epilogue

'Yes, yes? Come in! The door's open. Is that you, Harry, or –. No, it's *you*. Sit down. Or something… Shall we both stand? You look different. From what I remember. Of course, I've not see you since. Y'know, Monday.'

'Four days ago. Yes. A *long* time.'

'At The Rise. A long way away.'

'Y'know the house fell over just after you left?'

'I – um, heard.' And that was all they ever said about that. 'I wondered where you went.'

'London. To get clothes. Warm clothes.' For the weather had broken; it was a proper English summer again, chilly and sodden. 'Now I'm here to get books… Felix, you look twelve years old. Do sit down. *There*. I'll sit here. A good four feet off.'

'All right… Here we are.'

'Is that your *Quincentennial History*?'

'It is. Well, the galley proofs. A few more weeks and it'll – do y'want, say, a drink, Margot? I'm having gin. Well, you can see I'm having gin. Or something?'

'No, Felix.'

'Then I'm going. To dinner. Although you can see I'm not yet dressed for… Are you staying?' She shook her head, smiling. 'You're here to say goodbye?'

'Yes. I'm off to Stansted in a few minutes. A taxi's coming to the Lodge. I didn't want to leave time to be embarrassed with you…'

'But we seem to have enough time for that.'

'True…'

Felix took a gulp of gin.

'I suppose,' said Margot, considering him, 'we'll have more to say in the new term.'

'I shall miss you.'

'Probably you will, Felix.'

'How you disturb me when you're like this.'

'I know. I'm disturbed, too. It's so odd being back in College in midsummer. I had no idea things got so posthumous in July.'

'In…?'

'July.'

'Not Quin…?'

'No. The heathen stunt's over. Today's Thursday, the eleventh of July.'

'The feast,' remarked Culpepper, carefully, 'of St. Olga of Kiev, who forgave the Drevlian rebels on condition each household pay her a nominal tribute of a sparrow from its thatch-eaves. She had her soldiers tie smouldering chunks of sulphur to each little bird and set it free.' He regarded her under his brows. 'Every last Drevlian was burned up.'

'Oh? How thrilling. Talking of such thrills, I heard somebody chanting Latin in the chapel. That can't be Woolly, can it?'

'God, no. That'll be Trotsky Aloysius Benedict Dominic Augustine *et omnes sancti* Plantagenet.'

'Who?'

'The Master, dear heart. Our Master. The Master of St Wygefortis'. College.'

'*Juicy?*'

'He's asked for that name to be retired. I think you in particular ought to defer to him on that point.'

'Very well. Why is *Sir Trotsky* singing Marian anthems?'

'Because he's a neophyte. It's a peculiar story. I'm not sure I follow it. He's been gloomy since your – well, you know; your display with fruit and vegetables. Gloomy, gloomier, gloomiest. Sighing for no reason. Snuffling over his port. Conducting whispered dialogues with himself. One day last week he appeared at breakfast reeking of half-a-dozen colognes. Like a bombing in a cockney hairdresser's.'

'Ee-ugh.'

'On Monday, after the ambulance had borne away Mrs Elmsgall, I found him in Cocytus beating the air as if a bird were trying to land on his head. Whining "Go away, go away!" The next day he appeared with his halo of hair cropped to fuzz.'

'Ugh-ugh.'

'Yes. He'd hardly eat. Just sat murmuring "I can smell it, I can still smell it." Heavens knows what.'

'Aftershave?'

'No, that was only for one day.'

'How freakish you dons get out of term.'

'Perhaps. But the Master was different, it was serious. The stuffing was knocked out of him. On Tuesday I heard him *apologise* to Chyld for swearing after Chyld smashed a tureen.'

'He never apologises.'

'I know. The end, we assumed, was near. We began discussing the election. It's *murder* finding anyone willing to be Master of Wygefortis.'

'Had you thought of poor Sir Erskine?'

'No, Interpol called for *him*; he's had to vanish… Anyway, there's no need. Yesterday morning at nine Sir Trotsky's madness broke. For no particular reason. There was the usual breakfast hush. Someone had just asked for the cream jug or pineapple juice or some such – he started up like a guilty thing, choking. "Would you like some water, Master?" said someone, and he fairly shrieked: "That's it! The font, the font." Pulled Woolly up from his muesli, dragged him along.'

'Inconsequential nonsense,' declared Margot, demurely.

'I strolled after them, and sure enough, they were in Chapel. Woolly, was explaining, as he always does, that in a special sense all religions and irreligions are one so that conversions are not terribly affirming of the essential blah blah blah. But the Master, who was shivering feverishly and had him by the lapels, was saying he'd never been christened as a baby and wanted it now. "Now, by God, now, this instant!" He prevailed of course – he's the Master, and Woolly's Woolly – and he insisted on that slew of names. Woolly wanted to include Mohammed. Anyway: dunk, dunk, dunk. The moment it was done the Master started *sniffling*. Not tearfully. As if to smell. Shouted "It's gone, it's gone!" Kissed Woolly on both cheeks. Capered away. Now he's as happy as a boy in fresh snow. Frantically pompous. Odious to servants. Says he's growing his hair back and what do I think of orange dye. Quite his old self. Just pious, pious, pious.'

Culpepper recounted this story with a heavy air of innocence, which his enemy and lover did not quite credit. She shrugged. 'Nonsense. As you say. How uncouthly you all behave when we children aren't here to inhibit you. You surrender to inner disorder.' She glanced about his sitting-room. 'On the other hand, your rooms look… saner.'

This wasn't quite what she was thinking. Culpepper's sitting-room had always struck her as too perfectly well-furnished, and too calm about its perfection, to be quite sane; even with that black-and-pale-blue human-skull ashtray at the vortex. *Felix is sexually incomplete, so he can't be comfortable in his own rooms. He itches to spoil the effect.* What she said was: 'There's a freshness. A discernible absence of grease.'

'A Besslessness, in fact.'

'Besslessness? Does that mean you have a new bedder? Have you got rid of poor Mrs Elmsgall? You alleged horrible things about her.'

Culpepper told her about the holy water and the broken thigh. She wasn't impressed.

'So. You've terrorised, crippled and crazed a peasant.'

'Well, more than that. You've said yourself my room feels different. I don't think it's *only* a question of dirt. I mean, the warty tufted one had a distinct atmosphere to her. Don't you think? My rooms were always a bit smeared with her. Now that's gone.'

'You're making a mystery of nothing. She was slatternly, that's all. I can't think how you tolerated her. She did my rooms for a week last term when Peg was sick, and everything looked nasty after she'd been through.'

'Or *felt* nasty?'

'No, Felix. No mystification. Nastiness has no physical presence. Nor does niceness. They're just in our over-capacious brains.'

'Really...? Anyway, Mrs Elmsgall'll have more scope for whatever it is she does. Now I've promoted her to a permanent position at the Deepdell. They're sensitive to everything in madhouses. Madness; dirt; atmospheres...'

Margot sat looking at him for a few moments. 'Quite a bag, isn't it? Bess as well as my commune. *And* the Seacome house. *And* Sir Trotsky.'

'The Master was nothing to do with me. As to the others, they're just collateral damage. Side-shots. You were my quarry. And I've not bagged you yet, have I?'

'No you haven't. But at least I'm beyond Athena.'

'And Apollo – that is to say, Odingo?'

'Odingo? Yes, I'm beyond him.'

'Ah!'

'Or he's beyond me. Beyond us all. He's not coming back to Wygy's in the autumn. Did y'know? He's gone back to Kenya to join the family business.'

'Witch-doctoring?'

'Politics, Felix. His father's found him a place in the senate. I had a sweet goodbye email from Monaco. He's taking April with him. He's made her his wife. One of his wives.'

'I can't imagine the Minister will approve of her. And then what? I imagine they'll eat her.'

'Grump. Actually, they look quite sweet – there was a photo attached to his email. The two of them holding hands in front of a Mediterranean blue as blue fire. Odingo in red suit, white shirt, black tie. April in a grey frock with a pink ribbon round her neck, exactly like one of her pigeons.'

'It'll take me weeks to wash that image out of my head.'

'You have those weeks.' Margot rose, sighed, and fingered the infamous cruet, which was still standing on the pale green kilim covering Culpepper's desk, waiting to be smuggled back into the sacristy. 'I imagine I shall fall back in love with you next term. Although I'm not coming back as your sidekick. No more *Abishag* nonsense. It's going to be a proper partnership', by which she meant, of course, that she meant to supplant him. 'Yes, you'll duly bag me. But meanwhile you give me the shivers. You're so nearly evil. Do you realise?'

'Hmph.'

'I can see why Hell might eye you hopefully, and lure you out to the Westley Waterless pandemonium. You are "ambiguous".'

'I'm not.'

'And do you think I'm ambiguous, Felix? A barely-penitent sprig of heathenry?'

'Phrase-maker.'

'A gateway of darkness? A thwarted conspirator against monotheism?'

'Not at all. Darling.'

She removed the stopper and swilled the holy water about its cut-glass cruet, as if to bring out its bouquet. 'So I'm in no danger of being burned by this?'

'That sort of thing doesn't happen. I only said it to frighten the Elmsgall. Witches being superstitious. Really.' Nonetheless, he watched intently enough as she lowered two fingers into the cruet – and snatched them out, biting her lip with a gasp of sudden anguish.

'Just joshing,' she told Culpepper. He giggled weakly. She smiled. She rubbed her lips with wet fingers, came over, leant, kissed him on his forehead. 'Now hurry and dress for dinner. Have an interesting late summer.' She was gone.

For whatever reason that salty double-lip-shape on Felix's forehead did in fact tingle; it was a zone of mild fire. He didn't lose the troubling sensation until the end of the fish course.

The end of Quintember: The First Volume of the
Misdemeanours of Dr Felix Culpepper.

Felix and Margot will return in Parricide